ADVANCE PRAISE

"An *Animal Farm* for our times! Destined to be runaway
bestseller in the dystopian interspecies satire genre."
—ADAM CHODIKOFF, *The Daily Show*

"Fabulous...masterful...flawless...the satire is biting;
the humor razor sharp; the insights into 'human' relations,
social systems and corporate culture enlightening...
a superb fable for our times.
Every bit as good as Orwell, and timely, too."
—SARA PRITCHARD, *New York Times* Notable Book author/humorist

"Extremely clever, layered, sophisticated, funny...
a great book for the classroom!"
—J.L. POWERS, award-winning YA author and founder/ editor of
The Pirate Tree, a website on social justice and children's literature

"*Animals, Inc.* is a great concept and
Catherine Arne is just the writer for it."
—DAVID POYER, best-selling author

"Clever, well written...Catherine Arne is a big talent."
—JENNY BENT, The Bent Agency

"Resonant and timely...laugh-out-loud funny...
Animals, Inc., is a satiric cautionary tale exploring the pitfalls
of modern capitalism and contemporary corporate culture.
With a deft comedic hand, the author gently skewers
the foundations of modern society while simultaneously
crafting a character-driven story that is eminently readable
and potentially appealing to readers young and old.
A lucid, fresh, and entertaining page turner of a novel...
a timeless story about the uses and misuses of power."
—IBRAHIM AHMAD, senior editor, Akashic Books

ANIMALS, INC.

CATHERINE ARNE

ANIMALS, INC.

CATHERINE ARNE

OUT OF THE BOX

BOOKS

*To Chris, my favorite corporate refugee
and fellow adventurer on the road less traveled*

*and our buddies, Canute and Sassy,
who never let us forget what really matters*

CAST OF CHARACTERS

POE   **GIZZABELLE**   **GIZMO**

CLEO   **BUDDY**   **NEWTON**

HENRIETTA   **CLEMENTINE**   **SARGE**

XERXES   **XENA**

SAUSAGE   **PEANUT**   **MORDECAI**

FAE   **BANDIT**   **SHYLOCK**

EWINA   **JELLYBEAN**   **FLOSSY**

JOCK   **MILLIE**

*The worst sin towards our fellow creatures
is not to hate them,
but to be indifferent to them;
that's the essence of inhumanity.*
—GEORGE BERNARD SHAW, PLAYWRIGHT, HUMAN

CHAPTER 1

That which at first appears an ending
is only ever a beginning.
—SAUSAGE, PHILOSOPHER PIG

Buddy crested the hill at top speed, his lean, muscular body in full extension, ears flapping so furiously it seemed he might take flight and soar right over the cow pasture, past the sheep paddock to the big red barn beyond. He had but one thought, a merciless mantra that repeated again and again with every drumbeat of his paws.

Faster. Faster. Must. Go. Faster.

"Millie!" he barked to the cow grazing on the other side of the fence as soon as he got in hearing distance. "It's Farmer Bob. He's collapsed!" Skidding to a halt, his haunches dug into the soft earth, dirt spraying through the fence slats all over the cow's legs. "He's real crook, Millie," he panted. "You've got to get help quick smart!"

Before Millie could respond, he scrambled back onto his feet and took off in the direction from which he'd come. "I'm going back," he called over his shoulder. "He's just over the hump. Make tracks—*NOW!*"

Millie's eyes rolled to white, and she sprang away from the fence like she'd been jabbed with an electric cattle prod, hooves thundering across the pasture, clods of sod flying behind her. Startled from grazing, the other cows joined the mad dash, surrounding her in a pounding wave of panicked cowflesh.

Hearing the approaching rumble, the sheep gathered near the fence, bleating and milling about. As the stampeding cows neared, the sheep backed away, but didn't bolt, each one held back by its need to stay with the herd. The cows gave no sign of slowing as they barreled forward. Then—suddenly, impossibly, mere inches from the fence—they slid to a shuddering, quivering halt.

"It's Farmer Bob," Millie lowed. "He's hurt. Got to get help."

The sheep and the cows—who, except for Millie, hadn't known the cause of the hysteria until that moment—erupted in frantic questions.

"Mooooove out!" Millie bellowed into the din.

The sheep took off across the pasture toward the big red barn. "He's just over the hill," Millie called after them. Before reaching the fence they were already broadcasting the dire news. "It's baaaaad. *Baaaaaad.* Farmer Bob's hurt baaaaad! He needs help."

The hens in the barnyard were the first to hear the sheep's SOS. Although the chickens were confined to their yard at night, Farmer Bob gave them free rein of the farm in the daytime. The chickens scattered in all directions, carrying the message to the goat hut and the barn, where it leapt from stall to stall like wildfire. Animals snorted and squealed, paced and stomped. A thick musk of fear filled the air.

Slowly, the blind, instinctive panic subsided and confusion set in. Help? How could they? No other people were on the farm anymore since Farmer Bob had been forced to let go of his last full-time worker the year before. No neighbors lived nearby. Even if they had, the animals had no way of communicating with them.

The two draft horses neighed and stamped their hooves. The pigs squealed. Newton the mule paced round and round, pawing the hay and snorting in frustration. "Nothing we can do," he muttered.

There came a stirring, then heavy shifting from the next stall, the only one that had remained silent during the panic. A deep-timbred voice rose up, clear and calm. "We are not creatures of circumstance," it said. "We are creators of circumstance."

"Yes, creators of circumstance," a high squeal echoed from across the aisle.

Newton bridled at the implication. A self-taught engineer, anthropologist, and freethinker, he was the last animal on the farm to be guilty of being a mere creature of circumstance. No, he was as actively engaged with the world as it was possible to be from the confines of a stall. The mule gathered facts like other animals collected food. Nothing the humans said escaped his long ears. He could squeeze more from his fellow animals than they understood themselves, then piece it together with what he already knew to form uncannily accurate conclusions.

And yet, Newton had learned that on those rare occasions when his next-door neighbor spoke, it behooved him to listen.

Was there something he had missed? The mule applied himself to the problem anew, examining it from every angle, but still saw no solution. "We can't do anything," he declared. "Even if we got out of our stalls, what then? We can't fix Farmer Bob."

There was a long silence before he received a reply. "Each species has its own gifts. Hands for healing, wings for flying, voices for speaking."

"Only humans have hands, but even they don't have wings," muttered Newton. He glanced at the chickens fluttering around just outside the doorway, then shook his head. Suddenly he stopped short. "Voices for speaking..." he repeated softly, a grin breaking across his face. "Poe!" he brayed to the other animals. "We've got to get Poe. *He* can get the humans."

A wave of relief swept through the barn. Of course! Poe. Poe could help!

Poe was a raven Farmer Bob had rescued and raised himself. The farm animals had never seen him themselves, but they'd heard tell of him from the cat, Coco, and Buddy, who said the bird's powers of imitation were so convincing he'd been fooled several times into thinking Farmer Bob was calling his name when it was only the raven having a bit of fun. Coco never admitted to being hoodwinked. Then again she may have been spared Buddy's humiliation, not thanks to her superior powers of discernment, but by the handy fact that she never came on command anyway.

The chickens shared in the excitement over the new plan until they noticed the rest of the animals eyeing them expectantly. When the realization dawned that, as the only farm animals allowed to run loose in the barnyard, they were also the only ones who could get inside the farmhouse and free Poe, their happy clucking stopped. They suddenly developed an obsessive interest in the ground, scratching at the dirt with unprecedented industry and concentration.

Finally, the half-blind Sergeant Jebediah Bigg-Wattle straightened up, stretching his neck to crowing height. "*Aaaccchhechm,*" he cleared his throat. "As the farm's ranking rooster, it falls to me to lead this dangerous mission into unknown territory." Besides Buddy and Coco, none of the animals had ever been in the house. Certainly no chickens—not alive, that is.

"I'll go, too," chirped Gizmo, an impetuous young cockerel.

"Oh, no you won't!" said his adoptive mother, Clementine. A plump White Cochin, Clementine was the quintessential Mother Hen of the farm. She'd taken Gizmo and his older sister, Gizzabelle, under her wing after their parents died of bird flu when Gizmo was just an egg. "You're far too young for such shenanigans. Barely more than a chick."

"Am not!" Gizmo puffed out his chest. "I'm plenty old."

"You're not even crowing yet," said his mother.

Gizmo snorted. "I don't see any hens volunteering."

Clementine sighed. "*I'll* go, then. But you're staying right here."

"Aw, *man,*" he grumbled, kicking at the dirt. "It's not hen's work. It should be me and Sarge—"

"Mind your mother," Sarge said sternly. "Being a rooster isn't all cock-a-derring-do, junior. Learn some respect or you'll never be anything but a strutting prannock who thinks he can rule the roost just because he's got a big comb."

The young chicken hung his head.

"Gizmo," said Gizzabelle, "someone's got to look after everyone while Sarge is gone. I could keep Mom company while you stay here and watch the flock. We'll feel ever so much safer knowing you're... on duty here."

Gizzabelle was a rare bird. While most of the chickens on the farm were Rhode Island Reds and Jersey Giant Whites, she and her brother were Silver Sebrights, a smaller breed with striking black-laced white feathers. However, it was personality that set Gizzabelle apart as much as her unusual feathering. She had a reputation for being bright and inquisitive, which flummoxed the other chickens. How could the two possibly go together? Her detractors said she couldn't be as clever as she seemed or she wouldn't be as curious as she was. Everyone knew that questions were a clear sign of stupidity, and Gizzabelle asked nearly as many questions as her incorrigible little brother.

"Aw, alright," Gizmo said.

Sarge looked around and when it was clear that he wasn't going to get any more volunteers, he jerked his head at his two recruits, and they headed over to the house. Sarge stopped just in front of the back door and began scratching at the ground. Then, without any warning, he made a mad dash at the pet door. But whether it was his imperfect vision or that he had closed his eyes for his careening charge, instead of the pet door, he hit the jamb at full speed, sending him sprawling backwards onto his thinning tail feathers.

Clementine hurried over to help him up, clucking sympathetically. Sarge shrugged her off. "Door's jammed," he said gruffly. "No budging it. Absolutely impregnable."

Gizzabelle and Clementine looked at one another. "Oh, Sarge," Clementine cooed, "when you rammed the door with such force, I'm just *sure* I saw it move. Ever so slightly."

"Me, too," Gizzabelle agreed. "Let's see if we can't get in now that you loosened it up for us." With an easy hop, she pushed through the pet door and disappeared inside. A moment later, she stuck her head out. "Coast's clear," she chirped. "Come take a gander."

Clementine waddled up next and heaved her substantial weight against the door. But her momentum failed her midway and she tottered on the threshold. When it appeared she might fall backwards, Sarge rushed forward and gave her voluminous posterior a vigorous nudge, which pushed her over the edge and into the house.

Sarge followed, and the trio found themselves in a room like nothing they had ever seen before. It was filled with all manner of strange contraptions and paraphernalia. "What do you think it all is?" Gizzabelle asked, looking around in awe.

"This," pronounced Sarge, taking note of the canisters and vegetables on the counter, "must be the human feeding trough."

"Ah, yes," the ladies murmured, bobbing their heads.

"Eez called ze kitchen," said a voice from the corner of the room.

The chickens spun around. "Coco!" Clementine squawked. "I didn't see you there."

The sleek black cat slowly stretched and began licking her sable paw. "Looking *pour* Poe?" she purred. "*Venez*, I'll show you." Without waiting for a reply, she sauntered out of the room.

Although Coco had never hurt or even chased a chicken as far as they knew, there was no love lost between the chickens and the feline, and their relationship was an uneasy truce at best. However, the events of the day overshadowed whatever reservations they might have had under normal circumstances, and the birds hurried after her.

In the middle of the next room, Coco stopped. "*Voila*," she said, pointing her nose to the corner of the room, where a large cage stood beside an easy chair. "But *ez futile* if you ask *moi*. When have *ze humains* ever listened to *ze animaux*?"

"Well, we've got to try," Gizzabelle said.

Coco shrugged. "I hope *c'est un succès. Sincèrement.*" She rubbed up against the leg of the couch. "*Excusez-moi, poulets.* I will *adjourner*. We would not wish to scare *le petit* birdie off, *n'est-ce pas?*" With that, she strolled out of the room.

Sarge turned toward the cage and hopped up to the base of its stand. "Poe?" he crowed. "Can you hear me?"

There was no sound from the cage.

"You don't know us, but we're chickens from the farm. I'm Sergeant Jebediah Bigg-Wattle and these are Clementine and Gizzabelle," Sarge continued. "There's been some sort of accident. Farmer Bob's been badly hurt and we need your help."

The cage rattled and a dark form appeared at the bars. "*My* help? What can I do?"

"Buddy and Coco have told us about you and your gift," Gizzabelle piped up.

"My...gift?"

"Your gift of mimicry. Buddy tells us that you can call him into the room using Farmer Bob's own voice."

"Oh, that?" Poe said dismissively. "It's just a little something I do to amuse myself. I don't mean any harm. It's just I don't have anything else to do..."

"It's not easy to fool a dog's ears," said Sarge. "Your humanspeech must be first rate."

"I'm alright," Poe admitted. "I do *Poe's a pretty bird* and *Polly wanna cracker* for Farmer Bob and of course, his favorite, *nevermore*. He never gets tired of that one."

"That's why we need you now," said Gizzabelle. "You're the only one of us who can communicate with humans in their own language. We need you to tell the people what has happened."

"But how? I'm stuck in here. Unless…can you get me out? The latch isn't hard to move; I just can't get to it from my side."

"Well, my eyesight isn't what it used to be," Sarge conceded, "And we've all had our flight feathers clipped, but Gizzabelle here is as sprightly a young hen as you're likely to meet. I'm sure she can get up there."

"I'll do my best," Gizzabelle said, hopping up onto the chair beside Sarge and then onto its wide upholstered arm. From there it was just a few feet to the cage. Gizzabelle carefully gauged the distance and angle. "Here I come," she finally called, taking a deep breath and making a flying leap onto the cage. She grabbed onto the wire bars with her claws and beak. The cage swung wildly, rocking on its base and smashing its inhabitant against the bars.

Gizzabelle suddenly found herself beak-to-beak with the most ravishing specimen of bird she had ever beheld. His iridescent plumage glistened like an oil slick in the sun, perfectly setting off the obsidian eyes looking into her own. She clamped her eyelids shut, trying to stop the world from spinning.

Slowly the swinging eased into a gentle swaying and Gizzabelle hazarded a peek, only to find Poe still staring at her from behind the bars.

"You just about took out the whole cage there," he said.

Gizzabelle's face burned beneath her feathers. Although she was by no means large for a chicken, she felt like a fat, dumpy troll compared to the svelte raven. Why, oh why couldn't she have alighted on the cage as delicate and petite as a hummingbird? But chicken wings weren't much for flying, much less hovering. Which is why she was now in the ridiculous position of holding on to the cage bars with her beak.

She enunciated around the bar with as much dignity as she could muster. "Fo, whaddabow dalach?"

"What?"

"Dalach. Da *lach*."

"Ah, yes," he said. "The latch. You just pull that handle there

— 7 —

straight up and open the door. That's all there is to it."

Gizzabelle knew she couldn't stay aloft long enough to handle both maneuvers. "Wen I pull ub, you puzsh da duhr."

"Got it. On the count of three. One, two, three!"

Gizzabelle launched at the latch and held it up just long enough for Poe to throw open the door before she plummeted back down to the chair.

Poe stood in the cage doorway and flapped his wings tentatively. He looked down, then took a step backward into the cage.

The three chickens craned their necks, but the raven had disappeared from view.

"Poe?" Gizzabelle finally called up.

There was no answer. She glanced back at her mother and Sarge, and shrugged. What on earth could be the matter?

Then, with a jolt, she understood. Why, he'd never flown before! The poor bird must be petrified.

"Poe," she called quietly, "it's okay. You'll be fine." Still nothing. The little hen thought for a moment, then brightened. "Hey, Poe, do you ever *imagine* flying? Or do you fly in your dreams?"

Suddenly, there was movement in the cage. Poe stepped back into the doorway. He peered at Gizzabelle intently. "How did you know?" he asked. "Every night it's the same dream. I fly higher and higher, so high that the whole farm and all the animals are just little black specks on the ground." He sighed. "Sometimes it's more real than when I'm awake."

"Then you'll know just what to do," Gizzabelle said. "Just do what you do every night. It'll come naturally. It's what you were meant for."

Poe nodded slowly, then spread his wings. He gave Gizzabelle one last glance, and taking a deep breath, dropped off the ledge. At first he just glided down slowly, but instead of landing next to Sarge and Clementine as it looked like he would, he suddenly banked a hard right and swooped past them, ruffling Clementines's feathers with his tailwind.

Gizzabelle jumped off the chair onto the desk and joined Sarge and Clementine on the floor. Their heads zigzagged in perfect synchrony as they followed Poe's flight back and forth. Finally, after a couple of aerial somersaults, Poe touched down lightly next to them and shook his feathers in exultation.

"It's even better than in my dreams," he said, his eyes shining. "You can't imagine!"

Couldn't imagine? Indeed she could, thought Gizzabelle. She could tell him a thing or two about dreams. She might be a fat, dumpy, earthbound chicken by day, but at night, she was light as a hummingbird, swift as a falcon, agile as a sparrowhawk. She soared through the skies and touched the stars.

"It must be breathtaking," was all she said.

"It sure is," Poe said. "I didn't even realize how much I'd been missing..." His voice caught.

Gizzabelle's heart went out to him. She may have had her wings clipped, but at least she'd had her freedom. "It must have been so hard for you," she said softly.

The raven looked at her gratefully and their eyes locked.

Sarge cleared his throat and Gizzabelle started nervously.

"We've got to go," the rooster said. "We'll take you to Sausage."

"Sausage?" Poe asked. "Who's Sausage?"

How to describe Sausage? Gizzabelle wondered. Sausage was the wisest, most respected animal on the farm. At nineteen years old, he was also the oldest, although both Newton, the mule, and Mordecai, the goat, had come to the farm as adults and were decidedly long in the tooth as well. When Sausage was just a piglet, Farmer Bob noticed that he put on weight far faster than his littermates, which suggested prime show-pig promise. While his brothers and sisters frolicked and played together, Sausage was kept apart and plied with as much feed as he could eat. Farmer Bob's intuition soon paid off. Within just a few years, Sausage had grown to enormous proportions, and he'd taken the coveted "best in show" at the state fair every year since he was four.

But Sausage's award-winning physique wasn't what impressed the other animals on the farm. It was that he seemed to know everything—even things he had no conceivable way of knowing—and to understand them at their very core. Some speculated this penetrating insight was a result of his extensive travels to the fair every year, but others—including Gizzabelle—disagreed and thought it was Sausage's own peculiar meditative nature. Maybe it was the fact that he spent so much time alone as a piglet or his incredibly advanced age, but whatever the case, he was unquestionably an abnormally contemplative pig. Sausage himself joked that it was his name, providing as it did a constant *memento mori*, that made him so introspective. Like so much of what he said, the other animals didn't know exactly what that meant, but they were sure it must be profound indeed and repeated it, like his other "Sausagisms," with great relish in what they hoped were appropriate contexts.

"There's no explaining Sausage," Gizzabelle said to Poe as they scurried across the kitchen. "You'll just have to meet him."

When they got to the pet door, Sarge allowed the ladies to go first, and he followed, leaving Poe alone, staring at the door. Although he'd been able to look out the window next to his cage, he hadn't been out of the house since Farmer Bob had brought him home as a hatchling. Now he would finally get a chance to see the wide world on the other side of the glass.

Taking a deep breath, he pushed through the door. Immediately he was blinded by the sun. Once his eyes adapted to the light, he took off straight into the air. Up, up, up he went, without a backwards glance.

Panicking, Gizzabelle watched him soar over the barn and disappear out of sight. She scanned the horizon. Not even a shadow flitted across the roofline. Had he abandoned them? Why wouldn't he? He didn't owe them anything.

A moment later, though, he came flying over the roof, bearing down on the barnyard like a falcon after a fieldmouse. Just as it looked as if he was going to plow into the ground right in front of the chickens, he pulled up sharply and landed light as a feather.

"This is no time for tomfoolery," Sarge scolded sternly. "We've got important matters to attend to. Time is of the essence."

Poe hung his head. "Sorry," he said. "I just couldn't help myself. I've never been outside before. Not that I can remember, anyway."

"It's okay," Gizzabelle said reassuringly.

Poe shot her a grateful glance.

Sarge clucked impatiently. "Let's get moving. On the double."

"Yes, sir," Poe said, falling in behind him.

When they got to the barn, the animals went wild as soon as they saw the raven. "It's Poe!" whinnied the horses. "Poe! Poe!" squealed the pigs. "He's come!" brayed Newton.

Poe looked around at all the animals staring down on him, beaming and chanting his name. He hopped over to Gizzabelle. "What are they so excited about? Who do they think I am?" he asked in a low voice.

"Don't worry," she assured him. "They're just glad you're here. C'mon. Sausage will tell you what to do."

She set off down the aisle after Sarge, Poe following so closely on her heels that he stumbled into her when she stopped.

Sarge jerked his beak toward the last stall. Poe glanced at Gizzabelle, who nodded encouragingly. Poe flew up to the stall door and peered down. There, lying on the straw, was the biggest, most grotesquely corpulent hog Poe had ever seen. He didn't look anything like the cute, pink pigs Poe had glimpsed from his window. This enormous beast looked like a different species entirely. Indeed, he looked more like a stubby, hairless cow.

Poe suddenly realized his beak was hanging open. He snapped it shut and noticed for the first time the tiny dark eyes, nearly lost in the great mounds of fat, which were watching him intently. Poe quickly looked away, and shuffled back and forth on the stall door. When he reluctantly met Sausage's gaze again, instead of reproach, he felt only warmth and good humor.

"They told me to come see you?" Poe asked. He waited. When the silence became unbearable, he tried again. "The chickens said I could go for human help?"

"Indeed," said Sausage, but he made no move to elaborate.

Poe looked at the chickens questioningly. They shrugged.

He turned back to Sausage. "Okay...so where do I go? East? West?"

Again there was a long silence. "The way is not in the sky," Sausage finally said. "The way is in the heart."

"C'est Sausage," said Coco, who had materialized out of nowhere.

Poe shook his head in confusion. "I should just pick a random direction?"

Sausage shifted onto his side. "There is no such thing as chance," he said. "What seems to us as merest accident springs from the deepest source of destiny."

"Destiny?" Poe asked. "You think this is my...destiny?"

"Indeed."

Suddenly the weight of the responsibility of what he was being asked to do hit the raven. He drew himself up to full height. "I'll do my best. I'll try to get the people to come."

Poe stared at the ancient pig for a long moment before he turned around to face the other animals. They looked up at him expectantly, but he gazed over their heads, lost in his own thoughts. Without a word, he spread his wings and took off toward the barn doors. Then, just as he was about to pass through them, he suddenly circled back and swooped down. "Good-bye," he cawed, catching Gizzabelle's eye. "See you soon."

The little hen was speechless. Had he come back to say good-bye—to her?

"*Bon voyage, petit* birdie," said Coco as he flew away once more.

"Yes, and *adieu*," said Gizzabelle when she recovered her voice. It was something she'd once heard from Coco and she hoped it made her sound worldly and sophisticated.

"*Non, non, mon chéri,*" corrected Coco. "Not *adieu.*"

"Why not?" asked Gizzabelle. "Doesn't it mean goodbye?"

The cat shook her head. "*Adieu* means...how you say?"

"To God," supplied Sausage from behind the stall door. "*A dieu.*"

"*Oui,*" said Coco. "To God. *Final.* Vat you seek ez *au revoir*—until ve meet again."

"Oh!" Gizzabelle gasped, her wing flying to her beak. "Not *adieu!*" she cried, sprinting toward the barn doors. "I mean *au revoir! Au revoir!*"

But Poe had disappeared.

Gizzabelle stared after him, a horrible knot forming in her stomach.

"Not *adieu,*" she whispered. "'Til we meet again."

CHAPTER 2

After leaving the barn, Poe flew toward the driveway. It was how he'd always seen Farmer Bob come and go—and all other humans for that matter—so it seemed like the logical direction in which to look for people. He passed the sheep pasture and the cow pasture, and then several fields, brown and barren. When he reached the end of the driveway, there was a large road upon which a few vehicles zoomed along, and beyond that a patch of forest.

As he soared over the trees, Poe noticed a solitary figure perched in a giant oak. Hesitating, he circled around and touched down lightly on the branch. He cleared his throat. "Excuse me?"

The bird rotated his head and blinked owlishly.

"I'm sorry to disturb you in the middle of the day," Poe continued, "but are you familiar with these parts? Do you know where I might find some humans?"

"Whom?" the owl hooted, his golden eyes widening into perfect orbs.

"Humans," Poe repeated. "Could you tell me where to find some humans?"

"The only reason to look for humans," the owl said with asperity, "is to avoid them." He peered at Poe, his eyes narrowing to slits. "Why pray tell would you ever deliberately seek out those noxious bipeds?"

Poe explained the predicament of the farm animals as briefly as he could.

"They've got their chance to be free of one human and instead they're trying to fetch more?" the owl asked, his ear tufts bristling. "This slavish devotion to humans is inexplicable. I have never understood domesticated animals. I for one would never give up my independence."

"I'm sorry, but could you just tell me where I can find some humans?" Poe said, trying to keep the irritation out of his voice.

"I'm in a bit of a hurry."

The owl glared at him, unblinking. Then he shrugged his wings. "Do what you will. There's a farm that way," he said, pointing a wingtip. "They may help you."

"Thanks," said Poe, quickly taking off in the direction he had indicated.

The owl watched the departing raven crest the treetops and disappear into the distance. Shaking his head ruefully, he shuffled back and forth on his branch and settled back down for a good day's sleep.

Poe soon reached the edge of the forest, where he came upon field after field as far as he could see. He flew on, his eyes trained on the horizon, looking for any sign of human habitation. Finally, Poe noticed a faint scent upon the wind. As he flew on, it grew stronger and stronger. Then, in the distance, he saw another field. But unlike all those he'd flown over so far, this one was covered with dark spots. The indistinct dots quickly sharpened into discernable figures.

The field was jam packed with cows! Poe had never seen so many cows in his life. They were practically on top of each other there were so many in the compound, and they were standing knee deep in their own filth. There wasn't a blade of grass to be seen.

The cows watched impassively as he flew closer and alighted upon a fencepost.

"Hello," said the raven.

The cows nodded in acknowledgement, slowly chewing their cud.

"I'm from a farm not far away," Poe continued. "Our farmer has fallen and he's hurt. I need to find some humans to help him."

"What do you want to do that for?" asked a brown cow.

"Yeah, why would you wanna help a human?" another cow wanted to know.

"If *our* farmer got hurt, he'd be waiting 'til the cows came home before I'd bring him help," said a black steer.

"Why? Don't you like your farmer?" asked Poe.

"Are you kidding?" snorted the brown cow. "Do you think we *like* being held captive and mutilated and tortured?"

Poe drew back. "Mutilated and...tortured?"

The cow spun around and presented her backside. She flicked her stubby tail back and forth stiffly. "What do you call that?" she asked.

The other cows nodded vigorously, and the brown cow looked back at Poe. "Cut off!" she exclaimed before he had a chance to answer. "Now we can't even swat flies."

She did a quarter turn so she was broadside. "And how about this?" she said, jutting her chin at the blackened K on her hindquarters. Poe suddenly noticed that all the cows had the same mark. "Another gift from our beloved farmer. How would you like *your* flesh burned off with a red-hot poker? If that's not torture, I don't know what is."

Poe frowned. "Are you sure he didn't have a reason? Farmer Bob wouldn't do anything to the animals that wasn't for their own good."

"The only reason he had," she said, "was to prove his domination. To mark us as *his*."

Poe shook his head. "Surely there must be some mistake. Humans just couldn't be that cruel."

"Oh, honey," she said, shaking her head sadly. "You don't know the half of it..."

Back at the farm, the relief Poe had brought seemed to have left with him, and the tension built as the wait—for what exactly the animals didn't know—began. No one was even able to eat. The animals traded possible scenarios back and forth—where Poe was, what the humans would do, what had happened to Farmer Bob, what would become of the farm if Farmer Bob was too hurt to work...

After a while, conversation petered out and a melancholy silence descended over the farm. The chickens scratched listlessly at the ground; the cows chewed their cud, staring into the distance; the animals in the barn curled up in their stalls.

Gizzabelle couldn't stay still. First, she wandered aimlessly around the barnyard, but slowly, inexorably, she was drawn toward the fields. Eventually she found herself at the outer edge of the yard, smack against the fence to the sheep pasture. Although the bottom rail of the fence was plenty high for the chickens to go under, they never crossed into sheep territory. They weren't afraid of sheep, but the barnyard was the chicken's province and that's where they stayed.

For a while, Gizzabelle paced back and forth against the fence, but soon she'd worn a path in the dirt and she couldn't bear going up and down even one more time. Finally, with a sigh and a furtive look behind, she ducked under the fence and set out into the pasture.

Startled, the sheep stared at the little hen making her way across their field. It was an unusual sight, but then again, nothing about this day had been ordinary.

Gizzabelle scanned the horizon. "It's been so long," she said softly. "I hope he's alright."

"Chances are he's broken a leg," said the crusty old billy goat, Mordecai, who shared the pasture with the sheep during the day. "They'll have to put him down."

"Baaah, humbug," said a coquettish young ewe named Flossy. While the rest of the sheep were either standard white or more rarely, all black, Flossy had a white coat with a black face and legs. Her dramatic coloring made her stand out from the herd, a fact that was not lost on her. "Farmer Bob could already be at the vet, getting all fixed up. He'll be back in time for our evening feeding. He always is."

"Harumph," Mordecai snorted. "You and your woolly-headed rye-in-the-sky notions."

Flossy turned her back on the old goat, pointedly raised her tail and popped out a single, perfect dropping in Mordecai's direction, then ran away to snicker with her friends. Mordecai stalked away to the other side of the pasture and stood by himself, staring morosely over the fence at the deserted road.

Suddenly a sound like nothing they had heard before rose from over the hill. The unearthly, keening howl pierced straight through their hearts, and the animals knew instantly what it meant. Buddy's terrible baying lament waxed and waned, seemed to end, only to start up once more. Finally, there was silence again, which was even worse.

The sheep froze for an instant, then moved into small clumps where they began nuzzling one another in consolation. Gizzabelle was suddenly overwhelmed with the need to be with the other chickens and she took off toward the barnyard at a trot. When she saw Clementine in front of the henhouse, she raced over and fell into her mother's wings with an anguished sob.

"There, there," Clementine clucked. "It'll be okay."

"*Okay?*" squawked Henrietta, the farm's resident Chicken Little. "Okay? It'll be disaster! What will happen to us without Farmer Bob? We'll starve!" She began to hyperventilate.

Well accustomed to Henrietta's hysterics, Clementine tried to hush the terror-stricken hen before she began panicking the rest of the clutch.

"Nonsense, Henrietta," Clementine said. "Nothing's going to happen to us."

"That's right," said Gizzabelle, quickly drying her own tears. "I'm sure we'll be fine."

Henrietta moaned and began to sway precariously. "I can't breathe," she gasped. "I need air!"

Clementine shooed the other hens back and she and Gizzabelle began fanning Henrietta with their wings. They were still trying to calm the petrified hen when Poe swooped down from overhead. In the excitement, no one had noticed him approaching.

"Gizzabelle, I found another farm," he cawed from the air. "I didn't get any humans, though. You wouldn't believe what—"

"Poe," Gizzabelle interrupted. "It's too late."

"What?" he said, jerking up in mid-air. "You mean...?"

Gizzabelle nodded. The raven dropped onto the ground as if he'd turned to stone. "I can't believe it..." he muttered to himself, a dazed, faraway look in his eyes. "He's...gone?"

"I'm afraid so," said Gizzabelle, stroking his feathers with her wing.

The news that Poe had returned and no humans were on the way was immediately telegraphed around the farm. Fear gripped the animals anew. Back in the barn, amid the anxious oinking and squealing from the piglets, Newton tried to examine the situation rationally.

"Calm down, everyone," he said. "I'm sure the humans will

catch wind of what happened sooner or later, and then they'll come rescue us. We just have to be patient and wait."

The piglets quieted down, but the musk of fear was still heavy in the air.

After a few moments had passed, suddenly Sausage spoke. "The fences of the mind are stronger than any pen ever built by man," he intoned solemnly.

Newton's ears perked up. He knocked his hoof against his stall door experimentally. "Why, now that you mention it, I think you just might be right." He raised his voice so it could be heard down the barn: "Jock?"

"Yes?"

"Jock, do you think you can kick down your stall door?"

The mighty draft horse's head jerked backwards. Such a wild idea had never crossed his mind. He considered. "Well, I suppose I *could...*" he said reluctantly.

"It's alright, Jock," Newton said. "I know you're faithful to a fault, but no one will mind now. We need to be there for Buddy... and for Farmer Bob."

"Well, in that case. If you're sure..." Jock said. "For Farmer Bob." He squared himself in front of the stall door and gave it a single powerful blow with his hind legs. The door exploded outward, splintering into pieces. Jock turned around and stared at the shattered boards. His stomach churned. Every fiber of his being screamed it was wrong, wrong, *wrong*!

Jock tentatively pawed at a bit of board that still clung to the door frame, but he couldn't seem to put one hoof in front of the other and walk out.

"What's the matter?" called Newton. "There's nothing to be afraid of."

"Jock," counseled Sausage from his stall, "walk through the fear."

Jock took a deep breath and placed a huge, shaggy hoof through the doorway. In the blink of an eye, he was out and free—and all alone. He trotted directly to Newton's stall.

"If you move over," he said, "I'll break down your door, too."

With a nod, the mule pressed against the far wall and steeled

— 18 —

himself for the blow. Jock gave the door a swift kick and easily demolished it as well.

"Should I do the others, too?" the horse asked.

"Not yet," said Newton, who was already examining the latch to Sausage's stall. "There could be an easier way if I can just figure this out," he said as he nosed the sliding mechanism. After just a few tries, he was able to manipulate the latch with his teeth and began releasing the rest of the animals without wreaking further damage. This was a vast relief to the pigs, whose meticulous, orderly—some might say compulsive—natures recoiled at the wanton destruction the horse had caused.

"Mind over muscle," pronounced Peanut, Sausage's self-appointed protégé, when Newton swung open his stall door. He gave the mule a satisfied nod, then skipped over to Sausage's side. Like Sausage, Peanut's abnormal size had saved him from the slaughterhouse. But while Sausage put on weight at the mere smell of food, Peanut, who'd been the runt of his litter, was no bigger than a piglet even though he was full grown. The miniature pig and enormous hog were a curious pair.

After everyone was freed, Sausage led the animals out of the barn where the chickens were waiting just outside the door. The birds dutifully fell into line behind the other animals, and they trooped over to the sheep pasture. While they stopped to figure out how best to open the gate, Poe flew ahead to the cow pasture. He explained the situation to the cows and assured them that once the other animals freed the sheep, they'd do the same for the cows.

"Harumph," snorted Xena, a forward, take-charge cow. "If they can break out, so can we. C'mon, girls! Uh…and Xerxes." Her twin brother, Xerxes, used to being in the shadow of his dominant twin sister, didn't take offense at being thought of as "one of the girls."

"There's a section of fence up a piece I think may be rotting," Xena continued. "Follow me. We can break through if we all work together." Without waiting for a reply, she took off toward the fence. When she got to the rotted section, she barreled through as if it were nothing more than a row of corn stalks.

As she slowed to a trot on the other side, she noticed Sausage and the other animals coming up the road, and she jogged over to meet them. It was only then that Xena realized that none of the other cows were with her.

"Holy cow!" she exclaimed. "I just broke through the fence all by myself!"

"You are stronger than you know," Sausage said.

"It's the fences of the mind that are the most powerful," Peanut added knowingly.

"The fences of the mind...?" Xena repeated before the clatter of hooves interrupted her thoughts, as Xerxes and the cows caught up to her.

"Xena," Xerxes scolded. "Couldn't you have waited just a tail flick? You could have been hurt."

"Bollocks!" she scoffed. "You're such a nanny-goat. Did you get your cockles clipped or what? I'm perfectly fine. Besides," she said, softening, "I thought you guys were right behind me."

"And we would have been," Millie said, "if you'd have just given us a chance to wrap our heads around what you were planning. Remember who you're dealing with, dear. We need to chew on things a little, you know."

"What's important now is that we're all free," Gizzabelle said. "And going to Farmer Bob."

"Right, Farmer Bob," said Xena, hanging her head contritely.

The cows joined the solemn procession up the road and over the hill toward the cornfield. Sausage led the way, his grotesquely overgrown hooves giving him a pained, hobbling gait that was half as fast as most of the animals were used to, but fit the somber mood of the group. No one spoke and no one thought about what they would do once they arrived. All they knew was that they needed to get there.

When they reached the top of the hill, they saw Farmer Bob lying down near his tractor, Buddy tucked in against his side.

A blue merle Australian Shepherd, Buddy had copper and white points, one brown eye and one blue. As motley as his coloring was, though, his bloodlines were pure gold. Farmer Bob even had some sort of document to prove his superior extraction. "But you don't need papers to see his breeding," he'd told his friend Asa more than once, "it's as plain as the nose on his face." Every time he'd said that, Buddy's tail set to swishing and his mismatched eyes glowed with pride—not because he cared a whit about pedigree, but because of what it meant coming from his master. Like Buddy himself, Farmer Bob rarely put his emotions into words.

Even Farmer Bob's own wife—whose prized rose garden he meticulously tended five years after her death, whose favorite perfume he sprayed on his pillow before going to sleep—had only heard the word 'love' pass his lips nineteen times in their forty-one years of marriage, three of them on their wedding day. She'd never minded, though. She hadn't needed words to appreciate her husband's devotion—mute and enduring as the earth—any more than Buddy did. It was as plain as the nose on his face.

When he saw the animals approaching, Buddy sprang up. He bounded a few feet toward them, then circled back to stand by his master. "I'm so glad you're here," he said when they got closer. "I didn't know what to do, but I couldn't nick out on him. Not even after..."

Sausage nodded, his gaze warm. "T'would be easier to sever your own limb," he said. "Man never had a truer friend."

Gizmo hopped over to Farmer Bob. "Maybe he's just sleeping," he chirped. "There's no blood."

"You don't have the sense God gave a goose," Mordecai snapped. "Use your bleating brain cell. Don't you think Buddy knows the difference between sleeping and dead?"

Dead.

It was the first time the word had been spoken aloud. It hung in the air.

"He's gone," Buddy finally said. "He was out here busting his conk like he does every day, when the tractor carked it right in the middle of the field. He got out to have a squiz and next thing I know he was on the ground. I tried to get my nose under him to get him back on his stompers, but it wasn't any bloody good. He just lay there for a few secs, real quiet-like, his hand on my head.

"Then he started to talk. And you know Farmer Bob, he's never one to yabber. But suddenly there he was, rabbitin' on, telling me what a bonzer life he'd had, how he wouldn't have changed a thing. He told me about working the farm with his pa when he was just

— 21 —

a nipper, and when he'd brought his missus here for the first time and how she'd taken to farming like she'd been born to it. How he'd slogged all these years to keep it going, how he didn't want to muck it up and be the one to drop it down the gurgler, even if he didn't have a sprog to pass it to, but he reckoned it would all come good."

Buddy stopped, suddenly embarrassed, but the other animals nodded encouragingly. He swallowed and went on. "He told me what an ace mate I'd been. His best cobber. He told me to take care of the farm. 'Taking care,' he said. 'That's what matters.' Then he got quiet again. That's when I bolted for help. After I got back, he didn't say any more. I just sat here for yonks, listening to him breathing. It got quieter and quieter, until I couldn't even hear it. And then, I just felt him leave. I can't explain it, how I knew. I just did. He was here and then—just like that—he was gone."

The crowd was so still they could even hear the soft rustle of the chickens' feathers.

Then slowly, except for a few weak-stomached sheep who kept their distance, the rest of the animals gathered in around Farmer Bob's body. Most were satisfied just looking, but a few nosed him gently. Sausage closed Farmer Bob's eyes, while Gizmo gave his hand a surreptitious peck—just to be sure.

"What do we do now?" Gizzabelle finally asked.

The animals were so used to Farmer Bob taking care of such things that they'd never even thought about what to do with a dead body.

"I think the humans bury their dead under the ground," offered Newton, who always seemed to know how everything worked.

"Why can't we just leave him here?" Gizmo asked.

"Noooooooo!" Millie lowed so loudly that Gizmo scuttled to hide behind a particularly fluffy ewe. "We can't do that to Farmer Bob. He deserves better."

"That's right," said Peanut. "We're not leaving Farmer Bob for some nasty scavengers to peck the eyes ou—" He stopped short, looking at Poe.

Suddenly the raven could feel everyone watching him. He didn't know why they were staring, but he felt compelled to fill the awkward silence. "That's no way to treat Farmer Bob," he agreed. Then, out of nowhere, he had an idea.

"*We* should bury him, just like the humans do."

This caused a stir. "Us?" the animals murmured. Surely, they thought, the humans should bury their own.

"How could we possibly do that?" Mordecai scoffed. "I assume you've got it all worked out?"

"Um, no," admitted Poe. "But I bet we can figure out a way."

"That's the most bird-brained idea I've ever heard," said the goat.

"What do you think, Sausage?" asked Peanut. "Could we do it?"

"You're wasting your breath," harumphed Mordecai. "You can never get a straight answer from the great oracle of the mud pit. And if you ask again tomorrow, he'll probably say exactly the opposite. One day, it's look before you leap, the next it's the early bird gets the worm. He's full of hogwash, if you ask me."

Peanut trembled in rage, but the dig rolled off the older pig like water on a duck's back. "Everything of significance is a paradox," the older pig said. "The opposite of a simple truth is a falsehood, but the opposite of a great truth is often another great truth."

Mordecai looked heavenward and gave a beleaguered sigh.

Peanut trotted over and craned his neck in an attempt to look down his snout at the goat, who had, unfortunately, over a foot on the petite pig. "A foolish consistency is the hobgoblin of little minds," he said snootily.

"Who're you calling foolish, piglet?"

"The wise talk because they have something to say;" Peanut shot back, "fools, because they have to say something." It was one of his personal favorite Sausagisms. He'd found that, unlike so much of what Sausage said, everyone could catch its meaning, even the chickens, at whose expense Peanut most often used it.

"Peanut," Sausage remonstrated gently. "The tongue is like a sharp knife; it kills without drawing blood."

Mordecai smirked at Peanut's comeuppance, and the pig glared back in silence. Then he deliberately turned his back on the goat. "So, *Sausage*," he said, "do *you* think we can bury Farmer Bob?"

The animals leaned forward on their hooftips.

"The universe bends in the direction of belief," the great pig said at length.

The animals looked at one another. That was a yes, right? A surge of energy swept through the crowd. Excited chatter broke out as they discussed who could do what. The chickens were offended when they were told that, really, they were only good at *scratching*, not digging, but they were mollified when they realized none of the hooved animals were any good at making holes either. As it turned out, the only animal on the entire farm with any aptitude whatsoever for digging was Buddy.

"I'll give it a burl," he said gamely. "It'll be a chance to feel productive. It should be my job, anyway, seeing how I was his best mate. Just tell me where you want it, and I'll dig the deepest hole you ever squizzed."

This set off another debate on where the grave ought to be dug. Although there was a contingent of the lazier chickens and sheep who advocated putting it right there in the middle of the cornfield, the majority felt Farmer Bob should be laid to rest near the farmhouse. Eventually they decided that under the Great Tree on the edge of the barnyard would be the perfect place.

Newton suggested that they could use a cart from the garage to get Farmer Bob back to the farm, and a faction of animals followed Buddy to the farm to retrieve it.

"All that's left is planning the funeral," said Newton.

"What exactly *is* a funeral?" Peanut asked.

"I don't know exactly," admitted the mule. "Some sort of ceremony to commemorate the end of life."

"But Sausage, death isn't an ending, right?" squeaked Peanut.

Sausage smiled benignly at his eager acolyte. "Indeed. The lives of human beings and animals have no ending, just as their bodies have no corners. Nature wants things to be round. The universe itself is circular, and made up of earth, which is round, of the sun, which is round, of the stars, which are round. The moon, the horizon, the rainbow—circles within circles, with no beginning and no end."

"Why are the humans so backwards?" asked Peanut. "I thought they were supposed to be smart!"

"Intelligence is not wisdom," said Sausage. "Humans seek to

remove themselves from Nature. They find much pleasure in drawing lines and making distinctions. Borders and boundaries, edges and endings, boxes and buildings to separate one from the other."

"You're right," said Poe with surprising vehemence. "Cages and paddocks seem to be the humans' stock in trade."

Sausage looked at the raven placidly. Although he expressed disapproval in neither words nor demeanor, Poe suddenly felt his comment had been uncharitable in light of the circumstances.

"Perhaps you would like to assist with the funeral?" asked the hog. As the farm's de facto spiritual leader, it went without saying that he would be leading the ceremony.

"Me?" Poe croaked. "But I wouldn't know what to say."

"Music," replied Sausage, "is the language of the heart."

"I suppose I could sing something," Poe allowed. "I'm no songbird, but I can carry a tune."

The great pig started shambling toward the barn.

"Come," he invited. "Sit."

"You mean, ride on top...?"

Sausage nodded.

It seemed disrespectful, but so did declining the invitation. Poe uneasily alighted on Sausage's back, careful not to let his sharp talons dig into the pig's wiry-haired skin.

They rode quietly for a few minutes. "Sausage," Poe finally said. "I feel just awful. Everyone was counting on me and I let you all down. If it wasn't for me, Farmer Bob wouldn't be...dead." He was barely able to get out the last word. He tried to read Sausage's ears, but they were inscrutable.

At length, the great pig spoke, his voice kind. "Nothing ever dies," he said. "For life and death are one, even as the river and sea are one."

"What do you mean?" Poe squawked, involuntarily digging his talons in deeper. "We just saw his body! He's dead. Gone. Forever."

"There is no death. Only a change of worlds."

Poe shook his head vigorously, continuing on as if he hadn't heard. "It's all my fault. I should have tried harder. I shouldn't have wasted time talking to the animals at the other farm. Maybe I picked the wrong direction to fly in...I don't know. But I should have done *something*. I failed."

Sausage stopped walking and cupped his ears backwards. "One must be a god to be able to divine success from failure without error."

"But I was supposed to save him. It was my destiny, remember? And I blew it."

Sausage started forward again. The steady rhythm of his gait had a calming, meditative effect on the raven. As they walked on, Poe's talons slowly relaxed.

Finally, Sausage broke the silence. "The only real failure in life is not to be true to the best one knows."

It was Poe's turn to not to reply. At first he turned Sausage's words over in his mind, trying to make sense of everything the pig had said, but eventually, exhausted, he let go of his thoughts, his questions, his need to understand. Instead, he simply basked in the deep peacefulness the great hog radiated.

When they got to the barnyard, they could see Buddy under the Great Tree, busily digging. Although he was sorry to surrender the peculiar tranquility he had found with Sausage, Poe reluctantly excused himself to find a high branch where he could rehearse in private. The great hog retired to his stall, exhausted from the long walk.

The sky was almost dark by the time Buddy finished his digging and the other animals arrived with Farmer Bob's body indecorously in tow. Sarge gave a mighty crow to gather everyone together, and Poe and Sausage joined the rest of the animals at the Great Tree. They were just about to begin when Buddy noticed that Coco was missing. A quick search of her favorite lounging places turned up nothing.

"Couldn't be bothered, I suppose," Mordecai snorted.

Not knowing what else to do, the animals decided to proceed without her. Everyone gathered in close. Millie and Jock pulled Farmer Bob's body parallel to the grave, and the pigs nosed him over into it. The body landed with a sickening thud, face downwards and limbs splayed out at unnatural angles. The animals studiously ignored this final indignity.

Sausage climbed onto one of the piles of dirt at the head of the grave, and addressed the crowd. "Friends, we now remember Farmer Bob, who has passed from us this day. He touched each of our lives, and he will be missed. He treated the land and all he encountered upon it with dignity and respect. He was a good man, an excellent master, and a beloved friend. Anyone who wishes to speak may."

The animals blinked at one another. This was not something they had anticipated. At first no one spoke. Finally, Millie came forward and told of how Farmer Bob had delivered Buttercup—who'd been a breach birth—all by himself in the pouring rain when the vet hadn't been able to make it in time.

The sheep talked about how smoothly and gently he always sheared them; the cows recalled how he'd never missed a milking, not even once; Newton remembered how much he'd learned from Farmer Bob, not just facts, but how to analyze things and solve problems.

When the mule finished speaking, there was suddenly a commotion in the back as some of the sheep started bleating and jostling their neighbors. The crowd gave way before Farmer Bob's favorite straw hat, the wide-brimmed one his wife had given him their last Christmas together. It seemed to be making its way, slowly and deliberately, back to its owner. The hat propelled itself to the foot of the grave, stopped, and pitched forward into the hole. The animals spooked at the sudden movement and several of the chickens vaulted into the air before their brains registered what their eyes had seen.

"Coco!" Gizzabelle clucked in relief. "It's you. You brought Farmer Bob's hat?"

Coco shrugged nonchalantly. "*Oui*. It was *spécial* for him, no?"

There was shifting and whispering among the crowd, but for several minutes, no one else came forward. Finally, at long last, the one animal everyone had been waiting for made his way to the front. Buddy was limping, his paws raw and bloody from his hard day's labor.

He stared dolefully into the grave. "I'm rubbish at putting my feelings into words," he said apologetically.

"The deeper the sorrow the less tongue it has," Sausage said.

Buddy glanced at him gratefully.

"How can I explain what Farmer Bob was to me?" he said. "He was a true battler. He never whinged, no matter how hard things got. He was fair dinkum and as honest as the day is long. We were more than good mates. We ate together, slept together, worked together, played together. Sometimes when we were herding, we were so in tune I couldn't tell you where he stopped and I started." His voice caught. "He was my everything. I dunno what I'll do without him."

A reverent silence fell over the crowd.

Poe instinctively knew that the time was right. His sorrowful lament filled the air. It was not the silvery melody of a lark or a nightingale. His mourning-song was discordant, abrasive—its jagged edges tore at the heart. When Poe finished singing, no one stirred.

Sausage eventually spoke. "We now commit Farmer Bob's body to the ground."

He nodded to the pigs, who started filling the grave. The other animals lined up and each one solemnly approached the grave and added their own clump of earth. It was dark by the time Xerxes and Xena stamped down the last mound of dirt on the grave.

"He's gone on to The Great Nest in the Sky," said Clementine.

Mordecai snorted. "Poppycock. What would Farmer Bob do in a *nest* for all eternity? Lay eggs?"

"Why, you—" sputtered Gizmo, and a disgruntled clucking began among the rest of the chickens, who were offended that anyone would dare besmirch The Great Nest in the Sky. Meanwhile, the sheep and cows started muttering amongst themselves how bizarre it was to believe in a giant nest in the clouds when everyone knew that when you died you went to The Meadow Without End.

Newton shook his head vigorously. Although many suspected Mordecai shared his view, given the goat's frequent cutting remarks about religion and generally nihilistic attitude, Newton was the only admitted atheist on the farm. The chickens worshipped the fierce, vengeful rooster-god, Chikalita; the cows followed the serene, self-sacrificing Vishmoo; the sheep had a vague concept of Baa'l, but they were fuzzy on his attributes and requirements since they had never had any prophets. A few of the pigs were agnostic, but most of them believed in the Great Spirit, a divine power which transcended species.

Newton generally kept his opinions on religion to himself, not wanting to rob other creatures of their faith. But as he saw the other animals becoming increasingly hostile—and this at Farmer Bob's funeral!—he couldn't hold back. "Farmer Bob's not going anywhere," he said. "Dead is dead."

Everyone instantly turned on the mule. Peanut stalked over to face him nose to snout. "That's not true," he squealed. "He's wrong, isn't he, Sausage?"

Sausage often spoke of the Great Spirit, which was probably the reason he and Newton, who might have been expected to be fast friends given their stalls' proximity and similar age and intelligence, were not closer than they were. Sausage didn't proselytize or evangelize, and he never seemed bothered by Newton's disbelief, but the mule was distinctly uncomfortable with the pig's frequent allusions to spirituality and thus had never pursued a friendship with his corpulent neighbor.

Peanut trotted over to Sausage's side. "Sausage says Farmer Bob is still living, just, uh, somewhere else. You know where he's gone, right, Sausage?"

Sausage sighed. "Do not trouble yourself over what lies beyond. It is not an important question."

"Not important? What could be more important?" Peanut demanded, stung. He prided himself on his interest in deep philosophical and spiritual matters. It was what set him apart from his pedestrian barn-mates who only cared about food and mating.

"A wise man sees as much as he ought, not as much as he can. The veil over the Great Beyond can be penetrated," the hog said, dismissing the inconsequential exercise with a shrug. "But it is living that matters."

He turned from Peanut to the crowd. His eyes swept the fearful, angry, grieving faces.

"We have buried Farmer Bob's body," he declared. "But his spirit we do not bury. For spirit is born into nature and the soul, and for a time resides in flesh, yet is not flesh. Farmer Bob is no longer with us in this world, but he is not gone. His spirit has returned to whence it came, to the Great Spirit, the font of all life, the ground of all being. We wish you *bon voyage*, dear friend, on the Grand Adventure. Goodbye and Godspeed."

An unexpected peace settled over the crowd. It was not so much his message as Sausage's serene authority that affected the animals. They had the sudden conviction that no matter how upside-down things seemed, all was right with the world.

Sarge began a creditable rendition of Taps, its desolate notes slicing through the cool night air.

"Farewell," said Newton when he finished.

"*Adieu*," croaked Gizzabelle.

"Goodbye, Master," Buddy whispered.

The animals stood milling about in the moonlight, not sure what to do next. They all looked to Sausage.

The hog gazed into the starry sky. "Darkness has fallen," he said, "but on the morrow the sun will rise again, just as spring follows winter."

"Things may seem bleak now," Peanut interpreted, "but they'll look brighter in the morning. Everyone go to bed and get some rest, and we'll figure things out tomorrow."

"Right-o," said Buddy. "I'm dog-tired." Instead of going into the farmhouse where he normally slept at the foot of Farmer Bob's bed, he lay down right there on top of the grave, his nose tucked into his paws, and closed his eyes.

Poe watched the other animals make their way to their stalls and pens, all in little groups except for Mordecai who went to his hut by himself. Poe didn't relish the idea of going back to his cage, all alone in the empty house.

Gizzabelle, who hadn't left with the other chickens, seemed to read his mind.

"Would you like to stay in the henhouse?" she asked.

"Would I ever," he replied.

They hopped along together in companionable silence until they arrived at the coop. Gizzabelle ushered Poe inside. Although it was too dark to see the other birds, he could hear the rustle of feathers and occasional soft clucking, and it was curiously consoling.

"You can sleep up here next to me," Gizzabelle whispered. Inviting a strange bird into her nest wasn't anything she'd normally do, but today none of the usual rules seemed to apply.

Poe obediently jumped up onto her nesting spot, and they huddled together, both glad for the physical comfort after the trauma of the day's events.

Gizzabelle was just about to drift off when Poe stirred.

"Gizzabelle?"

"Mmm-hmmm?" she said drowsily.

"What did you think of my song tonight? Do you think it was okay?"

"Sure," she said. "Why?"

"You didn't think it was too...harsh?"

Gizzabelle, wide awake now, waited for him to go on.

"I've always loved Farmer Bob," he said. "He saved my life, after all, and took care of me all these years. But he also kept me in a cage. It's only now that I'm free that I realize how much he kept me from all this time. And it makes me furious!"

Gizzabelle considered her words carefully. "I think it's perfectly natural that you'd feel that way," she finally said.

"But shouldn't I be able to just get over it? He's *dead*, after all. It seems wrong to be mad at him now. Especially when I know he was a good man who loved me."

"Just give yourself time," she said, snuggling in closer. "Being angry doesn't mean you didn't love Farmer Bob."

"So, you don't think I'm awful?"

"Not at all," Gizzabelle assured him. "Not even remotely."

Poe sighed with relief. "You know, I've never had someone to talk to before. I had no idea it could feel this good."

Gizzabelle's innards hummed as if she had swallowed a thousand honeybees. "That's what friends are for," she said lightly.

Poe was quiet. "How about that?" He yawned and nestled deeper into the straw. "My first friend."

CHAPTER 3

The next morning when Sarge sounded his pre-dawn crow, he woke the farm not only to a new day but a new world. A world without Farmer Bob.

The animals were disoriented and anxious and hungry. No one had eaten much the day before. The cows were in even more desperate shape, not having been milked since the previous morning. Everyone assembled in the barn, which seemed the most natural gathering place. The crowd churned with questions. "What do we do now?" "What will happen to the farm?" "Who will feed us?" "Who will milk us?"

"We can't wait," Millie moaned. "We need to be milked *now*!"

"I'm about to pop," whimpered Buttercup.

She had no sooner stopped speaking than she went berserk. She started bucking and spinning like a rodeo bull just out of the gate.

"Why's Buttercup going off like a frog in a sack?" asked Buddy.

At first, no one could figure out what was wrong with the buck-wild cow. Then Gizzabelle saw the blur of black and white swinging around under her.

"Buttercup!" she squawked. "It's okay—it's just Gizmo!"

Sure enough, the young chicken had clamped his beak on Buttercup's teat and now he was hanging on for dear life as she furiously tried to dislodge him from her udder. Buttercup gave a particularly violent kick that sent Gizmo flying sideways into Flossy.

"Gizmo, are you okay?" Clementine asked, rushing over to the little bird who was laid out flat on his back. Buttercup stood trembling and blowing great puffs of air as she recovered herself.

To everyone's relief, Gizmo sat up and looked around woozily. "Yeah, I think so," he said.

"Well, I hope you learned your lesson, you silly chick," she clucked. "You know better than to startle someone like that, and you *especially* don't touch a cow there, in her special place, without asking. Do you understand me?"

"Yes, ma'am," he said, hanging his head. "Sorry, Buttercup. I was just trying to help."

"I know you were," she said, sides still heaving. "I didn't mean to throw you like that. You spooked me, that's all. Sorry for going crazy on you. Must've scared you half to death."

Gizmo perked up. "No way—that was fierce!" he raved. "Can I do it again?"

The hens were aghast. They fussed disapprovingly. "Gizmo!" Clementine scolded. "What are you saying? This isn't a game. You could have been killed."

"Awww, c'mon, Mom," he protested. "I'll be fine. That was totally *epic*."

"You come here, you foolish chick," Clementine demanded. "We're going to have to have a talk."

Gizmo slunk away after his mother to a corner of the barn. The muffled squawks of her lecture drifted back over the crowd as Peanut trotted over to Buttercup and circled around under her abused udder.

"May I?" he asked.

She regarded him skeptically, but nodded. Peanut sat on his haunches, took a teat between his front hooves and gave a squeeze. Milk shot out, spraying Mordecai squarely in the eye. He jerked backwards, sputtering and blinking frantically, and the other animals burst into laughter. Mordecai gave them what was meant to be a withering look, but his dripping horns and soggy beard ruined the effect.

As Mordecai stalked away, Millie tried to turn the attention away from the goat's humiliated retreat. "Don't pinch like that," she instructed Peanut. "Roll from the top to the bottom...slow and smooth."

Peanut tried again, and instead of just a squirt, this time produced a long, steady stream of milk.

"Aaaaahhh," Buttercup sighed happily. "That's it—you've got it."

A cry went up for buckets, and the sheep were dispatched to retrieve them. The pigs each positioned themselves under a cow, and soon a bustling little milking operation was up and running. Some of the pigs were more adept than others, and the other animals gathered around, shouting out encouragement and advice, and laughing at the occasional misfire.

When all the cows were milked, they emptied the buckets into the cooling tank and Coco stuck in a paw, swirling it slowly. "*Voyons.* Excellent color and clarity," she said. She withdrew her paw and licked it thoughtfully.

"And?" the animals clamored, eager to know if it passed muster with their resident connoisseur.

"Vintage *du porc*," she pronounced grandly. "*Sans pareil.* Second to none."

The animals cheered and nudged one another jovially in congratulations. The levity did not last long, but a ray of hope had shot through the gloom, and their mood was considerably brighter as they faced their circumstances anew.

"Maybe you could try the humans again, Poe," Gizzabelle suggested. "I know it didn't work last time, but maybe this time you can go to a different farm."

The animals immediately seized on the idea. "Yes! Fetch the humans!" they cried.

Poe looked around uncomfortably at the eager faces. He flew up to Sausage's stall door where he could be seen by everyone.

"There's something you need to know," he said, glancing at Sausage. "I don't know if bringing the humans in is really what we want to do. The other humans, they're not like Farmer Bob. The other farms aren't like here. I saw terrible things and heard even worse ones."

He told them about meeting the cows at the next farm.

"The things they told me were unbelievable," he said. "They told me about tails being lopped off and red-hot pokers burned into their flesh. Calves being taken from them at birth and kept in crates so small they can't even turn or lie down their entire lives."

The cows drew back, eyes white-rimmed and nostrils flaring.

"It can't be true," Millie lowed. "They must be tall tales to scare the calves with. No one would be so cruel."

"I know, I know," Poe said. "That's what I thought, too. But I saw their tails and the brands on their backsides. And they insisted that it wasn't just there. They said other farms were the same way. That humans are persecuting species of every kind, torturing them in unimaginable ways.

"And even then, even seeing the evidence with my own eyes, I just couldn't believe it, so I tried to find someone else to talk to. I looked around for any other animals; I could smell them—the stench was overpowering, just like with the cows—but there was nobody in sight. Finally, I found a small knot-hole in one of the huge windowless buildings. It was simply *packed* with chickens. It was the saddest thing you've ever seen. I had a hard time even talking to them. Most babbled like half-wits. Finally one chicken who seemed coherent enough came up to the hole. He didn't even have a name, just a number: 12947. He told me more horrible things. He said that as chicks, their owner had had them *de-beaked*! Can you imagine?"

Henrietta began to hyperventilate.

Poe pressed on. "He said they were kept in the dark all day, every day. Never allowed to forage or nest or even walk in the sun. Not that they could even enjoy a simple walk outside anymore anyway; they were so fat that their legs couldn't even support them. They were practically invalids!

"But that isn't even the worst part."

Henrietta stopped hyperventilating. In fact, she was so trained on Poe's next words that she stopped breathing at all.

Poe lowered his voice. "Some chickens couldn't take it, and well, it seems they went *mad*," he said. "They pulled out their own feathers and attacked their friends, and some…" He shook his head.

"What?" demanded Henrietta.

Poe felt as sick to his stomach as he had been the time he'd accidentally eaten some rotten pumpkin. "Some chickens even *ate each other*!" he blurted out.

Henrietta fell over in a dead faint, and the other animals drew back in horror.

Poe, though, felt better having spilled the secret, just like he had after he'd vomited up the putrid pumpkin.

"That poor 12947 begged me to help him escape," he continued, "but there was nothing I could do. I had to leave him there. That's when I came back to the farm. I'd seen enough."

"It puts my feathers on end just thinking about it," Clementine clucked.

"Is it really true?" Gizzabelle breathed.

"I wouldn't have told you if I hadn't seen it myself," Poe said.

A shocked silence fell over the crowd. The chickens, who'd been admirably stoic in the face of the atrocities visited upon the cows, were visibly more distraught after hearing the evils befalling their brethren.

"Hang on a tick," Buddy said. "Where were you? The next farm over, you say? Do you think that could have been Kratchet's place?"

"Why, I hadn't thought of that," Poe said. "K for Kratchet. I bet you're right. I bet that *was* Kratchet's farm." They gave each other a knowing look.

"What?" Peanut demanded. "What does that mean?"

"Farmer Bob grizzled a lot about That Dag-Blasted Kratchet," Buddy explained. "He's some yobbo trying to buy the farm out from under Farmer Bob."

"Yeah," Poe agreed. "No way I'll sell out to That Dag-Blasted Factory Farm trying to run me out of business," Poe said, mimicking Farmer Bob exactly. "Over my dead body."

Poe's imitation was so true to life, it was as if he had conjured Farmer Bob from the grave. The eerie prescience of his words sent chills up the animals' spines.

"You don't think...?" Peanut asked.

"Well," Buddy said, considering. "Kratchet *did* make him mad as a meat ax. And more than once he said that keeping up with That Dag-Blasted Kratchet was going to kill him."

"That's right," Poe said. "I heard him say that, too, on the phone. Lately, it seemed like all he could talk about. It really tore him up. This farm has been in his family for generations, and he didn't want to be the one to lose it. But he just couldn't keep his head above water, even when he was working himself to death."

"Maybe it was just too much for his ticker," Buddy said.

"Poor Farmer Bob," Gizzabelle said. "We never knew what a strain he was under. He never let on, just did his work every day, like nothing was wrong. I guess eventually his heart finally gave out."

Most of the animals were still absorbing Poe's words when Mordecai put his hoof on their ominous implications. "Well, if That Dag-Blasted Kratchet was already looking to buy the farm when Farmer Bob was alive, what do you think's going to happen now?" he bleated. "I'll tell you what's going to happen. We're going to become part of Kratchet Farms, that's what!"

Horrified squawks and squeals, braying and baying, filled the air. The cows lowered their heads and pawed the ground; the horses reared and high stepped.

"Whoa, whoa, everybody!" Poe shouted. "Don't panic! I've been thinking about it and I think I've come up with a way out." He paused.

The crowd was quiet.

"We can run things ourselves—without the humans," Poe declared.

Everyone stared at him as if he'd suddenly sprouted hands.

"Have you gone off the farm?" Mordecai asked incredulously. "I thought ravens were supposed to be smart, but you're as feather-headed as Gizmo over there. You're crazy as a loon if you think we can run the farm by ourselves."

"Yeah, what do we know about running a farm?" asked Buttercup.

"I heard about animals taking over a farm once," Newton said. "It didn't end well."

"It will be a disaster," squawked Henrietta, who had just roused herself. "We'll never survive!" The hens started fluttering and clucking frantically, and the sheep—who always followed the prevailing wind—picked up on their hysteria and began bleating nervously.

Gizmo didn't share the general apprehension. His mind was elsewhere. "If we ran things ourselves," he chirped, "does that mean we wouldn't have to go to the slaughterhouse anymore?"

There was a stunned silence.

"Gizmo!" exclaimed Clementine, aghast.

"What?" he said, looking around defensively. "That's where we all end up, and the cows and pigs too. Everybody knows it."

This was the great open secret on the farm, universally under-stood but hardly ever alluded to and certainly never spoken of directly.

"That's not something we talk about, Gizmo," Clementine said sternly.

"But—"

"Not another word, young cockerel."

Poe looked around the crowd in confusion. "What does he mean?" No one would meet his eyes. Comprehension began to dawn. "Surely not...?"

"You didn't know?" Gizzabelle said softly. "It's true. For most of us here on the farm, at least."

"But why?" asked Poe.

Buddy looked at him sympathetically. "You know the bangers Farmer Bob had with his hen fruits every morning for brekkie?" he asked.

"You mean the sausage and eggs?"

Buddy held Poe's gaze a long moment, then nodded almost imperceptibly.

"You mean," Poe gulped, "animals are...*meat*?"

The deafening cacophony of clucking and whinnying and lowing let Poe know in no uncertain terms that he'd stuck his foot in his beak.

"Easy, everyone," Gizzabelle shouted over the din of the outraged throng. "I'm sure he didn't mean it. Remember, he was raised in the house. He probably wasn't ever taught any better." She looked up at Poe. "We *never* use the m-word. Ever."

"Oh," Poe said miserably. "I'm sorry. I didn't mean to offend anyone."

"It's alright," Millie said gently. "It's not your fault. You didn't know."

As the animals settled down and smoothed their hackles, Coco rubbed up against the edge of Newton's stall door. "*Alors*," she said, smirking up at Poe, "vat did you think 'cheeken' was, *s'il vous plaît*?"

"I guess I didn't think," he admitted. "With humanspeech, it's hard to know what's real and what isn't. Farmer Brown called his tractor a caterpillar and his friend Asa a stubborn mule and the politicians on the TV rats and varmints. And besides, it sure didn't *look* like chicken..."

He scanned the crowd from his perch. "You knew this all along?" he said. "And you just went along with it? What's wrong with you?"

The animals looked at him blankly. Slaughter wasn't something they liked to think about, so for the most part they didn't; however, they accepted it as a fact of life, unpleasant but inescapable, just as stones were sharp and winters cold. To suggest that they could prevent it was like saying they should have stopped the sun from setting.

"Do *what*, pray tell?" asked Mordecai. "It's easy for you to look down your beak at us now, all high and mighty, but I didn't see you breaking out of your cage either."

"Cages are safety," squawked Henrietta. "They keep out foxes and raccoons and coyotes and skunks. Farmer Bob kept us safe in our cages."

"And fed! We'd starve without food," squealed Hamish, Peanut's corpulent brother. The very idea brought on hunger pangs.

"Farmer Bob gave us a good life," said Clementine.

"Yeah, a great life....right up until you got killed," Poe shot back. "How could you stand for it?"

The rabble rumbled indignantly. "Who does he think he is?" sniffed Mordecai.

"We need humans to take care of us," said Flossy petulantly. "We can't do it ourselves." The rest of the sheep nodded along.

"Maybe we can if we just give it a try," Gizzabelle said, but it appeared that she and Newton were the only ones who were even willing to entertain the notion. Buddy and the horses had been so close to Farmer Bob that bucking the rule of the humans seemed like a betrayal of his memory. The chickens feared anything new on principle; the cows felt duty-bound to maintain tradition above all; the sheep, who were dyed-in-the-wool slackers, objected to the very idea of work.

Flossy flounced over. She, even more than the rest of the sheep, wasn't one to get her hooves dirty. "Aw, can't we just wait and see?

Maybe it won't be so bad after all."

"Is that a chance you really want to take?" Poe asked. "The cows and chickens aren't the only ones the humans persecute, you know. They have something special just for sheep. They call it mulesing."

"Mulesing?" Flossy said nervously. "What's that?"

"It's when they not only cut off your tail, but they flay the skin right off your buttocks."

"B-b-b-b-but why?"

"To keep away the flies."

"But Farmer Bob never had to do that."

Poe shrugged. "I'm just telling you what I heard."

Flossy shuddered.

Millie stepped up. "Poe, I understand that other farm must have been horrific," she said. "But you can't judge all humans by what you saw there. Farmer Bob was good to us, and I think there are plenty of good humans out there. You can't blame them for eating other animals. That's just their nature, just like we're made to eat grass."

"Too right," chimed in Buddy, quick to jump to Farmer Bob's defense. "Some of us are just made that way. I'm a carnivore, too, you know."

"And what about us chickens?" asked Gizzabelle. "We're killers, too. We eat insects and worms."

The chickens were affronted. Predators were foxes and raccoons and chickenhawks; it was self evident that eating insects and worms didn't count as real killing.

Suddenly an ear-splitting *ffffrrrrrptptptpt* ripped through the crowd. Gizmo gasped and started gagging noisily. He staggered around in a circle before falling backwards onto the barn floor with a dramatic thud, his feet sticking straight in the air. His entire body twitched spastically; then he went completely limp.

Before anyone could react, he sat straight up and looked around. "Okay, fess up," he said. "Who cut the cheese?"

"Sorry, everyone," Millie said, hanging her head. "I get gaseous when I'm upset."

Gizmo waved his wing in front of his beak.

"What's the matter, Millie?" asked Gizzabelle. "What is it that's upsetting you so much?"

The cow looked at her hooves, sighed heavily, then raised her eyes to the crowd. "For generation after generation, my ancestors have been nourishing the humans," she said with quiet dignity. "And it's not because they were fools or duped into it either. It's our nature, what we're meant for, our life purpose. Our duty. I'm proud to follow in their hoofsteps someday."

Peanut shook his head and stamped his small hoof. "Calling it 'Nature' is just a way of protecting the status quo, saying it can't be changed. Who's to say it is our *nature* to be dependent?" he said. "Isn't that just one of the fences of the mind Sausage has warned us about?"

The animals didn't know whose side to be on. Everyone seemed right...while they were talking, at least.

"Isn't that right, Sausage?" asked Peanut eagerly.

The crowd waited for Sausage to tell them what to think.

Sausage shambled over to Millie and looked deep into her eyes. "There is no greater love than to lay down one's life for another," he said. The cow's eyes welled up with tears.

"Thank you, Sausage," she whispered.

Sausage turned to Peanut, his gaze tender. "Be wary of freeing a camel from the burden of his hump," he said. "You may be freeing him from being a camel."

Peanut flushed a deeper shade of pink than he already was. "But I'm trying to save her life," he protested, stung by the public rebuke.

"The measure of a life," said Sausage, "is not length, but depth."

Peanut was quiet. "So what are you saying? That sacrificing your life is a good thing?"

Then, before Sausage could respond, the little pig suddenly reversed direction all on his own. "Maybe you're right," he said softly. "Maybe self-sacrifice is the way." He looked around in excitement. "That's it! We should all follow Millie parents' example. We should all be *martyrs*!"

"What are you saying?" Henrietta screeched. "That we should sacrifice our lives? On purpose? You're loopier than your tail!"

Of all the animals on the farm, Henrietta might have been expected to embrace martyrdom, considering how often she played the part. She was hardly alone in her dismay, though. The hens were all squawking; the sheep were bleating; the cows murmured amongst themselves. Only moments before, slaughter had been an immutable fact of life, but now deliberately choosing death seemed as unimaginable as the idea of escaping it ever had been.

Sausage's deep voice cut through the din.

"Peanut?"

Peanut's little ears drooped. He could hear the unmistakable reproach in his master's voice. "Yes, Sausage?"

"Suffering should never be sought nor compelled."

Peanut wrinkled his snout in confusion. "But I thought you said—"

Sausage stilled him with an infinitesimal shake of his head. Peanut sat down on his haunches with a thump, determined to keep his snout shut.

"The highest manifestation of life consists in this," Sausage said to his perplexed protégé, "that a being governs its own actions." Sausage looked at Millie again. "But also know, my child," he said, "to give your life it is not always necessary to give *up* your life."

With that, the enormous hog lumbered back to his stall and disappeared inside, leaving the animals staring after him, not sure what to do next.

All eyes went to Peanut. As a runt, his opinion would normally have little influence, but he was generally acknowledged to be the spokespig of the farm's great sage. Whatever Peanut said, it came with the weight of Sausage behind it.

The small porker looked around uncertainly. Then he straightened up. "As Sausage has so eloquently said, it is right for every being to govern its own actions," he announced. "We are more powerful than we realize. We are intelligent creatures, strong and creative and brave. Long, long ago we allowed ourselves to become domesticated by men, but the covenant between our species has been broken and now is the time to part ways again. It's time for us to govern ourselves!"

"That's right," cawed Poe. "No species should enslave another. All species are equal. If we work together, we can create a farm where all animals have dignity and purpose beyond what they can produce for the humans. A farm where there will be no killing, no butchery, where no animal's life is sacrificed for another. A farm of the animals, by the animals, for the animals!"

The pigs, who had been largely absent from the debate up to that point as they waited to hear all the arguments, began oinking in support. The most intelligent and independent-minded of the livestock, the pigs were often slower than the others to make decisions since they relied less on instinct, but they were usually the first to embrace new ideas.

"Of the animals, by the animals, for the animals!" they began chanting. "Of the animals, by the animals, for the animals!"

With the pigs on board and—most importantly—an implied endorsement from Sausage, the other animals reconsidered their knee-jerk opposition.

Suddenly Gizmo launched forward. "HIIIH-YAH!" he screeched, slicing his wing horizontally in a swift karate chop. "Take that, you lousy old humans. You're not making *me* into a friggin' chicken nugget!" He kicked his small clawed foot in a sweeping arc and punched the air, all the while spewing a stream of inchoate gibberish noises at his invisible enemy.

Where rhetoric and reason had failed, theatrics succeeded. The crowd went wild. The chickens whistled and cheered. "Boo, humans!" they squawked. "Boo! Boo!"

The sheep, always emotional, quickly got swept up in the furor. Their chanting sounded more like baaing than booing, but it was every bit as loud as the chickens', despite the fact that not a single lamb from the farm had ever been sold for slaughter.

"We've been under the thumb of the humans for long enough," Peanut shouted over the growing din. "It's time for us to put our hooves down and take back our power. We won't be fooled into laying down our lives for slop and a warm stall anymore!"

"No more pork!" squealed the pigs. "No more beef!" lowed the cows. "No more fried chicken!" squawked the chickens.

"We'll never be taken advantage of again," croaked Poe. "Nevermore!"

Hoots and catcalls filled the air.

Buddy finally weighed in. "Seems like we've got to give it a go.

If it's just a matter of hard yakka, we can do it."

"Think about what we've *already* accomplished," agreed Gizzabelle. "Who thought we could have done everything we've done just since yesterday?"

"We freed ourselves," offered Jock.

"And milked ourselves," said Millie.

"And buried Farmer Bob," added Buddy.

Everyone began murmuring enthusiastically.

"We're stronger than we think," said Xena.

"It's the fences of the mind holding us back," Peanut said.

"The universe bends in the direction of belief," said Poe.

"We just need to walk through the fear," said Jock.

"We can do it!" the animals chorused with rising excitement. The chickens flapped their wings, and hopped up and down; the ungulates stomped their hooves. "Of the animals, by the animals, for the animals!"

Even grumpy old Mordecai admitted it wasn't *the* most idiotic course of action, all things considered.

CHAPTER 4

Having committed to running the farm themselves, the animals had absolutely no idea what to do next. Newton suggested that for the time being at least, they just keep to their normal routines and do what they always had. Being creatures of habit who disliked change, this suited everyone just fine.

"And don't damage anything or leave anything out of place from here on out," instructed the mule. "We can't do anything about the things we've already broken, but it's important that we make sure to keep everything looking just the same as it does now in case any humans come around."

"You sure like to tell everyone what to do," said Mordecai. "Next I guess you'll be telling us where we can take a dump."

"Absolutely!" cried Peanut, wiping the smirk off the goat's face. "Waste disposal is a major issue. You can't just go wherever you like."

Mordecai rolled his eyes.

To forestall the impending sewage problem, Peanut suggested an immediate moratorium on making waste inside the barn. The pigs' fixation on cleanliness was well known, but everyone had to admit that without anyone mucking out their stalls, it would soon be filthy by anyone's standards, so the inconvenience was grudgingly accepted.

With these items out of the way, they turned their attention to their main preoccupation, that which was always first and foremost in their minds: food.

Suddenly, seemingly out of nowhere, a chant took hold of the crowd. It didn't begin with any particular individual, but spontaneously issued forth from the collective as if they were a single animal. Within moments, it had risen to a deafening roar.

"To the corncrib!" they shouted. "To the corncrib! To the corncrib!" The still-chanting animals spilled out of the barn and across the farmyard. In no time, they were gathered outside the corncrib.

Jock was just about to kick in the door when Newton stayed his hoof. "Whoa, there!" he said. "Let me take a look at it! Remember, we don't want to cause any more damage than we have to." He quickly set about inspecting the latch. "It's not the same as the one on the stalls," he said, "but I might be able to figure it out anyway. Just give me a moment."

"Don't worry," Jock assured the chickens, who were pacing impatiently. "Between the two of us, we'll have you eating before you can say corncob!"

"Good, 'cause I'm *famished*!" whined Hamish, who was fairly obsessed with food. "I didn't eat anything yesterday except a few lousy acorns. I'm soooo hungry!"

"Ah, quit your bellyaching! No one wants to hear your complaining," Mordecai complained.

"What are you even doing here?" snapped Gizmo who regarded the goat with the warm feelings he normally reserved for poultry mites. "Why aren't you out grazing with the sheep?"

"Where are your manners, you impudent young whippersnapper?" Mordecai bleated. "Don't you know not to question your elders? Were you raised in the woods? Your mother would be ashamed!"

Gizmo glared at Mordecai defiantly.

"If you must know," Mordecai said archly, "I am a *browser*, not a grazer. I prefer *variety* in my diet. And today I—"

"Bingo!" Newton brayed triumphantly. "I got it!" He swung the door of the corncrib wide open. The animals rushed forward, then stopped dead in their tracks. Only in their dreams had they beheld such a sight. Big, beautiful piles of golden corncobs were stacked from floor to ceiling as far back as the eye could see. All theirs for the taking.

"Lord love a duck," Clementine exclaimed.

"It's like Shangri-La," Peanut squealed.

"Whoopee!" Gizmo shouted, streaking forward and diving headfirst into a pile of cobs. The rest of the animals followed, falling on top of one another in their rush to get into the crib. They immediately started gobbling down as much corn as they could cram in their mouths. The chickens jack-hammered the ears, spraying kernels in every direction, not bothering to finish one ear before attacking the next, while the pigs gulped down whole corncobs without even bothering to chew.

Only Gizzabelle didn't join in the exuberance. She picked half-heartedly at the corn.

"What's the matter, Giz?" asked Clementine. "Don't you want to plump up? You'll be nothing but skin and bones if you don't eat more than that!"

Gizzabelle dutifully finished off another row of kernels, but she darted out of the corncrib as soon as Clementine looked away.

When the animals emerged from their orgy of mastication some-time later, they were moaning and groaning in discomfort.

"Argh," grunted Hamish. He sat down hard on his haunches and rubbed his distended belly with his forehooves. "I've never been so stuffed in my life! It's fantastic!"

Peanut stumbled out after him. "I've got to take Sausage some breakfast." He belched heartily. "In a minute. I'll just sit for a second…" he said with a yawn.

When Peanut awoke a couple of hours later, he found himself alone, surrounded by half-eaten corncobs littering the ground out-side the corncrib. He jumped up and rushed to the tack room to fetch a burlap sack, which he hastily filled with corn and dragged to the barn for Sausage, who was still recovering from his exertion the day before.

"Here you go," he said, depositing the sack in front of the enor-mous pig, who was lying unmoving in his stall. "Eat as much as you want. And if you finish that, I can get more. There's plenty where that came from!"

Sausage sighed and shook his head. "Little one," he said affec-tionately, "satisfy your need, not your greed. To conserve today is to eat tomorrow."

Peanut's pink cheeks grew pinker. "Geez, I didn't think of it that way. There was just so much corn; more corn than you've ever seen! It's hard to believe we could ever eat it all, but you're right. It won't last forever."

Sausage started eating, his delicate chomping remarkably dainty for so hulking a beast.

"I'll never be as wise as you," Peanut sighed, kicking at the straw. "With Farmer Bob gone, now *I'll* never get to go to the fair." Going to the county fair was Peanut's most dearly-held ambition. He was sure it was where Sausage had gained his enlightened perspective.

Sausage chuckled. "You may gain as much wisdom from within a stall as from the whole world," he said. "The secret of the sea may be discovered in meditation upon the dewdrop."

Peanut wrinkled his brow.

Sausage beckoned the little pig to him. "A true journey is not made on hoof. The true journey is here," he said, placing his hoof over Peanut's heart.

"Here? But how...?"

"You must look until you see."

"Oh," said Peanut uncertainly. "I see. Look until I...*see*."

He went over to Sausage's water pail, squinted into it intently for several minutes, then looked at Sausage in dismay.

"But I don't see anything but water," he wailed.

Sausage nodded sagely. "Mind gets in the way."

"What?" squeaked Peanut, who had always prided himself on being a great thinker. "What's wrong with my mind?"

"You have an excellent mind," Sausage assured his devotee. Peanut relaxed. "Mind is the tiger in the path. Greater mind, bigger tiger."

Peanut didn't know what to make of this. He was still trying to digest that kernel of wisdom when there came a loud rustling near the grain bins. Peanut was torn between irritation at the interruption and relief. He'd had about as much enlightenment as he could handle for one day. His head was starting to hurt.

"I'll be back in two shakes of a lamb's tail," he said.

Releasing his disciple with an indulgent smile, Sausage returned to his corn. Peanut peeked around the door and discovered Buddy crouched in the corner, squinting his brown eye at the gap between two grain bins.

"What are you doing?" Peanut asked him.

"Shhhhh…"

Suddenly a mouse shot out from between the bins and Buddy took off after it, vainly swatting at the petrified rodent as it scuttled toward a hole in the wall and disappeared within.

Buddy sighed and sat down with a thump. Then he looked over at Peanut. "I can't stomach corn, you know, so Coco here's teaching me to hunt mice." He grimaced. "Giving it a bash, at least."

"*Coco's* teaching you to hunt?" Peanut asked incredulously.

Looking around, Buddy lowered his voice. "When she volunteered to show me the ropes, I was sure she was selling me a furphy. What does she think this is, bush week? I didn't just come down in the last shower! But she assured me she was fair dinkum. Claims we can kill more working together than alone, but I'm not sucked in. Just between you, me, and the barn walls, I reckon our pussy Coco's not quite the loner she makes out."

Suddenly he cleared his throat and said a bit too loudly, "And hopefully I'll start pulling my weight soon," as Coco appeared carrying a mouse delicately by the tail. She deposited the tiny carcass in front of Buddy and Peanut.

"*Pour vous?*" she said, examining her claws and tugging at one with her teeth. "*Pour moi*, another *n'est pas possible.*"

"Right-o," he said, scooping the tiny critter up and wolfing it down.

Much to Peanut's astonishment, Coco proceeded to instruct Buddy in the finer points of mouse hunting, and working as a team, they caught another luckless rodent. Soon Buddy proudly laid his first solo kill at Coco's feet.

"Maybe I'm not so old I can't learn some new tricks after all," he said, his tail thumping vigorously and a huge doggy grin on his face. "You'll make me into a tolerable ratter yet."

Coco merely arched an eyebrow.

By mid-morning everyone was fed and milked and ready for their midday nap. Although the horses had to be reminded more than once to make their droppings outdoors, and Peanut had to institute and enforce restrictions on corn consumption for the chickens, who, if given the chance, would eat themselves to death, for the most part the animals found adjusting to their new routines surprisingly easy. Their immediate needs taken care of, the animals were content.

Only Poe seemed to be having trouble figuring out what to do with himself. Having spent all his life in a cage, he didn't have a routine to return to. He tried hanging out with the chickens, but he didn't have much in common with the hens and felt like a third wing. Gizzabelle was the only one he could really talk to and he rarely left her side.

Poe was eager to learn everything he'd missed shut up in the house, and Gizzabelle tried to satisfy his curiosity as best she could. She recounted the major events of farm history as it had been passed down from generation to generation. She gave him a rundown of all the various personalities on the farm and described the relationship dynamics amongst animals and species. She even let him in on the farm secrets—the unspoken rules of behavior, the rumors, the speciest stereotypes that everyone knew but pretended they didn't. All except the ones about chickens and their limited intelligence, that is. She kept that to herself.

"Okay," Poe said. "So, no cracks about pigs and cleanliness or sheep not thinking for themselves." Gizzabelle had explained how the pigs' reputation for filth enraged them since they were, in point of fact, a particularly fastidious species, while the sheep's being called followers infuriated them for the simple reason that it was true. "Anything else I shouldn't talk about?"

"Well...I wouldn't mention Newton's mixed parentage," Gizzabelle said. "Or Xena's being a freemartin."

"What's a freemartin?"

"A cow that acts like a bull."

Poe raised his eyebrows. "That's not normal, is it?"

Gizzabelle shrugged. "It often happens with twins. Some of the animals think it's unnatural, but Sausage says that *is* her nature. And if anyone would know, it would be Sausage. He's always talking about Nature. He talks even more about it than the Great Spirit."

Poe's ears pricked up. "Nature, eh? What does he say?"

"Well, let's see," she said, struggling to remember everything the great hog had said on the subject. "Nature never hurries, yet all is accomplished; Nature is harmony; Never does Nature say one thing and Wisdom another; a domesticated lion is an unnatural animal, and whatever is unnatural is untrustworthy…" She tapped a claw in contemplation. "Peanut could probably give you even more. Oh, yeah. Just the other day Sausage said the difference between humans and the rest of the animals is that humans are the only ones to try to adapt Nature to themselves instead of the other way around. And of course, there's my all-time favorite Sausagism."

"And what would that be?"

"The goal of life is to make your heartbeat match the beat of the Universe, to match your nature with Nature."

"To match your nature with Nature," Poe repeated. "I like that." He paused, then looked at Gizzabelle thoughtfully. "You know, when we first met, Sausage talked to me about destiny. Do you believe in destiny?"

"Oh, yes," Gizzabelle said. "Everyone has a purpose."

Poe snorted. "I'm not so sure. I thought it was my destiny to save Farmer Bob and look how that turned out."

Gizzabelle thought for a moment. "That reminds me of something I heard Sausage say," she said. "'Life must be lived forward, but can only be understood backwards.' Maybe destiny's like that— you can't make sense of it until you've already fulfilled it."

Poe cocked his head. "Huh."

Suddenly Gizzabelle found the raven staring at her, a peculiar expression on his face. Her insides went as squishy as if she'd been deboned.

"It's not always easy to understand what Sausage means," she said, her words tumbling out in a rush. "I can't tell you how many times he's said something that didn't make a bit of sense when I first heard it. But later some completely different situation would crop up and what he said would come back to me and it would fall into place and make perfect sense."

Poe leaned in closer. Gizzabelle realized she was prattling like a popinjay but she couldn't seem to stop herself. "If Sausage said you've got a destiny," she chirped, "I'm sure you do. I've never known him to be wrong. And you've got such amazing gifts, I'm sure you have an extra-special purpose." Having come to the end of her breath, she stopped for a gulp of air.

"You know, you're some bird," Poe said, his voice husky.

Gizzabelle's mouth went dry, but it didn't matter since her thoughts had scattered like feathers in the wind. She wasn't aware of anything except the dark wells of Poe's eyes into which she seemed to be falling deeper and deeper.

"Gizzabelle—"

"Hey, guys!" said Peanut.

The two birds jumped apart like they'd been shot at.

"There's gonna be a farm tour!" squealed the little pig, his tail curling with excitement. "Buddy says he'll take anyone who wants on a tour of the farm. We're gonna see the *whole farm*! You wanna come?"

"Um....sure," croaked Poe. Gizzabelle hastily smoothed her feathers.

"Great," oinked Peanut. "With your being able to fly, you can be our forward scout. Make sure we don't run into any trouble. What about you, Giz?"

"Mmm-hmm," she said. "I'd love to."

As they set off to find Buddy, Gizzabelle and Poe gave the small pig their undivided attention as he prattled on about the grand adventure they were about to have. The birds didn't look at one another once.

When they found the group gathered at the edge of the barnyard, they were surprised to see how few animals had taken Buddy up on his offer. Most of the animals, it seemed, preferred the safety of home and were happy to let others brave the unknown for them. Newton would have been eager to explore the farthest reaches of the farm—and particularly to check out the tractor—but he was busy surveying the garage, which not only stored all Farmer Bob's tools, but was a graveyard of old equipment and supplies. For the mechanically-minded mule, it was an irresistible lure. He couldn't wait to get his hooves on Farmer Bob's machines, and see if he could get them to give up their secrets.

Although Jock, Xena, and Sarge had been induced to take part in the historic expedition on the grounds that a contingent of delegates that represented all the species should be assembled for such a momentous event, none of them were exactly champing at the bit.

The only one there who seemed genuinely excited about the prospect of exploring the farm was Gizmo.

"Oh, come *on*, Mom," he groaned.

"Absolutely not," said Clementine. "I'll not have you running around all over creation. Not at your age."

Gizmo saw Buddy approaching with his sister and ran over to them.

"I can come on the tour, can't I?" he demanded of the shepherd. "You said *anyone* could come, right?"

Buddy looked over his head at Clementine and quickly apprehended the issue. "Too right," he said. "I did say that. But you've got to listen to yer Mum, little fella. You're still knee high to a grasshopper."

"I bet *Gizzabelle* gets to go," he huffed. "And she's barely older than me. It's not fair!"

Clementine looked at Gizzabelle pleadingly.

The little hen sighed. "Don't look so down in the beak," she said. "How about this? How about we stay here and explore the farmhouse together?"

Gizmo snorted. "The farmhouse?"

"Sure," she said. "We'll have our own adventure, just you and me."

"Good call," said Buddy. "The farm is mainly just big, empty fields anyway. The house is full of all sorts of ripper thingamajigs and doovalackies. It's bonkers!"

Gizmo settled down a bit, but his feathers were still ruffled.

"Whatever you do, though," warned Buddy, "don't, under any circumstances, open the closet under the stairs."

Gizmo's pique instantly evaporated. "Why not?" he asked eagerly.

"*It* is in there."

"It?"

Buddy looked around. "The hoover," he said in a low voice, as if speaking its name might call it to life. There was no braver animal than shepherd, but his phobia of the vacuum cleaner was as absolute as it was irrational. "Just leave it alone. Got it?"

"Yes sir," Gizmo promised.

Gizmo stalked past Clementine, unspeaking, on his way to the farmhouse. Gizzabelle hurried after him.

Since none of the sheep had volunteered for the expedition, before setting off Buddy led the group to the sheep pasture to wrangle an ovine representative into joining them. Finally, a good-natured young ram named Jellybean valiantly stepped forward. At that point Mordecai, who refused to be lumped in with the sheep, insisted upon coming along as well and then promptly started grumbling about the imposition.

Their party complete, Buddy led the animals past the sheep and cows' pasture and through the fields. Poe flew in tight circles over the animals' heads so he could hear everything Buddy said. The fields, which had all looked the same from the air, turned out to be all different. Some were for wheat, some corn; others were for alfalfa and soybeans. "At least that's what they were last year," Buddy said. "Farmer Bob switches them around every few years. I don't know what he was planning for this year."

The animals marveled at the immensity of the farm.

"It's so big. I had no idea!" Peanut squealed. He skipped along beside Jock, snout in the air, breathing in all the different scents. Occasionally, he stopped to root around in the dirt, then hurried to catch up to the others.

When, at last, the animals came upon the big, green tractor, abandoned in the middle of the farthest field, they grew quiet. Buddy's ears sagged and his tail was tucked between his legs, but he soldiered on. He jumped up on his hind legs and rested his front paws on the side. "That is where Farmer Bob sat," he said, indicating the tractor cabin, "but I can't open the door. Even if we could get in, though, it's a skull-drag. All these sticks and knobs to push and pull at just the right time. I watched him do it more times than I can count and I still can't for the life of me figure it out."

The other animals sniffed at the tractor's enormous tires. Poe alighted on the windshield and peered into the cabin.

"What's this?" asked Peanut, pointing his snout at the evil-looking metal teeth on the long bar behind the tractor.

"That's the tiller," explained Buddy. "The metal bits go into the ground and claw it up, so you can go back and plant seeds in it later.

That's what we were doing when..." He stopped. "Somehow we need to pick up where we left off."

"You want us to dig up all these fields?" Mordecai snorted. "And how do you propose we do that?"

"We'll think of something," said Buddy much more confidently than he felt.

After a few more minutes of "inspecting" the tractor—more to say they had done it than with any real expectation that it would lead to anything—the animals moved on.

Soon they came to the intersection of the dirt road that ran down to the farmhouse and the paved road which marked the outer boundary of the farm.

"What's that?" asked Peanut, pointing his snout at the black metallic box attached to the fence.

"That's the postbox. The Postie puts letters and things there for Farmer Bob to pick up," said Buddy.

"You mean the mail?" Poe asked. He knew about the mail—Farmer Bob opened and read it at the desk just under Poe's cage—but he'd never known where it came from.

"What's the mail?" Jellybean asked.

"It's messages humans send to each other," Poe explained.

"They read things with their eyes the way we do with our nozzles," added Buddy. "They're handicapped that way; practically no sense of smell whatsoever. Why, Farmer Bob couldn't smell a skunk right under his shnoz!"

"How sad," Peanut said. "What would life be without its fragrance?"

"I wouldn't feel too sorry for them," Mordecai snorted. "They've got their damned opposable thumbs to console them. That's the only reason those naked apes have been able to subjugate us all these years, you know—those blasted thumbs that they build pens and make harnesses and run their confounded machine contraptions with."

Jock glanced at Buddy, who looked like he'd been kicked in the stomach. "Speak for yourself," said Jock. "*I* wasn't subjugated."

"Mordecai, you don't really mean that," Jellybean said gently. "Farmer Bob was always good to us."

"Well, he wasn't as bad as he could have been," Mordecai admitted, scruffing his hoof in the dirt. "A benign dictator."

"Plug your mug, Mordecai," growled Buddy, who almost never lost his temper but couldn't abide any slight to Farmer Bob's memory. "He wasn't a dictator. He was our master, and a bonza one at that. You'd be proud to call him master if you weren't such a mangy old drongo..." He took a step forward and Mordecai backed right into Xena.

"Easy, Buddy," said Jock, stepping between them. "Don't let him get to you; you know how he is. He'd say water's too wet. Just let it go." Then he walked over to the mailbox and Buddy followed him after giving Mordecai a final snarl for good measure.

"Let's see what we've got here," said Jock. Grabbing the tab in his teeth, he pulled the mailbox door open. It was filled with papers of all shapes and sizes.

"Grab as much as you can carry," Buddy instructed. "We'll take it back with us."

"We could just eat it," Mordecai suggested, but he was roundly ignored.

Sarge jumped up on top of Jellybean and clutched an envelope in his beak. Piece by piece, he pulled the mail out and dropped it on the ground, where the other animals nudged it into bite-sized piles. Finally, when the mailbox was empty, Sarge hopped down and everyone grabbed a mouthful of mail.

Since conversation was out of the question, the animals were lost in their own thoughts as they trudged down the dirt road to the barn. Now that no one was talking, Poe soared into the sky in wider and wider circles.

As he was flying overhead, he noticed a truck on the paved road slowing down to turn onto the dirt road toward the farmhouse. He could see the scouting party down below, oblivious to their danger, but he was too high to sound a warning.

Pivoting in midair, he tucked his wings to his body and aimed his beak at the earth. Faster and faster he went, picking up speed at a mad clip. The wind roared in his ears and the ground rushed at him. At the last possible moment, he pulled out of his nosedive right in front of the train of animals.

"Human coming! On the road!" he cawed as he whooshed by. "Run, run! I'll warn the others!" He took off toward the farmhouse.

The animals began to panic. They were hemmed in by the fence on one side, an open field with no cover on the other, and no way to outrun the vehicle.

"The broken fence!" Buddy barked. "Everybody, round up and get into the cow pasture. And whatever you do, *don't move*! Get a wriggle on, there's no time to lose."

Sure enough, the patch of fence that Xena had broken through was just a few yards down the road. The animals made a break for it, leaving a trail of envelopes and magazines scattered in their wake. Once they jumped over the broken railing, Xena and Jock hurriedly stationed themselves near the fence and the other animals scrambled around to crouch behind them.

They had no sooner gotten into position than the vehicle came over the hill.

"It's the milk truck," Sarge said, peeking out from between Xena's legs.

"Quiet," she hissed through clenched teeth. "Don't move."

No one moved a muscle, not even to breathe.

As the truck neared, Buddy started barking furiously from the other side of the road and then ran right into its path. Cursing, the driver swerved to miss him, then continued on down the road without even slowing down. The animals watched the truck speed away toward the barnyard.

When it was nearly out of sight, Buddy bounded over the broken fence and joined the rest of the animals in the pasture. "She's apples," he said, panting. "I reckoned it would work; humans aren't very observant as a rule."

"Now all we can do is cross our hooves that Poe gets to the barnyard in time to warn the others," said Jock.

CHAPTER 5

The animals set off across the pasture, keeping well away from the fence so the milkman wouldn't catch them on his way out. The group moved as fast as Sarge's legs would carry him, which wasn't very.

When they got to the barnyard, it was deserted. Poe glided over and landed next to Buddy.

"What happened?" asked the shepherd.

"The milkman just left."

"Did he see anything?"

Poe shook his head. "Luckily, Buttercup was the only one out of place, and I was able to get her inside the barn before the truck got here. He poked around for a minute, but then he just collected the milk as usual and left. I think we're safe."

"We were lucky this time," said Buddy. "But we can't count on luck forever."

"We should get everyone together to make a plan," said Peanut.

"Good idea," said Buddy. "Let's muster in the barn."

Each of the species reps rounded up their constituents. Peanut took it upon himself to personally fetch Sausage, while Poe went to get Newton and Buddy collected Gizzabelle and Gizmo from the farmhouse. He found them in the bedroom; Gizzabelle was looking in the closet and Gizmo's tail feathers were peeking out from under the bed.

"Hey there, chook!" Buddy said.

There was a muffled thump and then Gizmo's face poked out from the checkered bedskirts.

"Find anything?" Buddy asked.

"No!" Gizmo squawked heatedly before his sister had a chance to answer. "The vacuum cleaner was *lame!*"

Buddy flinched. "You saw it?" he said. "What did I tell you?"

"I don't know why you made such a big deal about it," the

cockerel shot back. "It didn't *do* anything!"

"Thank your lucky stars," said Buddy. "I guess it wasn't awake. A lot of the human thingamajigs sleep unless you know how to wake them up."

Gizmo snorted. "I don't know where all these 'amazing' things are that you claim are here. We didn't find anything but places to *sit*." He shook his head in disgust as he stalked out from beneath the bed. "How many places do they need to sit? Hard ones, soft ones, big ones, little ones, ones that rock, ones that roll around. Room after room of 'em. And if it's not a place to sit, it's somewhere to lie down!" He jerked his beak at the bed. "The only rooms that aren't for sitting are the drinking rooms."

"The drinking rooms?"

"Yeah," he chirped, his eyes lighting up, "that's the only cool thing we found. But it was pretty sweet. There're these big drinking bowls that you can refill just by pressing the bar. WHOOOOSSSHHH!" He enthusiastically mimicked the noise. "Ta-da! Beautiful, crystal-clear water!"

Gizmo was less than impressed when Buddy informed him that the "drinking bowls" were for sitting, too.

Buddy told them about the meeting in the barn and on their way over, he recounted their close call with the milkman. Gizmo was fairly livid that he had missed all the action. "I knew it!" he squawked. "I *knew* they'd have all the fun!" He kicked at the ground, throwing up a cloud of dirt.

Gizzabelle shot Buddy a look of rueful exasperation over the young cockerel's head. Gizmo's penchant for adventure was going to get him into trouble some day.

They arrived in the barn just as Peanut called the meeting to order. "Quiet down, everyone!" he squealed, rapping his tiny hoof on the floor. "We've got to focus. We had a couple of near squeaks today while we were out surveying the property, and if we don't get our act together, we're done for."

A hush fell over the crowd.

"For starters, we forgot about the post," said Buddy. Most of the animals looked at each other in bewilderment.

"And we also forgot about the milk truck coming today," piped up Peanut. "If it wasn't for Poe and Buddy, we would have been caught right then and there!" This created more of a stir; the milk truck was something everybody understood.

"Those are things that we should have been prepared for," Newton brayed. "What about surprise visits that we don't even know are coming? We have to start thinking ahead to the future and making plans." That wasn't something the animals had any experience with; they were used to living in the now and letting the future sort itself out.

"It's all well and good that we've remembered to collect the mail from the mailbox," said Poe, "but you know the mail *means* something, right? It's messages the humans send each other. Not answering those messages might be just as dangerous as leaving them in the mailbox."

"But how are we supposed to answer them when we can't understand them?" Gizzabelle said anxiously.

Poe began preening his feathers.

Gizzabelle eyed him suspiciously. "We can't, right? Understand them?"

Poe stopped his preening. "Well, actually I can," he admitted. "Farmer Bob's hearing had gone downhill in the last few years, so he'd started watching all his television shows with subtitles. I started teaching myself to read just to pass the time—I figured at the very least I could read the newspapers Farmer Bob lined my cage with. It was slow going at first, but I've gotten pretty good at it."

"So you think you can figure out what the mail says?" asked Newton.

Poe shrugged. "I don't know, but I can try."

"You're so talented, Poe," Gizzabelle gushed, her eyes wide with admiration.

"Now, don't get too excited yet," he said, although he was obviously pleased. "Let's see how it goes."

"If anyone can do it, you can," Gizzabelle said confidently.

"Okay, Poe can work on the mail," said Newton. "Everybody, put on your thinking caps and let's start thinking ahead."

"Our thinking caps?" Gizmo asked. "Mom, do I have a thinking cap?"

"It's just an expression, bird brain," said Mordecai, rolling his eyes. "It means to think hard. Really, you needn't bother. Your head's nothing but a place to grow feathers."

"Hey! I can think just as good as anyone!" Gizmo snapped, squinting and screwing up his face in his best approximation of serious cognition to prove his point.

"What about Granny Ann, The Egg Lady?" asked Gizzabelle. Granny Ann sold homemade breads and cookies at the local Farmer's Market, and she sold Farmer Bob's eggs for him at her booth.

"That's right," said Newton, looking over at the hens. "Winter's almost over. We'll need to gather the eggs so they're ready for her to pick up when she comes by. What else?"

"Farmer Bob usually hired on *travailleurs*—workers—around thees time," said Coco, who had deigned to attend the meeting.

"I don't reckon he's teed up anything for this year yet," said Buddy.

"Will it make the workers suspicious if they don't get hired back?" asked Peanut.

Buddy considered. "Not necessarily. The crew's been getting smaller every year, so they'll probably just assume he had to cut back again."

"Or that the farm went under altogether," said Poe.

"*Exactement*," said Coco. "*Entre nous*—between us—*ce n'est pas improbable.*"

"Okay, so maybe we don't have to worry too much about the workers," said Newton.

"What about blow-ins?" said Buddy. "Like Farmer Bob's best mate Asa. I don't reckon he'll lob in unannounced just yet but if he doesn't hear from Farmer Bob eventually, he's bound to think something's shonky."

"If we get surprised, we've just got to hope they don't notice anything unusual," said Newton. "With any luck, they'll just assume Farmer Bob isn't home and leave."

"But what if they catch us wandering about?" asked Millie. "The milkman almost caught Buttercup today."

Newton shrugged. "I guess the best you can do is stay in your pasture. Better safe than sorry."

"Bullcrap," lowed Xena. "We can't stay in our pasture all the time. We have to get milked."

"Or we've got to leave the barn to milk them," said Peanut.

"We'll be fetching the post now, too," Buddy reminded everyone.

"And animals are always going to and from the corncrib and the stream," said Gizzabelle. "It just isn't possible for us to stay in our usual places. What we need is some sort of warning so we can get out of sight. Like Poe gave Buttercup."

Peanut jumped in. "Yes. And then we can either get back to where we belong, or if there isn't time for that, find somewhere to hide."

"What about the security cameras Farmer Bob had installed?" asked Newton. "Could we use those?"

Poe shook his head. "They're fake. Farmer Bob didn't want to pay for a real security system; said it wasn't worth the price. He put up dummy cameras to make it look like the farm was monitored. Sorry."

Newton sat back, deflated.

"Lookouts," declared Sarge. "That's what we need. We'll post a sentry at the mailbox and set up a relay chain back to the barn. And drills. Lots of them. Until we can do it in our sleep." He puffed out his chest. "Give me command of the mission, and I'll have it running so reliable you could set your crow by it."

Everyone agreed that this sounded like a good plan, and Sarge was promptly deputized to coordinate an early warning system.

"Well, that seems to take care of that," said Newton. "Anyone have anything else?"

The animals thought and thought. Gizmo grunted with mental exertion.

Peanut cleared his throat. "There is something else," he squeaked. "It's about the corn."

"What about the corn?" asked Hamish tremulously.

"It may look like a lot, like it's going to last forever, but it's not," his brother said. "If we don't find a way to grow more, we're going to run out. And sooner than you think."

Henrietta began shrieking about starving to death and the crowd began to murmur anxiously.

"Hold on," Poe shouted above the rising rumble. "Give your-selves some credit. Farmer Bob did it, so why can't we?"

"But Farmer Bob had machines," Newton said glumly. "He couldn't have plowed the fields either without his 125-horsepower tractor."

"What's horsepower?" asked Gizzabelle.

"Horsepower is the number of horses it would take to do the same work as the tractor," Newton explained.

Gizzabelle gasped. "Did you say 125 horsepower? It would take *125* horses to do what the tractor does?"

All eyes instantly went to the two draft horses, who looked as though they wanted nothing more than to disappear through the barn floor.

"It's true we don't have 125 *horses*," said Poe. "But we've got a herd of cows, a flock of chickens, a mob of sheep, a drift of pigs, a mule, a goat, a dog, a cat....Surely, if everyone pitches in, we can do everything that needs to be done."

"We could have a legion of cows, or horses for that matter and it still wouldn't be enough to plow the fields," said Mordecai. "We already saw how good hooves are for digging. No one here can dig worth a damn except Buddy, and he's no bleating groundhog."

Henrietta's hysterical squawking was lost in the uproar of the rest of the animals. Everyone was panicking. Everyone except Newton.

"Actually," said the mule, who was suddenly grinning like he was eating briars. "I think I may have just what we need."

A hush fell over the crowd.

"When I was going through the garage," he continued, "there was lots of old stuff. Farmer Bob never threw anything away.... he always said you never knew when something would come in handy again. Some of it was so old that it probably went back to his father's or grandfather's time. A lot of it was broken and most of it was useless, but in middle of all that junk, I found an old-fashioned plow, the kind the humans used before they got tractors."

Newton looked around expectantly, but it was clear that the animals didn't grasp the import of his words. "It is designed to be pulled by horses or oxen," he explained impatiently. "Don't you see? It's made just for us animals!"

"So you mean we can plow the fields without the tractor?" Gizzabelle asked.

"Spot on," said Buddy, his tail beating back and forth uncontrollably. "Thanks to Newton here, now we've actually got a chance at making this work. I say, let's 'avago. Right-o?"

"That's the spirit!" cawed Poe. "We'll have the farm up and running before you know it."

"We can do it," Gizzabelle chimed in. "I know we can."

The crowd hummed with nervous energy. They didn't entirely understand what all these revelations meant, but from what they could deduce, they seemed to merit cautious optimism at the very least.

Under Buddy's direction, the animals split up to according to species to get started with their new responsibilities. Buddy and Newton took the horses and the cows to the garage to investigate the plow. Since the pigs already had their milking duties, the sheep were assigned mail pickup. Jellybean and Mordecai agreed to lead the first expedition since they knew the way, but they had a hard time convincing any sheep to join them. It was only when Mordecai began grumbling that you'd never see goats acting so cowardly that a few rams were sufficiently invested with species pride to volunteer.

Sarge sagely didn't rely on chickens volunteering; he conscripted. Although he exempted a few hens for medical reasons and Henrietta for psychiatric ones, the rest of the flock he divided into shifts for the lookout stations he strategically located across the fields and pastures, and once he deemed his squadron sufficiently trained, he began running farm-wide drills.

At first, the results were disastrous. When the final chicken on the lookout chain raised the alarm, the animals would instantly panic. Some froze in place, even if they were smack-dab in the middle of the farmyard where they were sure to be seen; others fled the scene at top speed, but without thinking about where they were headed, often ending up in an even more conspicuous place than they'd started from.

The chickens weren't required to take part in the drills other than in their role as lookouts since they had always had free range of the farmyard anyway. This suited them just fine since they, even more than any of the other animals, found it almost impossible to overcome their fear response. The notable exception was Gizmo, who, unlike his predominantly chicken-hearted brethren, actually enjoyed the adrenaline rush of the drills.

"Attention, attention!" he squawked, broadcasting the standard warning message Peanut had created to simultaneously alert and calm the animals. "Do not panic. Stop, think, and proceed to your nearest safe spot. Repeat, do not panic. Proceed to your nearest safe spot."

Flossy and her two sidekicks, Lulu and Ewina, who'd all been fast friends since they were lambs, dove behind a small outbuilding near the farmhouse, but no matter how they positioned themselves, someone's rump always stuck out into view.

"Lulu, I can still see your tail," Gizmo said. "Face it, that spot's only big enough for one. Why don't you try this woodpile over here?"

All three ewes set off toward the woodpile.

Ewina nudged Flossy. "He's staring at you again," she whispered.

"Who?" asked Flossy, looking around. "Oh, *him*," she said, rolling her eyes when she spied Jellybean coming back from the first mail collection. "Mr. Goody-Four-Hooves." Although she did appreciate Jellybean's good taste in ewes, Flossy had always gone for rebellious black-sheep types.

"I think he's cute," said Ewina.

Flossy blew a raspberry. She flicked her tail flirtatiously as they passed the besotted buck, who watched her mutely, his mouth full of mail.

"You're terrible!" giggled Lulu.

"You shouldn't tease him like that," chided Ewina, the more serious of the three.

"What?" said Flossy innocently. "Don't be such a fusspot. I just made his day." She ducked out of sight behind the woodpile.

Jellybean and the other mail carriers took the soggy, mud-spattered envelopes and magazines they had collected and deposited them in a pile on the farmhouse porch.

"Where would you like these, Poe?" Jellybean asked.

— 65 —

"Farmer Bob's desk, I guess," the raven replied. Somehow it just seemed like the appropriate place.

Although the sheep weren't much bigger than Buddy and probably could have fit through the pet door if they'd tried, they balked at venturing into the farmhouse, which was human territory.

"I can help you move it inside," volunteered Gizzabelle, who had just gotten off her first lookout shift and had gravitated to where Poe was.

"Thanks," Poe said. "I'd appreciate that."

Released from their responsibilities, the sheep happily set off for the pasture and the two birds laboriously began transferring the mountain of mail piece by piece to the desk in the main room. Gizzabelle tried not to let it bother her that while Poe could fly straight to the desk, she had to run through the house, then hop from the ground to the chair to the chair arm to the desktop.

"Do you need a break?" Poe asked when Gizzabelle dropped an envelope on the desk then bent over the mail pile, her chest heaving heavily.

"No," she gasped. "I'm fine." She glanced around and her eyes alighted on a large black object with a bright red knob near the desk. "What's that?" she wheezed, mostly hoping she could catch her breath while Poe explained.

"Oh, that?" he said. "That's a safe. Farmer Bob locked important things in there. But he always stood in front of it when he was opening it so I never saw how to unlock it."

"Oh, okay," chirped Gizzabelle, who had by then recovered enough to keep going. She jumped off the desk onto the chair arm and from there onto the floor. It wasn't until they had deposited the last pieces of mail on the table that the little hen finally allowed herself a proper rest. Before her respiration had even returned to normal, though, a loud ringing sliced through the air.

Gizzabelle looked around in alarm, but she didn't see anything. The ringing stopped as suddenly as it had started. She relaxed, but before she could say anything, it started up again, every bit as loud as before.

Poe called down over the ringing, "Don't worry, it's just the phone."

"The phone?"

"Yeah, just hold on and I'll explain..."

The ringing stopped and a voice filled the room. "This is Bob. You know what to do." Then there was a loud beep.

Gizzabelle's eyes bugged out. She stared at Poe. "That's.... Farmer Bob!" she exclaimed excitedly.

Poe shook his head and held up a wing. "Wait...."

Another voice started up. "Hey, Bob," it said. "You owe me a chance to redeem myself after our last match. Give me a call and we'll get together." There was a click and then silence.

"Who was that?" Gizzabelle said, not taking her eyes off the box. "Are there people inside?"

"It's called a phone," Poe explained. "It's a way for humans to talk to each other just like they are standing side by side no matter how far apart they actually are."

Gizzabelle was stunned. "So they can talk through the phone even when they're...*dead*?"

"Oh, no," Poe hurried to correct her. "That wasn't *really* Farmer Bob. It was just his answering machine. He recorded his voice into it....before."

Gizzabelle wrinkled her comb. "You mean that thing captures voices?"

"That's right."

"Does it hurt?"

"I don't think so. "

"Do they get it back?"

"Get what back?"

"Their voice."

"Oh, they never lose it."

Gizzabelle struggled to understand. "So who was the other voice?"

"That was Asa. He was talking about chess. That's a game where they move little wooden pieces around on a board," he explained before she had to ask.

"He's not dead too, then?"

"No, that really was him talking just now. Farmer Bob was just a recording. Now Asa's message is a recording. I know it's confusing.

Here, maybe this will help," he said, hopping over to the silver box next to the phone. "This is the answering machine," he said, examining the box.

"I wish I'd watched Farmer Bob closer when he did this," he said without looking up. He hopped onto the box and began stomping his feet willy-nilly. "You have to push something..."

"You have three new messages," a strange monotone voice from the box blared.

Poe nearly fell off the box in surprise.

"Message one," it continued. Then a high-pitched, slightly warbly voice: "Hi, Bob. It's Granny Ann. Just wanted to let you know the market opens next week so I'll be starting pickup next Tuesday. No need to call me back unless something's changed. Okay, well, bye!" Then the flat voice again: "To repeat, press nine. To delete, press seven."

"Seven," Poe said under his breath. "That's this one," he said, stomping on one of the small raised circles.

"Message deleted. Next message." A new voice: "Are you paying too much for your credit card? We have a new offer that can save you—"

"Message deleted. Next message."

Gizzabelle looked at Poe questioningly. He shrugged. "Farmer Bob never listened to those," he explained.

Then Asa's voice again: "Hey, Bob..." It was the message they'd just heard. Poe deleted it, too. "End of new messages," the flat voice said. Then silence.

Gizzabelle stared at the magical box for a long time. She was both mesmerized and terrified.

"So Asa is expecting to hear back from Farmer Bob?" she asked. "To *see* him? What are we going to do? He'll discover us for sure!"

"I don't know," Poe sighed heavily. "We can only tackle one thing at a time. Hopefully we'll figure something out before it becomes a problem." He looked at the mail pile by the door. "Should we get back to work?"

"Yeah, sure."

When they had retrieved the last of the mail from the porch, Gizzabelle offered to open the envelopes while Poe got busy decoding. "That'd be great," he said. While she set to work on the first envelope, he started with a big, glossy magazine with giant multicolored lettering all across the cover.

They settled into an easy work rhythm, with Poe occasionally reading snippets to her that he was able to decipher. The closer she got to being done, the slower Gizzabelle worked. But eventually she tore open the last envelope, extricated the paper and smoothed it out with her foot.

"I'm done," she said. "But I'd be happy to stay if you need me to."

Poe looked up from his pile of papers. "Thanks, but I don't think there's anything else for you to do."

"I can organize everything into categories if you want," she offered hopefully.

"That's alright. No need to bother. I'll have to read it all anyway."

"Oh, okay," she said gloomily. She brightened. "Maybe I could help with the reading? You could teach me the letters...?"

"Naw, that'd be too hard."

"Oh, uh, of course," she said, scuttling backwards. "Too hard for a *chicken*."

"Huh?" he said, giving her an odd look. Then his eyes widened in alarm. "Gizzabelle! Watch ou—!"

The little hen had backed right off the desk.

Poe rushed to the edge. "Are you okay?" he called down, but Gizzabelle had already skittered halfway across the room.

She made it through the pet door before the first tear fell. It appeared she hadn't been able to inoculate Poe from the prejudices against chickens after all, she thought. He'd picked them up as easily as he had reading.

Gizzabelle didn't want to go back to the henhouse where she'd have to put on a happy face for the other chickens, so she set off for the stream where she hoped she could be alone and pull herself together. But when she got to the brook, instead of drying up, her tears turned into wracking, inconsolable sobs.

"Now, now," said a kind voice behind her. "What is the matter, little one?"

"Oh, Sausage!" Gizzabelle cried, turning to the great pig who was lying in the shade by the water.

"Let not your heart be troubled," he said gently, heaving himself up. "Your task is not to seek for love, but merely to seek and find all the barriers you have built against it."

The little hen shook her head, not bothering to wonder how Sausage seemed to intuit what ailed her. "He'll *never*—" she hiccupped, unable to even say the awful thing aloud.

"Stop acting so small, my child," Sausage said, his tone at once both stern and yet infinitely kind. "You were not meant for crawling, so don't. You have wings. Learn to use them and fly."

"But I *can't* fly," Gizzabelle sobbed. "Can I?"

Sausage smiled enigmatically. "Only from the heart can you touch the sky," he said before turning and shambling toward the barn.

Gizzabelle watched him go, not sure what to make of his words. He was speaking figuratively, right? She couldn't *really* fly. Her flight feathers had been cut. Still....

Looking around to make sure no one was watching, she hesitantly spread her wings and took off at a sprint, flapping her wings furiously before making a huge running leap and pulling her feet into her body. For a split second she was gloriously airborne, then she pitched sideways, hit the ground hard, somersaulted tail over head, and skidded to a stop, wheezing and coughing up dirt.

She instantly popped up and looked around to make sure no one had witnessed the humiliating debacle. Seeing no one, she quickly dusted herself off and hurried back to the farm, berating herself the whole way.

You dumb chicken. Of course *he meant it figuratively. What kind of idiot are you, thinking that you could actually fly?*

CHAPTER 6

Over the next few days, the animals adjusted to their new routines. The pigs continued to milk the cows twice a day. Buddy and Newton divided the horses and cows into pairs and taught them how to pull the plow. Mordecai and the sheep collected the mail daily. The drills became so habitual that the animals were able to override their instinctive terror enough to give some forethought to their reactions. Hiding spots were identified all over the farm, which eventually even the most dull-witted of the sheep could find at a moment's notice.

Every day Gizzabelle helped Poe move the mail onto the desk, and each evening, he shared with her what he was learning. Every night he regaled her with tales of new amazing things the humans had invented. There were gadgets and doodads and contraptions; space-saving systems, time-saving technologies and labor-saving devices. There were lotions and potions that could make a human younger, skinnier, more buff, healthier, hairier, smoother, more beautiful, more popular, less smelly, better smelling, cleaner, hipper, happier and with whiter teeth. They were all new and improved, satisfaction guaranteed, and *on sale*. He wasn't sure what that meant, but it had to be good.

One evening Poe came in looking subdued. "I think I've made a big mistake," he admitted.

"What's that?"

"I've been concentrating on all the wrong things. I assumed that the biggest, brightest, most colorful pieces of mail were the most critical, but I realize now that the important things are actually quite dull looking. Just plain black and white. And even more strange, it seems that the really, really important things are written really small. In fine print."

"That sure seems backwards," said Gizzabelle.

"Doesn't it though?" said Poe. "I don't know if I'll ever understand humans."

He went back to his reading, this time ignoring the thick glossy magazines and multicolored fliers with lots of pictures of grinning humans for the thin plain white envelopes he'd previously ignored. After that, he no longer brought back breathless stories about brain-boosting super foods or the 'pick-me-ups' people could take to wake up from the pills that had put them to sleep. He didn't say much of anything, and grew increasingly distant and on edge.

Gizzabelle didn't mention the change until a few days later, when they were transferring the day's mail to the desk. Poe seemed even more tense than usual.

"Are you okay?" she asked. "You've been so quiet lately. Is something bothering you?"

Poe wouldn't meet her eyes. "I'm afraid so," he finally admitted.

"Is it something you read?"

Poe nodded. "It was something I saw in a magazine," said Poe glumly. "It was an ad for a seeder. It spreads 31,000 seeds in 18 minutes."

Gizzabelle shrugged. "So?"

"Don't you see? Once we're done plowing the fields, we'll have to plant them. We're not going to be able to run Farmer Bob's seeder any more than we were the tractor, and without it, we'll have to plant all those seeds ourselves."

Gizzabelle gulped. "Thirty-one thousand? We'd have to plant *31,000 seeds?*"

"No," Poe mumbled, looking at his feet. "It's actually 31,000 seeds per acre."

"*Per acre?* But the farm's over two hundred acres!" cried Gizzabelle. "Are you sure?"

Poe nodded dismally. "And that's not all. I've been running into these other things. I think they're what Farmer Bob used to call 'bills.'"

"Bills? Like on ducks?"

"No, not like that."

"Like what then?"

"I haven't got it quite figured out yet," Poe admitted. "But I've got a bad feeling about them. I know they used to upset Farmer

Bob a lot."

"Do you think Buddy knows what they are? Or Newton?" asked Gizzabelle. "If only there was someplace we could go to find the answers..."

Poe's eyes suddenly lit up. "I don't know why I didn't think of it before," he cawed, hopping over the flatish board in front of the phone. "This could be just what we need, if I can just figure out how to make it work..."

He examined the buttons. "I think it's this one," he said, stomping on it with one foot. There was a loud chime and the box behind the board flickered, then lit up. Gizzabelle stepped back, awe-struck. She waited to see what the amazing contraption would do next. When nothing else happened, she peered more closely at the glowing box. There was a long horizontal box with a single word above it.

"What does it say?" Gizzabelle wanted to know.

"Google." There were little eyeballs in the g's.

Poe stepped on one of the buttons with his foot. "That's 'B,'" he said. He jutted his beak at the glowing screen. "See how it appeared up there when I pressed it down here?"

Gizzabelle nodded.

"That's how the computer works. It's called typing. I have to do hunt and peck," Poe explained. "B-I-L-L-S," he said as he typed. "Bills. Let's see what we get with that," he said, hopping over to the side of the keyboard. "Now we go over here to the mouse..."

"The mouse?" Gizzabelle asked, looking around for one of the furry critters from the barn.

"Yeah, that's this thing," he said, laying his claws on a rounded white disc with a long tail. "It moves that arrow up on the screen." He scooted the mouse around on its pad until the arrow was where he wanted it, then jumped on the mouse with both feet as if he were attacking it.

The screen was suddenly filled with words.

"What does it say?" asked Gizzabelle.

Poe was already pointing and clicking with the mouse. "Hmmmm...Buffalo Bills," he read. He clicked some more, read silently, then shook his head. "This can't be right," he said. "It's all about football."

Gizzabelle looked at him quizzically.

"That's a game," he explained. "Farmer Bob used to watch it on the TV."

Gizzabelle groaned. "Every time you try to explain one thing, it just brings up more things I don't understand! It's hopeless."

"It's not hopeless," said Poe. "Of course you don't know about human things. Why would you? Let's look up something you do know about." He thought for a moment. "How about 'chicken'?"

"Oh, that's okay," Gizzabelle started. "You don't have to—" But Poe was already typing away.

Gizzabelle shut her eyes. Please, *please don't have anything about brain size*, she prayed.

On the first site—something called Wikipedia—Poe read that chickens are a type of Red Junglefowl and that there are three times as many chickens as humans in the world. They read about wattles and egg teeth and the world's oldest chicken (16 years) and—to their mutual embarrassment—the "circle dance" roosters perform as a courting ritual prior to mating.

They found pictures of every size and shape and color of chicken imaginable. Chicks and hens and roosters, red and black and white, speckled and plumed. Gizzabelle was mesmerized by the diversity of her kin. Transylvannian Turkens with long, red featherless necks. Golden Polishes that looked like dahlia flowers. Silkies who were walking furballs with beaks. Cartoon chickens. Rubber chickens. On something called YouTube, they watched humans doing The Funky Chicken.

Poe tried to keep Gizzabelle from seeing any of the recipes for chicken pot pie and casserole, but he couldn't shield her from the grisly pictures of naked golden-brown chicken corpses impaled on sticks and plates of crispy fried chicken legs that popped up unbidden in the middle of the rest. Gizzabelle's eyes widened in horror, but she didn't say anything. They hurried on.

They found tourist information for Chicken, Alaska, a gold-rush town with a population of 17, and a far-fetched game called highway chicken, where (if it could be believed) humans would skirt death just for kicks. Sometimes whole countries—millions of people at a time—would play it together. Poe had his doubts that it was true. "Don't believe everything you read, Farmer Bob used to say," he recalled. "Now I'm beginning to see what he meant."

Then they hit upon a series of pages all devoted to the question why the chicken crossed the road. There must have been a hundred theories.

"Why *shouldn't* a chicken cross the road?" Gizzabelle wanted to know. "Why does anyone cross a road? I'm sure there are as many answers as there are chickens and roads. I don't get what's so intriguing about it."

"Who knows," Poe said. "I guess maybe chickens are as much a mystery to humans as humans are to us."

Gizzabelle sighed. "I don't know if we'll ever understand them. They can create light and talk across space and get food to grow out of the earth, but they wonder why a chicken crosses a road. They can raise 24 billion chickens the world over, yet they don't even know which came first, the chicken or the egg!" They shook their heads in disbelief. Even a dodo bird knew the answer to that.

Just when Gizzabelle thought they'd never understand humans, tucked in between a raft of chicken soup recipes, they stumbled upon a collection of stories of human love and courage and everyday heroism that grabbed their attention. Each time they finished one, they decided to read "just one more." And there was always one more to be had. There was chicken soup for parents and chicken soup for kids; chicken soup for teens and preteens; chicken soup for pet lovers and business leaders and seniors and Canadians. Despite the gruesome name, the stories were so heart-warming, so poignant, the chasm between the two species shrank to a mere crevice. Sometimes Gizzabelle even forgot they were reading about humans. He didn't say as much, but Poe seemed to be affected as well. As he read aloud, his voice went thick and raspy, and Gizzabelle was sure he was misty eyed on more than one occasion.

"Achem," he croaked, after a particularly moving story about a human throwing stranded starfish back into the sea. "I think that's enough of that. We should move on." He clicked on another link. "Huh, here's something on chickenpox."

"What's that?"

"An illness humans get."

"*Chicken*pox?" Gizzabelle asked. "Are you sure that's something *humans* get?"

"Yep," said Poe. "I remember Farmer Bob saying once how he had to stay home from school when he had it as a kid so none of the other kids would catch it."

"So when one human has it, they can't see any other humans until they get better?" Gizzabelle stared at Poe so intently he shifted uncomfortably.

"Yeah, that's right," he agreed. "So what? What are you thinking?"

Gizzabelle was quiet for a moment. "You know when you were telling me about the phone?" she finally asked. "Could *we* talk into the phone, just like the humans do?"

"Sure, I guess. I don't see why not, if we wanted to. Why?" Poe asked.

"I think I've got an idea..." she said slowly.

Poe waited expectantly. "Well?"

Gizzabelle bobbed excitedly. "We can pretend Farmer Bob has the chickenpox!"

Poe cocked his head. "But how could we get the humans to think that?"

"The phone!" Gizzabelle chirped. "You can use the phone to pretend to be Farmer Bob!"

Poe was quiet for a long moment. "You know," he finally said, "I think you're onto something there. Yeah..." he said, his voice rising as he warmed to the idea. "I think I could do that. At least with Asa. He's on speed dial." He hopped over to the phone. "Shall we give it a try?"

Gizzabelle backed up. "You mean...right now?"

"Sure, why not? Waiting will just give us more time to get nervous."

"Shouldn't we ask the others or something?"

"Oh, I'm sure they'll agree. Think how relieved they'll be when we tell them we've *already* solved the Asa problem. They can use some good news, don't you think?"

"Well, if you're sure..." Gizzabelle said doubtfully.

"This is going to be a two-bird job," he said. "If you can help me get this"—gesturing to the handset—"out, you can hold it while I push the buttons."

Together they wrestled the handset out of the cradle, and Gizzabelle held it upright while Poe pressed buttons with his beak.

"I heard Farmer Bob call Asa so many times, all I have to do now I have to find out the right buttons..."

"There, I think that's it. It even says 'Asa' on the screen," he said. He cleared his throat. "This is Farmer Bob," he said in Farmer Bob's voice. "Wait, it should be more like this." He shifted down a register. "This," he croaked, "is Farmer Bob sick."

"That's amazing," marveled Gizzabelle. "You sound *exactly* like Farmer Bob! I'm sure Asa won't be able to tell the difference."

Poe shot her a grateful look. "Okay," he said, taking a deep breath. "You ready?"

"Ready when you are."

Poe pressed the button. Gizzabelle could hear a ringing coming from the handset followed by Asa's voice: "Hello?"

"Asa," rasped Poe. "I've been wanting to get back to you, but I've been sick."

"I can tell," said Asa. "You sound like a foghorn."

"Yes," Poe said, sniffing loudly and throwing in a cough for good measure. "I've got the chickenpox."

"Chickenpox?" snorted Asa in amusement.

Poe shot Gizzabelle a worried look. This was not the reaction he'd been expecting.

"Um, yeah," Poe said.

"Didn't you have that as a kid?" Asa asked.

"Yeah, but it's back."

"Ah," Asa said knowingly. "Shingles."

Poe blinked at Gizzabelle in bewilderment. *Shingles?* he mouthed silently. He thought those were something on the roof.

She shrugged back.

"Mmmph," grunted Poe noncommittally.

"Sorry, old pal. I thought you were pulling my leg there."

Poe looked relieved at his new serious tone. But before he had a chance to say anything, Asa continued, "Shingles is nothing to fool around with, not at your age…and with a cold on top of it. Have you been to Doc Green?"

"Uh, yeah."

"Then you must really be on death's door. Do you need anything? Do you want me to come over and take care of the animals?"

Poe started coughing uncontrollably. "No, no…" he finally said. "I'm fine. I've got everything under control. I've got help."

"You sure?"

"Mm-hmm."

"Well, okay…" Asa said doubtfully. "But if you needed something, you'd call, right?"

"Sure."

"Sure," snorted Asa. "When pigs fly. You stubborn old mule."

"Interfering old woman," Poe shot back. He'd heard their banter enough that it came easily.

Asa laughed. "Okay, take care of yourself, Bob. And call me if you need anything. I mean it."

"Yeah," Poe said, with another cough. "Bye, then."

"Bye." The line went dead, and Poe immediately sank onto the keyboard behind him.

"Whew!" he said. "That was close."

"Sure was," Gizzabelle said, letting the handset fall over.

"I can't believe it worked," Poe said, sounding dazed. "He really thought I was Farmer Bob."

"You were great," said Gizzabelle. "So convincing. You could have fooled me if I wasn't right here watching you! He won't be coming around the farm to visit now."

Poe nodded. "Not for a while, at least."

That evening when Gizzabelle and Poe shared their day's adventure with Buddy and Newton, Buddy commended them on their ingenuity and suggested Poe use the phone to call the milkman and cancel that service as well. Newton just wanted to hear about the computer. He couldn't get over the idea of a machine that contained all the knowledge in the world and was crushed that he couldn't fit in the pet door to see it for himself. Knowing that a miraculous portal to infinite information was right on the other side of the farmhouse door, just out of reach, was almost more than he could bear. He even suggested they break down the door, but the risk of humans seeing the damaged door was too great. Gizzabelle tried telling him that he wouldn't be able to type with his hooves anyway, but it was cold comfort.

Then next day, when Gizzabelle took in the mail, Poe was busy on the computer and barely even acknowledged her despite repeated attempts to engage him in conversation. And that evening, he didn't show up at dinner or come to the henhouse for bed.

As it grew later and darker, Gizzabelle got more and more anxious. She tried talking with Gizmo, but he got tired of repeating himself and getting one-word answers, and went to sleep. Gizzabelle listened to the chickens' soft snoring. She tossed and turned. She counted sheep. When she ran out of sheep, she counted chickens, then cows. Finally she hopped out of her nest and went down the henhouse ramp. Buddy was lying at the base of the ramp.

"Poe's not back," she said. "Do you think something's wrong? Should we check on him?"

Buddy sat bolt upright, his ears at attention and his muzzle quivering. He rushed around the side of the henhouse to where he could see the farmhouse. An eerie blue glow came from the window above the desk. Buddy watched it intently for a moment, then he trotted back around to the henhouse door.

"No worries," Buddy said. "The light is on and I saw a shadow move. He's fine; he's just working late. You can just go back to sleep."

Gizzabelle trudged back up the ramp, climbed into her nest, and fell into a troubled sleep.

She awoke to Poe nudging her shoulder. "Hey, Gizzabelle!" he said. "Wake up!"

"Wha—?" She groggily tried to focus. Poe looked haggard and talked like a bird possessed.

"I've got it!" he exclaimed; his eyes were unusually bright and glittering, and didn't seem focused on Gizzabelle at all, but seemed to look right through her. "I know what we need to do!"

"Do?"

"I've been researching all night and it's all so clear to me now.

We need to get everyone together. Yes, everyone together. Call a meeting! In the barn. And I'll tell everyone." He laughed, high and shrill.

"Poe, are you alright?" Gizzabelle asked.

"Yeah, yeah," he assured her. "I'm just tired. Was up all night. But I'm just so excited! I can't wait to tell you all." He squawked happily. "This could be the answer to everything! The salvation of the farm!"

"What is it?" Gizzabelle asked eagerly.

"Oh, no," Poe said with a naughty gleam in his eye. "You have to wait. Call a meeting in the barn and I'll tell you all at once!"

Gizzabelle spread the word that Poe was calling a meeting and as soon as the cows were milked (although many of the pigs did a slipshod job in their haste), everyone hurried to the barn to hear what he had to say.

Poe was waiting for them, perched on Sausage's stall door. As soon as it looked like everyone was there, he addressed the crowd. Gizzabelle was glad to see that he seemed more calm and lucid.

"Thank you all for coming at such short notice," he said. "But I've got important news. As some of you know, I have been learning to read human writing and to use their computer to find information. I think I've discovered what we need to do to save the farm."

The animals leaned in.

"We won't need to be afraid of the humans anymore. We won't have to hide from them anymore." Poe paused portentously. "Because we're going to *become* human!"

The animals bellowed and backed away in alarm. "But I don't want to be human!" Gizmo protested. Henrietta shrieked and swayed precipitously.

"Whoa, there. Easy! We wouldn't *really* become human," Poe hurried to clarify. "They'd just have to treat us like a person, according to their laws. It's called incorporation. We would become a corporation."

"And then we'd be, what? Like, *honorary* humans?" Gizmo asked.

"Even better," said Poe. "We'd have all the rights of a person and none of the responsibilities."

"So they couldn't do anything to us if they found out we were running the farm?" asked Peanut. "Since we'd be protected by their law?"

"Exactly!" said Poe, nodding enthusiastically.

Peanut looked questioningly at Sausage.

The great pig cocked his head to the side. "Corn cannot expect justice from a court composed of chickens."

The metaphor flew over almost everyone's heads.

"Sausage has a point," said Newton. Glad someone had understood their cryptic sage, the other animals waited for the mule to interpret. "I don't think we can expect fair treatment from a court composed of humans. Besides, human laws aren't like laws of nature."

"What do you mean?" Gizzabelle asked.

"Laws of nature can't be broken," said Newton.

"And human laws can?" asked Peanut, glancing over at Sausage.

"Laws are like cobwebs, which may catch small flies, but let wasps and hornets break through," said the great hog.

"Maybe they should call them whims instead of laws," Mordecai suggested snidely.

"The point is, I don't think we can count on human laws to protect us," said Newton. "Especially when they were made to protect humans, not animals."

"I think you're right, Newton," said Buddy. He looked at Poe. "It was a good idea, mate, but no sense taking any chances. I say we should still keep shtum."

The raven shook his feathers in agitation. "But that's not the only reason to form a corporation," he said. "It's not even the most important one."

"And that would be?" asked Mordecai, who opposed anything human on principle.

"Money," Poe said. "The main thing about corporations is that they make lots and lots of money."

"Money? Sausage knows *all* about money," said Peanut, wrinkling his forehead in concentration, trying to recall his master's teachings on the subject. "He said money is the root of poverty."

Poe frowned. "No, that can't be right. Money is the root of *pros-*

perity, not poverty. You must have it backwards."

"No, I didn't! I got it right, didn't I, Sausage?" Peanut insisted. But Sausage was staring into the distance, a strange faraway look in his eyes.

Peanut grunted, slightly miffed at not being corroborated. "Well, I know *for sure* he said money's like manure."

"Manure?" asked Millie.

"Of very little use unless spread around," pig-splained Peanut.

"Why would we want money?" asked Buddy. "I dunno what the humans see in it. It's not much to look at. Not even edible. I've tried. I'd take a bikkie any day." The mere thought sent great ropes of drool dripping out of his mouth. He hadn't had a biscuit since Farmer Bob died.

Flossy yawned. "Yeah, who cares about money?"

"You don't understand," said Poe. "Money's amazing. It can get you anything you want."

This caught the animals' attention.

"Anything?" asked Gizmo.

"What, like food?" asked Hamish.

"Absolutely. So much food you could eat yourself to death."

"How about safety?" asked Henrietta, who had recovered her senses.

"Sure," said Poe. "Money can buy all the locks and alarms and security cameras you'd need to be perfectly safe."

"What about love?" asked Ewina shyly. "Can it get us mates?"

"It can get you everything you need to attract a mate."

"She doesn't need anything to attract a mate," said Jellybean. "She's fine just the way she is." Ewina looked at him gratefully.

"Well, sure, if you're satisfied with *fine*..." said Poe.

"I don't see what we need money for," continued Millie. "We've already got everything we need."

"Actually," said Poe, "that's another thing corporations are really good at: helping you discover needs you don't even know you have."

Everyone just stared at him.

"What a load of human hooey!" Mordecai finally said.

"Now, Poe," said Millie. "I know you're into this whole corporation idea, but I have to say in this case I agree with Mordecai. I just don't see the point."

Poe sighed, then shrugged. "Okay," he said. "I didn't want to have to tell you this, but we've got to have money. And lots of it."

"Why?" asked Buddy, his brow furrowed with concern.

"We've got bills to pay. And if we don't have money to pay them, we're going to lose the farm."

A nervous titter rippled through the crowd.

"Lose the farm?" asked Buttercup. "But...where would it go?"

"It's not where the farm would go, but who would come to the farm that you need to worry about. And you know who that would be, don't you?" Poe swept the barn with a piercing glance. "Jim Kratchet, that's who!"

At the mere mention of Kratchet, terror shot through the crowd. The animals started shifting and stomping and fluttering, and murmuring nervously among themselves.

Suddenly an eerie voice rose over the uproar. "Aaaaahhhhh.... the monster!"

It was Sausage. His eyes were glassy, and he was staring fixedly at a point in the middle of the crowd.

Henrietta immediately fell over in a dead faint. The animals who were standing near the spot Sausage was staring scattered in all directions. They watched the empty area nervously as if they expected a monster to materialize there at any moment.

"The monster devouring with a thousand mouths," Sausage moaned softly, swaying back and forth, "trampling with a thousand hooves."

Fear set feathers and fur on edge. Everyone looked at one another, not knowing what to do.

"*It is the Great Butcher!*" Sausage bellowed. "*Coming, coming!*" Then his eyes rolled back in his head and he collapsed onto his side.

"Sausage?" Peanut squealed, racing over to his master's side, his snout trembling with concern. "Stay back!" he commanded. "Give him breathing room."

Clementine fanned Sausage with her wing. As Henrietta's best friend, she was used to offering such ministrations. Slowly, the hog's shallow breathing steadied.

Now the animals were twice as terrified as before. First Kratchet, now Sausage raving about monsters and butchers like a creature possessed...

Buddy tried to rein in the panic. Being a dog of action, he believed that having a plan—any plan—was better than sitting around worrying. "So you reckon we should give this corporation scheme a fair go?" he asked Poe.

"I do," said Poe.

The animals were desperate to grab on to anything that promised answers, and Poe made corporations sound like paradise on earth.

"Yes! Yes!" they cried. "Let's incorporate! Incorporate now! Incorporate now!" Crows and whistles from the chickens rose over the crowd's fervent chanting.

"The farm has spoken!" Poe crowed over the din. "We hereby incorporate!"

There was more whistling and ecstatic cheering. When that died down, the animals began to look around.

A cricket chirped.

The fridge hummed.

Water dripped onto a tin can.

"So what exactly does that mean, incorporate?" asked Newton, thinking that they'd really put the cart before the horse this time.

"Well, I don't know all the ins and outs yet," admitted Poe, "but there's something about an invisible hand that brings everyone what they need."

"An invisible hand?" scoffed Mordecai. "Horsefeathers!"

"Are you talking about Santa Claus?" asked Newton. "He's supposed to bring presents down the chimney, but I'm pretty sure he's not real."

Poe shrugged. "I don't know. But one thing I do know is it's really important for everyone to have a job, and for everyone to be organized into a pyramid according to what job they have."

"A pyramid..." said Newton, nodding his head slowly. "Like the food chain."

"Oh! Oh! Oh!" Gizmo squawked, jumping up and down. "I know this! The food chain...plants are at the bottom, and then the insects and bugs are above them, and then we're next, and then foxes and chickenhawks, and then the humans at the very top."

"That's right," said Poe. "And at the bottom of the corporate pyramid are the workers, and above them are the middle managers, and then the upper management and at the very top of the pyramid is what they call the CEO."

"So the ones at the top are the predators?" asked Gizmo. He looked around and lowered his voice. "They eat everybody else?"

"No, no, no!" Poe said impatiently. "Not like that at all! There's no eating involved! No one eats anyone else in a corporation."

Gizmo eyed him skeptically. "Well, if the ones on top don't eat the others, what *do* they do?"

"They tell the others what to do and make sure they do it."

"Hold on," Newton brayed. "So you're saying the CEO tells the upper management and the upper management tells the middle managers and the middle managers tell the workers and the workers actually do it?"

"Exactly," Poe said, nodding eagerly.

"And that makes it *more* efficient?"

"Uh-huh," Poe said. "Because you're maximizing talent. We all have different skill sets. Some of us are good at doing and others are better at telling others what to do."

"So who gets to be CEO?" Gizmo asked.

Poe didn't answer immediately. "Well...I guess that's something we have to decide. We have to choose someone everyone can agree is the right animal to lead the farm. He should—"

"Or she!" interrupted Xena.

"He or *she*," agreed Poe, "should be smart and a good decision maker and someone we can all trust and respect. A strong leader.".

The animals looked around, and all eyeballs came to rest on a single head.

"I think it should be Buddy," said Jellybean. "No one's more qualified to take over from Farmer Bob. He knows the farm better than anyone."

"And you can't find a more decent, honorable creature anywhere," added Millie.

"Buddy's born to lead. He's a *purebred*," said Flossy, who'd always been impressed by pedigrees and fancied some blue blood concealed in her own lineage. A sheep of her beauty and refinement simply couldn't come from common stock.

"Aw, shucks," Buddy demurred modestly, but his tail started swishing back and forth in the dirt. He always wore his heart on his coat, which was one reason everyone loved him. With Buddy, what you saw was what you got. "I'd be happy to give it a burl, if that's what everyone decides," he said.

The animals nodded and murmured agreeably. It was settled. The big-hearted shepherd seemed like the obvious choice for CEO.

Just then, Peanut trotted to the front of the crowd. "I like Buddy as much as the next pig," he said, his high-pitched squeak barely making it over the din, "and for getting things done day-to-day, I couldn't agree more...Buddy's your dog. But for this, we need someone with vision. Someone with insight and judgment. Someone with wisdom." He paused dramatically. "Sausage should be our CEO."

All eyes went to the great hog, who was still lying on his side, his eyes closed. Sausage was without doubt the wisest animal on the farm. Surely he should be their leader?

"When pigs fly," Mordecai bleated. "Sausage for CEO makes as much sense as horseshoes on a goose. How's he going to lead us when you can never make heads or tails of what he says? You ask him if we should go left or right, and he'll say it isn't the path but the walker or water runs downhill in a storm or some other pigswill that passes as wisdom."

"Oh, shut your hayhole!" snapped Peanut. "You're just jealous!"

As little as they wanted to admit it, though, the other animals knew Mordecai had a point. Sausage was clear as mud. Still, openly agreeing with the contrarian goat would mean revealing that they didn't really understand Sausage half the time, and no one wanted to do that.

"Sausage isn't well," said a spotted cow.

"Yeah," a sheep agreed, "maybe we shouldn't tax his strength."

"Actually, I'm not sure wisdom is all that important for a CEO," added Poe. "Vision, yes. Expediency, decisiveness, the killer instinct—"

"The killer instinct?" Henrietta squawked, who'd only just revived.

"Hey," said Gizmo, narrowing his eyes, "I thought you said the CEO wasn't a predator?"

"Well, he...or *she*," Poe said, shooting Xena a glance, "isn't, but they do have to be willing to do whatever it takes to succeed."

"Does Sausage even *want* to be CEO?" asked Millie doubtfully.

"Of course he does!" squealed Peanut.

"Maybe we could have some sort of vote since we've got two candidates now," suggested Newton.

"Three, actually," said Gizzabelle. "I've got another nomination." She looked down at her feet shyly. "I'd like to nominate Poe."

Poe? The animals stared at the raven in surprise.

"Think about how he's already been leading us even from the beginning, when he told us we should bury Farmer Bob," continued Gizzabelle, gaining confidence as she spoke. "It was Poe who warned us about Kratchet and convinced us we could run the farm ourselves, and he's the one who told us about corporations in the first place. And he can fly and read and humanspeak, too. No one else can do any of that."

"But he doesn't know anything about running the farm," protested Peanut. "Up until a few weeks ago, he'd never even been outside."

"Yeah," bleated Flossy. "He's not one of us. Are we going to trust some scavenging bird we don't even know to lead us?"

"Some bird!" screeched Henrietta. "Not one of 'us'? It's nothing but anti-avian prejudice! You mammals think you're so superior just because you've got legs and fur and....and—"

"And an infinitely superior brain," Mordecai supplied helpfully.

"And an infin...*hey*!" Henrietta shot him a look of death, which wiped the smirk off his face.

Always sensitive about the size of their brains, now all the chickens had their dander up. They flapped their wings and clucked angrily.

"Hold on, everyone," Newton said, trying to smooth the ruffled feathers. "I don't think Flossy meant it that way. She wasn't saying anything against birds. Just that Poe hasn't been one of us *farm animals* very long, so he might not know our ways yet."

The chickens refused to be mollified. Mordecai's barb stuck in their craws.

"Poe's smarter than any sheep that ever lived," yelled Gizmo. "Much less a bow-legged old billy goat!"

"Show some respect, you impudent cockalorum," said Mordecai.

"Birds before herds!" shouted Gizmo, completely undeterred.

"Zip your trap, bird brain!" bleated a sheep.

"Nappy-haired muttonhead!" Gizmo squawked.

"Guano for brains," the sheep snapped back.

Gizmo screeched incoherently and lunged after the offending buck.

Buddy jumped between them and fixed them with The Eye, instantly riveting them to the spot. "Easy on!" he barked. "This is no time for biffo. We're up the gumtree here and we've got to get it sorted."

"Look, I don't want to be the cause of any conflict," said Poe. "It's true. I *haven't* been here long. I'd understand if you don't feel like I've been here long enough to trust me. Maybe I should just withdraw—"

"No," Buddy cut him off. "We're going to have an election. Fair dinkum, mate. I'm not winning by forfeit." With a mere glance, he sent Gizmo and the sheep scampering back to their kin.

"You all know me," he said to the crowd. "And you know Sausage. But you may not know Poe. I've probably had more time with him than anyone here, except maybe Gizzabelle. And you can take it from me, this bird's the full bottle. He may not be 'one of us,' but he's chosen to be here. In fact, he's the only one here who has. He didn't have to come back to help us. He could have flown the coop and buzzed off to the great blue yonder—still can. But he's here. He's a battler. And if you ask me, without him we have Buckley's chance of making this work."

Poe peered quizzically at his rival, who seemed to be doing his campaigning for him.

"What I'm saying is Poe's a good bloke, and if he wins, I don't want to hear any whinging. Whoever wins, we have to get behind him 100%. We can't let this tear us apart. We're going to move forward together as one farm. Right-o?"

The cows, horses, and pigs nodded eagerly, and the chickens and sheep grudgingly followed suit.

"Good. Is there anyone else who wants to run?" Buddy said. "Speak now or forever hold your peace."

No one came forward. Newton was a bit disappointed that no one had seen fit to nominate him. As the only mule on the farm, he told himself it was his lack of a natural constituency, but deep down, he suspected that even as smart as he was, he just didn't have that certain *je ne sais quoi* that made others want to follow him.

"Newton," Buddy said, "you're so clever and organized. I was thinking..."

"Yes?" Newton asked eagerly.

"If no one has an objection, I think you should run the election for us. You'd make an ace marshal. Whaddya say?"

Newton sighed, then smiled ruefully. "Sure, I'd be happy to."

"We should have a secret ballot," said Peanut. "So no one will be unduly influenced by how anyone else votes." He looked pointedly at the sheep, who were all standing together in a huddle.

Everyone agreed a secret ballot was fair, and under Newton's supervision, the animals began setting up the voting booth. They found three cans that they maneuvered into one of the empty stalls. In front of each they set a marker to represent one of the three candidates: a feather for Poe, a bone for Buddy, and for Sausage, a coil of metal which reminded them of his curly tail. Each animal was given a pebble to drop into their candidate's can.

"May the best animal win," said Buddy.

"May the best animal win," the animals repeated, and they lined up to take their turn in the voting stall.

Predictably, the voting fell out along species lines. The sheep and cows, who had experienced Buddy's shepherding and leadership in the fields, voted for the dog, while the pigs and horses, who shared neighboring stalls in the barn, supported Sausage. Whether from species solidarity or Gizzabelle's impassioned plea, the chickens voted unanimously for Poe. Coco placed her pebble in Buddy's can, then furtively removed one pebble from each of the other cans and put them in as well. Newton followed the cat into the voting booth, and after circling the cans several times, he too deposited his stone in Buddy's can. But then he turned back, fished it out and dropped it in Poe's instead. Buddy voted for Sausage, Poe voted for Buddy, and Sausage, who had still not awoken, didn't vote. Mordecai was the only animal to actively abstain, setting his pebble on the ground in conspicuous protest.

When all the animals had voted, Newton and a delegation he had chosen went in to tally the results. But as it turned out, they didn't need to count the votes. The winner was clear. One can was nearly overflowing.

The chickens, by far the largest voting bloc, had given Poe a landslide victory.

CHAPTER 7

The counting committee emerged from the barn and Newton addressed the eagerly awaiting crowd. "The animals have spoken," he said with as much fanfare as he could muster. Public speaking was not his forte. "Our new CEO is...Poe the raven!"

The chickens cheered raucously, and there was polite applause from the rest of the animals. All except Peanut.

The pygmy pig sprang to his feet, his entire body trembling with rage. "How could you do this?" he demanded. "How could you not see that Sausage is the best leader?"

On the other side of the barn, Poe absorbed the news in stunned silence. "Wow," he finally said. "I thought it'd be you for sure, Buddy."

"No worries," the shepherd said with a shrug. "That's the way the bikkie crumbles. I guess you're the better animal, mate. I'm behind you go to whoa. You just tell me what to do, and I'll do it. Just like I did for Farmer Bob."

"Thanks, Buddy. I may be CEO now, but I can't do it alone. We need you on the management team, too. I would like to appoint you Chief Operating Officer—COO—of our animal corporation. You'll be in charge of day-to-day farming operations, just like you've always been."

"Right-o," said Buddy, his tail beating furiously back and forth. Everyone cheered. There was something so solid and dependable about Buddy, even the animals who hadn't voted for him were heartened to know he would be part of the leadership team.

"Well, besides Buddy, we'll need animals to head each of the farm's departments," Poe said. Peanut was named Milking Manager and Sarge was appointed Head of Farmland Security.

He looked over at Gizzabelle. "Would you be willing to be Director of Egg Collection once laying season starts?" he asked her. "You've shown real leadership potential over the last few days."

"Of course," she breathed.

Mordecai snorted. "Birds of a feather..." he muttered loudly.

This opened the door for the sheep to begin bleating their gripes. Sarge was one thing, but now a *second* chicken manager? Even though the sheep were natural followers with the leadership skills of celery and no real desire for authority, they couldn't bear being passed over for chickens, the one species they felt superior to.

Although generally an easy-going species, the cows picked up on the sheep's discontent. Since pigs were acknowledged to be the smartest animals on the farm, the cows had willingly accepted a non-bovine milking manager, but now that *chickens* were being put in charge...

Even a few of the old guard hens were provoked that a pullet so young—and particularly that odd bird, Gizzabelle, who wasn't one of *their* breed—should be put in a leadership position, and added their voices to the fray.

Poe scanned the increasingly restive crowd. "What is it?" he asked. "What's wrong?"

At first no one spoke.

"We don't think Gizzabelle is...appropriate leadership material," a cow finally said.

Poe shot Gizzabelle a questioning look. The hen looked away. "Not appropriate?" he asked. "What do you mean?"

The mammals looked at one another, annoyed that they had to explain the obvious. "She's a *chicken*."

"Yeah," Poe said, shrugging. "So?"

"Well, everyone knows that chickens are—"

"It's okay," Gizzabelle interrupted. "I don't need to be Director of Egg Collection. Someone else can do it. I'm sure someone else could do it better."

"No," Poe stopped her, turning back to the cow. "Everyone knows that chickens are what?" he said, his eyes narrowed.

"You haven't been here long enough to know..." the cow began.

Poe glowered at her. "To know *what*?"

"That, um, chickens are..." she stammered, looking at her hooves.

"Dumb," Mordecai finally finished for her. "Chickens are dumb as dirt."

The chickens exploded in outraged clucking.

"I'll resign," Gizzabelle said in a strangled whisper, staring at her claws in mortification.

"No, you won't."

Could he still...? Gizzabelle snuck a peek from under her eyelids. Her stomach dropped. Anger or contempt she could have dealt with, but not the look she saw on Poe's face.

"I don't need your pity," she said fiercely.

"My...what?" He just stared at her for a moment, then shook his head. He looked out at the birds and mammals hurling insults at each other.

"Listen up, everyone!" he cawed. "I've made my choice. Gizzabelle here is going to be my Director of Egg Collection. And it's not because of cronyism or payback or"—he looked over at Gizzabelle—"*pity*. It's because she's the bravest, most compassionate, most creative animal I've ever met. If you don't think she's one of the smartest animals on this farm, then you just haven't taken the time to get to know her."

The animals were quiet. Gizzabelle felt dizzy; all the blood had rushed down to her feet and she suddenly had to remind herself to breathe.

"He's spot on," said Buddy. "I didn't really know Gizzabelle very well myself until the past few days, but she's a corker. A bonzer Sheila."

"She's always been a good egg," chimed in Clementine.

"And an egghead besides!" quipped Newton.

Poe nodded. "Gizzabelle has already proven invaluable," he continued. "She's the one who got me out of my cage, she had the idea to use the phone to get rid of Asa, and if it wasn't for Gizzabelle, we wouldn't have gotten on the computer in the first place, which led to us incorporating. We wouldn't be where we are without her. And I know if she's on the leadership team, she'll give us even more great ideas."

There was some appreciative murmuring in the crowd. A few chickens whistled.

"Actually, I had been thinking," Gizzabelle said shyly, "what if, instead of laying in the usual places, the hens laid in the barn, near the fridge? It might save us a lot of time rolling them across the barnyard."

Poe grinned. "See, what did I tell you?"

Gizzabelle felt three feet tall.

"If no one has any more objections," said Poe, scanning the crowd before he turned to Gizzabelle, "I'd like to welcome you aboard as Director of Egg Collection."

"Thank you," she twittered happily. She was floating on Cloud Nine.

The animals' applause was strong and sincere.

"And last but not least," Poe said when the noise died down, "there's mail collection." He surveyed the crowd, his eyes coming to rest in a most unexpected quarter.

"Will you be our Postmaster General, Mordecai?" he asked.

The crowd gasped. Mordecai's eyes grew wide as saucers. For once, the goat was speechless. He nodded slowly. Poe didn't linger or explain.

"Okay, now that that's all settled," said Poe, "I think our first order of business is to figure out a new name."

"What's wrong with the one we've got?" asked Buddy, who was fiercely protective of all things Farmer Bob.

"Well, it's not technically the McMann Farm anymore," Poe said carefully, not wanting to offend the loyal shepherd. "This is a brand-new enterprise, and I think it deserves a new name, don't you?"

Buddy cocked his head to the side as he considered, then nodded his assent.

"Good," said Poe. "We certainly don't want to disrespect Farmer Bob or his memory, but we can't cling to the past. We've got to move forward. So...does anyone have any suggestions for a new name?"

The barn was quiet.

"The farm used to be named after Farmer Bob. Now that Poe's at the helm, how about Ravenscroft?" offered Gizzabelle finally, thinking that had an awfully romantic ring. "Or Raven's Haven?"

Poe shook his head vigorously. "No," he demurred. "I may be

CEO, but I'm no more important than anyone else. We're all equals here."

"How about Hog Heaven?" said Peanut, who still thought Sausage should rightly be recognized as the spiritual leader of the farm.

"Or Udder Bliss?" suggested a cow.

"Maaaybe Ewe-topia?" offered Ewina shyly.

"Happy Hooves Farm?" suggested Newton.

"Happy *Hooves*? *Ewe*-topia?" Henrietta screeched. The hens clucked noisily about the arrogance of ungulates and cast around for more chicken-centric ideas, but it was a tall order for their limited cognitive skills.

"Well, I for one think it was very creative," Jellybean said to the mortified Ewina, who gave him a grateful look.

"What about Winging It?" suggested Gizzabelle.

"I'd say that hits the nail on the head," said Poe appreciatively, but the other animals cried fowl.

"Brilliant," bayed Mordecai. "If this was a bleating *bird* farm."

"Don't you ever have anything nice to say about anything, you sway-backed, knob-kneed, cootie-covered old dungbag?" squawked Gizmo.

"Shut your wormhole, insolent young cockatoo, and leave the thinking to your betters," shot back the old goat. "Everyone knows a smart chicken's scarce as hen's teeth."

"Cluck you, you clucking cluckwit!" Gizmo screeched, too angry to formulate a more nuanced comeback. "You sh—"

Suddenly the little cockerel found himself laid out flat on the ground, his beak clamped shut. "I won't have you talking that way to your elders," declared Clementine. "No matter *how* much they deserve it," she finished, sending the goat a withering look.

Soon insults were flying back and forth. Every species had been excluded by at least one suggestion, and griping about how they'd been oh-so-outrageously insulted was much easier—and more fun—than coming up with a new name.

"Whoa, everyone!" Buddy barked over the din. "Easy on. Obviously, we don't want to leave anyone out. Whatever name we pick needs to include everyone."

"*Exactement*," purred Coco, who had just materialized. "*Ma suggestion est La Ferme des Animaux.*"

The barn was quiet. For the first time, no one could come up with any objections.

"The Animals' Farm," Buddy repeated, trying it on for size. He gave Coco a cock-eyed grin. "I reckon that's a goer, mate."

"Maybe it should be The Animals' Farm, *Incorporated* since we're a corporation now," said Poe. "Or just Animals, Inc.," he amended. "That's shorter, catchier."

Gizzabelle nodded approvingly.

"I second the motion," Newton said, and the crowd rumbled enthusiastically.

"Alright, then, let's put it to a vote," said Poe. "A motion has been made to change the name of the farm from McMann Farm to Animals, Inc. All in favor, say 'aye,' all opposed, say 'neigh.'"

The "ayes" clearly had it.

"The animals have decided," said Poe. "Animals, Inc., it is."

With that issue out of the way, Poe moved on to the next order of business. "Next," he said, "we need a mission statement."

"Where do we get one of those?" Gizmo asked. "Can I go?"

"It's not something you go get; it's something you make up," Poe explained. "It tells the purpose of the corporation, its reason for being."

"That should be easy," said Newton. "Didn't you say the goal of every corporation is to make money? There's our mission right there."

"I don't know..." Poe said uncertainly. "I think that's understood. There's got to be more to it than just making money."

"You're CEO now," Flossy said, yawning at all this talk of money. "Why don't you just come up with a mission statement for us?"

"Because if I do it myself, you won't be invested in it," Poe said. "It's got to be something we can all get behind."

"Words, words, words," Jock muttered. "I've got no use for the lot of 'em. Words won't fill your belly or keep you warm at night."

Other animals started grumbling, too. It seemed like a lot of meaningless human mumbo-jumbo to them as well.

"Trust me, Jock," Poe said. "This is important. It's like Newton in the fields; seeing him out in front of you helps you plow straight, right? Well, this is the same. It's what we'll use to stay on track and not run off in a ditch somewhere." He appealed to the crowd. "C'mon, guys, what is it we're aiming for? Obviously no one cares about money. What is it you *really* want?"

All signs of boredom and apathy vanished instantaneously, and a torrent of excited chatter flooded the barn. Hamish wanted double corn rations and Clementine suggested softer nests. Henrietta wanted hawk-free skies and fox-proof fences. The cows extolled the virtues of salt licks and clover, while the horses lobbied for carrots and apples. The pigs and chickens got into a heated argument over mud versus dirt baths.

Poe watched with alarm as the discussion slipped out of his control, and his hopes for reaching any sort of consensus evaporated. Just when it appeared the meeting was going to devolve into a complete free-for-all, Gizzabelle asked Sarge to get everyone's attention for her. He obligingly complied, letting loose an ear-splitting crow that stopped everyone in their tracks.

Gizzabelle hopped up on an empty crate. "I think we're getting too bogged down in details," she said. "We can work those out later. What we need is a mission statement we can all agree on. How about: 'to give all the animals a good life'? In the end, isn't that what we all really want?"

Although they were loath to let go their individual demands, the animals reluctantly agreed, and Poe suggested they take a quick voice vote before any objections could be found. The 'ayes' were unanimous, and the mission statement was adopted on the spot.

"So what else do corporations do?" Peanut asked Poe.

"Meetings," the raven relied. "Meetings are very important."

"Why?"

"That's where everything gets done."

"I thought things got done in the fields," corrected Xena.

"Well, yes, of course," backtracked Poe. "But we need meetings to keep everyone on the same page."

"The same page?" asked Buttercup, the metaphor completely escaping her.

"To keep everyone informed of what's going on," rephrased Poe. "Just like we're doing now. I propose that we have regular All-Animal Meetings to go over all the farm news and make any announcements or decisions that need to be made."

That sounded sensible enough to the animals, and their first act after instituting All-Animal Weekly Meetings was to adjourn the meeting. Everyone was tired and hungry, and it was nearing the cows' milking time, so it was decided that enough had been accomplished for one day, and the meeting was disbanded with instructions that everyone should meet at the corncrib the following morning.

When the other animals left to find their dinner, Poe, Gizzabelle, Buddy, and Newton stayed behind to go over the day's events.

"I think it went well, don't you?" Poe said, once they were alone.

Newton couldn't contain himself. "Okay, can I just say... *Mordecai*?? Really?"

"Yeah, mate, what were you thinking?" Buddy teased. "We need that old knocker on the leadership team like a fish needs a ukulele."

"Maybe if he's part of the decision making, he won't be so likely to criticize," said Gizzabelle.

"My thoughts exactly," said Poe, shooting her a conspiratorial grin.

"Well, maybe you're right," snorted Newton good-naturedly, "but I think you're underestimating our dear Mordecai. It's going to take more than a title to sweeten up that cantankerous old goat."

As they chatted away, a curious feeling swept over Gizzabelle that she couldn't put her feathertip on immediately. She had never had much interaction with any animals outside of her own species before and now she found she had more in common with the shepherd, mule, and raven than she ever had with her own species, with whom she'd always felt out of step. This cross-species camaraderie filled a void she hadn't even known was there.

"Well, I dunno about you," said Buddy when the conversation hit a lull, "but I'm ready to eat a horse and chase the jockey."

"No kidding," agreed Poe, "I'm ravenous."

Deciding to break for dinner, they said their good nights. Buddy headed over to the farmhouse where Coco said there were mice in the crawlspace, and Newton went out to the pasture, while Gizzabelle and Poe set off for the corncrib.

The barn was empty except for Sausage and Peanut. The younger pig lay beside his master, listening to the rhythmic sound of his breathing, somewhat comforted by its steady regularity. He wondered what was wrong with Sausage. Had he been dreaming? Hallucinating? Did he have second sight? Had he had a vision?

Then the thought that he'd been trying to avoid broke through and washed over him like a tidal wave. What if Sausage was sick, even dying? The very idea took his breath away. Peanut loved Sausage with every fiber of his being. He couldn't imagine life without him.

Suddenly Sausage shuddered and gave a small grunt. His eyes fluttered open.

Peanut sprang up. "Sausage!" he cried. "You're awake! Are you okay?"

The great pig struggled to sit up. "Indeed," he said at length, but he seemed to be having difficulty focusing.

"Thank goodness you're back to yourself!"

Sausage gave a derisive snort. "The Self is not so easily shed as that," he said. "It is the work of many lifetimes."

Peanut's spirits lifted. Sausage was indeed back, back to his usual incomprehensibility.

Satisfied his master was on the mend, the little pig erupted into questions. "What was that you said about a monster?" he asked excitedly. "Do you remember? Were you having a vision? Is there really a monster coming to kill us, like Henrietta says? Or is Kratchet the monster?" While the chickens were literalists, Peanut suspected Sausage had been speaking metaphorically.

"Fear not monsters from the outside," said Sausage. "The only real dangers lie within."

"Whew," Peanut said with relief. "No monsters." His fears put to rest, he hurried to tell Sausage the travesty that had occurred while he was insentient. "The animals incorporated and they chose Poe as CEO!" he exclaimed. "It should have been you! I tried to tell them, but no one would listen. It was all the chickens' fault. They voted for Poe just because he's a bird. You're clearly the superior candidate, and not just because you're a pig either. I'd vote for you if you were a garden slug!"

Sausage chuckled. "Be at peace, little one," he said. "As I would not be slave, so I would not be master."

"But you are so much wiser than anyone else!" Peanut insisted. "You should have been CEO."

"The attempt to wed wisdom with power has rarely been successful, and then only for a short time," Sausage said.

"So you're saying they made the right choice?" Peanut asked doubtfully.

"They are walking their path," said Sausage. "What is in the end to be shrunk must first be stretched. Whatever is to be weakened must first be made strong. What is to be overthrown must begin by being set up."

"I don't understand," said Peanut. "So, like, things have to be bad first in order to be good?" That didn't make a bit of sense to him. "But everything eventually has a happy ending, right?" he implored.

"There are no happy endings—" began Sausage.

"No happy endings?" squeaked Peanut three octaves above his usual squeal. "But what about everything you've always said about everything having a purpose, everything working together for good? Now you're saying there *won't* be a happy ending?" The little pig trembled in indignation.

"There are no happy endings," said Sausage calmly, "because nothing ever ends."

"Oh," said Peanut. "That's right. You did say that. Everything's a circle." He sat down with as hard *thump* as his tiny frame allowed. "I don't know *anything*!" he wailed. "I'm never going to know as much as you. How did you get to be so wise?"

"By three methods we may learn wisdom," began Sausage. Peanut perked up eagerly. "First, by reflection, which is noblest; second, by imitation, which is easiest; and third, by experience, which is the most bitter."

"Reflection, imitation, experience," Peanut recited, committing them to memory. "*I'm* going to take the noblest path."

"The noblest path?" asked Poe, who had suddenly appeared at

Peanut's side. "What's that?"

Peanut glared at him. "Nothing you'd understand," he said snootily. He was still resentful of the bird's victory, no matter what Sausage said.

"Don't mean to interrupt. I just wanted to make sure Sausage was feeling better. And I brought you both some corncobs in case you're hungry," Poe said, gesturing to the sack at his feet.

"Ah, victuals!" said Sausage appreciatively. "There is no happiness like a good friend, a clear conscience, and a full belly."

"Thanks," said Peanut. He opened the bag and laid a couple of cobs in front of Sausage.

"I also had something to discuss with you, Sausage," Poe said as the two pigs began their dinner. "You have more wisdom in the tip of your hoof than the rest of us put together. I don't think the farm can make it without you. I wanted to ask you if you would agree to be Chairpig Emeritus of our new corporation."

Peanut thought Chairpig Emeritus sounded very dignified and erudite indeed, just perfect for Sausage. "What does the Chairpig Emeritus do?" he inquired eagerly.

Poe shuffled his feet. "Well, it's a, uh, non-executive position," he said.

"Which means he doesn't do anything!" Peanut practically spat. "It's an empty title, just for show."

"That's not true!" Poe insisted, his feathers bristling angrily. "There are no official duties per se, but we'll look to Sausage for his wisdom and advice. It's not empty...not at all." He looked at Sausage. "Honestly."

Sausage cocked his head. "We do not receive wisdom; we must discover it ourselves after a journey no one can take for us or spare us."

"So what are you saying?" Poe asked, shifting back and forth in agitation. "That we all have to learn the hard way? I don't believe that. I can take advice. Just tell me: how can I be a great leader?"

Sausage looked at the raven speculatively, and then although he did not actually move, something in his mien suggested a shrug of his great shoulders.

"To be great," he said, "you must first be good."

Poe's wings slumped in disappointment. "Is that all?"

Sausage's eyes suddenly lit up like burning coals, boring into Poe and pinioning him in place. "The loss of a feather, a foot, a mate, is sure to be noticed," the hoary pig said, all traces of warmth and humor suddenly gone from his voice, "but the greatest danger—the loss of one's self—may pass off as quietly as if it were nothing."

Poe felt icy rivulets trickling through his innards. He tried to speak, but only managed a croak.

Sausage held Poe's gaze. "What profit is there to gain the whole world, but lose your own soul?"

Poe stared back, slack beaked.

Then Sausage returned to his corn cob, and Poe had the definite impression that he had been dismissed. He ruffled his feathers, trying to shake off the oppressive feeling of impending doom that had suddenly settled over him. He made his way to the henhouse and went to sleep without even saying goodnight to Gizzabelle, who heard him thrashing and mumbling throughout the night.

The next morning, everyone assembled at the corncrib after breakfast to discuss seeding. Poe, exhausted and bleary-eyed, explained the planting process: each of the kernels would need to be taken off the cob, transported to the fields, put in the ground and covered over with dirt. Then the tiny kernel would grow into a big corn plant with many, many more corncobs that would be collected and start the whole process over again.

"What we need to do now," said Poe, "is figure out who can do what."

"We chickens can peck the kernels off the cobs," Gizzabelle volunteered. "Our beaks are practically made for it."

Poe nodded. "Yes, absolutely," he agreed, "the chickens will be in charge of seed production."

The chickens grew restive.

"We've already got jobs!" crowed a querulous chicken. "We've got lookout duty, not to mention laying! And now you want to give us even *more* to do?"

Poe and Gizzabelle exchanged worried glances. The other animals had no idea of the gargantuan task they were up against, and what it would take from each of them if they had even a hope of succeeding.

Mutinous muttering erupted from the birds. "Yeah, what do you want us to do, work all day long?" another hen shouted, outraged by the very suggestion.

The sheep couldn't contain their glee that Poe was giving the chickens extra duties.

"Thought they'd feathered their nests, electing one of their own," chuckled one sheep to his neighbor. "Bet they're rethinking their vote now!" The sheeps' opinion of Poe soared, now that it seemed he wouldn't be catering to the birds as they'd feared when he appointed two chicken managers and not a single sheep.

"We've already got our claws full," objected Henrietta vehemently. "We do enough already. Let someone else take a turn!"

"Try plowing a field some day," lowed one of the younger cows.

"And it's no picnic getting up before dawn to milk you cows," grunted a pig with an upturned snout.

Henrietta snorted. "And what do the sheep do? Nothing, that's what! Sit on their rumps and watch their wool grow!"

The sheep stopped grinning and bleated angrily. "That's rubbish, you nit-picking old windbaaaaag!" Flossy fumed.

"We've done everything we've been asked to," said Jellybean quietly.

"It's true," Buddy said to Henrietta. "Unfortunately some animals are being asked to do more than others, but that's just because some animals can do more things than others. Chooks just happen to have the misfortune of being a particularly talented and gifted species, so they're being tapped for more things."

"That's right, to whom much is given, much is required," chimed in Peanut with an oft-repeated Sausagism.

Henrietta was slightly mollified. Those condescending mammals might have big brains, but what were brains compared to everything chickens had to offer? "Yes, well, there is no question that chickens are a superior species," she said, preening her feathers, "but still, we can only do so much."

"Henrietta's right. We should help the chickens," said Jellybean. Ignoring the icy glares from the other sheep, he continued, "Their beaks might be best adapted for plucking kernels, but we can take the seeds to the fields and plant them. The cows and horses are too big for work like that. We're just the right size."

"Us, too!" said Peanut. "Our hooves are perfect for planting seeds. When we're done milking in the morning, we can help, too."

When the chickens saw that the sheep and pigs would also be getting more responsibilities, they grudgingly acquiesced to the additional duties. Poe shot Gizzabelle a relieved glance. They had dodged a bullet. In the turmoil over who would plant the seeds, no one had thought to question if it would even be possible.

Although they'd thought they'd get into dekerneling and planting right away, it soon became evident that the first order of business had to be the much more difficult and tedious task of scheduling. Between lookout duty and laying and now dekerneling corn cobs, the chickens' time in particular was getting more and more cramped, but all the animals were having trouble keeping track of where they needed to be when, and not accidentally committing to be in two places at once.

Someone proposed all-day shifts to cut down on the confusion and avoid the time lost to shift changes, but that nearly started a riot. Expecting anyone to work *all day* was clearly cruel and unreasonable, and the animals were having none of it. Finally Poe hit upon a solution. He brought a gadget—Farmer Bob's treasured pocket watch—from the farmhouse and asked Sarge to use it to break the day into segments. In addition to the morning wake-up call, Sarge would crow at evenly spaced intervals throughout the day. These would be called First Crow, Second Crow, and so forth.

Sarge was too well-disciplined to challenge a direct order, but his brusque manner made his opposition crystal clear. It had taken the rooster an entire year to master the many variables and intricate calculations involved in determining when exactly to give his wake-up crow each morning. He hardly thought the complex task could be replicated by a little black "hand" traveling around in a circle.

Poe, however, was resolute. The season and weather and light and circadian rhythms would not influence the timing of the wake-up crow. From now on, rain or shine, summer or winter, First Crow would be held at six'o'clock sharp. The animals would not eat when they were hungry or sleep when they were sleepy or stop working when they were tired, but whenever the clock told them to. "I actually think everyone will prefer this way once they get used to it," said Poe. "Being told when to do everything will be so much easier than having to figure it out for themselves."

Using the new time blocks, the managers were able to make a shift schedule and plug the animals into it. Noticing there was one time slot—right before bedtime—that everyone still had available, Poe decided to offer after-dinner reading lessons for anyone who wanted to learn.

"For *anyone*?" asked Gizzabelle.

"Sure, why not?"

"But I thought you said it would be too hard for me."

Poe frowned. "When did I say that?"

"In the farmhouse. When I asked if you'd teach me, you said it would be too hard."

Poe rolled his eyes. "That's not what I meant, featherhead. I just meant it would be too hard to teach you while I was still trying to figure it all out myself."

"Oh," said Gizzabelle, who was both giddy and embarrassed all at once. She determined then and there to prove Poe's confidence had not been misplaced. *Chickens can learn just as well as anyone else*, she told herself.

As it turned out, though, most of the other animals weren't much interested in learning to read. They couldn't see any merit in connecting words to black squiggles. Poe didn't push the issue with the rank and file, but he encouraged the members of the management team to give it serious consideration.

In the end, only Gizzabelle and Newton were excited about the new learning opportunity. Buddy agreed to give it his best shot, although it wasn't something he was looking forward to, being more of a doer than a thinker. Sarge begged off on account of his poor eyesight, and Mordecai outright refused to take part in learning a human discipline. Peanut was raring to go until Sausage politely declined, saying that the trees and clouds and stars were his books, after which the smaller pig's enthusiasm was decidedly dampened. Clementine saw reading lessons as a convenient means of keeping Gizmo occupied and safely out of trouble for at least a few hours a week. Although he tried mightily, the young cockerel couldn't come up with an excuse to get himself off the hook and he resigned himself to attending the classes until he could think of a way out. At the last minute, Jellybean and Millie volunteered as well. They weren't that interested in reading per se, but they thought their species should be represented.

Meanwhile Buddy began training the chickens on their new duties. The shepherd quickly discovered that managing chickens was an entirely different animal than anything he was used to. While the sheep and cows were born followers, the chickens fought him every step of the way. They didn't respond well to The Eye like the sheep or appeals to Duty like the cows, and you couldn't reason with them like you could the pigs. If someone wasn't standing over them, making sure they stayed on task, they were slacking off, or worse, snacking away the very kernels they were supposed to be producing. Buddy had his work cut out for him.

He tried hard to strike a balance between cheerleading and gentle correction, but Gizzabelle noticed that as the days wore on, the chickens were starting to chafe under his watchful eye.

"I know shepherds are bred for their work ethic," said Henrietta, who was the most vocal of the hens, "but not everyone's made that way. I can't keep up this pace."

"He chewed me out for eating one lousy kernel!" sulked Gizmo.

"If he wants to work himself to the bone, that's his business," grumbled a hen with a crooked beak, "but leave the rest of us out of it."

"He doesn't need to put so much pressure on us, watching every kernel, always wanting us to go faster, faster, faster," said another. "What's the big rush?"

Only Gizzabelle knew the answer to that, and she, of course, kept her beak shut.

At the next leadership meeting, which they held in the corncrib, they took stock of their progress. Newton reported that his workers were nearly finished plowing the last field, and he'd soon be ready to start training the sheep and pigs to plant the corn the chickens were preparing.

Poe inspected the seed pile.

"How many do you think we have so far?" Gizzabelle asked.

"I don't know," Poe said. "But you can bet your feathers it isn't 31,000—and that would just be one acre's worth. And we've got acres and acres."

"You're a regular beam of sunshine," Gizzabelle said. "Don't you ever have anything *good* to say?"

"I'm a raven, chickadee. We didn't get our gloomy reputation for nothing."

"I'm afraid Poe's right," Buddy said. "We didn't get nearly as much accomplished as I'd hoped. I just don't know how to motivate the chooks. It isn't at all like mustering jumbucks or pigs. You give a pig a little constructive criticism and you don't see them carrying on like a pork chop. But chooks, they just can't handle any kind of correction. Henrietta gave me an earbashing today for being too rough on them. And maybe I was, but I was at the end of my rope. When I bark or give them The Eye, instead of egging them on, it just seems to make them work *slower*."

"Scaring them's the worst thing you can do," Gizzabelle said. "It only paralyzes them. I think you have to go positive. Inspire them. Tap into their Higher Chicken."

"Sounds like what they need is a dose of that chicken soup we were reading about," Poe said dryly.

Instead of laughing, though, Gizzabelle cocked her head at him.

Poe nodded thoughtfully as if she'd spoken aloud. "You may be onto something there," he said. "I think I know just what we need to do."

CHAPTER 8

"A rally?" asked Buddy.

"Yes," Poe said confidently. "A motivational rally."

"I don't know…" Newton said skeptically. A firm believer in things that could be seen and felt and quantified, the practical utility of a rally stuck him as highly dubious. "Sounds like a lot of touchy-feely tail waving to me."

"No," Gizzabelle said eagerly, "I think it can really help. You didn't hear those stories. You'd have to have a heart of stone not to be inspired." She looked at Buddy inquiringly.

"I'm game," he said. "What have we got to lose?"

"Well, I don't want to be the wet blanket," said Newton. "We've already got one of those on the farm, and I'm not looking to take his place. Let's give it a try and see what happens. Like Buddy says, if it doesn't work, we haven't really lost anything."

"Exactly," Poe said.

They planned to have the rally in two days, to give themselves time to organize and generate "buzz" amongst the animals. They announced that there would be a big event in the barn at Fourth Crow, but refused to give any further details. The more the animals pressed, the more smugly close-mouthed they became. "You'll just have to wait and see," was their stock reply. Only a few chickens who were enlisted to help out were let in on the plan, and then only on a need-to-know basis.

Since he loved the limelight, Gizmo was enlisted as MC. After swearing him to silence, Poe brought Gizmo into the farmhouse and showed him how to use the computer to find material. Although Poe had to read all the text to him, Gizmo was immediately captivated by the Internet. He wanted to know what every icon meant and where every link went. He asked so many questions and took them on so many tangents that Poe thought they'd never finish their task.

"The Web is so awesome!" Gizmo raved when they were done, eagerly showing off the new lingo he'd just learned. "Can I come back and 'surf' it myself?"

"Not unsupervised," said Poe. "Not at your age. Too many disturbing images."

"I'm not a chick!" Gizmo cheeped angrily.

"I know," Poe said, "but you're not a rooster yet, either. I'm afraid it's just too violent. Your sister and I ran across some awful things online and she'd have my feathers if I exposed you anything like that. Not to mention your mother!"

"Jeez," Gizmo grumbled, "I never get to do *anything*."

"How can you say that?" Poe asked. "What about what we're doing now? You're going to be a star!"

Gizmo just snorted, but Poe could tell he was pleased. He perked up even more when Poe reminded him of the secrecy of what they were doing.

"You can trust me," Gizmo said, puffing up his chest. "My beak is sealed."

By the day of the rally, the animals were beside themselves wanting to know what all the mystery was about. The barn was full long before the appointed time, and the animals were atwitter with speculation. None of the principal players—Poe, Buddy, Gizzabelle or Newton—were anywhere to be seen. The only evidence of anything out of the ordinary at all was a makeshift stage at the back of the barn.

Finally, Sarge heralded Fourth Crow and the crowd grew quiet.

Gizmo hopped up on the stage and began warming up the audience with some ribald tales he'd found on the Internet. He played his part to perfection, parading and preening and winking lewdly at some of the prettiest pullets. Some of the older, more forward hens started whistling. Even the straight-laced cows couldn't resist snorting at the cockerel's outrageous antics, not even when he made an off-color joke about interspecies mating. When he was done, the young comic took multiple bows in every direction, basking in the thunderous applause.

Before the hilarity died down completely and the animals had time to wonder what was coming next, Sarge began a rousing

"Pomp and Circumstance" processional. There was movement behind them, and the animals turned around to see Buddy standing in the barn doorway with Gizzabelle on his back.

Buddy began to march forward, keeping time with the beat of the music. The crowd parted so they could pass through. When they reached the stage, Newton appeared in the doorway. He wore a purple blanket, and Poe stood astride his back, looking very regal indeed. When they reached the back of the barn, Newton took his place on the opposite side of the stage as Buddy and Gizzabelle. Poe glided onto the stage and stood in stately silence center stage as Sarge finished the last heart-swelling notes of his march.

After several more moments of silence, Poe addressed the crowd. He thanked them for their hard work and acknowledged how much they had accomplished to date. He told them that what they were attempting was revolutionary, a pioneering enterprise that could mark the beginning of a whole new era for animals everywhere. He impressed upon them the weight of their responsibility to history, to their species.

"I know it seems daunting," he said. "There are many obstacles in front of us. But the greater the obstacles, the greater the glory in overcoming them. The humans understand this. They delight in doing the impossible, achieving the unimaginable. You may think that this is because they are smarter than we are."

The animals all nodded.

"You're wrong. They don't succeed because they're smarter. They succeed because they believe they can."

He followed with several inspiring stories of humans beating the odds, rising from humble beginnings or overcoming enormous physical disabilities or setbacks to achieve astonishing things, all because they believed they could. Then he told the story of the two seeds, the industrious little seed who worked and worked and eventually became a great tree, and the other seed who was afraid to send her delicate tendrils into the earth and decided to stay a seed because it was safe. That little seed got eaten by a chicken.

"We have to imagine great things for ourselves and be willing to do what it takes to make those things happen," he concluded.

Most of the animals were right there with Poe, swept up in

grandiose dreams of fame and fortune. They imagined bottomless feed troughs and vast open pastures. They envisioned attaining old age and seeing their children and grandchildren and great-grandchildren and great-great-grandchildren and great-great-great-grandchildren grow up. They basked in the anticipated adoration of future generations of animals throughout the world, who would look up to them as great liberating heroes.

But Flossy was not going to have the wool pulled over her eyes. She knew what those pretty words really meant. More work.

"Work, work, work! We don't need any more work," she bleated, breaking through the gossamer web Poe had spun. Gizzabelle grimaced. Everything had been going so well.

"That's right," clucked Henrietta, who agreed with a sheep for once. "We're already working hard enough."

Poe couldn't afford to let the tide turn. "Enough is yesterday's word," he cawed. "Today's word is MORE. We have to do more to get more! Enough was alright, but more is better! More is better!"

"But—" started Henrietta.

"MORE IS BETTER!" Poe thundered over her. "MORE...IS...BETTER!"

Gizzabelle picked up the mantra. "More is better!" the two birds squawked in unison.

"More is better!" Buddy and Newton joined in.

The animals started to chant, "More is better! More is better!" Any further grumbling from Henrietta was drowned out by the racket.

"Do you want more food?" asked Poe.

"Yes! More food!" they shouted. "More, More!"

"You can have more than you've ever imagined!" Poe shouted. "You just have to want it! You have to believe you can have it! If we just work hard, we can have everything we want!"

"More! More! More!" they shouted. Along with the chanting, they started stamping their feet and lowing and bleating and squealing and clucking.

The herding animals knew the terror of collective panic, but they'd never felt the near-ecstatic thrill of a riot before, and for animals like the pigs and chickens, it was a new experience altogether.

Their frenzy rose to a fevered pitch. It demanded expression. They started kicking and butting the stall doors and grain bins and whatever else they came across. Soon they couldn't be contained in the barn anymore, and they spilled out into the barnyard, chanting and stomping.

Once they hit the wide-open space and fanned out across the yard, however, the mob's energy quickly dissipated. Their chants trailed away and they milled around aimlessly, not knowing what to do with themselves. Eventually they drifted off for a quick snack or a nap before the next shift started, but some of the more industrious ones went in early to get a jump on their job. "Got to *do* more to *have* more," Jock mumbled as he set off for the field.

Back in the barn, only a few animals remained behind. Poe, Gizzabelle, Newton, and Buddy surveyed the empty barn with a mix of wonderment and relief. Poe had been even more successful at stoking the animals' enthusiasm than they'd dared imagine, but things had slipped out of his control there at the end. They felt lucky that more harm hadn't been done.

Newton studied the cow damage to one of the stall doors. "The hinge is just bent, not broken. I think we can knock it back into shape without too much trouble," he told the others. "But what were they thinking, kicking the door to start with? Everyone knows we need to keep things looking good! That was one of the very first rules we agreed on." He shook his head. "Doesn't make a lick of sense."

"*Mon Dieu,*" said Coco, uncurling herself in the hayloft, "*émotion* always trumps *logique*. When will you *apprendre* that *animaux* aren't ze *rationnel* creatures you wish for, *mon ami?*"

"Well, they *should* be," Newton said mulishly. Although he was generally flexible and easy-going, he took after his father's side of the family when it came to his most cherished principles. "Anyone can feel. Reason is what separates us from the invertebrates."

"Be that as it may," said Poe, "as long as we can channel all that emotion constructively, I'll take it! Hopefully this is going to translate into increased production. That was the whole point, after all."

"It's almost Fifth Crow. The next shift is about to start," said Buddy. "We'll see soon enough if it worked."

Sure enough, they did see a spike in production immediately following the rally. The sheep and pigs planted three times as many rows, and the chickens nearly doubled their seed piles. But, alas, the effect was only temporary. Within a few days, the numbers were down to their original levels.

"Back to the drawing board," said Poe with a deep sigh. "I really thought that was going to be the answer to the TOTSPA situation."

"The totspa situation?" Gizzabelle asked.

"TOTSPA. It's an acronym for thirty-one thousand seeds per acre," said Poe. "I came up with it myself." He went on to explain what acronyms were and how everything important had one. "The shorter something is, the more important it seems to be."

Gizzabelle nodded, remembering the fine print.

"Another thing about acronyms," Poe said, "is that they separate those who are in the know from those who aren't. So I could say 'TOTSPA' in a barnful of animals and nobody but you would know what I was talking about, even if they were standing right there."

"I see," said Gizzabelle. "Sort of like secret code."

"Exactly!" said Poe. "Of course, you've got to be able to read to do acronyms. But we're getting there, aren't we?"

The reading lessons had begun and Poe had proven to be not only an excellent reader but also teacher. He had a way of explaining things so they related to things the animals already understood. In their first lesson, he taught them that letters were like the animals themselves: they came in pairs, big and little, like parent and offspring. And like the different species, each letter made its own special sound. Poe animated each letter, giving it a unique personality as well as sound.

Despite Poe's skills as a teacher, however, progress was slow. The lessons were held after dinner, when everyone was already tired and what little brain currency they had, spent. Jellybean and Millie, in particular, had a hard time keeping up. Although they seemed to catch on to the letter of the day while Poe was explaining it, by the next lesson, they had forgotten everything they'd learned and Poe would have to start over again nearly from scratch.

Meanwhile, Gizmo seemed to pick up reading as easily as breathing. He barely seemed to pay attention to the lessons and he never did homework, but he never fell behind. Indeed, except for Newton, he was at the head of the class. Poe assured Gizzabelle that Gizmo's sponge-like memory was a function of his youth, but she couldn't help but be annoyed that he'd taken the role of star pupil she'd coveted for herself. At least he put in a good showing for chicken-kind, she consoled herself.

"If only I was reading already," she told Poe, "I could help you look online for other ideas to motivate everyone. The rally worked for awhile. You just need to keep it out in front of them. Maybe there are more soup stories or something you can use."

"Good idea," said Poe. "No sense in re-inventing the wheel." This was an expression he'd picked up from Newton, who made no secret of his admiration of the wheel. It was among his favorite human inventions, along with the internal combustion engine and the flyswatter.

Poe immediately set to work researching. He discovered not one but a whole host of programs designed to boost productivity.

The first was the *Who Moved My Cheese?* Program, which Poe proudly unveiled at the next All-Animal Weekly Meeting. Although it was designed for mice, he thought it could be adapted for other species.

"Success is all about change!" Poe explained. "Some of the lack of productivity we're seeing is just plain resistance to change. It's always, 'we never had to do this when Farmer Bob was here' and 'in the good old days, blah, blah, blah.' We need to learn to not just tolerate change, but embrace it, and this program will help us do that."

To get the animals accustomed to change, Poe wanted the managers to hide everyone's food in a different place every day so they had to look for it. However, the managers immediately objected to that plan, saying it was completely impractical. Hiding enough corncobs for nearly a hundred animals wasn't as easy as moving the cheese for a couple of mice. Newton argued that they would spend all their time hiding food and no time managing their workers, and the workers would waste time and energy looking for food, which they could better spend producing it.

Poe couldn't be talked out of the idea altogether, but he did finally agree to a compromise in which the animals would have to find a hidden token to get their food rations. However, instead of making the animals more tolerant of change, having to find the tokens only seemed to make them cranky and insubordinate. Within days, the workers were planting spies to watch where the managers hid the tokens and passing around the whereabouts of the secret location before each meal. They gave up the program by the end of the week. Even Poe agreed it had been a disaster.

The next week came the *Fish!* Program.

"Success is all about play!" Poe explained. "Work shouldn't be drudgery. If the animals are having fun, they'll be willing to work longer and harder, and they'll get more done. It's a win-win for everyone."

According to the fish philosophy, one of the most fun things to do was throw things. Animals were no longer allowed to *give* anything to another animal if it could be *tossed* instead. In seed production, this meant that corncobs had to be tossed from chicken to chicken as it went through the dekerneling process. However, the chickens' aim was not very good and so many injuries and concussions were sustained that this program too had to be discontinued.

The third week, Poe rolled out Scientific Management.

"Success is all about efficiency!" he exclaimed. "Analyzing workflow using scientific principles can pinpoint waste and inefficiencies, and identify best practices." He asked all the managers to do time-and-motion studies of all their workers' activities, and based on the results, make recommendations on improving efficiency. Most of the managers agreed with this in theory, but in practice they found the meticulous measuring incredibly dull.

Newton, on the other hand, couldn't get enough of it. He was constantly analyzing numbers, coming up with new ways to shave a second here or cut an extraneous motion there. He even volunteered to help the other managers with their breakdowns, and the biggest success of the initiative—the assembly line for seed production—was at least as much his creation as Buddy's.

The process was broken down into parts, and each chicken was given a specific task. First came the huskers, who took the husks off the cobs. The husk went to a composter, who transported it outside to the compost pile, while the cob was passed to a gripper. The gripper held the cob for her partner, the dekerneler, who would strip off the kernels with her beak. Sweepers periodically came by each gripper/dekerneler pair and used their wings to brush the kernels into a pile for the sheep and pigs to pick up. Finally, more composters disposed of the naked cobs. As soon as the assembly line was implemented, seed production skyrocketed.

But he hadn't eeked out all the efficiency in the system yet. In the course of conducting the time and motion studies, he observed that one dekerneler had a very unusual technique whereby she was able to gouge out all the kernels in an entire row with a single motion, instead of the usual one-by-one method. He immediately seized on her innovation and had her teach it to the rest of the group. It quickly became evident that only certain chickens were capable of performing the difficult maneuver, and positions had to be shifted around so that only the most dexterous hens were selected as dekernelers.

At first, the prestige of being a dekerneler was enough to induce the hens to accept the grueling work. However, after a while, knowing they couldn't be replaced, the dekernelers began demanding shorter shifts, arguing that they should be compensated since their job was more difficult than any of the other tasks and led to beak problems. When they heard this, the huskers complained that they, too, were subject to repetitive-motion injuries and the sweepers brought up the feather loss they endured. Soon all the hens were pressing for shorter hours.

After much discussion with Gizzabelle and Newton, Poe and Buddy decided to give in to the dekernelers' demands. They didn't have much choice since the dekernelers had them over a barrel, and they knew it, but as Poe pointed out, it made sense in terms of productivity anyway. Dekerneling *was* very difficult and there had to be some incentive to do it. Also, shorter shifts might reduce burnout and beak issues, which would bring down efficiency in the long run anyway. However, they couldn't afford to let all the chickens have shorter hours. Therefore it was decided that only dekernelers would be eligible for the added benefits since theirs was the only job requiring special skills and training.

Predictably, this caused much resentment among the chickens, and the grumbling and disgruntled hen-pecking threatened to eat into the gains made by the more efficient systems. After more furious computer research, Poe found an answer to this dilemma, too.

"Success is all about teamwork!" he declared, announcing his newest initiative. "You have to work together to get things done."

Poe decided the best way to teach teamwork was through sports. At first he couldn't figure out what sort of sport would be best for the lessons he wanted to get across. "We need everyone to start on a level playing field," he said. That immediately eliminated many sports, since most gave an unfair advantage to one species or another. The cows were strongest, the horses fastest, and the pigs were by far the best at strategy.

However, Poe soon settled on the perfect solution, a sport he knew well from years of games he'd watched on television with Farmer Bob.

"Football!" he announced. "We'll have the first-ever all-animal football game."

"Footie?" asked Buddy skeptically.

"Sure," said Poe. "There's an old football in the garage, and we have plenty of open pasture that can serve as a field."

After some initial fractiousness over the name (the ungulates wanted to rename it hoofball, which the chickens vigorously resisted), Poe explained the rules of the game. The animals all liked to play, but games with rules were foreign territory. The herding animals instinctively understood teams, but the concept of scores went over everyone's heads.

"Can you explain points again? I don't get it," Flossy said.

"If you score a touchdown, you get points," Poe explained patiently, "and whoever gets the most points, wins."

"Can you eat points?" Hamish wanted to know.

"No, you can't eat points," Poe said. "They're not something you can see and touch."

The animals weren't impressed.

"What do we win with these so-called 'points?'" Gizmo asked.

"Nothing, you just win," Poe said in exasperation. Then, seeing the skepticism on the animals' faces, he thought the better of it.

"Bragging rights," he amended.

Still nothing.

"And extra corn rations."

Finally he got the reaction he was seeking. An excited murmuring arose from the crowd.

"Yum," said Hamish, smacking his lips. "How do we start?"

"First we need to set up the field," said Poe.

Using an old can of paint—another of Newton's garage finds—they painted an end zone and 50-yard line on their flattest pasture. But when they looked around for something to build goal posts with, nothing was the right size or shape. Even Newton was stumped.

"What about scarecrows?" suggested Gizzabelle.

"Good thinking," Newton said. "And they belong in the fields anyway, so they won't raise any eyebrows if they happen to be spotted."

Once the scarecrows were erected in the end zones, Poe gathered everyone together and assigned teams and positions. Everyone except Sasuage, who was too unwell, had a role. Buddy and Newton were team captains and quarterbacks. Xena, Xerxes, and the horses were linebackers; the pigs, full, tail and cornerbacks; cows, tackles and guards; sheep, centers and wide receivers; chickens, safeties; Mordecai and Peanut were kickers; Coco and Sarge were placekickers.

"And I'll be referee," said Poe. He gave a loud warning whistle, just to show how it was done, and they found some colored rags for him to use as flags.

Next came finding some way of differentiating the teams. Initially, they decided to try a skins and shirts, but they couldn't get any of Farmer Bob's old shirts to fit. The cows and horses were too big to even tie a shirt around, and the chickens couldn't get their wings into the sleeves.

They were stuck until Newton had an idea. "What if we dyed one team with the marker spray Farmer Bob used to use on the sheep?"

"I know just what you're talking about," said Buddy. He led them to where Farmer Bob kept the marker spray and selected the blue can. "We can call our team True Blue." Although the aerosol cans were hard to manipulate and Gizmo accidentally sprayed himself in the face as they were figuring it out, eventually everyone on Buddy's team had been streaked bright blue. All except Henrietta, who was convinced that chemicals were poisonous and insisted on swapping teams with Clementine. She wanted nothing to do with the "death spray," as she called it.

After everyone had rubbed charcoal on their cheeks for eye black and a couple of old tennis balls had been found to stick on Xerxes' horns, Poe deemed them properly "suited up" and led everyone onto the field for practice.

Training started with a warm-up run. "Ten times around the field," Poe instructed, assembling everyone on the starting line, then giving a sharp whistle to send them off. The poor chickens were already being lapped by the horses before they even got a quarter of the way around the field, and Poe exempted them from the rest of the run after Clementine collapsed from heat exhaustion on lap two.

After Hamish—the last to finish—stumbled in and took a few minutes to catch his breath, Poe led everyone in squats and side-shuffles and high knee drills. They even attempted push-ups, although that was mostly a failure. They learned how to block and pass and tackle, taking special care that the larger animals refrained from demolishing the smaller ones. Buddy and Newton devised some simple plays. Mordecai and Peanut practiced their kicking.

Finally Poe deemed them ready to compete.

The team captains picked their strongest athletes to start and led them onto the middle of the field. Everyone else stayed on the sidelines to watch.

Flossy, who had fallen in love with cheerleading as soon as she learned of its existence, had been preparing for her moment in the spotlight with a dedication no one had suspected she had in her. She pranced out in front of the crowd and bleated the cheer she'd made up all by herself:

"We are true and we are blue,
We are gonna slaughter you!
Dice you up for dinner stew,
Cordon bleu or vindaloo!
We are gonna butcher you,

'Cuz that's just what we like to do!
Go, Team, Go!"

Then she jumped up and down, and dropped to the ground in a double split.

The blue team cheered and took up the refrain. "Go, Team, Go! Go, Team, Go!"

Not to be outdone, Henrietta fluttered to the front of the crowd and led her team in their own chant:

"Predators are made to kill
Slaying you will be a thrill
We'll rip out your throats
And eat your guts.
Peck out your eyes
And kick your butts!
KILL, KILL, KILL!"

It wasn't as poetic as Flossy's, but it got the job done. The Predators went wild. Although the cheer skirted the bounds of decency, it fed into the latent predator fantasies that all herbivores held in their heart of hearts, even if they never admitted to them.

"KILL! KILL! KILL!" the Predators yelled.

"We are gonna slaughter you! We are gonna butcher you!" the blue team screamed back.

Gizzabelle suppressed a shudder. This was teaching teamwork?

Out on the field, Poe raised his voice to be heard over the din of the crowd. "First," he announced, strutting around the two huddles of animals, "is the coin toss." He looked around. "Anyone have a quarter?"

"What's that?" Gizmo asked.

"It's a coin with a head and tail," Poe explained.

"Oh," said Gizmo, then he perked up. "Hey, *I've* got a head and a tail! Flip me! Flip me!"

Poe studied the young bird. "Only if your mom says it's okay," he finally said.

Gizmo swelled up like a blowfish. "Why? I'm old enough to

make up my own mind!"

Poe was resolute, though, and the two went over to the stands to ask for Clementine's permission.

"Absolutely not," she said. "It's much too dangerous."

"No, it's not!" insisted Gizmo. "I'll be careful. I promise. Pleeeease?"

After much begging and pleading from Gizmo, Clementine finally relented after Poe suggested they use the sheep as a sort of landing pad to break his fall.

"You're sure it will be safe?" she asked Poe.

"Sure," he said. "We'll just put Gizmo on top of Xerxes, who will buck him right over to the sheep. It'll be just like landing on a big, fluffy pillow."

"Wait just a tail flick," Xena interjected. "Why Xerxes? Just because he's a bull?" She scowled. "I buck twice as much as he does! Twice as high, too."

Xerxes looked at Poe. "It's true," he admitted. "Xena's the firebrand in the family."

Xena glared at Poe, arching a brow expectantly. When nothing happened immediately, her breath quickened and started to come in snorts. Her tail began flicking from side to side.

They quickly perched Gizmo on Xena's haunches.

"Okay," said Poe. "When Xena throws Gizmo into the air one of the team captains calls 'heads' or 'tails.' Whichever end he lands on determines whose side gets to choose whether to kick off or receive."

"That would never work with *félin*," said Coco, shaking her head.

"You can call it," Buddy offered Newton.

The mule accepted with a nod. "Awfully generous of you."

"No, no, no!" Poe said in exasperation. "You're supposed to be adversaries! None of this chivalry nonsense." He rolled his eyes. "Okay, Gizmo. Are you ready?"

Gizmo saluted the animals on the sideline and blew a kiss to Clementine. "Sayonara, baby!" he chirped happily.

At Poe's signal, Xena gave a single tremendous kick, launching the little blue chicken high into the sky. All the animals watched as he soared heavenwards.

"Tails!" Newton brayed as Gizmo crested and began his head-over-heels descent. As he tumbled down, a horrified gasp rose from the crowd. Xena had thrown him farther than they'd expected and he had passed right over the knot of sheep he was supposed to land on.

"He's going to hit the ground!" Clementine cried.

Buddy was in motion before she finished her sentence, his herding instincts snapping into high gear. "Everyone, up and *over*!" he barked, racing toward the sheep.

The sheep scrambled to their feet and tripped over one another in their panicked attempt to flee the barking dog.

They had barely gotten up when Buddy was already shouting a new command. "Down, down, down!"

As one body, the sheep flopped down and squeezed their eyes closed just as Gizmo dove headfirst into their midst and landed with muffled thud. He popped up before anyone else had a chance to recover themselves.

"That was *fly*!" he squawked. He looked around. "Heads wins! Who had heads?"

No one answered. On the sideline, Henrietta, who had fainted, began to moan, and two hens rushed to her side.

"Well?" Gizmo said impatiently. "Who goes first?"

Buddy sighed heavily and shook his head. "That would be us, I guess," he said at last.

"Awesome possum! We win!" Gizmo said, strutting around in a victory dance, oblivious to the danger he had so narrowly avoided. "So do we kick or receive?"

"We'll receive," said Buddy.

The players took their places on the field as Poe had instructed them. The cheerleaders got the crowd riled up with increasingly blood-thirsty chants.

At Poe's whistle, Newton gave the football a mighty kick. It sailed through the air, right toward none other than Gizmo, who flew up to catch it. The two collided in an explosion of feathers and fell straight to the earth. The football rolled away from the stunned bird.

Everyone on the field took off toward them, and the ground trembled with the force of the stampede. This was enough to alarm even the brave-hearted little chicken. As the cows and horses and pigs and sheep thundered toward him from all sides, Gizmo scrambled to the football, sank his claws into it, and covered his head with his wings.

Luckily for Gizmo, Millie got to him first and shielded him with her body as the rest of the animals piled on. By the time it was all done, there was not a single animal left standing.

They began the process of peeling away the pileup. Everyone was moaning and rubbing bruised shins and crushed wings. A sheep had gotten a black eye, and a cow had broken her tail. Finally, they unearthed Gizmo, who was miraculously unhurt and still clutching the ball.

"You've got more lives than Coco," Buddy marveled.

The animals who were able headed for the thirty-yard line while the wounded and malingerers who had already had their fill of football limped off the field to be replaced. The two sides lined up across from one another and locked eyes with their opposing counterparts, grunting and growling in their most menacing manner.

"Fifteen, twenty-four, fifty-two!" barked Buddy, diligently reeling off the random numbers as Poe had instructed. "Hike!"

As soon as Jellybean, his center, hiked Buddy the ball, the nice, orderly formation instantly fell into chaos. Although the rules and objectives of the game had seemed clear enough when Poe explained them during training, in the harum-scarum pandemonium of the play, with everything coming at them all at once, it was all the animals could do to hold one thing in their heads. Some remembered to chase the football, others focused on tackling the opposition, still others simply panicked and tried to get away from the action as fast as they could.

There was holding and clipping and illegal blocking, not to mention kicking and pecking and tail pulling. Poe whistled frantically and threw penalty flags left and right, but no one paid him the slightest attention.

Buddy weaved through the defense virtually unchecked, easily outmaneuvering even the faster animals. He was just about to cross the goal line when Xerxes, who had been behind him the whole time, suddenly head-butted him and sent him sprawling across the field.

With the quarterback down, Poe gave a single ear-splitting whistle that stopped everyone their tracks.

Buddy slowly got to his feet. "What'd you do that for?" he asked the bull. "You're supposed to be on my side. You're my guard!"

Xerxes hung his head. "I'm sorry. I thought that we're supposed to tackle whoever's got the ball."

"That's when you're on *defense*," Buddy said in exasperation. Seeing Xerxes' wounded expression, he relented. "It's alright, mate, we're all just learning."

"That's right," said Poe. "You're not the only one by any means. I counted twenty-two fouls altogether, and that's just the ones I saw!"

Calculating where to mark the first down turned out to be a major production. Many of the fouls weren't even covered in the rules and were open for debate. Should tail pulling be counted as holding for a 10-yard penalty or a personal foul for 15? Was pecking unnecessary roughness? Could you get a penalty for fouling your own teammate?

Poe made a hatch mark in the dirt for every penalty point awarded, and soon there were so many he completely lost count.

The two sides were deeply embroiled in an argument over whether scratching should be considered illegal use of hands and feet when Poe happened to glance up and notice someone on the sideline, behind and apart from the spectators, who were still cheering enthusiastically, unaware of anything amiss. Poe froze, staring at a face which perfectly mirrored the horror and disbelief he felt.

It was Granny Ann, the Egg Lady.

CHAPTER 9

The next thing Poe knew, Gizmo was shaking his wing vigorously.

"They are not, are they?" the young cockerel demanded.

Poe struggled to focus. "Are what?"

"Paws aren't feet, right?" Gizmo said, rolling his eyes.

"Um…yes," Poe said distractedly, trying to catch Buddy's eye. Gizmo beamed. "They are."

Gizmo's face fell. "Yes, they *are*, or yes, they *aren't*?" he insisted.

"Are." Poe finally caught Buddy's attention, and beckoned him over.

"But—" Gizmo began.

"I mean aren't. Whatever." While Gizmo sashayed triumphantly in front of the now-irate Predators, who immediately began protesting the decision, Poe motioned for Newton to join Buddy at his side.

"Don't look now," he hissed, "but we've been found out. Granny Ann's over there on the sidelines!"

Without moving his head, Buddy scanned the crowd until his eyes landed on the human, who was still rooted to the spot.

"Castration!" he cursed under his breath.

"What are we going to do now?" asked Newton.

"Just act natural," said Poe. "As unobtrusively as you can, let everyone know she's there and *not to panic*. It is imperative that they keep playing as if nothing's wrong. No time to explain, but I've got an idea that just might work."

Poe gave a loud whistle. "Okay everyone, huddle up! First down's at the 30-yard line!" He hadn't actually totaled the hatch marks, but he knew that none of the other animals had either. No one except Newton and Sausage could possibly count that high.

While Buddy and Newton apprised their teammates of the situation in their huddles, Poe flew over to Gizzabelle and hurriedly explained things to her. "She's right over there to the left, behind Buttercup," he whispered, nodding almost imperceptibly in the human's direction. As they watched, Granny Ann took a tentative step forward, craning her neck to see the animals on the field as they lined up at the 30-yard line.

Gizzabelle shot Poe a worried look. Then, thinking fast, she addressed the crowd. "I've got a new cheer. True Blue and Predators, repeat after me!" she commanded. "I need *everyone* for this one!"

Do not panic; do not fear,
But there is a human near!
Act as normal as you can;
Poe will save us with his plan!

The import of the words sank in as they shouted them back, and the animals shifted uncomfortably and surreptitiously glanced from side to side, but with the exception of Henrietta, who had fainted yet again, they didn't panic or break rank. Gizzabelle repeated the cheer over and over, knowing that having something to occupy them would go a long way in keeping the animals calm.

When Poe saw that Gizzabelle had things under control, he took off again. This time, he flew over the crowd and landed right in front of Granny Ann.

"Achem," he said, clearing his throat loudly.

Granny Ann dragged her eyes away from the field to settle on the small bird at her feet.

Poe stared up at her. "I see you are enjoying our game," he said in his best humanspeech. "Do you follow football regularly?"

Granny Ann blanched and took a step back.

"Would you care to join us on the sidelines for a better view, Granny Ann?" Poe invited, his voice oozing with courtly charm. "Do you mind if I call you that? The hens talk about you so much, I feel as if I know you, but please let me know if I am being too familiar."

Her mouth began working, but no words formed.

"The Easter Bunny will be joining us shortly," he continued. "And the purple elephants and the Mad Hatter. You don't want to miss them. Oh, and of course, dear old Cuckoo. How could I forget! You are acquainted with Cuckoo, are you not?" He looked at her expectantly.

Granny Ann blubbered some more unintelligible noises and shook her head.

Poe narrowed his eyes. "No?" he asked, his tone suddenly ice-cold. "Really? I have reason to think you are." He flew up and alighted on Granny Ann's shoulder. He tucked his beak in her ear.

"CUCKOO!" he squawked at the top of his lungs. Granny Ann screamed and jerked away. Poe lost his footing and started flying around her head. He swooped down and tangled his claws in her hair while she swatted him away.

"CUCKOO! CUCKOO!" he shrieked.

Granny Ann took off toward the house. Poe followed her, diving and pecking and screeching all sorts of wild nonsense. "Jabberwocky, jubjub bird. Why is a raven like a writing desk? I will rend thee in the gobberwarts with my blurglecruncheon, see if I don't! Hey, wocky, watch me pull a wabbit out of my hat...he's a wascally wabbit, he is! Guess who? It's Woody Woodpecker. Wha ha hahaha! Wha ha hahaha! Hahahahahahahaha!" he laughed maniacally.

Granny Ann jumped into her car and peeled out so fast, the stench of burning rubber filled the air. Poe watched the car careen down the driveway. As it disappeared over the hill, he took off toward the field.

The animals had quit any pretense at playing football and were huddled together, muttering anxiously amongst themselves. When they saw Poe returning, they grew silent.

He circled over their heads. "I'm going to follow her," he called down. "While I'm gone, you've got to dispose of all the evidence of the game. Not a single trace of anything suspicious, understand? I've got to go before I lose track of her car, but I'll be back as soon as I can!"

With that, he took off in the direction Granny Ann had gone. Buddy looked around. "You heard him," he said. "Let's skedaddle!" He led his teammates to the creek, which was soon blue with dye, while everyone else stayed behind to turn the football field back into a pasture. They dismantled the scarecrows, and stomped and scratched and chomped the painted lines off the field. When they were done, they scoured the barnyard for any telltale signs they might have missed.

Then they settled in for the hardest part: waiting.

Buddy and Gizzabelle gathered outside Newton's stall.

"What do you think's going to happen?" Gizzabelle asked the others in hushed tones. "Do you think she's gone for good?"

"Dunno. I don't reckon she'll come back by herself," said Buddy. "Not after the walloping Poe gave her." No one had been close enough to hear what Poe had said to Granny Ann, but they'd all seen him run her off the farm. "But she might bring others."

The feathers rose on Gizzabelle's neck as she imagined great swarms of humans descending on the farm in retaliation, turning out the barn, overrunning the henhouse. "What do you think they'll do?" she asked tremulously. "Give us over to Kratchet?"

"They could do that," said Newton, "but if they find out we've been running the farm ourselves, it's impossible to know what they'll do. Maybe they'd want to observe us for scientific purposes." Being a part of the great march of progress, even as an object of observation, didn't strike him as all bad.

"Or they might put us on display," suggested Buddy. "Remember the brouhaha they made over the two-headed chicken a while back? Farmer Bob took me for a squiz —they were carting the poor chook all over the countryside—and you should have seen it! The humans queued up for hours just for a bo-peep."

"Yes, humans do seem to love anything weird and unusual," agreed Newton. "On the other hoof, they can be terrified of things that are different, too." His expression darkened. As much as he envied the humans their science, he was under no illusions that they were an entirely rational species. "I'd hate to think what might happen if they see us as a threat..."

Gizzabelle twittered anxiously. "What? Surely, it wouldn't be worse than Kratchet, right?"

Newton didn't answer.

Buddy hastened to reassure her. "No worries, Giz. Most humans are fair dinkum. Besides, Poe said he had a plan. I reckon he knew what he was doing. He hasn't let us down yet."

He'd said just the right thing. Gizzabelle wasn't convinced in the benevolence of the humans, but she had consummate faith in

Poe's ability to see them through.

It wasn't until well after dark that Poe returned to the farm. He immediately sought out his three friends and found Gizzabelle and Buddy snoozing in front of Newton's stall. He poked them awake.

"I think it worked!" he said excitedly.

"What worked?" asked Buddy groggily.

"My plan."

"Which is?" asked Newton, sticking his head out of his stall. "Drive her away? Sure, we can scare off one little old lady, but don't you think the humans will come back with overwhelming force? Are you prepared for full-scale war?"

"No, no, no," said Poe, shaking his head. "You've got it all wrong! She wasn't running because she was scared...not of me, at least."

"What do you mean?" asked Gizzabelle.

"Well, I got the idea when I saw Granny Ann's face," Poe said. "She obviously couldn't believe what she was seeing. It was like I could read her mind; she was thinking she must be dreaming—or crazy. And then it came to me in a flash." Poe paused; his audience leaned in. "Why not convince her that she was?"

"Was what?" asked Gizzabelle.

"Oh, I see..." Buddy said, his eyes twinkling merrily. "You want her to think she's got a couple kangaroos loose in the top paddock."

"Exactly," Poe chirped. "It's not nearly as hard as you might think. Humans are more inclined to believe what they've been taught to expect than what their own senses tell them. I talked to her in humanspeech, which was apparently upsetting in and of itself, and then I made some inane comments and mussed around in her hair, and that was all it took. You saw her—she was completely freaked out!" A large, self-satisfied smile spread across his face at the memory.

"But I couldn't be sure. I wanted to follow her to make sure it had worked, that she wasn't just leaving to get reinforcements. I followed her car to a house and she went inside. I didn't know what to do. For a long time, I just peered in the windows, but the curtains were drawn and I couldn't see inside. Then I remembered what Newton said about Santa Claus and I decided to go down the chimney. I flew up to the roof but just as I was about to go down, a raccoon appeared on the roof and stopped me. He said he'd been 'casing the joint'—whatever that means—for days and wanted to know what I was doing. So I explained our whole situation to him—"

"A raccoon?" Gizzabelle said sharply. "You told a *raccoon* about us?"

"Yeah, why not?" said Poe. "He was very interested to hear about our little enterprise."

"I bet he was!" Gizzabelle snapped. "A henhouse unprotected by humans! I'm sure he was licking his chops just thinking about it."

"No, no," Poe protested. "You've got it all wrong. It wasn't like that at all. Bandit just wanted to help me—help *us*—out. He said he was a master burglar, claimed he could find a way into anything. Then he said something really smart. He said that it's not getting in that's hard. The hard part is getting *out*. Told me to always have an exit strategy. I hadn't even thought of that! See, Giz, he really was being helpful."

"Harumph," was all she said.

"Anyway," continued Poe, turning to Buddy and Newton, "Bandit told me it was no good trying to fly *up* the chimney once I got inside. I'd never make it out that way. He said that when I wanted to get out, I should hide in the trash. They'd put it out at night and he promised he'd come and get me out."

"And you trusted him?" asked Gizzabelle.

"Why not?" asked Poe. "You didn't meet him. If you had, you'd understand. He was so friendly. And sharp. You couldn't help but like him. So, anyway, I went down the chimney. I was afraid Granny Ann would hear me when I landed in the fireplace, but I don't think she would have noticed if there was a dancing bear in the middle of the room! She was completely distracted. She kept pacing from room to room, muttering to herself. That went on for a while. She'd lie down and toss and turn and then get up, and then pace, and then lie down some more. Then her mate got home. That's when I knew we'd done it. She didn't mention anything about us to him at all. Instead, she asked him if he'd noticed anything unusual about *her* lately!"

"So…it worked?" Buddy asked. "She believed it? She reckoned she'd gone troppo?"

"I guess so," said Poe. "Her mate said he hadn't noticed anything and she told him she hadn't been feeling well and she hadn't finished her egg pickups that day and would he mind helping her out tomorrow and he said he could. And that was that. They didn't talk anymore about it. In fact, they didn't talk about much of anything. They didn't eat at the table like Farmer Bob did. They took their food into the room where the TV was and watched it while they ate."

"So anyway," he continued, after he explained to Gizzabelle what TV was, "while they were watching TV, I snuck into the kitchen and jumped into the trash can. I covered myself with garbage just like Bandit had told me to and waited. After what seemed like forever, Granny Ann's mate came in and tied the bag shut and took it outside. He threw it in the trashcan and I heard the lid slam down. When I was sure he was gone, I pecked through the bag—that was easy; just like breaking out of an egg—but I couldn't get the lid to open. I pushed and pushed, but it didn't budge."

"What about the raccoon?" asked Buddy. "Wasn't he supposed to come get you?"

"Well, that's what was *supposed* to happen," Poe said. "But, honestly, when he didn't come after a while, I have to admit that I started to wonder if he was going to show up at all. When you're trapped all alone in the dark, it's easy to get a little paranoid. I started thinking maybe he'd forgotten or maybe he'd just been stringing me along after all."

He looked around sheepishly. "So then I sort of panicked and started squawking really loudly about all the delicious garbage that was in there with me. 'Yum, yum. Sardines! Apple pie! Potato chips! How could they throw stuff like this away?' That sort of thing. And then, just when I was about to give up, I heard scratching outside and then the lid lifted and there he was! He said he'd been unavoidably detained and he was so sincerely apologetic that I felt like a real cad for doubting him. He had to have known, too, because there wasn't any food in there except a melon rind and rotten onion. He was too polite to call me on it, though. That made me feel even

— 131 —

worse."

"I wouldn't lose any sleep over it," Gizzabelle grumbled.

"Anyway," continued Poe, "I told him what had happened inside and that I needed to get back to the farm to warn you that Granny Ann would be coming back tomorrow with her mate."

"What will we do?" asked Gizzabelle. "Act like everything's normal?"

"Well, that's what I thought at first, too," said Poe with a twinkle in his eye. "But Bandit had an even better idea. Wait 'til you hear it..."

The next day when Granny Ann and her husband drove up the driveway to the farmyard, the animals were ready. Any animals who were still tinged blue with dye were safely hidden away and the football field had been meticulously returned to its original state. The key players were in place and knew their roles.

Granny Ann opened the van door and stepped out, looking around anxiously. She noticed the empty driveway. "I guess Bob's not here," she told her husband, who was still sitting in the van. "The fridge is in the barn. You're coming, aren't you, Hank?" Her voice was high and tight.

Hank grunted. "I don't know why you need me here," he said. "You seem just fine to me."

"Please, Hank," Granny Ann pleaded. "I'm feeling a little shaky again." Sure enough, she did look pale and her hands were trembling.

"Oh, alright," sighed Hank, heaving himself out of the van and getting the hand truck out of the back. Granny Ann led the way to the barn. Hank kept his head down as he followed, but Granny Ann's eyes darted back and forth, nervous as a field mouse.

Suddenly, Buddy came trotting across the barnyard, Coco perched on his back like a bareback circus performer. She struck several graceful poses, balancing on three legs and maneuvering her tail into various positions.

"Hank!" Granny Ann screeched.

He jerked his head up to look at his wife. "Huh?"

"Do you see that?" she demanded, staring at her husband

imploringly.

"See what?"

Granny Ann pointed at Buddy and Coco, her eyes following her finger. Buddy was casually scratching his ear with his hind leg and Coco rubbing against the fencepost, paying the dog—and Granny Ann—no mind.

"Um, nothing," she said, her voice wavering. "I thought I, um, saw something..."

Hank gave her a look, and took the lead into the barn. Granny Ann hurried after him.

Inside, she directed Hank to the refrigerator. When Hank disappeared behind the fridge door and began stacking the egg cartons in the hand truck, Peanut appeared in the doorway of the stall across the aisle. He was standing on his hind legs, leaning against the door frame, a beanie on his head and a bottle of Coke between his hooves. As she stared at him, dumbfounded, he took a swig of the soda, tipped the bottle at her, and stepped into his stall, closing the door behind him.

"Hank?" Granny Ann said urgently, rushing forward toward the stall. When she got to the door, she looked over into the stall, only to find Peanut seemingly asleep in the hay, the beanie and soda bottle nowhere to be seen.

"What now?" Hank said absently from behind the fridge door.

When Granny Ann looked up from Peanut's stall, Newton and the horses were staring at her. They began rolling their eyes and wiggling their ears maniacally. They stuck out their long tongues and tossed their heads from side to side. Then Newton gave Granny Ann a sly wink.

"N-n-n-n-nothing," Granny Ann stammered. "Never mind. Let's just go. Hurry!"

"Hold your horses!" Hank snapped. "If you're so frigging impatient, you could come help."

But Granny Ann wasn't listening; she was already out the barn door. There, she was confronted by a barnyard filled with chickens dancing to music that apparently only they could hear. Gizzabelle pirouetted and pliéd and ran around on her tippy-toes; Henrietta did the Twist; Sarge led Clementine in a foxtrot; one gaggle of hens formed a conga line while the rest did the Electric Slide. Gizmo showed off some impressive break-dancing moves, moon walking and executing a very respectable back spin.

Granny Ann, though, missed out on most of the chickens' dance spectacular. She made a beeline to the van, looking neither left nor right, but only straight ahead, blinkering her eyes with her hands.

Poe flew over from his perch on a nearby fencepost. "Welcome to the funny farm!" he cried, swooping down toward Granny Ann's head. "Stay here on the funny farm! You can be as loony as you like here on the funny farm! Cuckoo! Cuckoo!"

Granny Ann shrieked and put her hands over her ears. Then she broke into a jog. Poe followed so closely that his wings ruffled her hair. He hissed into her ear. "Or leave now and never, never come back! You hear? Nevermore!"

At that moment, Sarge gave a mighty crow, signaling Hank's emergence from the barn. The chickens instantly ceased their dancing. Poe made himself scarce. Granny Ann had reached the car and sat shuddering in the passenger seat.

Hank crossed the barnyard, paying no mind at all to the chickens, and loaded the eggs into the back. Although he was not generally a very observant man, even he couldn't miss his wife's ashen pallor. "You're not looking too hot," he said when he got in the car. "Are you alright?"

"Let's just go!" Granny Ann said sharply.

"Well, excuuuuse me," he grumbled under his breath, starting the engine. As they headed back up the dirt road to the street, Granny Ann made the final mistake of looking out her window as they passed the sheep pasture.

Lining the fence, the sheep stood on their hind legs, waving her a cheery goodbye.

The animals were full of self-congratulatory back slapping when they returned to the barn.

"That was awesome!" Gizmo squawked. "Didya see her face?" He bugged out his eyes and let his jaw drop in a fair imitation.

Buddy chuckled. "She reckoned she'd gone bonkers alright. Barmy as a bandicoot."

Everyone was eager to tell the story of *their* encounter with Granny Ann and tried to buttonhole the others into listening, which they did only in order to have an audience for their own story. They reenacted their respective crazy-making tricks for one another. Peanut modeled his now-crushed beanie for Sausage. The chickens boogied down; the horses made goofy faces; the sheep waved to the imaginary car.

"B-bye, and don't come baaaaack!" Flossy bleated.

Miffed that Granny Ann hadn't made it out to the cow pasture, Xena demanded that the entire barn sit through the tap dance routine she'd rehearsed so diligently. Considering her vast size, Xena was fairly light on her hooves, but even so, she had about as much grace as a hog on ice.

"Queerer than a pigeon-toed platypus, that one," said a snarky hen to her neighbor as the obligatory applause died away.

Newton trotted over to Gizzabelle. "That dancing sure was a stroke of pure genius," he said.

"Oh, it was nothing," Gizzabelle said. "Poe's the one who found it online."

"Nonsense," insisted Newton. "Not only was it your idea, but you're the one who worked your tail feathers off choreographing the whole thing. I have to admit, when I saw where you were starting from—it was chaos out there in the barnyard for a while!—I didn't think you'd be able to pull it off in time, but you sure proved me wrong. You had everyone dancing like they'd been born to it."

"Dancing!" Henrietta sighed happily, rolling her hips back and forth. "I adore dancing!" said the hen, who had been so caught up in her twisting, she hadn't even remembered to be scared.

"Me, too," agreed Clementine. "Takes me back to my pullet days. It's like being light as a feather, like you're floating on air." She shot Sarge a glance from beneath lowered lids. "Of course, it helps having a strong partner," she said. Sarge guffawed gruffly.

Poe watched the proceedings from a slight distance without taking part himself. When he felt they had reveled in their accomplishments long enough, he called them to order.

"Attention, everyone!" he cawed. "I want to congratulate all of you for the excellent job you did today. We couldn't have done it without each and every one of you doing your part. Our timing had to be perfect; if Granny Ann's mate had seen even one of our pranks, that would have been the end of us! But, together, we pulled it off. This was a great day for the farm."

Everyone cheered, and engaged in another round of enthusiastic back patting.

When the clamor died down, Clementine hesitantly raised a wing. "And what about the eggs?" she asked softly. "What will we be doing with the eggs now that they aren't being collected and sold? Could we...hatch them?"

Poe paused. Sarge was the only rooster on the farm and it had been many moons since he'd mated with anyone except Clementine. "I don't see why not," he said.

Clementine almost swooned in ecstasy. She was a broody hen, and she couldn't imagine anything better than sitting a nest, unless it was caring for hatchlings. She didn't know which was worse: having your babies taken before they were even out of the shell, or raising chicks knowing all along that they'd be taken away as soon as they reached frying size. Gizzabelle and Gizmo were the apples of her eye, and more than most hens ever got, but the prospect of having her own chicks and getting to raise them to adulthood thrilled her to her very core.

"Can we, really?" she breathed. "Imagine," she clucked to Sarge. "We can have a family!" As soon as the words were out of her mouth, she covered her beak with her wing. "Of course, you're our family, too," she rushed to assure Gizmo and Gizzabelle. "No one will ever take your place in our hearts, no matter how many chicks we hatch. There's room for all of you."

"Don't worry," Gizzabelle said, smiling. "We know what you meant."

"So what now?" asked Newton. "Are we going back to the football game?"

"No," said Poe. "Everyone can have the rest of the day off. I think you deserve it."

A cheer went up, and the animals streamed out of the barn to enjoy the sunshine.

"I don't really think football teaches teamwork," Poe said to

Buddy, Newton, and Gizzabelle when they were alone. "Did you see how intense the animals got arguing about penalties? Even the animals in the stands looked like they were about to tear each other's heads off!"

"Yeah," said Newton, "I guess football was a bust."

"Nonsense," said Poe. "It was fantastic!"

"Fantastic?" echoed Gizzabelle.

"Sure, we just need to figure out how to channel all that energy into work. Forget teamwork. Success is all about competition!"

"*Another* program?" groaned Buddy. He felt like he was only just beginning to get the hang of one program when another one came down the pike.

"Do we really want to encourage competition?" asked Gizzabelle. "Even if football didn't foster teamwork like we'd hoped, I think working together is still the best approach."

"I'm afraid the urge to win is far more powerful than the cooperative spirit," said Poe. "I'm not saying I like it; it's just the way things are. Nature's red in tooth and claw, no matter what your soup stories say."

"I'm not so sure about that," said Gizzabelle dubiously. "But even so, do we need to pander to our lower instincts? I thought we were making our numbers as it is." She looked at Newton. "Aren't we producing enough already?"

Poe stared at her like a second beak had sprouted in the middle of her forehead. "There is *never* enough," he said sternly. "Enough is for losers. We always have to be looking for ways to get *more*. That's our job as leaders. More. Never forget it. Remember, that's our motto: More, more, more!"

"Right," Gizzabelle sighed. "More."

"So we're going to play football to learn competition now?" asked Newton.

"I don't think we have to teach it," said Poe, "we just have to harness it."

The raven immediately set to work devising a system which would take advantage of the animals' competitive spirits. Utilizing the groundwork laid during the Scientific Management phase, he helped the managers break everyone's jobs into parts and quantify them. Then each manager kept detailed records of how each worker did in relation to his peers and to his or her own past performance, and whether the department as a whole met their weekly goal, which was constantly rising. Using mathematical formulas Newton developed, it was even possible to compare widely dissimilar divisions in terms of their productivity. Reading lessons were temporarily put on hold for math lessons, and this time, none of the managers were exempt.

Poe expected weekly totals on all seeds produced, seeds planted, mail collected, and drills run. He even wanted to track eggs laid and gallons of milk produced, even though their output wasn't really relevant anymore. He said it would help keep the animals in the right mindset. "More is better," he reminded. At the end of each week, the results were announced at the weekly All-Animal Meeting. Top-ranked workers and managers were honored, poor performers faced public ridicule.

The impact of the new system was dramatic. The animals quickly fell out into three groups. The top performers of every species acquired a new strut in their step and quickly rose in status and prestige, toppling the old pecking orders where they had existed and creating new ones in the species which had previously been more egalitarian. While their predecessors at the top had risen to their positions of prominence slowly, the newcomers were apt to allow their meteoric rise to go to their heads and became perfectly insufferable to be around.

By contrast, the animals who consistently found themselves in the poor performers category became listless and apathetic, losing all interest in food and mating, and withdrawing from farm life in general. They had no energy, slept all day, and complained of headaches, back pain, and other unexplained ailments. Friends and family reported that they weren't themselves.

Most of the animals, however, fell into the middle group, never knowing for sure if the weekly meeting would find them in the top or bottom group. Although they were used to brief spurts of panic when spooked, the constant, unrelenting anxiety the weekly meetings created was unprecedented. They began to have trouble sleeping and digestive problems skyrocketed. Sheep got the shakes;

cows developed nervous tics; pigs got hives; hens began molting out of season. Everyone was short-tempered and on edge, and fiercely protective of their turf. Gone were the days of cooperation and collaboration. Now that everyone was a rival, no one was willing to offer assistance unless a clear advantage could be seen. Rumors abounded and occasionally out-and-out fighting broke out between workers. On the flip side, the managers, who were in charge of the record-keeping, were all courted and fawned over in hopes of currying favor.

Buddy, in particular, was having trouble with his new role. Numbers were no more his forte than letters had been, and he felt like he was spending all of his time counting and calculating productivity and not enough time in the field, developing his workers. But worst of all was the continuous toadying up, which was almost more than the shepherd could bear. The insincerity cut straight to his core. However, he pressed on doggedly, refusing to say anything to Poe. He believed any complaint would be a sign of insubordination and a betrayal of his promise to support Poe's agenda 100%.

"You've got to tell him," pleaded Gizzabelle. "He's not down here on the ground like you are. He needs to know what's going on."

"No," said Buddy resolutely. "I'm not going to be a grumble-bum. I've just got to buck up and deal with it."

Finally, one evening after listening to Buddy's travails over dinner again and unsuccessfully exhorting him to take his concerns to Poe, Gizzabelle could stand it no longer. She'd been avoiding Poe ever since she started molting, too embarrassed to let him see her patchy plumage, but something had to be done.

She headed up to the farmhouse and ducked into the pet door. She found Poe in his usual spot on the desk, in front of the computer and surrounded by papers.

"Oh, hi, Gizzabelle," he said when he saw the little hen. "*Whoa*! What happened to you?"

Gizzabelle wished she could sink into the floor.

"I'm, uh...molting," she said hastily. "I need to talk to you. I don't know if these latest productivity measures are worth it. The numbers may be improving, but something's wrong with the animals." She explained about the animals' insomnia and irritable bowels and other symptoms. She couldn't bear to bring up her revolting feathers, although they were clearly the elephant in the room.

"Ah, yes," Poe said, nodding his head knowingly. "Nothing to worry about. Perfectly normal."

"Normal?" squawked Gizzabelle. "You think everyone having the squirts is *normal?*"

"I know exactly what it is," said Poe. "It's called stress."

"Stress?"

"Yeah, like I said, it's nothing to worry about."

One of Gizzabelle's feathers chose that moment to release and it drifted down to the ground, settling on the desk between the two birds.

"I think we need to re-think the new measures," she said stubbornly.

"I'm afraid that's just not possible. In fact, we need to up our numbers."

"What do you mean? We may not have gotten all the fields planted, but we did more than half. That's a good deal better than what Newton thought we'd need to get through winter. Isn't that enough?"

"What did I tell you about 'enough,' Gizzabelle?"

"There is no enough," she recited grudgingly.

"That's right. We may have done 'enough' to get us through the winter, but we need more."

"But why? *Why* do we need more?"

Poe's eyes shot over to the papers next to the computer. "Trust me," he said, "we do."

Gizzabelle looked over at the papers and although she didn't recognize all of the letters—they'd only gotten halfway through the alphabet before they'd started studying math—she noticed that each page had the same seven letters written in large red print. The pages had a lot of numbers on them too.

"What're those?" she asked.

"What, those?" Poe asked nonchalantly, stepping between Gizzabelle and the papers. "Nothing. Just mail."

"Oh," she said, trying to see around the raven. He sidestepped so he was right in her line of sight again. He gave an exaggerated yawn. "I'm exhausted. C'mon, let's go to roost." He walked over to the edge of the desk and glided to the floor.

With Poe out of the way, Gizzabelle had a clear view of the papers. She stared at the red letters. She didn't know them all yet, but she could memorize them for when she did.

"Gizzabelle?" Poe called from the floor.

"I'm coming," she said. She took one last look to fix the unfamiliar shapes in her memory before she glided down off the desk and the two birds made their way out of the farmhouse and to the henhouse.

Newton, who was on guard duty that night, was snoozing in front of the henhouse door. They nudged him gently. Barely rousing, he moved aside just enough for them to pass. Then he rearranged himself in front of the door and promptly fell back to sleep.

The whistling snores of the hens filled the house; not a chicken stirred. Gizzabelle could hear Poe rearranging his nest before he settled in for the night.

"Pleasant dreams, Gizzabelle," he said quietly. "See you tomorrow."

"Good night, Poe," she said absently.

Her mind was still back in the farmhouse. What was Poe keeping from her? What did the ominous red letters say? She traced them out in the dirt beside her nest so she'd be able to remember them later.

PAST DUE

CHAPTER 10

With seeding finished, the animals looked forward to a much-anticipated break from their demanding workloads. For several weeks there would be little to do except watch for the first tender corn shoots to appear. Surprisingly, even though the animals had more time to devote to them, egg and milk output actually fell, lending credence to Poe's contention that productivity thrived on scarcity and competition, not satiety and ease. Drills too were at an all-time low since by now everyone could practically do them in their sleep. The only division unaffected by the downturn was the mail collection, which carried on unabated, as Mordecai was quick to point out at every All-Animal Meeting.

The stress symptoms of the animals began to clear up, but as the days wore on, a strange new malaise fell over the farm. Instead of enjoying the rest and relaxation that they had looked forward to with such enthusiasm, the animals were restless and jittery.

"I'm all out of sorts," lowed Mille one day at morning milking. "I feel like I should be *doing* something, but I don't know what."

"I know," agreed Peanut. "I can't sit still anymore. I can't put my hoof on it, but something just doesn't feel right."

Poe was quick to diagnose the problem.

"I know exactly what's wrong," he told the animals at the next All-Animal Meeting.

"Is it stress again?" asked Jock.

"Not exactly," said Poe. "It's called boredom. You're all bored."

Bored? Boredom was an utterly unfamiliar concept.

"Is that a disease?" asked Jock, who was one of the hardest hit.

"Is it fatal?" Henrietta gasped. "It is, isn't it?"

"Don't worry," Poe assured her. "It's not a disease. It comes from not having enough to do."

At first it seemed impossible, but gradually the animals began nodding in agreement. It was true; the cud chewing and napping

— 142 —

and post rubbing and mud rolling and cloud gazing and sun bathing they'd done before somehow just didn't seem like *enough* anymore. Looking back, they didn't know how it ever had been.

"How do you make it go away?" they wanted to know.

"Reading, surfing the Internet, playing games, working out..." said Poe. "Anything that's a distraction."

The animals weren't interested in reading or computers, and their disastrous experience with football had soured them on games. When Poe explained what "working out" was, they nixed that idea too. Exercise seemed even more pointless than scoring points had.

"Actually," said Poe, grinning broadly, "I thought you might feel that way. But I think I have just the thing for you. It's the ultimate cure for boredom." He flew over to a barrel at the back of the barn and landed on the odd-shaped burlap-covered object on top. He had gotten Buddy and Peanut to drag it out from the farmhouse under cover of darkness the night before. Gizzabelle and Newton looked at each other curiously. Even they didn't know what was in store.

"This," Poe said, pulling off the sack with relish, "is a TV."

The crowd stared at the black box, unimpressed.

Poe alighted on the TV. "Peanut," he instructed, "turn it on." He grinned expectantly as Peanut, who was holding the remote, pressed the small button with his hoof.

Nothing happened.

Everyone looked at Poe.

His feathers ruffled, the raven bent over so he was looking at the blank screen upside down.

"Doesn't it need to be plugged in?" asked Newton.

Poe straightened up and shot the mule a grateful glance. "You're right. Buddy, could you plug it in?"

With some help from Gizzabelle, the shepherd was able to maneuver the black plug into the outlet on the barn wall.

"Okay, try it again," Poe said to Peanut.

Peanut pressed the remote again and the television sparked to life. Startled by the sudden noise, the animals jumped back in alarm, then tentatively approached to see the wild psychedelic light display. The chickens, who had a special fondness for bright, sparkling things, were particularly entranced by the flickering electric glow.

Poe hurried to adjust the rabbit-ear antennae and images soon began to appear. The animals oohed and aahed. Poe had Peanut flip through the channels, and they finally settled on a story about a man whose family had been killed by another man, and who killed a lot of other men in his search for revenge. There were lots of guns and shooting and things exploding. There was also a female human, but she didn't do much except get into harm's way.

Most of the animals didn't care for the story, which was altogether too violent for their tastes, but what they really enjoyed were the short programs in between. Each one featured an exciting new human invention, many of which the animals had never seen before. When they couldn't figure out what the product was for, lively debates about its purpose and function ensued.

The animals had always considered the clothes and tools and other accoutrements that humans came with as much a part of them as feathers were to a bird or claws to a cat, but now, for the first time, they realized that products weren't something people were born with at all. Poe explained that each item had to be bought. Although most of the items weren't things the animals had any use for, they made the people look so deliriously happy that the animals wished they had unsightly shower mildew just so they could use the miraculous bathroom cleaner to get rid of it.

After that first night, the animals decided to institute a regular TV time right after dinner as a way to while away the evening. Poe didn't join them, having work that he needed to attend to back at the house. So it wasn't until they had been watching for nearly a week when he accidentally discovered from an offhoof comment by Newton that the animals were suffering under the delusion that everything on the television was true. Poe quickly set them straight, explaining that while *some* shows were true, many were make-believe.

"Oh, that explains it," said Newton with relief. "I couldn't figure out why those people on the news shows were always so composed when they were talking about such horrible things—murder and war and environmental destruction—like they didn't have any feelings about it. But now I see. It was just *pretend*. I should've guessed."

"Actually..." Poe admitted reluctantly, "I'm afraid those are some of the true bits."

The animals were utterly confused. How could they tell what was real and what wasn't? They peppered Poe with questions, and were astonished to find that some of the most unbelievable things, the things they'd been most sure were imaginary—cities so full of humans that they had to live in concrete boxes in the sky and huge metal ships that could float on the water and invisible creatures called "germs" that caused disease—were actually real. Meanwhile Poe told them that, from what he could tell, most movies could be safely assumed to be works of fiction, as could all advertisements and political speeches.

Poe said if they really wanted to know that what they were watching was true, they could stick to "reality shows." This suited the animals just fine. Even though banishment—the worst fate the animals could imagine—seemed like a needlessly harsh punishment for failure, elimination contests were especially popular since even the most dim-witted of the chickens could follow the plot. Singing, skating, cooking, losing weight, eating bugs and jumping off buildings, racing around the world—it seemed like the humans could make anything into a contest.

Little by little, television time expanded and soon the animals' viewing options grew as the distinction between fact and fiction began to seem less important. It didn't take long for squabbles to begin over what to watch. Flossy was crazy about makeover shows; Newton lobbied—mostly unsuccessfully—for documentaries; Hamish was addicted to the food network; Sarge preferred the history channel; Clementine fancied dance-offs; Gizzabelle liked all sorts of dramas, but her guilty pleasure was a reality show where the contestants tried to find their true love. Of all the animals, Gizmo was perhaps the most obsessed of all. He loved comedies and action movies and especially anything to do with martial arts.

Of course, everyone especially liked seeing their own species on TV. The pigs had *Babe*; the chickens, *Chicken Farm*; and the sheep had a whole series, *Shaun the Sheep*. The cows tried to get into *Back to the Barnyard* since its protagonist was a bovine, but when they discovered that the presumably-male Otis was—inexplicably—in possession of an udder, they found the anatomical ambiguity too disconcerting. The cows were a deeply conservative species and gender fluidity was beyond their ken. Luckily Mordecai didn't watch TV or he would have been sure to kick up a row over the complete lack of caprine representation.

Soon the TV was on all day long and anytime the animals didn't have to be somewhere else, chances were good that they could be found in the back of the barn with their eyes riveted to the set. The hens, especially, put up a huge squawk if they couldn't have their afternoon soaps. Heaven forbid if anyone got between Henriettta and her "shows."

Newton initially enjoyed all the television shows for their anthropological value, but soon he felt he had culled all the useful information he could from them and began to chafe at the repetitiveness of the programming. Since he was rarely ever able to convince the other animals to tune in to any of the documentaries he wanted to see, his TV viewing waned to the occasional trivia game show.

"It's the same old thing over and over," he complained to Poe one day. "I don't see how they can stand it. You say it's the cure for boredom, but I couldn't be more bored!"

Poe, who rarely ever watched TV since he was constantly in the farmhouse researching and strategizing, didn't say anything, but the next day he had Buddy and Gizzabelle help him deliver a present to Newton's stall.

"Here's a little something to occupy your time," Poe said after he'd set down the bag he'd had in his beak. He gestured to the checkered object Buddy had laid on the barn floor. "That's Farmer Bob's chess board. And these are the chessmen." He emptied his bag of ebony pieces and Gizzabelle dumped out her ivory ones. The animals admired the delicate carvings, especially the exquisitely-rendered horses' heads.

"Those are called 'knights,'" Poe said. He showed them how the pieces were arranged on the board and then explained the rules. Newton instantly grasped the object of the game, and he handily beat Poe in their first match. After enduring much good-natured ribbing from the others, though, Poe excused himself to return to the farmhouse. "Sorry I can't stay longer," he apologized. "I've just got too many important things to do."

Newton's first hope was that Buddy would be his chess partner since the shepherd, ever the doer, couldn't sit still to watch television and therefore also had a lot of time on his paws. As it turned out, though, Buddy couldn't sit still for chess either.

"Maybe I'll go patrolling or check the fields to see if we've got any shoots yet," he said. "I've got to get out and about, or I'll go fruit loops."

That left Gizzabelle, who couldn't whip up any enthusiasm for the game but stuck with it, partially because she didn't want to leave Newton in the lurch and partially because she was afraid quitting might mean chickens weren't smart enough for such a complex challenge. However, eventually it became clear to both her and Newton that her heart really wasn't in it.

"You're beating me so badly, it can't be much fun for you any-way," she told the disappointed mule. "You need someone who can give you some competition."

Newton tried to wheedle Coco into playing with him, but she would have none of it. For a while, he played both sides, which helped him hone his skills, but soon got old. Then one day, on the spur of the moment, he invited his next-door neighbor to play, not really expecting him to accept. Although Sausage never watched television, Newton doubted he would be much interested in games, which no doubt seemed trivial and frivolous to the metaphysically-minded pig. To his surprise, however, Sausage cheerfully consented.

From that day forward, the two became regular chess partners. Their games were long and intense. They played in companionable silence, punctuated only by the occasional observations or congrat-ulations for a particularly brilliant move. If Newton had expected the pig to be a soft touch, he found instead a tough competitor with razor-sharp strategic skills who wasn't afraid to go for the jugular. In fact, the hog won almost all their games, and Newton sometimes had his suspicions about those he didn't, although Sausage was a pig of such integrity, it was hard to believe he would deliberately throw a match.

Peanut sat at Sausage's shoulder during the matches. "Well played!" he exclaimed every time Sausage moved a piece. "Checkmate!" he would squeal whenever Newton's king was even marginally threatened. Occasionally Peanut would take a stab at playing himself, but he was no match for either player, even when they didn't fully apply themselves.

One day while they were in the middle of a match, Mordecai stopped by on his way to look for his workers. "There's mail to deliver and where do you think my do-nothing mail carriers are? Ten to one they've got their noses stuck in front of that despicable peace-wrecking, time-killing, mind-numbing contraption you've got in here," grunted the goat. "That's all they ever do anymore."

"Napping with eyes open," Sausage chuckled.

Mordecai snorted appreciatively.

Peanut shot him the stink eye. "Yeah, Sausage," the small pig said, jumping between his master and the goat, "it's like they are only half awake, in a kind of dream."

"Who looks outside dreams. Who looks within awakens," said Sausage.

While Peanut puzzled over the latest Sausagism, the elder pig returned his attention to the board. He and Newton resumed their play; Mordecai continued to watch. No one spoke.

After several moves, Sausage looked at the goat. "Mordecai, we have reached the endgame. Will you join us?"

Peanut scowled and Newton raised his eyebrows in surprise.

"No thanks!" Mordecai bleated. "I'm not going to waste my time with more human nonsense." He stalked off toward the blaring television to find his mail carriers.

"I don't know why you'd waste your time with *him*," Peanut said when Mordecai was out of earshot. "Always bleating and moaning about everything. He's insufferable!"

Sausage picked up his bishop and moved it across the board, simultaneously capturing Newton's knight and putting the mule's king in check. "A cynic is only an idealist disappointed," he said.

"The only way there's an idealist inside him is if he ate one!" scoffed Peanut. He looked to Newton for backing.

But instead of laughing along with him, the mule was strangely quiet. "You know," he said, "now that I think about it, when I first came to the farm, an old cow told me a story." He shook his head thoughtfully. "Wow, I haven't thought about that in years."

"Thought about what?" Peanut asked.

Newton turned to the runty pig. "It was long before your time, Peanut. It was before everyone's time—everyone but Sausage, that is. Seems Farmer Bob was looking to diversify and he'd decided to try goat milk and cheese. Mordecai was one of the first goats he acquired, and the only billy. It was going to be his responsibility to sire many kids and grow the herd."

"So what happened?" Peanut asked.

"Something went dreadfully wrong with the nannies," said Newton. "One by one, they got sick and died. Farmer Bob brought in the vet, but he couldn't save them. Soon, Mordecai was the only one left. For a while, I guess everyone thought Farmer Bob would get some new nannies and try again, but he never did. So Mordecai was left all alone."

No one spoke for a long moment.

Newton finally continued. "The thing is, I remember that cow describing Mordecai when he first came. High-spirited and self-confident and full of a young buck's vim and vigor. She said he was always talking about his plans for the future, almost what you'd call...a dreamer."

"*Mordecai*??" Peanut sputtered.

"I know," said Newton with a wan smile. "Hard to believe, isn't it?"

Peanut shook his tiny head in disbelief. "Well, I guess that's enough to make anyone bitter. It's like you always say, Sausage, 'be kind, for everyone is fighting their own battle.' I should have been kinder."

"The greatest wisdom of all is kindness," Sausage said.

Peanut flushed crimson and Newton's ears drooped in shame. "It's true. Sometimes I put things ahead of animals," said the mule, remembering all the conversations he'd instigated just to glean information from someone.

"You," Sausage pronounced, "are a lettuce."

Newton looked at him in bewilderment, not knowing what that meant and if he should feel insulted or not.

"Your heart is in your head," the great pig continued, with a merry twinkle in his eye. "But it is none the smaller for it."

Newton shook his head. "But I knew how hard a time Mordecai's had, and I didn't show him a grain of compassion. It's unforgiveable."

Sausage tutted gently. "Sometimes the hardest kindness to practice is kindness towards oneself," he said. "You, as much as anyone in the entire universe, are deserving of your love and compassion."

With that, he heaved himself up and disappeared into his stall, leaving Peanut and Newton staring after him.

That evening at dinner, Peanut noticed Mordecai eating by himself in the corner of the corncrib.

"Hold on," he told Newton.

"What are you doing?"

"I'll be back in a minute."

Peanut approached the old goat.

"Mordecai?" the young pig said, drawing an invisible design on the corncrib floor with his hoof. "Are you sure you won't join us for chess? We'd, um, really like you to play with us."

"I told you, I don't go in for any of that human crap," Mordecai snapped.

"Oh, okay," mumbled Peanut, hurrying back over to Newton, his tail between his legs.

The next day, though, Newton extended the invitation and Mordecai declined with somewhat less vehemence. From then on, hardly a day went by when either Peanut or Newton didn't try to get Mordecai to play, never getting offended or discouraged no matter what the cranky old goat said. Eventually a guarded curiosity replaced his knee-jerk refusals and finally, with a show of great exasperation, he grudgingly agreed to a game, "just to get you pesky critters off my back."

Mordecai listened to the rules and watched closely as Newton and Sausage played a match. He didn't utter a single sarcastic word the whole time; in fact, he didn't say anything at all other than to ask a question here or there about the rules or strategy. Newton could tell from Mordecai's questions that he was catching on quickly.

When Sausage won the observation match, Newton suggested that he and Peanut and Mordecai take on the great pig as a team. "Between the three of us, maybe we've got a shot at beating the

Grand Master!" Newton said.

As the match progressed, Newton and Peanut were careful not to point out any of Mordecai's missteps nor praise his good moves too loudly lest he think they were patronizing him. Surprisingly, Mordecai didn't seem to mind being bested, but he was acutely sensitive to any whiff of condescension. When he made a move that allowed Sausage to capture their queen and neither Newton nor Peanut commented on it, Mordecai narrowed his eyes suspiciously. In his experience, things that were too easy or tasty or nice weren't to be trusted.

Newton saw Mordecai's hackles rise and quickly surmised the cause. "Good play, Mordecai," he said dryly, rolling his eyes. "That's what's called a rank amateur move."

Peanut glared at Newton and was about to leap to the goat's defense when Sausage stilled him with an almost-imperceptible shake of the head. Peanut wrinkled his brow curiously, but stayed quiet.

Mordecai, who had missed the interplay between the two pigs, grumbled something about the fact that indeed he *was* an amateur, but Newton could tell that he had relaxed. And when, just a few moves later, Sausage put them in checkmate in a stunning masterstroke, Mordecai looked as pleased as if he had carried it off himself.

"Well played," he said to Sausage, without a trace of irony.

From then on, Mordecai joined them every day. Although he wasn't in Sausage or Newton's league, by observing the superior players, his skills quickly rivaled Peanut's, and the bitter enemies soon became passionate opponents. Not nearly as chivalrous as the older pig and mule, their insults could be heard throughout the barn.

"Pint-sized pipsqueak!"

"Cranky old curmudgeon!"

"Bacon bit!"

"Fleabag!"

While their barbs were every bit as sharp as before, they no longer drew blood. Although they would never admit it—especially to one another—Peanut and Mordecai looked forward to their games as much as Henrietta did her shows.

The days passed and as edged closer to summer, the temperatures began to rise. The sheep started to complain about their unsheared coats. "I'm roasting," grumbled a squat, thick-wooled sheep. "I'm going to have heat stroke," another bleated.

Newton offered to try his hoof at shearing. He'd seen Farmer Bob do it and it hadn't looked too difficult. He got out Farmer Bob's electric shear and trawled the sheep for any takers. As usual, Jellybean was the first to volunteer and he obligingly rolled over on his back, hooves in the air. Newton turned on the shear and it buzzed to life. The mule tried to maneuver it using his front hooves, but no matter how hard he tried, he just couldn't manage to keep it on an even path. It jerked and bucked and pulled, causing Jellybean to wince in pain more than once when it caught his skin.

When Newton was finally finished, the sheep stared in horror. Jellybean's coat was a zig-zag crazy-quilt of crisscrossing stripes. Knots of wool sprinkled his back haphazardly. Jellybean couldn't see most of it himself, but he could tell by the looks on the other sheeps' faces that it was bad. Very bad.

"Well, look what the cat dragged in," giggled Flossy to Ewina. "He looks like he got chewed up and spit out."

"Flossy!" Ewina bleated reproachfully.

Jellybean's ears drooped. "Well, it *feels* better," he assured Newton, who looked mortified.

The rest of the sheep quickly scattered, preferring to seek relief from the heat watching TV in the cool barn than risk a shearing.

Every day Buddy would check the fields to see if the corn had sprouted yet. By the time the tender green shoots started breaking through the ground, however, the animals were firmly ensconced in their new leisure-time routines and the shepherd had a hard time getting anyone back to work. The shepherd had to call on all of his skills as a herder. Eventually, with a lot of barking and prodding and nipping, he wrangled everyone out into the field.

The chickens were assigned pest control. They fanned out into the fields, hunting out any bugs and worms that might destroy the crops.

Then Buddy started working with the pigs, cows, and sheep to help them be able to identify corn. "And everything that isn't corn is a weed," he explained. "All the weeds need to be eaten."

The sheep and pigs caught on quickly, but the cows had a difficult time. Their eyesight wasn't as good as the other animals and they were so large that maneuvering in the narrow rows was tough. While their front halves were pulling up weeds, their back halves were often stomping on corn shoots. When it became apparent that the cows were ruining a good portion of the crops, Buddy had no choice but to relieve them of duty.

As soon as they learned that the cows were being sent off to pasture, the sheeps' performance took an immediate nosedive. They "accidentally" began nibbling corn, while passing right over weeds. Their coordination also seemed to suffer; suddenly they were stepping on plants left and right.

At the end of the day, Buddy dismissed the chickens and pigs for dinner. "And you can go, too, Jellybean," he said to the unsightly sheep. "You've been working hard."

"What about the rest of us?" asked Flossy.

"You're all staying behind," said Buddy. "Your work's gotten so lousy, you need some remedial training."

Gizmo grinned. "See ya later, suckas!"

The sheep grumbled loudly as the other animals went off to the corncrib, laughing and jeering at the detainees on their way.

"That's not fair!" said Lulu, watching Hamish prance past. "We're hungry too!"

"We're too hot to work. You try working in the fields wearing a wool coat! Jellybean doesn't have to deal with what we do," said Flossy, irritated that he was always making the rest of them look bad.

"He's just trying to do a good job," said Ewina.

"The cows didn't have to do extra training," whined Lulu. "Why do we?"

"The cows weren't shirking," said Buddy. "You'll stay late every night until you can figure out how to do your job right."

The remedial training proved to be incredibly effective. The sheep instantaneously recovered their capacities and never required a refresher course thereafter.

CHAPTER 11

One balmy June night Gizzabelle was roused from her sleep by a commotion outside the chicken coop. It was pitch black in the henhouse. She could hear Newton's clipped, measured speech and Buddy's low growl. And there was a smooth, conciliatory voice she didn't recognize.

"What do you think is going on?" she whispered to Poe, who was stirring beside her.

"I don't know," he said. "Let's go see."

As their eyes adjusted to the dark, the birds hopped off their roosts and made their way to the door. Gizzabelle saw Buddy and Newton at the base of the ramp to the henhouse. Newton's back was toward her, but she could see Buddy in profile, muscles rigid, hackles raised, and paws planted squarely on the ground. And beyond him, facing the shepherd and mule, she could just make out another form. Backlit by the moonlight was a large gray raccoon.

"Bandit!" exclaimed Poe, brushing past Gizzabelle and racing down the ramp. "Is that you?"

The raccoon was sitting back on his rear legs in a submissive posture, but his tone was deliberately casual. "In the flesh," he drawled. "As I was explaining to your friends here, I'm looking for my buddy Poe."

"This a mate of yours?" Buddy asked Poe, never taking his eyes off the masked stranger. "Newton caught him trying to sneak into the henhouse."

"Sneak?" said Bandit, sounding hurt. "I wasn't sneaking. I was just coming to visit."

"Really?" Gizzabelle said skeptically. "In the middle of the night?"

"Granted, it's a somewhat unconventional time for you," he said evenly, "but I'm nocturnal, you know, and it's perfectly normal for me."

Gizzabelle felt the feathers on her neck stand up. His explanation sounded plausible enough, but she didn't buy it.

"It's okay," said Poe. "This is the raccoon I met at Granny Ann's. He's the one who saved my neck."

"You're the...master burglar?" asked Newton tentatively, feeling as if the term was offensive even though it was the raccoon himself who'd first used the label.

"At your service," Bandit said, making a courtly bow. "I see my reputation has preceded me. Not necessarily an advantage in my line of work."

"Your line of work...you mean, stealing?" asked Gizzabelle coldly.

Bandit swung around to look at her. His eyes flashed for a moment but his voice was like honey when he spoke. "And this must be the lovely Gizzabelle." He looked her up and down appraisingly. The hen's skin crawled.

"For there to be stealing, my dear, there must first be ownership," the raccoon said. "In my view, all property is theft," said Bandit.

"That's absurd!" said Gizzabelle.

"Is it?" the raccoon countered. "And on what grounds does legitimate ownership rest? Native rights? Animals once occupied all the lands that humans now claim as their own. They conquered us by sheer force, killing indiscriminately, young and old, and destroying our ancestral homes. Everything they possess now is fruit from the land they stole from us, is it not?"

Gizzabelle didn't answer.

"Tsk, tsk, my darling," he continued, shaking his head. "Does might make right? I never would have taken you for one to defend power. I'm just righting historic wrongs. Anything I take through cunning and wile isn't stealing. It's recovery."

Gizzabelle stared at him dumbly. She had no rebuttal. His argument made a certain sense—coming from someone else, she might even have agreed with it—but she couldn't shake the conviction that the whole speech was merely an elaborate rationale to obscure the raccoon's self-serving motives, not the product of any deeply-held principles.

"So you're a lock pick?" Newton butted in, eager to explore the practical, not philosophical, dimensions of Bandit's work.

"Among other things."

Newton looked at the raccoon's nimble-fingered hands. "Those paws must come in handy," he said enviously. The mule had always wondered what he might have been able to accomplish were his hooves more dexterous.

"It is a common misconception that burglary is a skill of the hands," Bandit sighed dismissively.

"Isn't it?"

"No. Picking locks is only a part of what I do—and a minor one at that. Burglary is not in the hands; it's in the mind. It's evasion, artifice, misdirection. Knowing when and who to hit, how long to stay, when to cut your losses and get out...You can be the best lock pick in the world, but without understanding the mind game, you will never be a master burglar."

For the first time since she'd met him, Gizzabelle believed the raccoon was speaking sincerely. His pride in his chosen profession was genuine. She was just about to ask him what he was doing on the farm when Poe spoke up.

"Bandit," he said. "It's late. Way past everyone's bedtime. Why don't we let them get back to sleep? I'll take you up to the farmhouse, show you around. I'm a bit of a night owl myself."

"Excellent," said Bandit. "That's your control center, I assume? CEO headquarters?"

"It's where I work out of," Poe admitted. He seemed embarrassed but pleased.

"We don't want to keep you from your slumber any longer," Bandit said to Gizzabelle, Newton and Buddy. "Please do excuse my unforgivably rude intrusion. I didn't mean to disturb you. We'll let you all get back to sleep now."

Somehow, his use of "we" stuck in Gizzabelle's craw.

"Good night," said Poe over his shoulder as he hopped the rest of the way down the ramp. "We'll see you tomorrow."

The hen, shepherd and mule murmured their goodnights as the raven and raccoon set off together to the farmhouse. As they disappeared into the dark, Gizzabelle noticed that where Bandit should have had a bushy striped tail, there was only a knobby stump.

A shiver shot up her spine. "I don't like him," she said with surprising vehemence. "Something about him gives me the creeps."

"Well," said Newton, "it's natural you wouldn't like him. He is a raccoon, after all. Not exactly a chicken's best friend."

"Maybe," she said, "but I don't trust him."

"If you think he's dodgy," said Buddy, "I'll keep my blinkers on him."

The next morning, Poe took Bandit on a tour of the farm and Gizzabelle didn't see Poe again until dinnertime, when he showed up at the corncrib, alone.

"Where's Bandit? Did he leave?" Gizzabelle asked hopefully.

Poe started. "No, he's just getting his own dinner. He doesn't care much for corn." He looked at Gizzabelle nervously. "You don't really think he'd leave, do you? He'd be such an asset to the farm."

Gizzabelle gaped at him. "You're not suggesting he stay here permanently, are you?"

"Sure," said Poe. "Do you realize what his hands alone are worth to us? I can read, but Bandit can write. And he's so worldly and well traveled. He knows as much about humans and their ways as Newton. Maybe more. He's been studying them for years."

"We don't need a raccoon on the farm," Gizzabelle insisted. "He's bad news."

"That's where you're wrong, Gizzabelle. He's very probably saved our hides twice, just today!"

The little hen narrowed her eyes. "Saved us, how?"

"Well, when I was showing him around this morning, he had a fantastic idea. He suggested we lock the gate to the farm—locks are his specialty, you know—to keep the humans out. So that's exactly what we did. We found a bunch of old locks in the garage and Bandit even wrote a sign to put on the gate. It says, 'KEEP OUT – NO TRESPASSING.'" Poe grinned broadly. "Can you believe it? I don't think we have to worry about humans any more!"

As much as she didn't want to admit it, Gizzabelle couldn't deny this was excellent news. "You said he saved us twice?" she asked irritably.

Poe looked around to make sure none of the other animals could hear. "His other plan may be even more brilliant," he said in a low voice. "He taught me what to do when you don't have the money you need."

"So?" she said. "We don't need money."

"Well, actually we do," he said, "I didn't want to worry you before, but now that the problem's solved, I don't mind telling you. Farmer Bob had a lot of overdue bills that needed to be paid. Every month in the mail we get new 'past due' notices."

Gizzabelle immediately thought of the papers she had spied that day in the farmhouse. Once she'd finished learning the alphabet, she had figured out what the letters spelled, but still hadn't known what it meant—not until now.

"You told Bandit about the overdue bills, but not us?" asked Gizzabelle.

"Oh, now, Gizzabelle, don't take it that way. I didn't want to upset you. Aren't you glad you didn't have to worry about it?"

Gizzabelle didn't answer. "So Bandit's found a way to get money for us?" she asked instead.

"No," said Poe. "We don't need money."

Gizzabelle shook her head in confusion. "I don't understand; I thought you just said we did."

"We've got something better than money," Poe said, grinning. "We've got *credit*!"

"Credit?"

"It comes on a card," Poe said eagerly. "The card has a string of numbers on it and all you have to do is tell people the number and you can pay for anything you want. Just like money!"

It sounded like a sneaky raccoon scam to Gizzabelle. "Are you sure that's all there is to it?" she asked skeptically. "If it was that easy, why wouldn't everyone do it?"

"Everyone does!" Poe said. "Don't be such a worrywart. We already tried it and it worked just like Bandit said it would. I remembered the numbers from when Farmer Bob ordered things over the phone, and Bandit and I used them to pay off all the bills this afternoon. Problem solved! Isn't it great?

"And if we ever run out of credit," he ran on, without waiting for an answer, "Bandit says we can always get more. It's simple; all you have to do is get a new card to 'pay off' the old one! He's even going to learn to copy Farmer Bob's signature so he can fill out an application for us when the time comes. I'm telling you, Gizzabelle, he's a godsend. You have no idea!"

For the rest of the meal, Poe enlightened the little hen with Bandit's views on everything from evolutionary economics and incentive structures to risk assessment and information management. It was all "Bandit says this," and "Bandit thinks that." Gizzabelle thought that the raccoon may as well have joined them for dinner after all; he couldn't have been more present if he'd set up shop in the middle of the corncrib.

When Gizzabelle couldn't take listening to one more of the raccoon's theories, she tried to change the subject to something more enjoyable. "So," she said, "do you know how Bandit lost his tail?"

"I don't know the details, but he said something about a job gone wrong."

"Serves him right," Gizzabelle said.

Poe drew back. The look he gave her was positively withering.

Gizzabelle's feathers fluffed out. "I'm not *glad* he lost it," she stammered. "I'm just saying that when you play with fire, you have to expect to get burned."

Poe didn't reply. The silence stretched out awkwardly.

"Um, I guess I'll be going to the henhouse now…" she finally said, wishing he would stop staring at her like that.

"You go on along," Poe said. "I don't think I'll be coming."

"What do you mean?" she said sharply.

"I think I'll go back to sleeping in the farmhouse. The henhouse really isn't the right place for me."

Gizzabelle eyed him. "Let me guess. That wouldn't be another of Bandit's ideas, by chance?"

"Actually, yes, it is," said Poe. "He thinks there needs to be a separation between the CEO and the rest of the animals…"

"I see. You're above sleeping with the *commoners*."

"It's not like that," said Poe. "It's not that I think I'm any better than anyone else. It's just that they need to respect me, and that's hard to do when they see me drooling in my sleep and waking up with disheveled feathers and morning breath!"

"So let me get this straight. It's not because you think you're better," said Gizzabelle, "but so they think you are?"

Poe's expression hardened. "Well, I think he has a point."

"I'm sure you do." With that, Gizzabelle stalked out of the corncrib and back to the henhouse. Although she had a hard time sleeping, she refused to even look over toward the farmhouse to see whether Poe was up. He could do whatever he liked for all she cared, she told herself.

The next day, Bandit wandered around the farm on his own, making small talk with the animals. He noticed the sheeps' over-grown coats and volunteered to give a trim to anyone who wanted one. His paws were much more suited to the shears than Newton's hooves had been, he assured them. He ushered the sheep into the back of the barn where the electric shear was plugged in.

"Fleecing the flock?" snorted Sausage as they passed his stall.

The raccoon shot him a look, but kept on walking.

"Don't you like Bandit?" asked Peanut. "Poe says he's going to fix all our money problems."

"The faults of the burglar are the qualities of the financier," Sausage said philosophically. Peanut didn't know what a financier was, but he nodded vigorously nonetheless.

"Who's up first?" Bandit asked when they got to the back of the barn, but not a sheep came forward. It was normally hard to get a sheep to take the lead in anything, but after the disastrous wool-butchering Jellybean had gotten, they were even more reluctant than usual to take the risk.

Finally, Jellybean stepped up. "Maybe you can tidy me up," he said with a shrug. "Can't get much worse that it already is."

"Have a little faith," said Bandit, as he went to work evening out Newton's hack job. The shears were smooth and steady in his hands, and he loped off swaths of wool in long, even strokes. Soon the barn floor was covered in fleece.

When he was done, Jellybean looked like any newly-sheared sheep, which was still plenty ridiculous enough. Satisfied that Bandit knew what he was doing, one by one the other sheep went under the shear. Flossy went last. She'd wanted Bandit to perfect his technique on the others before she would allow him near her coat.

Bandit looked her over appreciatively. "My, aren't you a looker?" he said. "What's your name, little lady?"

"Flossy," she murmured.

"I bet you've got a real sense of style, Flossy. I can tell just by looking at you. Do you mind if I try something on you? A special 'do' for a special ewe? Not everyone could manage it, but you, you could pull it off."

"Alright," Flossy acquiesced enthusiastically.

Bandit set to work clipping and shearing. More reams of wool fell onto the ground. Finally he stepped back to admire his handiwork. He gave a low whistle. Flossy's hindquarters were shaved closely, but her front half had only been trimmed and manicured, not shorn, and Bandit had left little round poofs of wool on her forehead and tail.

"It may have been introduced by the poodle," he said, "but you wear it better. Mark my word, next season all the ewes will be begging for 'The Flossy.' Just you wait. It'll be all the rage."

Flossy bleated happily and loped off to show off to Lulu and Ewina, who were out enjoying the breeze in their lighter coats.

Thus began what Gizzabelle deemed Bandit's campaign to win the hearts and minds of the farm animals. Nearly every morning the raccoon returned from his nighttime forays—or raids, as Gizzabelle thought of them—with some sort of gift in tow. There were bones for Buddy and fish heads for Coco, and apples for the horses and pigs, small and underripe, but still impressive for late June. Mordecai was the beneficiary of a wide array of scraps: wilted vegetables, a loaf of crusty bread, the remnants of a bag of potato chips, a box of cookies, which the goat ate box and all. Bandit's *coup d'état*, though, was the salt lick that appeared one morning in the cow pasture. When everyone clamored to know where he got it, the raccoon just smiled.

Bandit seemed to be working overtime to charm everyone on the farm, everyone except for Sausage, that is. Ever since he had offered the pig an apple and Sausage had declined, saying something about a serpent and a garden, the raccoon had given the hog a wide berth. It was almost as if Sausage didn't exist for all the attention Bandit paid him. His frostiness toward Sausage was all the more obvious when compared with his extreme friendliness to everyone else.

"Why's Bandit going to all that trouble?" Gizzabelle wondered to Newton one day as they noticed the raccoon across the barnyard giving Jock some sugar cubes. "He doesn't need our food. He never even comes in the corncrib. So what's he getting out of all this? What's in it for him?"

"Maybe he just wants to help out," said Newton, who had become quite chummy with the raccoon. Bandit was the ideal informant—observant and articulate—and he seemed happy to let the mule pick his brain about human goings-on, sometimes for hours on end. They shared a fascination with mechanical devices and could often be found in the shed examining various contraptions and machines, flipping switches and pushing buttons, disassembling and reassembling innards. With Bandit's deft paws, they were able to do things Newton had only fantasized about before.

The chickens seemed to be the only ones who weren't won over by the raccoon's overtures. Not only did they carry millennia of inherited distrust, but they were also immune to his gifts of food. The fields were overrun with aphids and corn rootworms and earworms, and the chickens ate so much in the course of their work they didn't even have room for corn anymore, much less anything else.

One afternoon Gizzabelle was gratified to hear Henrietta reject Bandit's offer of a fat, juicy earthworm. "I don't take food from 'coons," she snapped. Even after Bandit's much-vaunted locking of the gate, Henrietta would only tolerate the raccoon's presence in broad daylight when there were plenty of other animals around and even then she couldn't bring herself to be civil to him.

"I know one thing you'd like," said Bandit.

Henrietta snorted in derision.

"Really? What?" asked Clementine politely.

"Something to calm your nerves."

Henrietta's head perked up. No one appreciated how much her hyper-vigilance cost her, how incredibly taxing it was to constantly be on the alert. "You know something that can do that?" she asked, her eyes narrowed in suspicion.

"Sure do," the raccoon replied nonchalantly. He glanced at her over his shoulder. "But I'm sure you wouldn't be interested..."

He started to saunter off toward the farmhouse.

"Wait!" clucked Henrietta. "What is it? Can you get some?"

Bandit paused, smiling slowly. "Indeed I can. Wait here."

He returned a few minutes later rolling a shiny can in front of him. He stopped in front of Henrietta, righted the can, and popped open the tab. Henrietta squawked in terror as white spray erupted in every direction.

Bandit grinned and licked the foam off his fur. "It's called booze," he explained. "It can really take the edge off."

Henrietta watched with fascination as the frothy fizz ran down the sides of the can and formed a puddle. "You first?" she asked, still leery of anything the raccoon had to offer.

"Don't mind if I do," Bandit replied easily, tipping the can to his mouth and taking several big gulps. He put the can down with a loud belch.

Henrietta tentatively took a sip. Then a swallow. Then a swig. A goofy grin spread across her face. "I feel funny," she said. "Dizzy. Fizzy-dizzy!"

"You've got a buzz," said Bandit.

"A buzzzzzzzzzzz," she repeated, cackling loudly. "I like it! More! More booze! Clementine, you've got to try this!"

"There's plenty where that came from," said Bandit.

By the time he returned from the farmhouse with a couple of six-packs of beer, a group of curious animals had gathered around to see what Henrietta was going on and on about. Everyone wanted to try the booze. Although it didn't have much effect on the cows because of their vast body weight, the rest of the animals immediately took to the heady feeling.

Soon everyone was guzzling beer and reveling in the new sensations. They all talked over one another, trying to put their experiences into words.

"It's like dancing," said Clementine. "Like I'm dancing on air."

"Yeah, my head's light," said Hamish, "but at the same time my tummy's all warm and gooey."

"This is wicked cool!" shouted Gizmo, who had managed to commandeer an entire beer for himself. "Cock-a-doodle-doo! I am rooster! Hear me crow!" Then he lit off for the henhouse—which he had suddenly decided would make an excellent launching pad for backflips—with Gizzabelle, who refused to partake of Bandit's booze, in hot pursuit.

Bandit kept making trips back to the farmhouse for more beer, until they'd run through Farmer Bob's entire stockpile. When they ran out of beer, he broke out the homemade wine and when that was gone, they started in on an old jug of hooch that had sat untouched for years.

Everyone was funnier and smarter and more brave and attractive than they ever had been. Laughter and banter filled the air, and as dusk fell, several of the animals paired up and went off looking for some privacy for necking and tail sniffing. Jellybean was even emboldened to approach Flossy, who had finished off nearly an entire bottle of raspberry wine.

"Flossy?"

The ewe struggled to bring the blurry young ram into focus.

"Jellybean?" she asked, then gave a delicate hiccup.

"Yeah. Um, I've been wanting to tell you, I mean, I was wondering if you'd consider..." he cleared his throat and looked at his hooves. He found it impossible to look at Flossy and talk coherently at the same time. "I've noticed you out in the pasture and I think you're the most beautiful ewe on the farm. Heck, you're probably the most beautiful ewe anywhere. But you're so much more than that, you're so vivacious and spirited. I think you're just wonderful. I was wondering if I could be so forward as to ask you if you would consider making me the happiest sheep in the world. Flossy, will you...will you be my mate?"

She didn't respond.

"I know I don't have a lot to offer," he finally said. "I'm nothing special myself. But I am a hard worker. And I can promise you I'll do everything in my power to make you happy."

When Jellybean could stand Flossy's silence no longer, he looked up to find the ewe lying down next to the overturned wine bottle, fast asleep.

He sighed. Without waking her, he gently nosed the snoring ewe away from the bottle so the spreading puddle of wine wouldn't get in her wool. Then he lay down next to her, making sure none of the other rams took advantage of her inebriated state.

"Awww, Baaandit," slurred Henrietta as the evening wound down. She stumbled against the raccoon and put a wing over his shoulder. "I don' know why I've been so suzzzpichus of you all dis time. Yuur a jolly good fella. Jolly good. Hear that evryone? Bandid here izz a jolly good fella! Less hear it for Bandid…" She sat down with a thump and promptly puked all over her breastfeathers.

Most everyone staggered back to their beds, but a few animals spent the night passed out in the barnyard.

The next morning, Gizzabelle woke to terrible moaning and groaning throughout the henhouse.

"Quiet, everybody," whined Gizmo, squeezing his eyes shut against the sunlight. "My head is killing me!"

Gizzabelle went from nest to nest, checking on the hens and, without exception, they were all sick as dogs.

"We're dying," gasped Henrietta when Gizzabelle reached her nest. "Poisoned, I tell you! I feel it in my bones!"

Gizzabelle raced outside and found the rest of the animals just as bad off as the chickens. Could it be that Henrietta was right? she wondered. Had Bandit really poisoned them after all?

She half-ran, half-flew to the farmhouse. "Poe! Poe!" she called. She nearly ran smack-dab into the raven on her way in the pet door.

"Poe, it's the animals! Bandit gave them booze last night, and now they're all sick! I think they might be dying."

"What—?" said Poe. "Booze? Are you sure? Farmer Bob would have a beer nearly every night, and it never seemed to make him sick."

"I don't know," said Gizzabelle with a shrug. "Maybe it's poisonous to animals? Can you look it up online? Maybe there's a cure."

Poe took off for the living room. By the time Gizzabelle made it up onto the desk, he was already online. He clicked through a few pages, muttering to himself. He finally turned away from the screen. "Looks like there's nothing to worry about," he said. "They're just hungover. It'll go away in no time. They just need to sleep it off."

"Thank goodness," Gizzabelle sighed with relief. "But they just have to wait it out? There's no pill? No medicine? There's nothing we can do to help them feel better?"

Poe shook his head. "Not really. Just make sure they drink plenty of water."

Gizzabelle spent the morning taking water to the animals. By the middle of the day, everyone seemed to be feeling better. Strangely enough, though, the experience hadn't turned the animals against Bandit as Gizzabelle had been sure it would. In fact, just the opposite. It seemed to have warmed them to the raccoon, and whetted their appetite for booze to boot.

"I don't get it," she told Poe. "They're constantly asking Bandit when he can get more booze. It's like they don't even remember how sick they were afterward."

"Apparently, from what I read, alcohol—booze—is addictive."

"What does that mean?"

"When something can make you want it even when it's bad for you."

Gizzabelle shook her head. It didn't make a bit of sense to her.

Poe frowned. "I hope this doesn't turn into a problem. Addiction to alcohol is serious business. It can significantly affect productivity."

He needn't have worried, though. As much as the animals wished he could, Bandit wasn't ever able to provide them with any more "giggle water," as Henrietta called it.

Over the next days and weeks, Gizzabelle found herself increasingly distanced from Poe. Reading lessons had long since ended. Once the class had finished learning the alphabet and had the basics of phonics down pat, Poe had pushed them out of the nest, with instructions to keep practicing on their own since that was the only way they'd improve. And now that Poe slept in the farmhouse and egg collection was irrelevant to "the bottom line"—whatever that was—Gizzabelle had no real reason to see him outside of the All-Animal Meetings. He never even seemed to come to the corncrib for dinner anymore. At first, she thought they were simply missing each other, but his absence grew so conspicuous, she began to think maybe he was deliberately avoiding her.

Finally, one day she could stand it no more. She gathered her courage in her claws and marched over the farmhouse. She stuck her head in the pet door and called out tentatively, "Poe?"

There was a rustling from the living room. Then the raven alighted in the kitchen doorway.

"Gizzabelle!" he said, a wide grin splitting his face. "What are you doing here?"

The little hen relaxed some, glad that Poe looked so happy to see her. She launched into her pretext for coming. "Um, we've got a bit of a situation," she said. "I wanted to talk to you about it. It has to do with the eggs."

"Yeah? What about them?"

"We're about to run out of space for them in the fridge," she said. "What should we do? We can't have eggs rotting all over the property. They'll stink to high heaven, not to mention the hygiene issues."

Poe furrowed his brow. "Good point. I hadn't thought about that. There are so many things to do to keep the farm running properly. Every time you think you've got it all worked out, something else comes along." He thought for a moment. "I'll ask Bandit. Maybe he'll have an idea."

"Yeah," Gizzabelle said sharply, turning to go. "You do that."

"Gizzabelle, wait!"

She paused.

"There something I've been wanting to tell you. Do you remember Asa?"

She looked over her shoulder. "Farmer Bob's friend, the one who called on the phone?"

"Yeah. He called again."

"Really?" she said, turning around and taking two hops forward. "What happened?"

"Well, it's a pretty unbelievable story, actually," he said. "I was on the phone with him again, pretending to be Farmer Bob and I happened to mention those modified seeds by Monstroso that Bandit told us about. I said that they sure would make life so much easier. He didn't say anything so I started explaining how you don't have to till the ground or pick the weeds anymore, and how much time and money it saves you. And then suddenly, he just *flipped out*! Yelling about 'Frankenseeds' and calling me a coward and a sellout. Said I was 'in bed' with Monstroso and he didn't know who I was anymore and no wonder I'd been avoiding him lately. We got in this huge screaming match. I called him a close-minded old mossback who wouldn't know progress if it ran him over. He had a few more choice words for me and told me never to call him again and then he hung up!"

"Wow!" was all Gizzabelle could say.

"Yeah, what about that, eh? I don't know what his problem was, but it couldn't have worked out better if we'd planned it. I don't think he's going to want to see Farmer Bob ever again!"

"That's great," Gizzabelle said.

"I wanted you to know."

They were both quiet.

"Well, I guess I should go..." Gizzabelle finally said.

"Yeah, okay," said Poe reluctantly. "I'll get back to you about that egg issue."

The next evening as she was leaving the corncrib, Poe showed up at her side.

"Good news," he said. "Bandit came up with the solution to your egg problem."

"Oh?" she said unenthusiastically.

"Yeah, we can use the root cellar near the farmhouse. It's cool, just like the fridge, and way bigger. Isn't that a great idea?"

Gizzabelle had to admit to herself it was pretty ingenious. Whatever else he was, Bandit was no idiot. Still, she couldn't bring herself to praise the raccoon aloud. She managed a curt nod.

Neither spoke for a moment.

"Corn's looking good," Poe said. "'Knee high by July, as they say."

"Mmm-hmm."

The awkward silence fell again.

"You know, I really enjoyed talking to you yesterday," Poe finally said. "I miss our talks. I was wondering...would you mind if I moved back to the henhouse?"

The little hen couldn't have been more shocked if he had announced his intention to fly to the moon.

"B-u-u-t why?" she stammered.

"Well, it's pretty lonely up there. Buddy always sleeps out under the Great Tree if he's not on guard duty, and Coco and Bandit are both out at night, so, it's just me..." He trailed off and stared at his feet. He looked up shyly. "And I...well, I miss you."

Gizzabelle's heart soared. It was as if the past month hadn't happened.

"Sure," she croaked, "I'd love it if you came back. I've missed you, too."

"Really?" Poe said, grinning.

He returned to the henhouse with her that very evening. When they got there, she led him past their roosts to Clementine's nest.

"Shhh," Gizzabelle said, "I've got something to show you." Clementine smiled at them and raised her tail feathers to reveal five newborn chicks nestled against her ample posterior. Disturbed, the little yellow fuzzballs started peeping angrily at the top of their tiny lungs.

Poe's eyes widened.

"Aren't they adorable?" asked Gizzabelle. "And get this: Gizmo has been sneaking off in the middle of the night recently. I think he and that sweet little pullet, Sunny, might be lovebirds. It's only a matter of time before he's mating, if he's not already. Just a few days ago I heard him crow for the very first time! It was a little scratchy, to be sure, but no question it was an honest-to-goodness crow. Can you believe he's almost a rooster already? Seems like just yesterday he was a chick himself."

Poe continued to stare at the chicks, a far-away look in his eyes. Gizzabelle wondered whether he was pondering the miracle of life, the innocence of newborns, or perhaps even contemplating having a family of his own.

"Do you know what this means?" Poe said.

Gizzabelle shook her head.

"We're headed for a population explosion!" Poe exclaimed. "Once these chicks get to be full grown, we're going to have a bunch of roosters. And more roosters means more chicks. And more chicks means even more roosters. Can you imagine what would happen if every hen had a mate? The chickens'll outgrow the henhouse in no time. We're going to have to expand—and soon!"

"Oh. I didn't think of it that way," said Gizzabelle uncertainly.

Poe spent the rest of the evening ruminating on the coming crisis. He considered building additions onto the existing henhouses, re-purposing other structures, or even instituting a one-chick policy for each hen. "I don't think we need to consider that just yet," he said, "but someday we might have to."

Gizzabelle listened, but she just couldn't get as worked up about it as Poe did. She knew what he was doing was important, but she preferred to see chicks as a blessing to be enjoyed, not a problem to be solved. She realized that as CEO, this was a luxury Poe had given up, and felt a stab of sadness that no one but her would probably ever even be aware of it. They would see the power and prestige, but never the sacrifice.

He was still muttering to himself as she drifted to sleep.

The next day, Poe sought Gizzabelle out again. This time he was distraught. "Bandit's gone!" he said. "He never came home this morning. I talked to him last night right before dinner and he didn't mention going away. Do you think something happened to him?"

"Did you tell him about going back to the henhouse?" Gizzabelle asked.

"Yes, I mentioned it. Why? Do you think that offended him? He didn't say anything."

"No, no, I'm sure it didn't," she assured him, although she was sure of no such thing. She suspected the raccoon was just playing with Poe's emotions and would reappear at any minute, but she couldn't help hoping he had left for good once he realized he'd lost Poe's ear. "Maybe he decided to take the opportunity to get away for a while, knowing he wouldn't be leaving you all alone," she said carefully. "I'm sure he'll be back."

"Oh, do you think?" Poe said, considering. "That could be." He wasn't entirely convinced, but he seemed somewhat placated.

The next day, Poe spent the day flying over the farm and the surrounding properties looking for any sign of the raccoon. When his efforts turned up nothing and Bandit still didn't show up on the third day, Poe began to resign himself to Bandit's disappearance and Gizzabelle, finally allowing herself to believe that they had seen the last of the raccoon, stopped looking for the masked mammal around every corner.

Mid-morning, Poe came out and visited Gizzabelle in the fields, even eating a few aphids and corn rootworms himself, then asking her to come with him back to the house to work on some mail, just like old times. They were on their way to the farmhouse, happily speculating on Gizmo's amorous pursuits, when Gizzabelle froze in her tracks.

There, on the kitchen stoop, sat the raccoon.

"Bandit!" Poe cried, hopping up to the stoop. "Where have you been? I've been worried sick!"

"I didn't mean to upset you, old chum," Bandit said to Poe, his voice smooth and unhurried. "It's just when we talked the night I left, I suddenly realized how lonely you must be here, everyone else with their families and loved ones, and it hurt me. Hurt me deeply. You not having anyone." He looked pointedly at Gizzabelle, who glared back. She could've happily pecked out his eyes.

Bandit oozed on. "You know how I like to give gifts, make folks happy, and here you are, my very best friend, and I haven't been able to do anything for you."

"Oh, that's alright," Poe rushed to assure him. "I never expected anything like that. I'm just glad you're back."

"Well, isn't that just like our Poe?" Bandit said to Gizzabelle. "So selfless, never asking anything for himself." He looked back at Poe. "Which is what makes this so satisfying. For you see, I've been able to bring you what you've been missing out on all these years, what you've yearned for your whole life. What you never thought you'd have."

His eyes glittering, he glared at Gizzabelle. His lips drew back in a sharp-toothed smirk of victory.

"Poe," he said, "meet your family."

CHAPTER 12

"My...*family*?" Poe croaked.

Gizzabelle's heart sank like a stone. The heartrending hopefulness in Poe's voice was so obvious she knew at once. Bandit had won.

"Indeed," said the raccoon. He jerked his chin in the air and from nowhere, a handful of dark shapes dropped down onto the stoop behind him. "They're crows, not ravens," Bandit said. "But you're relatives."

"What does it matter?" Poe said breathlessly, unable to tear his eyes away from the smaller black birds. "It's family."

Bandit introduced the crows one by one. "This is Shylock, Drake, Jinx, Rune, Odile, and Nessa. And this pretty little *ingénue* is Fae."

Fae hopped down the step to stand in front of Poe. She looked up at him. "So the raccoon says this all," sweeping her wing to encompass the whole barnyard, "is...yours?"

"Well, not exactly..." said Poe. "I'm the CEO. "

"The CEO?" she asked, batting her lashless lids.

"The leader, I guess you'd say."

"*Oh.*" The single syllable was loaded with enough adulation to choke a horse, thought Gizzabelle. Surely, she told herself, Poe wouldn't fall for such obvious fawning.

"Would you like a tour?" Poe asked Fae, tearing his gaze away to look up at the other crows. "We could fly around the farm, get the bird's eye view, then I could show you the house."

Gizzabelle realized she would necessarily be excluded from the tour. She already felt like a hulking beast next to the exquisitely petite Fae, and now she was acutely aware of being earth-bound too.

"I've got to get back to the field," she hurried to excuse herself. "There's something I forgot to tell Buddy."

"Oh, geez, Gizzabelle, I didn't think..." said Poe, clearly realizing her predicament for the first time. Gizzabelle wondered if he'd overlooked the fact that she couldn't fly or simply forgotten she was there at all.

"It's alright," she said breezily. "Really. Don't worry about me. Take the grand tour with your, your...with them."

"Yes," said Bandit. "You all go ahead without us. You should have some time to yourselves to get acquainted, *family* time. Gizzabelle and I wouldn't want to intrude." He grinned at the little hen. "Would we, my dear?"

Poe looked relieved. "Well, if you really don't mind..." To the crows, he said, "Did Bandit tell you we're growing corn? The other animals are out in the fields right now, weeding and keeping the bugs off the crops. I don't mind saying, I think we've got a pretty nifty little operation going, what with having just started. I think you'll be impressed. Follow me!"

Without a backwards glance, they took off toward the fields, leaving Gizzabelle and Bandit alone together.

"Aren't you glad I found Poe his family?" the raccoon gloated. "*Kissing* cousins, you might say."

Unwilling to give the raccoon a chance to rub her beak in his coup, Gizzabelle turned her back on him and headed out to find Buddy and tell him and the other animals—as impartially as she could—about the new arrivals.

From the fields, Gizzabelle watched Poe and the crows flying overhead until they finally disappeared from sight. She had finished her shift by the time they returned. She watched from the chicken yard as they leisurely circled the barn, the milk parlor, the corncrib and the silo, before finally flying back to the farmhouse and alighting on the kitchen stoop. Instead of going through the pet door as she expected, though, they just stood there, looking up at the living room window. Gizzabelle narrowed her eyes. Bandit was leaning out the window. Apparently he had unlocked and opened it for them, and now he seemed to be calling down to them. One by one, the crows flew up to the windowsill and hopped inside. Poe was the last to disappear within.

They didn't come out that evening, not even for dinner. Didn't they like corn either? Gizzabelle wondered. Had they already eaten while they were out? Did they prefer a late-night dinner? She speculated on what they were doing in the house. Swapping chickhood stories? Comparing likes and dislikes, figuring out all the things ravens and crows shared? She tried to push away thoughts of Fae and her fluttering eyelids.

Unsurprisingly, Poe didn't come back to the henhouse to sleep.

Over the next few days, Poe and the crows spent all their time either in the skies or in the house. Unlike Bandit, the crows didn't try to ingratiate themselves with the farm animals. In fact, they didn't even try to get to know them. Poe didn't introduce his new "family" to anyone, not even his leadership team. So it was a surprise when, along with Bandit, the entire murder showed up at the next All-Animal Meeting.

"As you may have heard," Poe said to the crowd, "we have added some new members to the farm."

This caused a ripple in the crowd. Since the crows had made no efforts to meet anyone, the animals had begun to assume that they weren't planning on staying long, much less forever.

Poe introduced each of the crows by name, and they each ducked their head in a small bow. "Having my family here is obviously important to me personally," he continued, "but I believe they are also going to play a vital role here in the organization. It has come to my attention that our corporation has been functioning without one of its core components."

He paused. "We've been operating all this time without a higher authority."

A higher authority? Several animals looked heavenward. A few chickens genuflected.

"This higher authority," he went on, "is the supreme governing body of the corporation: the board of directors. That is a serious oversight that we must correct *immediately* if we are going to succeed. Therefore, I hereby recommend that we elect these new members of the corporation to the board, with Bandit as chair."

The animals shifted uneasily. Even though they had accepted Bandit for the most part, the crows were complete strangers and it seemed like a big leap of faith to put them on the "supreme governing body."

"Smacks of *crow*-nyism, if you ask me," said Mordecai.

"What exactly does the board do?" asked Gizzabelle.

"For one thing, they prognosticate the weather," said Poe. "If we know what sort of climate we'll be facing, we're in a better position to make good decisions about the future."

"And have they demonstrated any aptitude for predicting the weather?"

"Well, of course, forecasting is a tricky business," Poe said. "You can't expect anyone to get it right all the time."

"But how do we know they're any good at it?"

"They fly. So they can get right up in the clouds to see what's coming," said Poe.

Gizzabelle was quiet. It was true, the crows could fly.

"It is also the board's responsibility to support and advise the CEO, and to make sure the corporation keeps to its mission," Poe continued.

"Isn't that the job of the leadership team?" asked Newton. "Don't you get advice and support from us?"

"And what about Sausage?" demanded Peanut. "Didn't you say that's the role of the Chairpig Emeritus? Have you even gone to him for advice even once?"

"Of course, all my senior leaders give me valuable feedback," Poe said, "but they're too close to the ground to see the big picture."

"But what qualifies them to give advice?" asked Gizzabelle, jerking her beak at the crows, who observed her with cool detachment. "They don't know anything about farming, and what's more, they don't know us!"

"That's exactly what they've got to offer," said Poe. "They don't know anything or anyone. They come in with no biases, no preconceived notions to overcome. No personal attachments. They can be completely impartial and unbiased, and make decisions based on reason alone without letting their emotions get in the way; they won't be swayed by any nostalgic ties to tradition or how a course of action will impact this animal or that group. They can look at what is best for the farm as a whole."

This made a lot of sense to the animals. They were always afraid of being in the out-group, and an objective outside perspective certainly sounded like a good thing.

"And besides," continued Poe, "the counsel you get from peers is different than what you can expect from subordinates."

"Subordinates?" lowed Xena, her eyes flashing.

Poe was quick to correct himself. "What I mean is, my co-workers might not feel like they can be completely candid with me, given my position. The board is independent, therefore they are completely free to share their real opinions."

"I'm no fibber," Buddy said quietly. "I've always been ridgy-didge with you."

"Of course you have," Poe said. "And this isn't replacing your input, only adding to it. I'm perfectly open to hearing other nominations to the board. It's just that the board of directors and the senior leaders serve two entirely different roles and they aren't allowed to overlap. So if you want to suggest other candidates, that's fine, but they can't be any of the senior leaders unless they are willing to step down from their current position. And, personally, I think they are more valuable where they're at."

He scanned the crowd.

"Are there any other nominations?"

The animals were quiet. All the strongest leaders were already on the leadership team and no one wanted them to move out of their positions just to serve in an advisory role.

"Good," nodded Poe.

Since the candidates were running unopposed, he decided they didn't need to go to the trouble of a formal vote.

"Congratulations on your new posts," he said to the crows. "I look forward to working together." His eyes lingered on Fae, who smiled back coyly.

After clearing up a few small business items, the meeting was adjourned. Bandit and the crows left the barn without having spoken a word to anyone.

The next day, when Gizzabelle met the mail carriers on the porch to start bringing the day's mail inside, she found Poe barring the way. "You just leave the mail here on the porch," he told Mordecai and the sheep. "We'll take it from there."

"But...don't you want me to help you bring it in?" asked Gizzabelle.

"No need," said Poe. "The board would like their own space where they can have some privacy. Besides, you have enough on your plate as it is without having to worry about the mail, too."

Not knowing what to say, Gizzabelle just watched as the raven picked up a small package wrapped in brown paper and disappeared back into the house.

"Privacy?" Mordecai sniffed, when he related the story to his chess-mates later that day. "What are they afraid of?"

"A door may be closed to keep out the darkness," mused Sausage, picking up a pawn and studying it, "or to keep out the light."

For once, Mordecai thought he understood the pig's meaning, and just as surely wished he hadn't. It gave him a nasty case of foreboding, as if he needed any more cause for gloom.

Although the board was almost never seen personally after their introduction, their presence was certainly felt. A voluminous amount of paperwork began to spew forth from the farmhouse. Bandit was obviously putting his writing skills to use and the board quickly started churning out policy guidelines for every conceivable activity. The reasoning behind this was a little murky since almost no one could read them—and even those who could, didn't. Gizzabelle tried to slog through the first few, but she found them virtually incomprehensible, and soon gave up. She suspected the memos weren't meant to be understood at all. The more unintelligible they were, the more brilliant the animals seemed to think Bandit and his board must be for having written them.

After the first tidal wave of policies passed, there came addendums and revisions and occasionally, outright reversals. Sometimes a policy could change two or three times a week. Poe tried to keep abreast of the changes and pass them on to the managers, but it was hard even for him to keep track, and as a result, the official policy and the way things were actually done often bore little resemblance to each other. Initially this discrepancy upset the animals, particularly the conscientious cows, but when no oversight or penalties ever materialized, eventually everyone stopped paying the policies much mind.

Occasionally the board also sent down recommendations for the animals to approve. The resolutions were just as dense and impen-etrable as the policy memos, so the animals generally passed them without knowing anything but the title.

One day Poe brought something else from the board.

"This," he said, unveiling a large, carefully-printed sign, "is the mission statement. Bandit wrote it out himself."

Of course, most of the animals couldn't make heads or tails of the charcoal lettering.

"But that's not the mission statement," said Gizzabelle when she finished reading it.

"Sure it is," said Poe. 'To give all the shareholders of Animals, Inc. the highest possible standard of living,'" he read.

"But our mission statement was, 'To give all the animals a good life,'" said Gizzabelle.

"This means the same thing; it just uses slightly different words."

"All shareholders?" asked Newton. "What's a shareholder?"

"You're all shareholders," said Poe. "It's just another way of saying all the animals on the farm."

"If it means the same thing, why change it?" asked Gizzabelle.

"Well, it's more precise. It limits it to animals who have a stake in the farm, who have made an investment in its success. How fair would it be for some animal from outside to come in after the harvest and reap the rewards of our labor?"

"Yeah, we wouldn't want that," said Mordecai dryly. "Outsiders swooping in and reaping the rewards of our labor."

Poe ignored him.

"What's that about standard of living?" asked Peanut. "What was wrong with good life?"

"It's not quantifiable," said Poe. "It's vague, means different things to different animals. Standard of living is tangible, concrete, measurable. And besides, if you've got a high standard of living, you're bound to have a good life, too. Can't have one without the other; they go together like a bird and its shadow."

The animals shrugged. It seemed like needless hair-splitting to them, but they saw no reason not to go along. They hung it in the back of the barn for everyone to see, if not to read.

A few days later, Gizzabelle, having just gotten off her shift in the field, was perusing the barnyard for something soft to plump up her nest with when Gizmo stomped by.

"I wish those dumb crows would just go back to wherever they came from!" he snapped, surprising Gizzabelle with his vehemence. He'd been cranky ever since the All-Animal Meeting where the board was elected. She'd also noticed he hadn't been leaving his nest at night since then, so she figured he and Sunny must be having a young lover's quarrel. She sighed. She hoped he'd have better luck in the romance department than his big sister.

Gizmo stalked around, kicking the dirt and glowering at the farmhouse. "Stupid crows! Taking over the house like they own it!"

"*Exactement,*" said Coco, who was licking herself nearby.

Gizzabelle's ears perked up. Now that the pet door was locked, the cat was the only non-board member who could get in the farmhouse, and Gizzabelle was dying to know what she'd seen inside. "So..." she said casually, "what do they do over there? Write policies all day?"

"*Au contraire,*" said the feline, flicking her tail disdainfully. "I have never seen zem working on zeez preposterous policies," Then she shrugged and gave a languorous stretch. "*Je suppose* that ez what zey do at ze board meetings."

"Board meetings?" asked Gizmo.

"*Oui,*" said Coco. "*Tout d'abord*—first thing—every day zey have ze board meeting."

"They meet every morning?" Gizmo asked. "Where?"

"In Farmer Bob's *chamber.* Zey keep ze door *clos. Très mystérieux.*"

"So if they're not coming up with the policies all day, what are they doing?" asked Gizzabelle.

Coco licked a paw, then ran her paw over the back of her ear. "Zat Bandeet, he ez always with his ear to Farmer Bob's safe. Turning ze dial, listening, turning ze dial again. But non, it does not open. *Quelle folie!* Zome 'master burglar' he ez." She groomed her whiskers contemptuously.

"And ze *corbeaux,* ze are *constamment* on ze computer." Gizzabelle couldn't help thinking that if the crows hadn't come, it could have been *her* at the computer. Her and Poe.

"What are they doing on the computer?" she asked.

"*Je ne sais pas*," Coco continued, "I hear many words. Zey talk about 'seeds' and 'harvesting' and 'golden *fontaines*' and 'XP'—"

"FarmVille?" squawked Gizmo. "They're playing *FarmVille*?"

Gizzabelle and Coco both started at his sudden outburst. "What's FarmVille?" asked his sister.

Gizmo dropped his head and stared at his feet. "Um, I think it's a computer game," he mumbled. "Poe must've told me about it."

"A *game*?" Gizzabelle said. "They spend all day playing *games*?"

"Yeah!" Gizmo exclaimed, echoing his sister's indignation. "That's right! How dare they!" He puffed out his chest in apparent outrage.

"They expect us to work all day," sputtered Gizzabelle. "They shouldn't get to spend all day playing games."

Coco shrugged. "*Peut-être*," she said philosophically, "or *comme alternatif* perhaps it would be better if zey did more game playing and less policy writing."

As the first cool winds of autumn began to blow, everyone had settled into a comfortable, familiar routine. While they might not consider their job a "calling" and often grumbled about the hassles and demands it put on them, the animals' work gave them structure and a certain sense of purpose and solidarity. The only one on the farm not to have a steady job was Sausage, who had never fully recovered after his strange seizure and rarely left his stall. Peanut brought his dinner each night and relished the opportunity to have private one-on-one time with his sensei. The other animals were so busy that Sausage's withdrawal from farm affairs went largely unnoticed.

Poe's absence was nearly as total as the great pig's and certainly more conspicuous. He never visited the workers and seldom saw even the leadership team outside of their regular meetings, where they talked only of corn height and bug counts and the implementation of the new manure fertilization plan.

Gizzabelle was just as surprised as the rest of the workers when Poe announced a special All-Animal Meeting to prepare for harvest. He hadn't even mentioned it at their last leadership meeting. She wondered what he had in store.

On the appointed day, everyone gathered in the barn. Even Bandit and the crows were there, which alerted the animals that this must be an auspicious day indeed.

"I've called you all together today," Poe said to the assemblage, when the crowd's murmuring had quieted down, "first of all to thank you for all your hard work. You have done a fantastic job, first planting then keeping the corn free of weeds and bugs. The yield looks to be tremendous. As good as any human farmers. Better than some even. You should be extremely proud of yourselves. Congratulations are very much in order."

The animals stomped their feet in applause. They whistled and bleated and lowed and made all manner of ruckus.

When the clamor died down, Poe grew somber. "However," he said gravely, "we cannot rest on laurels. All our hard work will be for nothing if we do not master the next feat before us. It is time for harvest. I'm not going to sugarcoat it. It will be hard. It will be difficult. It will be our greatest challenge yet. It will take all of our strength and endurance and determination if we are to succeed. But everything that we have done so far has prepared us for this moment. We are ready to meet the challenge! I know that working together we can do it! *We can do it!*"

Again, there were hoots and catcalls, and more hoof stomping.

"Of course, Buddy and Newton will be heading up the operations in the fields. And the board will be setting the production goals for us. First, we'll replenish the corncrib, which is, as you know, nearly empty."

The animals nodded. They were down to the dregs; it was getting hard to even find a decent corncob anymore.

"And starting today," continued Poe, "the corn will be distributed according to the guidelines of the Corn Compensation Plan."

The animals looked at one another questioningly and murmured amongst themselves.

"The Corn Compensation Plan that you passed last week," Poe reminded them, seeing their confusion. "It says that each animal gets a daily allowance of corn as compensation for their day's labor. Remember?"

The animals nodded obligingly, although none of them did. They'd voted on a good many items, none of which they rightly understood.

"And the rest of the corn we'll put in the silo," Poe said. "It's not for eating."

"What's it for then?" asked Gizmo.

"Well," explained Poe, "that's our profit. It's up to the board to decide how best to use it, but some of it will be put back into the company."

"We'll need seed for next year," Newton said knowingly.

Poe nodded at the mule. "We'll also take the CEO and board compensation out of that pot. And anything left over gets distributed among the rest of the shareholders. That's you all. So if you all work hard, you can expect a big, fat dividend when all is said and done. The harder you work, the bigger everyone's dividend!"

This was greeted with great enthusiasm. Even though they always had enough corn to satisfy their hunger, the animals salivated at the thought of a big end-of-season windfall. This "profit" scheme didn't sound half bad.

They began harvest the very next day. Everyone—cows, pigs, sheep, chickens, horses—had a job to do. Buddy and Newton took them all out to the fields, assigned them to a work group, and trained them on their individual tasks. True to Poe's prediction, it was harder than anything they had done before. It was brutal, backbreaking work, and it stretched out in front of them as endless as the horizon.

That night, when the animals trudged in from the fields, exhausted and starving, they arrived at the corncrib to find Bandit escorting out the chickens who had been working inside. He stood in front of the doors.

"Now it is time for you all to collect your hard-earned wages," he said to the crowd. He consulted the stack of papers in his paw. "This list tells how many ears of corn each worker will receive."

A disgruntled rumble arose from the animals. They were hungry and they didn't want to be told how much they could eat.

Bandit looked at them, his eyes widening in surprise. "This is the Corn Compensation Plan you voted for, right?"

No one knew how to answer.

Bandit nodded and looked back at his paper. "Now, get in line to get your wages. I will let you know your pay rate and then you can collect your day's wage from one of the crows." The crows, who had been out of sight inside the corncrib, came forward to stand behind the raccoon.

Although Bandit made a point of whispering each animal's corn allotment so that none of the others could hear it, the animals could see with their own eyes that some were getting more than others. As hard as they tried to figure it out, though, the reasoning behind the income distribution remained obscure. It certainly wasn't based on need. Some cows got less than some chickens. It also was clearly not related to industriousness or hard work, as was obvious when some of the slacker sheep were given just as many ears as Jellybean.

"I'd better get a fair wage," Mordecai grumbled. "We get more and more packages in the mail every day, with no extra workers. I'm constantly having to look for ways to cut corners, do more with less. Just you watch, now they'll probably try to stiff me in pay, too."

However, his dire predictions proved completely unfounded. Mordecai's pile of corn was so enormous that even the impossible-to-please goat couldn't complain.

"Harrumph," he snorted. "It'll do."

"What's our compensation based on?" Newton asked when his turn finally came.

"Job function," Bandit said. "The more important the job, the greater the compensation."

"But everyone's job is important. There isn't a single job on the farm that isn't absolutely essential." The mule looked Bandit right in the eye. "Unless it's yours, maybe."

Anger flashed in the raccoon's eyes, but he remained outwardly calm.

Newton pressed on. "Poe says we're all equal."

"Equality may be okay in principle," said Bandit, "but you can't expect principles to bear out in practice."

"I see. So in *practice* some animals are more equal than others?"

Bandit gave an exaggerated sigh. "It's very complicated; I

— 183 —

really can't explain all the ins and outs of compensation right now. Physical jobs earn the least. Thinking jobs earn more. Anything related to numbers or counting earns the most.

"How good you are at your job might increase your take-home some," he continued, "but not nearly as much as how long you've been doing it. And of course, jobs that require special skills earn more too."

"But dekerneling is skilled work," argued Newton. "And they're not being paid more than some of the field laborers."

"They're hens," said Bandit brusquely. "Female work automatically gets paid less."

"But that's not fair!"

Bandit arched an eyebrow. "Whoever said it was fair?"

The raccoon consulted his list. He found Newton's name and ran his paw across the page to his pay rate. "You've got nothing to grumble about. As an upper-level manager, you're in the highest earning bracket."

Newton glared at him stubbornly.

"This isn't the time or place," Bandit finally said. "Please move along now. You're holding up the line."

Newton stalked over to Jinx who pointed him to a pile of corn. The stack was so big he couldn't even manage it himself. He called over some of the cows in his workgroup who had been seriously shortchanged.

"Please, take as many ears as you like," he said. "I can't eat it all myself anyway."

Buttercup and Rosemary eagerly accepted the offer, but Millie demurred.

"I couldn't possibly," said Millie. "This is yours."

"Nonsense," said Newton. "It's not charity. You *earned* it. You worked every bit as hard as I did today."

"No," she insisted. "I'm fine. There's plenty of grass in the pasture. I don't need corn."

Newton gave in. He would have persisted, but it wasn't worth trampling on Millie's pride.

The animals grew increasingly restless as the line progressed. Other than the few animals in management who, like Newton, had more corn than they knew what do with, most of the animals had less than they were used to. And everyone was incensed by the unfairness of the system.

"Are you kidding?" Henrietta screeched when she heard her pay rate. "I get less than *her*?" She glowered at Flossy. "She spends half the day at the scratching post and the other half filing her hooves. It's not fair!"

"Yeah! It's not fair!" the other animals echoed. Their dissatisfaction threatened to ignite.

"Quiet, everyone!" Bandit shouted before the protest could get traction. "We've got to hurry! This is TV premiere week, you know. We've got to get everyone through the line and fed so you don't miss any of the new shows."

As irate as they were, they were also bone-tired and sitting down in front of the television sounded a lot more appealing than fighting over compensation. The shouting subsided to a low grumble, and the line inched forward. Soon, most of the animals were scattered around the corncrib, hurrying to finish their dinner so they could get to the barn to watch their shows.

Clementine, who Gizzabelle had fetched from the henhouse, was the last animal in line. When she got to Bandit, though, he shook his head and gestured for the crows to come outside.

"You're not on the list," he said over his shoulder as he turned to shut the corncrib doors.

"What?" she clucked. "There must be some mistake!"

Bandit stopped and looked back at the hen. "You're not a worker," he said. "You have to have a job to be paid."

Clementine's beak fell open.

"She hasn't been working in the *fields*," said Buddy, who had been off to the side, quietly observing the proceedings, "but she's raising chicks. That's just as important."

"Staying in the henhouse taking care of chicks isn't a job."

"What do you mean it isn't a job? She's raising the next generation of workers!" said Newton, outraged.

"Jobs make corn," Bandit said briskly.

"But what will I eat?" Clementine asked, her voice finally recovered.

"That's not really our concern," said Bandit, shrugging indifferently. "But Sarge gets a good wage. Plenty to take care of you and your chicks. Talk to him." He turned back to the doors.

"As COO, don't I have a say in compensation?" interrupted Buddy. His tone was easygoing, but his eyes were hard.

"The budget," Bandit declared, "is the domain of the board." He slammed the doors with a bang.

That evening, while the other animals were zoned out in front of the television, Buddy, Newton, Gizzabelle, and Mordecai gathered in the mule's stall.

At first, they just stared at each other, mute as scarecrows.

"I wouldn't believe it myself if I hadn't seen it with my own eyes," said Newton finally.

"I know," Gizzabelle said. "Imagine not feeding some of the animals!" She shuddered. "It's unspeakable."

"I never did trust them," Mordecai said. "Scavengers, every last one of 'em. Something smells foul to me."

"Poe must not know what's going on," said Gizzabelle with conviction. "He couldn't possibly have sanctioned such a thing. I'm sure he'll put things right."

However, at the next leadership meeting when Buddy raised his concern that the animals' compensation wasn't enough, Poe waved away his worries.

"That's by design," he said. "Satisfaction saps motivation. We want everyone to be a little hungry."

"But I thought our mission was to provide the highest standard of living possible," Gizzabelle said. "Doesn't a high standard of living come from high wages?"

"It's a high standard of living for *shareholders*," Poe reminded her. "Not workers. In fact, worker pay is an expense we need to keep down so shareholder profit can go up."

"But the shareholders *are* the workers!" squeaked Peanut. "They're the same animals!"

"I know it sounds confusing," admitted Poe, "but you've got to let the system do its job. The system knows best. It knows just how to spread the wealth around so everyone gets more in the long run. A rising tide lifts all boats."

Mordecai snorted.

"In fact," said Poe slowly, "if you think about it, this could even be *good* for the animals."

"How do you figure that?" asked Newton.

"Deprivation is an excellent character-building experience. Think of all it teaches: thrift, appreciating what you have, delayed gratification, long-term thinking...values we need the animals to adopt if they're going to succeed." He looked at Peanut. "Don't you think those are all important virtues, virtues Sausage would approve of?" As Chairpig Emeritus, Sausage didn't attend leadership meetings.

Peanut thought for a moment. "I guess so..." he said reluctantly.

"Good," Poe said, sitting back with satisfaction. "That's settled then."

The other animals left the meeting not sure how to feel. It didn't seem quite right, but Sausage *did* teach the meaning that could be found in overcoming adversity. Maybe it would be good for them after all.

CHAPTER 13

Just as the animals were grudgingly beginning to acclimate to the reality of low wages and rationed food, a brand-new problem reared its head: the animals' production goals were ballooning out of control. Every time the animals met their goals, the board would reset them even higher, putting the workers in a terrible double bind. Although they were desperately afraid of the potential consequences should they fail to achieve their goals, they knew that making them would only ensure even higher goals the next day. No matter what they did, they lost.

"You can't keep raising the bar forever," Buddy told Poe. "There has to be a point where enough is enough."

"If they're meeting the goals, they can't be too high," said Poe. "They're called 'stretch' goals."

"You'd have to be made of rubber to stretch that far," grumbled Newton.

The animals had no choice but to start working longer hours if they were to make their ever-rising quotas. At this, Newton put his hoof down. Although he drove his teams hard, he refused to keep them past quitting time and always let his work groups off right at Fifth Crow, whether they'd met their goals or not.

"Staying late sets a bad precedent," he said to Buddy, who, having somewhat workaholic tendencies himself, wasn't as viscerally opposed to overtime as the mule. "I'm telling you, if you give an inch, they'll take a yard. I'm taking a stand."

The leadership meetings became increasingly tense as, day after day, Newton had to defend his low numbers. Poe never came right out and told Newton to work longer hours, but he was exhorted to "be a team player" and "do whatever it takes" to get the numbers up. "Work smarter," Poe suggested.

"What's the 'smarter' way to harvest corn?" Newton groused to Mordecai at an after-dinner chess match.

"Sounds like what you need isn't smarter workers, but smarter corn," offered the goat. "Then it could walk itself to the corncrib."

"Gee, thanks," said Newton.

At the next leadership meeting, they were joined by Shylock, who stood behind Poe, unsmiling.

Poe looked at the crow, then at Newton. "Newton," he said, clearing his throat. "It has come to my attention that there have been some, um, irregularities in your teams' procedures."

"Irregularities?"

"Yes," he said, not meeting the mule's eyes. "Shylock here has noticed that your team has not been following policy. There have been several instances." Shylock read off a list of trivial policy violations.

"But *everyone* violates policy," Newton brayed. "It's not just my teams. Half of those policies don't even make sense!"

"That's not your call," Poe said. "I was hoping this wasn't the case, Newton. If this was just an oversight, I might have been able to do something, but if you *knowingly* violated policy, I'm afraid I have no choice." He looked back at Shylock. "I'm afraid I'll have to remove you from your post."

Newton was stunned. "You're getting rid of me?"

"No," Poe said. "Although I could have. It's certainly a serious enough offense. But you're lucky. You're just being demoted, not terminated. We're going to be lenient..." he looked around at the other managers, "...this time."

Newton stumbled out in a fog.

Gizzabelle was no less shocked. Her head spun as she tried to understand Poe's actions.

"He said he had no choice," she said to Newton and Buddy later. "That must be it. There's probably a *policy* about violating policy."

"It wasn't about the stupid policy violations," Newton said furiously. "If it had been, everyone'd have been in trouble. They got rid of me because I wouldn't roll over on the overtime issue. I wasn't being a 'team player.' If you don't believe me, just look at my replacement: Jock! It's no accident they picked a horse. Horses don't know when to quit. They'll work themselves to death if you let them."

Sure enough, the work groups under Jock's leadership worked longer and longer hours, and Buddy's workers had to do the same to keep up. Although he hadn't minded putting in a limited amount of overtime, Buddy saw the animals getting increasingly depleted and stressed out as they tried to do more and more work on limited food supplies. They weren't even watching television in the evening anymore; they'd stumble to bed right after dinner.

"This can't go on," Buddy declared to Newton, Gizzabelle and Gizmo one day. "We've got to say something."

"I wouldn't if I were you!" warned Newton. "They'll just demote you like they did me. Or worse. You heard what he said about termination."

"I'm sure Poe will listen to us," Gizzabelle argued. "If he's only hearing from the board, of course he's going to go along with them. Once he knows what's really going on, he'll do the right thing. I'm sure of it."

At the next leadership meeting, Buddy raised his concerns with Poe. Gizzabelle seconded his opinions. "They've got to have better working conditions," she said. "They can't keep working longer and longer on less food. It's not right."

"As much as I'd like to improve conditions," said Poe, glancing at Bandit, "I'm afraid we've got to run as lean as we can. We have to trim all the fat from our operation—"

"Now, now, don't be hasty," Bandit admonished, drawing astonished glances from everyone, not least the raven. "Those seem like reasonable demands. We have to consider the long-term viability of the workers." He turned to Gizzabelle. "The board will consider your requests and offer a solution."

Buddy and Gizzabelle stared at one another. It was too easy. Was he just humoring them?

But true to his word, the board almost immediately passed down two resolutions—an overtime reduction measure and the Supplementary Corn Option—both of which the animals enthusiastically approved. Upon their passage, the animals' hours immediately dropped and any worker who elected to exercise their supplementary corn option was given a 25% increase in their daily take-home ears. Everyone took the option except a handful of animals including Buddy, who didn't eat corn to begin with, and the rest of the managers who were already overpaid.

"I think the new measures are working," Gizzabelle said the next time the raven came out to observe the workers. "You can't imagine what an improvement in morale there has been. Everyone's so much happier now that they're not hungry anymore."

"Aren't hungry anymore..." Poe repeated, watching a couple of hens scratching lackadaisically for rootworms.

Gizzabelle followed his gaze. "I mean, they're still hungry enough..." she amended quickly.

Poe didn't seem to hear her. He continued to stare glumly at the chickens. Gizzabelle wished they'd pick up the pace a little. Suddenly Poe brightened. "Of course!" he exclaimed. "Why didn't I think of it before? There's more than one way to be hungry."

"Huh?" said Gizzabelle, but Poe had already taken off toward the farmhouse.

Over the next few days, Poe and the crows started making as many as ten or twelve trips a day away from the farm. They would take off in all directions, disappear from sight, and return a while later carrying small objects in their beaks and talons. No one knew what the purpose of these forays was.

"Probably looking for roadkill," said Mordecai.

Gizzabelle refused to even dignify his outlandish insinuations with a response. But she too wondered what the birds were up to.

They found out at the next All-Animal Meeting, when Poe addressed the animals from atop a large cloth-covered pile that had appeared in the barn overnight.

"You've probably been wondering what we've been up to lately," he said. "Although we've been happy to have been able to raise your wages recently..."—he paused to let the applause die down— "there is more to life than corn. The crows and I have been working on a new project which will allow you to earn something for your labor besides just corn."

"This," Poe announced grandly, whisking away the cloth to unveil a heap of various shiny items, including coins, scraps of foil, electronic components, bottle caps, broken glass, screws, beads, jewelry, and metal buttons, "is what's called *bling*."

The chickens were immediately bedazzled by the bright, sparkly objects and rushed forward to get a better look.

At first, the sheep were nonplussed. But when they saw the hens cooing and clucking with such gusto, they couldn't help but be intrigued.

Flossy was the first to step forward. As the most beautiful and popular ewe, Flossy was, if not a leader among the sheep, at least a trendsetter and influencer. When the other ewes saw Flossy poking around in the bling, they followed suit.

"Hopefully, if they'll take to the bling," Poe murmured to Gizzabelle, "they'll want more and more of it. Keep your claws crossed."

"But what about deprivation and frugality?" she asked.

"What? Oh…yeah. I might have been wrong about that. We don't need to encourage frugality any more. *Consumption* is really the engine that drives everything."

He looked on eagerly as Flossy nosed through the objects. Discarding a gold necklace inlaid with glittering rocks, she picked up a set of keys in her mouth and shook them experimentally, liking the pleasant jingle they made.

"Where'd they come from?" Bandit asked sharply.

"I found them in the field over the hill," answered Nessa. "In an abandoned tractor."

"I'll take those," the raccoon said, snatching the keys right out of Flossy's mouth.

She barely noticed. Her gaze had fallen on something infinitely more captivating.

"It's *beautiful*," she breathed, unable to tear her eyes away.

She carefully put out a hoof and extracted a large green medallion of a four-leafed clover from the pile. Each cloverleaf was stamped with a large "H" and there was more lettering encircling the entire medallion.

"What does it say?" she asked Poe.

He peered at lettering. "Head, heart, hands, health," he read. "Clover of Excellence."

"Clover of Excellence," Flossy repeated, savoring each word. "How do I get it?"

"You can trade corn for bling," Poe explained to all the animals. "Of course, a piece like this won't come cheap. You'll have to work hard and save up. But in addition to your regular salaries, we've decided to institute performance-based bonuses to give you more ways to earn bling. You can buy bling whenever you have enough corn, but at the end of the season, we'll have a big auction for the best pieces."

Flossy kept staring at the medallion. "Can I try it on?" she asked.

Smiling tolerantly, Poe nodded, and Lulu helped Flossy get the green ribbon over her head.

"How do I look?" Flossy asked Lulu and Ewina.

"Wait," said Poe. "You can see for yourself."

Everyone stopped to watch, curious to see what he meant. From the bottom of the heap, Poe dragged out a round object. Using his talons to open it like a clam shell, he held it up for Flossy to look at. "This is a mirror."

If Flossy had been beguiled by the medallion, she was utterly transfixed by her own reflection, which she'd never had the pleasure of seeing before. She looked this way and that, admiring herself from every direction. She'd known her dramatic black-and-white coloring was unique from what other animals had told her, but seeing it herself was something else. Her natural beauty was perfectly set off by the cutting-edge fleecing Bandit had given her weeks ago, and now the magnificent Clover of Excellence.

"Can I see?" Lulu asked.

"Me, too!" bleated Ewina.

All the chickens and sheep started clamoring for a peek.

Poe snapped the compact shut. "Everyone can have a look," he said. "But only at a price. You've got to earn it."

From the moment they were introduced, bling and the mirror proved to be incredibly effective motivational tools. The prospect of seeing themselves for the first time consumed the animals. Physical appearance suddenly dominated everyone's thoughts and conversation. They looked forward to their day of revelation with equal parts anticipation and dread, wondering if they would like what they saw. They fished for clues to their attractiveness from their friends to brace themselves for what they'd see. Everyone wanted some bling so they would look their absolute best on the big day.

The animals put beaks and noses and snouts to the grindstone. No one talked in the fields. They came in early and left late, despite the restrictions on overtime. Everyone wanted to get ahead, but instead, they just kept raising the bar for everyone.

Flossy had a different strategy. "Jellybean," she cooed, sidling up to the hard-working young sheep, "I'm just *dying* for that Clover of Excellence. I couldn't stand it if someone else got it. It looked *so* good on me."

"You're beautiful just like you are," Jellybean said.

Flossy tossed her head and shook her tail flirtatiously. "But I could be even *more* beautiful with the Clover of Excellence," she said. "Don't you think?" She waved her tail at him coyly as she pranced away.

"She's just using you, you know," Mordecai said. "Vain as a peacock and shallow as an August rain puddle."

Jellybean just shrugged.

Only a few of the animals seemed immune to the appeal of the crow's offerings. Sausage gently declined Peanut's offer to secure him some bling befitting his station. "The greatest wealth is a poverty of desires," he said. "What is essential is invisible to the eye."

The cows, too, were nonplussed by the bling and mirrors. This was partially because their eyesight wasn't very good and, being so large, they wouldn't be able to see much of themselves in the small compact anyway, but it was just as much a factor of their temperament. The bovines didn't put much stock in superficial appearances, and they didn't have a vain bone in their bodies.

"Most everyone else's productivity has jumped, but the cows' output has barely budged," Poe complained as he went over the numbers at the next leadership meeting.

"I reckon that's because they were already working at capacity," said Buddy. "They're not bludgers like the sheep, playing silly buggers all day long. They always give 100%."

"We need 110%," said Poe.

"Why set your sights so low?" asked Mordecai. "I say we settle for no less than 120%. And we can raise it to 125% next week."

"They can do better," Poe insisted. "They will do better. We've just got to incentivize them."

"Incentivize?" asked Gizzabelle.

"Implement impactful motivation-enhancing strategies to maximally optimize their deliverables."

Gizzabelle's eyes bulged and she blinked rapidly.

"That's corporatese," Poe said proudly.

"Sounds like you've mastered it."

Poe preened himself.

"Well, if you ask me, *incentivizing* isn't going to work on the cows," said Buddy. "They don't respond to external rewards; they're more internally motivated."

"Everyone responds to something," said Poe. "Either carrots or sticks. We just haven't found the right buttons to push yet." He tapped a talon. "What we need is to think outside the box..."

"Outside what box?" asked Gizmo.

"That's just an expression," explained Gizzabelle. "It just means that it's like we all live in our own box and we can't see beyond the boundaries of what we're used to. We have to imagine new possibilities."

"What did you say?" Poe said.

"Huh? We have to imagine new possibilities?"

"No, the part about living in your own box..." said Poe vaguely. "Never mind."

The other animals looked at her, but Gizzabelle just shrugged. She seemed to have lost the ability to know what Poe was thinking anymore.

The next morning, Poe and the crows were in the cow pasture with stakes and string, parceling off the land.

"Each cow will get their own private plot," Poe explained to the curious bovines. "We're going to keep track of everyone's productivity and at the end of harvest, we'll hold a plot-pick. The cow with the highest production gets first pick of plots and second highest gets second pick and so on down the line. Until then, feel free to check out all the parcels; find the one that suits you. Some plots will be larger than others. You may want a property with a shade tree or a scenic view or high-quality grass. Or a location close to the farm. Real estate is location, location, location!"

"How can you 'own' land?" Millie wanted to know. "Doesn't it belong to everyone?"

"Now you'll own your *own* land," said Poe. "You'll love owning. Once you get a taste of it, there's no going back. You'll see."

Poe had found the cows' soft spot. The bovines were intimately connected to the land; it was an integral part of their identity. Although they didn't feel any need to own their own land, when they realized that after harvest, they would be cut off from most of the pasture they had enjoyed their entire lives, they became intent on at least retaining access to their favorite corner.

There was an immediate chilling effect on relations between the cows, as everyone tried to hide which parcel they were interested in from the other cows. They deliberately avoided the plots they had their eyes on, while loudly lowing the praises of less desirable parcels to anyone who would listen.

This breakdown bled over into the fields as well. Instead of pulling together as a team as they always had, Buddy noticed a decided unwillingness to help one another out. And it wasn't just the cows either. While in the past, one animal's success had not impeded another's, now everyone was competing for the best bling and nicest digs.

Tempers flared as everyone tried to catch their fellow workers doing something wrong. Sometimes they would go so far as actual sabotage, getting in each other's way, spreading misinformation, or taking credit for another animal's work.

Buddy was at his wit's end. And then, just when he didn't think things could get worse, one morning Newton went missing. Buddy was worried. Ever since his demotion, Newton had been downright despondent. No matter how his friends tried to tell him no one thought less of him, he felt like everyone looked at him differently now that he'd been stripped of his position. "I know I shouldn't," he said, "but I feel like less of a mule."

When he couldn't find Newton in the fields, Buddy went to look for him in the barn after work, thinking that he might have been too depressed to get out of bed. However, he found the mule's stall empty.

He poked his head in Sausage's stall. "Have you seen Newton?"

Before Sausage could answer, Newton trotted in, grinning from ear to ear.

"Where've you been?" asked Buddy, irritated that he'd been worried about the mule when it appeared he'd been out gallivanting instead of working. "I could've really used you in the fields; the workers are at each other's throats. Everything's gone to buggery. Jock's doing his best, but he's just getting his hooves wet as a manager."

"I was working on a project," Newton confided. "And if it's successful, it will solve all your problems. It's a game changer." He grinned impishly at Buddy and Sausage.

"What is it?" Buddy asked.

"It's the corn picker," he said, his eyes twinkling.

Buddy's eyes widened. The corn picker had been sitting somnambulant in the garage, utterly useless since its keys had never been found.

"Nessa found the keys," Newton explained, "and Poe looked up how to use them, but they needed my help to actually drive it. Bandit can't do it all himself and the birds aren't strong enough to help out."

"You've been working with Bandit?" asked Buddy in disbelief.

"There's certainly no love lost between us," Newton acknowledged, "but I have to admit, it feels good to be needed again. We're going to take it for a trial run tomorrow."

"Well, blow me down!" said Buddy. "Good onya if you really can get it working."

"It will free up everyone," Newton agreed. "You won't have to drive the workers so hard; it'll really take the pressure off. We'll be able to do twice as much in half the time." He looked at Sausage, who hadn't said anything. "Isn't it great?"

The hog didn't answer.

"Oh, c'mon, Sausage," Newton insisted, "You're not afraid of a little human technology, are you?"

"Men have become the tools of their tools."

"It's all in how you use it," Newton said obstinately. "Technology is the road to progress."

Sausage was quiet for a moment.

"There is more to life than increasing its speed," he finally said. "Take care not to outrun your soul."

Newton hardly thought there was much danger of that, since he didn't believe in souls in the first place. "Just wait 'til tomorrow," he said. "You'll see. You'll change your tune when you see how much work the corn picker saves." He paused. "Assuming we're able to get it up and running, that is."

At dinner that evening, Newton told Gizzabelle about how he and Bandit were working on the corn picker, and soon the whole corncrib was abuzz with the news. Everyone chattered happily about how they would use their new leisure time. Of course, number one on everyone's list was watching more television. The cows imagined themselves sun bathing and chewing cud in their own private plots, and the rest of the animals looked forward to spending more time acquiring bling, and admiring and shining up and showing off the bling they already owned.

When Newton and Bandit got to the shed in the morning, there was already a crowd gathered out front.

"Maybe I shouldn't have told anyone until we actually got it running," Newton said nervously, looking at all the expectant faces.

"You'll make it work," said Bandit. "Everyone's counting on you." He climbed onto Newton's back to reach the door handle. Opening the door, the raccoon sprang inside and Newton awkwardly followed him and positioned himself in the driver's seat.

He put a hoof on the clutch and maneuvered the gearshift into low. "Okay, give it some gas," he said.

Bandit grabbed the throttle and pulled it toward him. Taking a deep breath, Newton let his hoof off the clutch and they lurched forward. A thunderous cheer erupted from the crowd. The animals ran out of the corn picker's way as it left the shed, and they followed alongside, whistling and shouting, as it chugged up the road to the fields.

Newton sat up higher in the driver's seat, listening to the jubilant cheering down below.

"Get ready to turn," he said, as they approached the closest unharvested field. "Okay, now!"

Bandit clasped both paws around the top of the wheel and yanked downwards with all his might. "Keep going!" Newton cried. Bandit let go and lunged for the top again, letting his weight pull the wheel down. The corn picker turned into the field.

"Now let it go," Newton instructed, and the raccoon let the wheel slip through his paws until it returned to its original position. Newton pressed on the brake, and the engine continued to purr. He looked at Bandit.

"Okay, here's where the rubber meets the road," he said. "Let's see if we can make this baby work."

"This one?" asked Bandit, putting his paw on a lever.

Newton nodded. "Let 'er rip!"

Bandit pulled the lever. The corn picker started to hum, softly at first, then louder as the thresher picked up speed. Bandit and Newton's eyes met; they both grinned. "Here we go!" Newton said, taking his hoof off the brake. They moved forward again, and the stalks of corn in front of them started to disappear into the harvester.

"Hooray!" shouted the animals. "They did it!"

"Well, I'll be a son of a..." Buddy said, smiling and shaking his head.

In what seemed like no time, they had gone the entire length of the field, harvesting an area that would have taken the animals all day to do. Although they had some trouble turning the corn picker around when they got to the end of the row, they eventually figured it out and were soon running the harvester like pros.

The animals were ecstatic. They treated Newton and Bandit to a heroes' welcome when they returned from the field at the end of the day. "Hip-hip-hooray!" they shouted. They threw wood chips and sang, *For he's a jolly good fellow.*

Bandit hushed the crowd. "I don't know what to say," he said modestly. "When I first tackled the corn picker, I didn't know if I'd really be able to make it work. And now here we are. Believe me, no one is as surprised as I am. It just shows you what patience and good old-fashioned animal ingenuity can do."

Bandit looked at the mule. "Of course," he said, "I can't take all the credit. I couldn't have done it without Newton, here. This was a joint effort. Newton worked the brake for me. Let's have a round of applause for him, too!"

The animals stomped their feet in appreciation. Newton gritted his teeth in what he hoped was a semblance of a smile. He couldn't think of anything he could say to set the record straight that wouldn't sound petty and self-serving.

"Bandit acts like getting the corn picker running was all his doing," he complained to his chessmates later. "I contributed just as much, if not more! But I'm sure if I'd said anything about it, they would have said I wasn't being a good *team player*." He tossed his head. "What being a team player *really* means is letting someone else take the credit for your work!"

"Credit flows upwards, blame flows downwards," quipped Peanut, debuting an original Peanutism.

"Exactly."

Newton tried to bite his tongue the next day, but he couldn't help himself. "Oh, please, let me get the brake," he said pointedly when he and Bandit climbed into the corn picker's cab.

Bandit looked at him evenly. "Something on your mind?"

Newton stared at the raccoon for a long moment, then shook his head. It wasn't worth it. They continued their work in uncompanionable silence, talking only to exchange necessary information.

The animals' enthusiasm about the corn picker lasted two whole days. On the third day, Poe called a special meeting to announce some coming changes.

He cleared his throat and glanced back at the board members lined up behind him.

"As I am sure you are aware, Bandit's recent success in getting the corn picker running has been a huge step forward for us. It has exponentially increased our efficiency, and I'm sure it will go down in our history as one of our greatest triumphs," he said. He allowed some time for the animals' applause to die down.

"As a result of this success, we're going to be restructuring. We don't need such a large, bloated workforce now so we'll be streamlining our operations. Rightsizing."

Restructuring? Streamlining? Rightsizing? None of the words had any meaning to the animals.

"As head of operations," continued Poe, "Buddy will be in charge of head count reduction."

Buddy jerked his head around in surprise.

"What exactly does that mean...head count reduction?" asked Gizzabelle, although she had a sinking feeling she already knew.

"Eliminating redundancies," Poe explained.

The animals looked at him blankly.

"Pink slipping?"

Still nothing.

"Dehiring unnecessary workers," he finally said.

"*Dehiring*?" cried Newton. "You're getting rid of our jobs?"

"But only animals with jobs get paid wages," clucked Clementine.

"No corn?" squeaked Hamish.

"We'll starve!" screeched Henrietta. "Starve to death!"

Fear shot through the crowd. The chickens squawked; the pigs squealed; and the sheep and cows were on the verge of a stampede.

"You can't just eliminate animals' jobs!" brayed Newton. "We won't take it! We'll rebel! We'll organize!"

Bandit shot him a lethal stare.

"Calm down, everyone!" Poe cawed loudly, trying to make himself heard over the din. "Don't panic. No one will starve. The board is offering all sunsetted workers a very generous severance package and they will receive transitioning assistance!"

The animals didn't know what that meant exactly, but it sounded promising. Maybe things weren't as bad as they seemed. There was a plan. They settled down, ready to hear more.

"If we pull together," Poe said, "we can weather the storm. It will be hard, but in the end, we're going to come out of this leaner and stronger and better than before. Buddy will be announcing his decisions at the end of the week. In the meantime, everyone just return to your jobs and in this time of uncertainty, don't allow yourselves to lose sight of the most important thing: driving our efficiency even higher. That is what will assure both our corporate and your personal survival and success."

With that, he ended the meeting.

CHAPTER 14

As the animals staggered out of the barn, shocked into silence, Poe called the senior leaders into the tack room for a private meeting. Bandit and the crows joined them.

Poe got straight to the point. "Okay, Buddy," he said, "we need you to cut 50% of the workers."

"Come again?" Buddy said.

"I know it's a lot, but the corn picker is amazingly efficient. Even keeping on 50% is hard to justify."

"What happens to them after they're fired?" Peanut wanted to know. "You mentioned a severance package. What's that?"

"It means the animals will get a full three months wages," said Poe. "I insisted on it."

"Three months," said Mordecai. "That takes them to the middle of winter. What then?"

Poe looked at Bandit, then back at the goat. "They can use that time to figure out what to do next..." he faltered.

"What about the transitioning assistance?" asked Gizzabelle.

Poe brightened. "That's right! I forgot! New technology opens fantastic job opportunities for highly-trained workers. And as high-skill positions, they're better than the jobs that are being eliminated."

"Like what?" Gizzabelle asked eagerly.

"We'll need someone to learn how to operate the corn picker with me," Bandit said.

"Doesn't Newton already do that?" Jock asked.

"Yes, but he should have a back up," said Bandit. "Cross-training is important. I was thinking Jellybean would be a good choice. He's smart and pliable."

"Pliable?" asked Mordecai, his eyes narrowing.

"Trainable," said Bandit. "Able to pick up new things."

"Okay, that sounds good," said Gizzabelle. "So what other new jobs will be created?"

Poe shifted uncomfortably, but Bandit and the crows looked unruffled.

"That's it?" Gizzabelle said. "You're getting rid of half the workers' jobs, and replacing it with *one* new position?"

No one said anything.

"I could use some more lookouts," Sarge finally suggested.

"That's an idea," said Poe, looking toward Bandit.

"I'm afraid we can't use any 'make-work' jobs," the raccoon said. "We just have to accept that progress comes with some winners and some losers. We can't hold back the tides of change." He looked at Buddy. "I trust we can rely on you to handle the layoff process?"

"Fire them yourself," said Buddy. "It's your decision, not mine."

"Now, Buddy," said Bandit, "I know it's not pleasant, but leadership means making the tough choices. Nobody likes it, but we need to present a united front, show that we're all on board with this."

"But I'm *not* on board with it," Buddy said quietly but emphatically.

The other animals stared at him in shock. Coming from the faithful shepherd, this defiance was unthinkable.

"It goes against the mission statement," he continued. "This directly affects the standard of living of half the shareholders. It's not even a close call."

"Quite the contrary," said Bandit. "Eliminating workers increases profit which benefits the shareholders."

"I know, I know," said Buddy, "you say workers are different than shareholders. But even if the laid-off workers get a bigger payoff at the end of the year, it won't compensate for weeks of no wages. They need to eat *year-round*; getting a lump sum is no substitute. Call a vote. They'll vote it down in a jiffy."

Bandit met his eyes. "We could call a vote," he said, "but we thought it would be a pointless formality."

"How do you reckon?" scoffed Buddy. "You'd be lucky to get a single vote. The workers will all be against you."

"Most likely you are right," said Bandit. "But the workers don't get a vote."

"*What?*" the managers all nearly shouted.

Bandit smiled his jagged, sharp-toothed smile. "That's right. They don't get a vote, since they aren't shareholders."

"What are you taking about?" asked Gizzabelle.

"The workers gave up their shares when they exercised their supplemental corn option. The senior leaders were the only animals who chose not to take the option."

"Of all the low down, underpawed tricks…" said Gizzabelle.

"It wasn't a trick. It was spelled out very clearly in the resolution."

"But you know they can't read!"

"Well, you shouldn't vote for anything you don't understand. We can't take responsibility for making sure the animals educate themselves on the issues. Reading lessons were available to everyone." He eyed Gizzabelle. "But what about you? *You* read, don't you? Why didn't you read it?"

"I did," Gizzabelle said. "At least I thought I did. I read most of it, just not…"

"…the fine print?" Bandit supplied.

She hung her head.

The raccoon looked around the room triumphantly. "So, I believe a vote at this point would be academic."

"Wait," said Gizzabelle. "There are eight of us—me, Buddy, Gizmo, Sarge, Peanut, Mordecai, Newton, and Sausage—and eight board members. That still leaves Poe to break the tie." She turned to the raven. "Poe, you can't lay off half the workers. It's heartless!"

"I know it's hard," Poe said. "But they just aren't needed anymore."

"Well," said Gizzabelle, "what if instead of laying animals off, we cut everyone's hours in half? Then everyone could stay on the payroll."

Poe looked hopefully at Bandit, who shook his head. "That would mean cutting everyone's compensation in half, and the workers can't survive on half rations," said the raccoon. "They'd be too malnourished to work. Weren't you *already* complaining they are underfed?"

Gizzabelle gritted her beak.

"Sorry, Gizzabelle," Poe said, "If it were up to me, I'd try to help you out. Really, I would. But I don't have a choice."

"What do you mean, you don't have a choice? You're CEO!"

Bandit spoke for him. "He's right, Gizzabelle. He has no choice. He can't make a decision that negatively affects the shareholders."

Gizzabelle turned on the raccoon. "Who says? What's to stop him?"

"He has a fiduciary responsibility as CEO to put the shareholder's interests first," said Bandit. "He can't violate that trust."

"Or what?"

A gleam appearing in the raccoon's eyes. "Or the board will replace him."

Gizzabelle gasped and whipped around to Poe, who hung his head, acknowledging the truth of the raccoon's words. Bandit smiled his pointy-toothed smile.

"Well, I reckon it's clear what we have to do," Buddy finally said. "Corporate policy is clear. Still, we should follow proper procedure and put it to a vote. But once the decision's official, I'll support it and give them the bullet myself."

"Buddy!" Gizzabelle cried. "I know you're loyal, but how could you go along with *this*?"

"It's policy, Gizzabelle," Buddy said. "It's not our job to set policy; it's our job to follow it."

"I'm glad you've come to heel," said Bandit, nodding with satisfaction. "You'll go far with that attitude. The rest of your colleagues could learn a thing or two from you."

"Yeah, like how to fink," muttered Gizmo.

Ignoring him, Buddy turned back to the raccoon. "Why don't you go nut out the resolution while we round up Sausage, and then we'll meet back here to vote?" he said.

"Excellent," said Bandit. "I'll get right on it."

After Bandit and his board members left for the farmhouse, the other animals turned on Buddy.

"How could you do this?" hissed Gizzabelle. "I can't *believe* you!"

"Yeah," said Gizmo, "are you really going to just roll over on this?"

"The code of honor is clear," said Sarge sternly, "leave no animal behind."

"I never thought you'd do something like this, Buddy," squeaked Peanut.

"What did you expect?" said Mordecai. The goat seemed more sad than snide. "He knows who holds the leash."

"Easy, everyone," Buddy said, smiling grimly. "I haven't gone over to the dark side yet. I reckon I know how we can get that extra vote."

Gizzabelle looked at him cock-eyed, but then her eyes lit up.

"You're right!" she chirped. "There *is* a vote they didn't count. Let's go get her!"

When the board returned from the farmhouse with the new organizational rightsizing resolution, Jock, Sarge, Gizmo, Mordecai, Peanut and Sausage were waiting for them.

"Where are Gizzabelle and Buddy?" asked Poe.

"Relax," said Gizmo. "They'll be here in a jiffy."

"*Alors*, are we going to vote *ou pas?*"

Everyone whipped around. A decidedly smug Coco emerged with Buddy right on her heels. She stretched luxuriously.

"Coco?" asked Poe.

"Coco doesn't eat corn so she never gave up her share!" crowed Gizmo triumphantly.

"I'm tired of waiting. *Allons-y?*" she purred.

Bandit's eyes burned with fury; his fur puffed out in all directions, swelling him to twice his normal size. Then, slowly, a grin spread over his face. "That is only nine votes even if the little hen shows up."

"Don't worry, she'll be here!" snapped Gizmo.

"Even so, it's still a tie," said Bandit. "And in the event of a tie, the CEO's vote takes it."

Poe's head jerked up.

"You're just making this up as you go along!" squealed Peanut, who'd seen Poe's obvious surprise.

"I'm sorry you don't like it," said Bandit smoothly. "But policy is policy."

"So are there any more of these *policies* we should know about?" Peanut sneered. "Like you have to be over three months old to vote or chickens are only 3/5 of an animal or some other rubbish?"

"Now, Peanut," Bandit remonstrated. "What are you implying? We'd never try to deprive anyone of their rightful share. You can't blame the system just because you don't get your way. You simply don't have the votes."

Just then, Gizzabelle appeared in the door. "I'm back," she chirped. Clementine was at her side. "We're ready to vote."

"But, she can't vote," burst out Bandit. "She's not even a worker!"

"You're right," agreed Gizzabelle. "She's not a worker, but she's still a shareholder. Since she wasn't getting a wage to begin with, she wasn't eligible for supplementary corn. So she never gave up her share."

Gizmo strutted around in a circle, jabbing his head back and forth with exuberant neck swagger. "That's ten to nine, *losers*!"

"So shall we take that vote now?" asked Buddy, who was barely managing to keep a straight face but whose tail was sweeping a clean patch on the floor.

Even Poe seemed to be repressing a smile.

"We will withdraw the resolution," Bandit said, stalking toward the door. "For now."

When they were informed that the layoffs had been averted and that all the workers would be kept on at full wages, the animals rejoiced and eagerly looked forward to working less. However, they soon discovered the reality was less appealing than they had envisioned. Instead of enjoying their leisure time, they found themselves once again plagued with boredom. Even television didn't help. In fact, it seemed as if the more television they watched, the more listless and dispirited they felt. To make matters worse, with the reduced hours, there was no way for them to earn bling. It continued to dominate the animals' minds, though, and they spent a considerable portion of their free time imagining the bling they might have had if only their jobs hadn't been scaled back.

Jellybean was the only animal who seemed to benefit from the new arrangement. Under Bandit's watchful eye, Newton began teaching the young ram how to operate the corn picker. Although he was initially worried that he wouldn't be able to meet the demands of the job, Jellybean proved to be a quick study and picked up the machinations of the gears, clutch and brake far easier than he had reading.

"Just because you're not book smart doesn't mean you're dumb," Newton told him. "You're just better with your hooves."

"You've got excellent potential, Jellybean," Bandit said. "I did the right thing recommending you for this post. If you keep up the good work, I can see a real future for you with the farm. You've got what it takes to be an important part of the team, if you want it."

Newton narrowed his eyes. "Just because he's a sheep, doesn't mean he's a *sheep*," he said.

Bandit ignored him. "Of course, the position comes with a generous compensation package. We take care of our talent. Not only will you be getting more corn, but you'll also be entitled to top-of-the-line bling."

"I'll do my best," said Jellybean.

The animals had barely started to settle into their new routines when Poe called another All-Animal Meeting in the barn. Everyone wondered what sort of announcement he would have this time. First the corn picker, then layoffs, then part-time hours. Things were changing so fast it made their heads spin.

Bandit and the crows stood behind Poe as he addressed the crowd. After a few introductory remarks, Poe got down to business.

"We have some exciting news to share," he said. "Some of our colleagues are taking the next stage in their journey. After their long service to the farm, our valued co-workers Sausage and Newton will be stepping down."

"*What?*" brayed Newton.

"Bull dust!" barked Buddy. "We agreed, no layoffs!"

"They're not being laid off," answered Bandit calmly. "They're retiring."

"Retiring?"

"Yes, going out to pasture. Don't you remember the Happy Golden Years provision you passed?"

"But that was supposed to be a *benefit* to workers!"

"It is," said Bandit. "It assures animals that they don't have to work in their old age."

Newton glared at the raccoon. "So you had me train my own replacement, eh? I should have seen this coming. You've just been waiting to get rid of me!"

The raccoon only smiled.

"I don't understand," Peanut said, glancing uncertainly at Sausage, who appeared as serene as ever. "You're sending them out...to pasture? Which pasture?"

"Well, that's just an expression," said Poe. "They won't actually be going to the pasture."

"So what will they be doing?"

"They'll be...moving on," Poe said uncomfortably.

"Moving on?" Newton asked. "To where?"

"Wherever you want," Poe said with forced enthusiasm.

A shocked silence fell over the crowd.

"What are you saying?" Gizzabelle finally choked out. "That they can't stay on the farm? That they're being *banished*?"

The crowd rumbled threateningly. Leaving the farm was the worst fate they could imagine.

"Winter's coming!" squalled Henrietta. "They'll die!"

Gizzabelle turned on Poe and Bandit. "You can't do this."

The animals murmured their agreement.

"I assure you, we can," said Bandit. "And we can arrange an early retirement for anyone else who wants one."

Silence fell like a hammer.

"But Sausage isn't well," Peanut said to Poe. "He can't be wandering around in the wild with no food or shelter."

"He looks fine to me," said Bandit.

They looked at Sausage, who sure enough, looked better than he had in months.

Peanut turned on the raccoon. "You've always had it out for Sausage. And don't think I don't know why either. You're just trying to get rid of him because you're scared!"

"You're looking at it all wrong," Poe said. "Retirement is a good thing. It's an opportunity for them to reinvent themselves. To travel, see the world...Bandit says the forest is just lovely."

"Horsefeathers!" said Mordecai. "You can roll a turd in sugar, but it's still poop. They're being run off the farm and you know it."

"Mordecai," said Bandit coldly, "you must be getting close to re-tirement age yourself. We had thought we could retain your services for a while longer, but perhaps it is time for you to retire as well."

Mordecai locked eyes with the raccoon. Neither backed down, and no one spoke for what seemed like an eternity.

"Well, overseeing the mail has been memorable," said Mordecai finally, "but I think I may be ready for something new. Maybe it is time for me to 'reinvent' myself."

The animals gasped in surprise.

Mordecai gave Newton and Sausage a wan smile. "I've always wanted to see the world."

"No!" squealed Peanut. "No one's going anywhere. Not you, not Sausage, no one! We'll...we'll...we'll *revolt*! That's what we'll do!" He looked at the crowd. "Who's with me?"

No one would meet his eyes. The chicken-hearted hens were too afraid; the cows never bucked authority; the sheep weren't about to be the first to speak out. The pigs would have liked to stage a rebellion, but considering their fellow animals' timidity, they didn't want to risk their curly tails being left hanging out in the wind if the others didn't back them up.

Gizzabelle and Buddy looked at one another questioningly, their loyalties hopelessly divided. Newton was raring to join the little pig, but he was muzzled by his fear that everyone would think his sup-port was merely self-serving.

"*I'm* with you!" cried a voice from the back. The animals whipped around to see where it came from.

It was Gizmo. "Let's do it!" he squawked.

Peanut tossed the cockerel a grateful glance. "C'mon, guys!" the little pig urged. "We can do it." He trotted over to Xena. "We're stronger than they are. You could crush that raccoon with one good stomp. Let's run *them* off the farm and see how they like it!"

Xena looked toward Sausage. The rest of the animals held their breaths. What would the great pig say?

Sausage was quiet for a moment. "Returning violence for vio-lence multiplies violence," he finally pronounced, "adding deeper darkness to a night already devoid of stars."

"So we should just accept it...let them get away with it?" oinked Peanut indignantly. "Let them *win*?!?"

"Darkness cannot drive out darkness; only light can do that. Hate cannot drive out hate; only love can do that."

Before anyone had a chance to respond, Bandit signaled the crows and they flew out into the crowd, each carrying a lumpy bag in their talons. At his cue, the crows dumped the contents of their bags into the crowd. Corn kernels, bits of food, and small pieces of bling rained down. The animals fell over themselves trying to collect the treats and trinkets, completely forgetting their distress over the retirements.

"Corn and circuses," Newton said to Gizzabelle as they watched the frantic *mêlée*.

She just shook her head sadly.

Peanut was undeterred. "I can't believe they're pushing you off the farm," he said miserably. "It's the worst fate that can befall an animal. It's practically a death sentence! You can't leave!"

The hog smiled. "Goodbyes are only for those who love with their eyes. Because for those who love with the heart and soul there is no such thing as separation."

The tiny pig gazed deep into the elder's eyes. Suddenly he brightened. "I know! I can come with you!" he cried. "I can, can't I? I can come with you?" He held his breath, his tail taut with anticipation, waiting for his master's answer.

When Sausage gave no response, Peanut's snout began to quiver and his eyes filled with tears. "You said the highest manifestation of life is that a being governs its own actions. *You* said it! I want to follow you wherever you go. This is *my* choice!"

"Indeed," said the hog, his eyes crinkling with pleasure. "We each must choose our own path. I would be blessed to walk the same trail for a ways longer. True companionship is a treasure beyond price."

Peanut's heart exploded with joy. He made a series of tiny love grunts and rubbed his head against the big pig. "Oh, thank you! Thank you, Sausage. I never want to leave your side!" He would have happily followed Sausage to the slaughterhouse gates.

When the snacks had been consumed and the bling claimed,

Poe quieted the crowd. "Can we have the honorees up front?" he asked.

Everyone was surprised when Peanut joined Sausage, Newton, and Mordecai in stepping forward.

"I'm going with Sausage!" he oinked proudly.

"Are you sure?" asked Poe doubtfully. "We could still use you on the farm."

"Absolutely!" Peanut exclaimed. "I only want to be with Sausage."

"Um, alright. I guess it's your choice," said Poe. "Before you go, I want to thank you all for your service and present you with a token of our deep appreciation."

He signaled the crows, who dragged out two largish objects from behind a bin.

"These are for the next step of your journey."

"What are they?" asked Peanut.

"They're golden backpacks," Poe announced proudly.

"Golden backpacks?" asked Peanut. "What are they for?"

"They're filled with corn," explained Poe. "They'll help cushion your transition. Unfortunately, we only prepared two."

With some difficulty, Newton and Mordecai were fitted with the golden backpacks. When the packs were in place and the straps had been tightened, Poe looked out on the crowd.

"Join me in thanking our co-workers once again and wishing them good luck for a long and happy retirement."

There was lackluster applause from the animals. Then Bandit led everyone out of the barn. Poe and the crows flew overhead while the rest of the animals trudged along beside the retirees as they walked up the road to the gate. Everyone was quiet, remembering the last time they had made such a trek together, when they had gone to bring Farmer Bob back to the farm. The mood was no less funereal.

"Wait!" lowed Mille.

The animals turned to see Gizzabelle, Gizmo, and Buddy hurrying to catch up. They each had something in their mouth.

The crowd parted so the three latecomers could get through.

Gizzabelle placed the bag she'd been carrying at Newton's hooves. "You should have these," she said.

Gizmo dropped his bag, and Buddy laid down the board he'd been carrying.

"The chess set!" squeaked Peanut.

"A delightful gift, indeed," said Sausage. "Sustenance for the mind is as essential as sustenance for the body. Thank you, my friends."

Newton removed his backpack and he and Peanut struggled to fit the board and game pieces into it, happily sacrificing some corn for their beloved chess set.

"Oh, Sausage," clucked Clementine, bursting into tears. "It's not right for you to leave. This is your *home*!"

"Do not cry, my child," he said. "I am not born for a corner. The whole world is my native land."

"B-b-but how will you survive?" Henrietta spluttered.

He smiled tenderly. "The forest is no more fearsome than the farm."

"What about *us*?" oinked Hamish. "What will we do without you to teach us?"

"There is no teaching, only reminding," he replied, "no learning, only remembering."

Then Sausage raised his gaze to the crowd and a reverent hush fell over the animals as they waited for their massive maharishi to speak.

"Do not be led by others," he proclaimed, his warm, melodious voice like a soothing balm for their spirits. "Awaken your own mind, amass your own experience, and decide for yourself your own path."

Bandit began pushing his way to the front of the crowd.

"Peace I leave with you; my peace I give to you," Sausage continued. "Let not your hearts be troubled, neither let them be afra—"

"Okay, folks," interrupted Bandit. "Newton's got his pack on again. We're ready to go now. Let's get moving." The animals murmured angrily. The least they could do was let Sausage impart a few final words of wisdom before he left!

"I said, let's go!" Bandit ordered threateningly. He gave Sausage a shove, and the enormous pig began lumbering toward the gate.

Gizzabelle ran to the great pig's side. "Take heart, my child," he said as they walked. "Do not spend so much time looking into the darkness that you forget that you yourself are made of stars. The light you seek has always been within."

The crowd surrounded them, pushing and shoving one another in their efforts to get close to the hallowed hog. As the throng pressed in, Gizzabelle was smashed right into Sausage's side.

He lowered his snout to Gizzabelle's ear. "Watch out for Poe," he grunted softly. "One sees clearly only with the heart. Let your heart lead you."

Just then a black sheep butted in between them and Gizzabelle was thrust into the rushing tide of animals. "Peace be with you, little lamb," Sausage said to the young buck. "Chin up, Buttercup," he told the tender-hearted cow, who was delighted to have been singled out *by name*. "Fear not," he murmured to the animals on his right, each of whom was sure words were meant just for them. The other animals surged forward, each hoping for an acknowledgement or assurance or even simply a touch from the great porcine sage.

Gizzabelle tried to fight her way back to the hog, but the small chicken had no chance against the far larger cows, sheep, and pigs, and she was steadily pushed farther and farther away.

The last thing she heard Sausage say before she was swept out of earshot was his message to Millie, "Trust in your own wisdom. There is a voice that doesn't use words. Listen."

When the animals reached the gate, the raccoon unlatched it and swung it open. Everyone rushed to nuzzle their departing friends one last time. There was whimpering and whining; weeping and wailing and gnashing of teeth. Henrietta turned on the waterworks. Sausage continued to dispense benedictions; Buddy and Newton said a deeply emotional—if mostly wordless—farewell; Hamish and Peanut had a final snuggle; and Mordecai got his nicest send-off, surprisingly, from Gizmo of all animals. Gizmo thought it was "totally kick-ass" how the goat had stood up to Bandit. Poe looked on from his perch on the fence, appearing decidedly uncomfortable. He didn't even try to say goodbye to any of the departing animals.

Before they knew it, Bandit was herding the exiles through the gate. Gizzabelle tried to push her way to the front of the crowd. She hopped up and down, straining to see over the others, to no avail.

It was nothing but rumps and tails.

Finally Bandit called an end to the leave-taking and slammed the gate shut. Sausage, Peanut, Newton and Mordecai set off down the lane, the tearful goodbyes and well wishes of their fellow farm-mates at their backs, buoying them forward into the unknown.

One by one the animals drifted away until only Gizzabelle remained. She stood at the gate for a long time, staring through the slats at the empty road.

Adieu, she said silently. *Adieu* to you all.

CHAPTER 15

After the forced retirement of their fellow co-workers, an icy frost settled over the farm and lodged itself in the hearts of the animals. Although their grief was deep, their fear cut even deeper. Banishment was no longer a hypothetical concern, but a very real danger.

Gizzabelle realized what many did not: with Newton, Mordecai, Peanut, and Sausage all gone, the board had an absolute majority and could now pass any resolutions they wanted. Certainly neither of the two newly appointed managers were likely to give them any substantial opposition. A toadying, brown-nosing cow named Maybelle had been chosen as milk manager, and a dirt-dumb sheep named Nimbus took over for Mordecai. Sausage was not replaced. The threat of layoffs loomed overhead like a butcher's blade.

For the first time, Gizzabelle considered out-and-out revolt. With the rules of the corporation rigged in favor of the board and Poe's wings tied behind his back by his "fiduciary responsibility," she was beginning to doubt that workers could find any justice within the system. But when she casually floated the idea to various animals she thought might be receptive, she was shocked by how vehemently it was shot down. No matter how overworked they were, no matter how hungry, no matter how likely they were to be laid off or driven off the farm into forced retirement, they still clung to the current system like a lifeline. Anything was better than the unknown and in their minds, the corporation was their only defense against the greatest bugbear of all: being taken over by Kratchet Farms. The animals felt their only choice was collaboration.

Everyone worked as hard as they could, but since everyone was working above and beyond, there was no sure-fire way to distinguish oneself through work alone. So the animals looked for other ways to set themselves apart. Cozying up to Buddy and the board became the animals' primary preoccupation. They fell over themselves to loudly proclaim their complete and total agreement with each decision that was made by the leadership. They obsessively analyzed and mirrored back their superiors' every interest and opinion, and jealously guarded any new nugget of information about them like it was a delectable morsel of food. They adopted Bandit's mannerisms and mimicked Poe's expressions of speech; some even went so far as to roll in rot, which everyone knew was like catnip to Buddy.

But no matter how hard they worked, the sense of dread was ever present and when Poe announced an emergency All-Animal Meeting, Henrietta voiced what everyone was thinking.

"It's layoffs!" she screeched. "I know it! I can feel it in my bones!"

Buddy looked at Gizzabelle. "Don't they have to at least run it past the leadership team for our approval first?"

The hen shrugged. "Why bother? It would just be a rubber stamp now that they don't need our votes." She was afraid that Henrietta's prophesies of doom might be right for once.

They followed the rest of the animals into the barn, where Poe was waiting for them. Bandit and the crows were nowhere to be seen.

When it looked like everyone had arrived, Poe addressed the crowd.

"I have some bad news," he said, sparing any preamble. "It's going to affect everyone's jobs. Right now, you are all working part time. But that's just not going to be feasible anymore."

A nervous murmur rippled across the crowd. They steeled themselves for the coming blow.

"The corn picker has stopped running," announced Poe.

The animals stared at him, uncomprehending.

"The corn picker has stopped working," repeated Poe, "and we're not going to be able to get it running again."

"I bet they wish they hadn't gotten rid of Newton now," said Gizzabelle to Buddy. "He could fix it."

"No, he couldn't," said Poe, who'd overheard her. "It's not exactly broken."

"Then why'd it stop running?"

"It's out of gas."

"What's gas?" everyone wanted to know.

"It's what the corn picker eats," explained Poe.

"What about corn?" asked Hamish. "Can't it eat corn instead?"

"That would be nice," mused Poe. "But unfortunately, no."

"Can we get more gas?" asked Millie.

"I'm afraid not. The drum's dry as dust."

"But you had to have known this would happen eventually," said Gizzabelle, hurrying to his defense, "so you must have been working on a plan, right?"

The raven looked at his feet. "Well, I wouldn't say that exactly. We knew we'd run out *someday*, I guess, but we never thought it to be so soon..."

"That's pretty dumb," snapped Gizmo.

Poe shot him a look. "We can't look backwards," he said sternly. "Blaming and Monday morning quarterbacking will get us nowhere. We have to concentrate on moving ahead. Luckily, there is a clear path forward." He scanned the crowd. "Until we're done with the harvest, which should be in a week or so, you are all going back to full-time employee status. Effective immediately."

The animals were stunned. The news wasn't bad after all! They had their old jobs back!

They eagerly accepted the extra hours. Instead of resenting the hard work as they had before, they now saw it as a blessing. It was *job security*. The animals' mood started to improve. They even began to think about bling again.

"Don't you think the Clover of Excellence would set off my wool perfectly?" Flossy asked Nimbus, who had taken Mordecai's place as postmaster. As soon as Jellybean had lost his plush job running the corn picker, Flossy had noticed that Nimbus possessed a certain attraction that she had never appreciated before.

By the end of the week, not an ear of corn could be found in the fields. The silo was packed with golden kernels; the corncrib was practically overflowing with cobs. The animals were full of pride in their accomplishment. They had done it! They had planted and tended and harvested the corn crop *all by themselves*.

Everyone looked forward to a well-deserved rest and a well-provisioned winter, but most especially they couldn't wait for the big end-of-harvest bash that Poe had promised them.

The kickoff to the festivities was the much-anticipated auction.

Even Hamish, who always consumed everything he earned forthwith, had managed to put away a few cobs for the event, and the managers and most productive workers had stored up so many that they were being held in personal accounts at the corncrib. They double-checked their balances with Shylock before Poe gathered everyone together to explain how the bidding would work.

He started with ordinary bling like coins and jewelry before moving on to the more valuable items. There was a particularly spirited bidding war for a large metallic disc with decorative cutouts. Poe, getting into his auctioneer's role, whipped up the crowd.

"Who'll give me seven?" he cawed. "Seven cobs for lot number fifteen? You'll be the envy of your neighbors with this exclusive, one-of-a-kind bling. C'mon, who'll give me seven?"

The bidding reached an unprecedented twenty-two cobs before Gizmo was, at last, declared the winner and gleefully rolled his cherished trophy—a "hubcap," Poe informed him—back to the chicken coop.

Of course, the prize jewel of the auction was the Clover of Excellence, which Poe held until the end. Practically everyone—chickens, sheep, pigs, and cows alike—dreamed of owning it. Even the animals who'd already spent all their corn stuck around to see who went home with the coveted item. The bidding started at fifteen cobs. Most of the animals were quickly priced out, but Henrietta got several hens to pool their cobs, and they went head-to-head against Nimbus who quickly matched every bid they made. Flossy watched with rapt attention.

Back and forth it went between Henrietta and Nimbus. Thirty-six, thirty-seven, thirty-eight. When they hit forty, it looked like the chickens had run dry until Henrietta convinced a reluctant Clementine to ask Sarge for some cobs. This influx of funds kept the hens solvent for another few rounds.

But finally, at fifty-six, the bidding ground to a halt. Henrietta couldn't finagle a single more cob. The chickens were out.

Everyone turned to Jellybean, ready for a showdown between the rams. Nimbus shot his rival a nervous glance. Everyone knew Jellybean was by far the hardest worker on the farm and consistently got the biggest bonuses, not to mention his time as a high-wage cornpicker driver. He had to have more corn in the bank than Nimbus who'd only recently been promoted to postmaster.

"That's fifty-six," Poe repeated, staring at Jellybean. "Who'll give me fifty-seven?"

Jellybean, though, was silent. Flossy flicked her ears back and forth in annoyance. She'd been looking forward to watching the bidding shoot into the stratosphere. The higher, the better, in her opinion. Show everyone exactly how much her affection was worth.

"Fifty-six, going once?"

Gizzabelle nudged the young ram. "What's wrong, Jellybean? Are you short on corn?"

"Do you want to borrow some cobs?" asked Buddy. "I know you're good for it, mate."

"That's okay," the sheep said, "but I'm not bidding."

"Why not? Don't you want to win it?" asked Gizzabelle in surprise.

Jellybean shrugged. "As long as Flossy gets it, I'm happy. I know that's what she wants."

"Fifty-six, going *twice*," Poe said. A gleam of hope appeared in Nimbus's eye when Jellybean still made no move to bid.

"But," pressed Gizzabelle, "don't you want to be the one who gives it to Flossy?"

"I'm sure she'd rather get it from Nimbus," he said matter-of-factly. "They've been spending a lot of time together."

"But, Jelly—" Gizzabelle began.

"SOLD!" squawked Poe. "For fifty-six corncobs."

Nimbus rushed forward and accepted the Clover of Excellence from Poe. He immediately took it over to Flossy and clumsily slipped it over her neck.

"How do I look?" she asked, stepping back so he could admire her.

"Very…pretty," he finally managed.

"You're a peach!" she said, casting a glance at Jellybean as she nuzzled Nimbus. Then she pranced away to show off her new acquisition to Ewina and Lulu. Sighing, Jellybean trotted over to Poe. Gizzabelle just looked at Buddy in bewilderment as the raven and ram started off toward the cow pasture for the next event: the plot pick.

The plot pick worked just the opposite of the auction: the best items went first. Millie, who got first pick, surprisingly chose a modest plot near the back fence. She said it had sentimental value since it was where Buttercup had been born. That meant the prime plot, the one with a shade tree *and* a clover patch, went to the number two cow: Xena.

"Wouldn't you know it would go to *her*," grumbled a disgruntled cow who'd been eyeing the parcel for herself.

"What do you expect?" said her companion. "Of course she can pull more than the rest of us. Look at those bulging muscles. So un-cowlike. It's revolting!"

"Whaddya expect from a bull dyke?" chimed in one of the cow's calves. Millie was aghast. She never would have *dreamed* of saying such a thing about an adult cow when she was his age. Her mother would have had her hide! But this year's calves had been left to virtually raise themselves while their mothers worked in the fields and they had no respect for their elders.

"Let her have her fancy plot," sniffed his mother.

The three cows nodded knowingly, and when their time came, chose adjoining tracts of land on the opposite side of the pasture from the plot with the shade tree and clover patch. The "right" kind of neighborhood, they said. Xerxes and Buttercup pointedly chose lots on either side of Xena's, even though they weren't the best available real estate.

"What could matter more than having good neighbors?" asked Buttercup.

"That's right," said her mother, proud to have raised such a good-hearted cow.

Eventually, after all the parcels were distributed, everyone headed back to the barn for the third and final event of the day.

The Big Reveal.

Poe told the animals that because they had all worked so hard, everyone would be given mirror time. Instead of the little compact he'd shown them before, he had brought a large framed mirror from the farmhouse, and he instructed them to form a line in front of it. Everyone nervously groomed and preened themselves while they waited.

"How do I look?" Clementine asked Henrietta.

"Just fine," said Henrietta, smoothing one of her friend's stray feathers into place. "How about me?"

"Elegant as a swan," Clementine assured her.

"Of course, if I hadn't been saving my corn for the Clover of Excellence, I could have bought some nice bling," Henrietta groused. She shot Flossy, who was first up at the mirror and taking her sweet time, a deadly look.

"I can't wait for you to get a look at yourself," Clementine told Gizzabelle. "Maybe then you'll believe me when I say you need to put on some ounces."

"Too right," said Buddy. "You're so skinny you'd have to run around in a rainstorm to get wet!"

Gizzabelle just shrugged. She hadn't been actively watching her weight for weeks; she just didn't feel like eating much recently.

"Of course, you'll always be beautiful to me, no matter your size," Clementine hastened to assure her.

As Flossy continued to admire herself in the mirror, turning this way and that, the other animals began shifting and grumbling amongst themselves.

"No need to linger," Poe finally told her. "After today you'll have as all the time in the world to look at yourself."

"What do you mean?" she asked.

"An anonymous benefactor bought the mirror," the raven explained. "Just for you. It'll be all yours after today."

Flossy tilted her head. "For me...?" she echoed, stumbling out of the way as the other animals crowded forward to get their look.

Everyone's reaction to their reflection was different. Some tried to hide their pleasure; others, their disappointment. Hamish loudly lamented his size, but his good-natured chortling belied any real mortification. Coco nonchalantly washed her face and whiskers, as if she looked in the mirror every day. After briefly squinting into the mirror, Sarge stalked away, muttering under his breath that he didn't see what all the commotion was about. Gizmo admired himself unabashedly, strutting back and forth until the other animals forced him to let someone else have a turn. Gizzabelle was surprised to discover that, while she was still heavier than she would have liked, she found her plumage quite fetching; her post-molt feathers were even sleeker and shiner than before. Ewina was similarly pleased with her appearance, but Lulu took one look at herself and ran out of the barn, bleating hysterically.

"Why didn't anyone say something?" she moaned to Flossy and Ewina when they caught up with her. "How could you not tell me I'm *cross-eyed*?"

"Because we don't even notice it," Ewina said. "We don't care what you look like. We love you."

"Don't cry," said Flossy, who was on the verge of tears herself. "Would you like to wear my Clover of Excellence? Would that make you feel better?" She buried her head in her good friend's neck.

"No, thanks," said Lulu miserably, blowing her nose all over Flossy's shoulder. "It would just make me look ridiculous. I'd rather no one looked at me at all, ever."

"Oh, Lewie," said Flossy. "Don't say that."

Only after much coaxing and cajoling were the two sheep able to convince Ewina to come back to the barn with them.

They returned just in time to hear Poe make a startling announcement. "I didn't want to ruin your fun before you could enjoy the rewards of all your hard labor," he said, "but now that you've had a chance to celebrate, I'm afraid I have some bad news."

You could have heard a kernel drop.

The raven continued on. "We're going to have to decrease everyone's rations to get through winter. We're going to be moving some of the corn out of the corncrib and putting it in the silo."

"What?" the animals cried in alarm.

"But those are *our* cobs!" shrieked Henrietta. "We earned them!"

"Yeah," said Gizmo. "You and your thieving scavie friends can't have them!"

"They're not for us," said Poe. "We'll be selling them. We need money."

"Money?" asked Gizzabelle. "I thought you said we didn't need money anymore now that we have credit."

Poe wouldn't meet her eyes. "Unfortunately, we've run out of credit."

"First petrol, now credit?" asked Buddy.

"You said we could always get more credit," said Gizzabelle. "So get more."

"Well," Poe admitted, "we already did that. After the first credit card maxed out, we got more and after we maxed those out, we took out equity on the farm. But it turns out we weren't quite right that you can *always* get more credit. There is a limit. And we've hit it."

"But...what'd it all go to?"

Poe shifted back and forth. "Well...of course there were bills. Those came first. And the board's salaries and bonuses are paid in money..."

How much are those?"

Poe looked around nervously. "That is, uh, privileged."

An angry murmur rose from the crowd.

"I don't know the numbers off the top of my head," Poe said.

"You can tell us your salary," said Buddy.

"Surely you remember *that*," Gizmo said sarcastically.

Poe's reply was too soft to hear. When he was forced to repeat the figure, Gizzabelle's beak fell open.

"You make..." she did some quick calculations, "...*over 300 times* more than I do?" she squawked.

"Whoa, dude, that's *messed up*," Gizmo said. The animals rumbled in agreement.

"No wonder you can't pay the workers more," said Buddy.

"I didn't set it myself," Poe said. "It's the industry standard."

Gizzabelle stared at him.

"It's below average, actually," he said. "Some CEOs make even more."

"So you paid yourselves an exorbitant salary with this *borrowed* money—money we never had—and now there are bills due and *we're* supposed to cut back?"

"It's called austerity," said Poe.

"That's dodgy," said Buddy. "Wouldn't it be more fair if you gave some of the dosh back to cover the farm's debt?"

"I'm afraid that's not the way it works, said Poe. "You can't just take money back once it's been paid out. That would be *income redistribution*." The way he said it made it seem as if this was *obviously* a very, very bad thing, but Gizzabelle didn't see why it was so obvious. Was she just too dumb to understand? Was everyone else in possession of some instinctive knowledge that she had been born lacking? Although she was deathly afraid of revealing the depth of her own ignorance, she couldn't help but ask more questions.

"Okay, it might be too late to change salaries, but what about bonuses?" she asked. "Aren't bonuses supposed to be dependent on performance? If the farm is *failing*, how can the leadership deserve bonuses?"

"I hear what you're saying, but even if we didn't pay out bonuses, that wouldn't solve the problem," Poe said. "It's the debt that's the real issue. We're up to our ears in it."

"I don't understand."

"Well, you see, the crows were looking for things to do with their money, ways to multiply it, and they discovered this thing online called gambling," he explained. "It's another game the humans play where you try to predict the future. You can play with just about anything: sports, card games, horse races…they picked the stock market—"

"The stock market…what's that?"

"It's made up of a bunch of 'stocks' which are things that go up and down. If you guess which ones will go up, you win money; but if they go down, you lose money. The crows got into it and they made out pretty well. But then Bandit go into it and whoa! I mean, he was a savant! He was making money hand over fist in something called 'day trading.' Everything he touched turned to gold. It was going great until he got into derivatives."

"What are they?"

Poe shrugged. "Heck if I know. But Bandit said it was a *sure thing*. It was going to solve all the farm's financial problems *forever*! So we sank everything we had into it. We leveraged the whole farm." He stopped.

"And…?" Gizzabelle said.

Poe sighed. "And then the bottom fell out of the market. We lost everything."

"You mean—you mean we lost the farm, too?" Gizzabelle asked

in a strangled whisper.

Poe nodded miserably.

Gizzabelle's comb quivered with anger. "I guess Bandit wasn't so brilliant after all."

"You can't blame him," Poe said. "Turns out no one *really* understands derivatives."

"Then why would you risk everything on them?"

"I don't know. I guess we got caught up in the excitement. We just never thought we'd lose."

"And now you expect *us* to pay for *your* losses?"

The animals began grumbling loudly.

Poe sighed. "I know it doesn't seem fair, but I'm afraid there isn't a choice. If we don't pay our debt, we'll have to declare bankruptcy and the humans will come after us, and then we'll *all* be done for."

Suddenly, a single whispered word—from where no one knew—swept through the crowd, barely audible, but bone chilling.

Kratchet.

Angry oinking and squawking instantly turned to panicked squealing and screeching. Cows bellowed; sheep bleated. With the threat of Kratchet hanging over their heads, the animals practically fell over themselves in their haste to implement the proposed austerity measures. They spent the next few days transferring corn from the corncrib to the silo, and watched, uncomplainingly, as their daily rations were cut by a third. At first, the animals compensated by selling their bling back to the crows for more corn, although they got far less for it than they had paid. Soon, however, they had sold back all their bling, except for Flossy, who refused to part with the Clover of Excellence no matter how hungry she got.

After they had eaten the proceeds of their bling, the cows and sheep spent more time grazing in the pasture and the chickens hunted for insects to supplement their diet, but the closer winter got, the slimmer the pickings. Everyone was hungry all the time, and all the workers started losing weight. Although their wages would have been more than enough to meet their nutritional needs, even the managers were slimming down since they were sharing their corn with the less fortunate. Only Poe and the board appeared to be as healthy and well nourished as ever.

The cows were doubly distressed. Not only were their bellies empty, but they were cold too. Since everyone kept to their own private plots now, they couldn't reap the benefits of shared body heat that they'd always had in the past. But no one thought of going back.

Since everyone was cranky and irritable, when some of the sheep began lashing out and even charging one another at the slightest provocation, at first the animals put it down to hunger. But when they started developing strange mannerisms—an odd high-stepping gait, excessive lip smacking, tremors, and uncontrollable post rubbing—it was clear something was very wrong.

"It starts with the personality changes," Jellybean told Buddy, "but before you know it they're scratching themselves bloody. We don't know what to do."

"Make sure they're eating and drinking," said Buddy, "and try to keep them from doing too much damage to themselves. Maybe it will just go away on its own in time."

But it didn't just go away. The sheep got sicker and sicker, and more sheep developed symptoms every day. Some of the sheep who had been sick the longest began collapsing with convulsions and became lethargic and unresponsive, refusing even to go to the corn-crib. The healthy sheep brought them their daily rations and tried to make them as comfortable as possible.

The other animals offered assistance, each according to their own beliefs. The pigs gave practical suggestions: medicinal mush-rooms and mud poultices for the itching. The cows held healing cir-cles with praying and laying on of hooves. The chickens performed an ancient sacrificial ritual involving elaborate ceremonial strutting and squawking, and offerings of unfertilized eggs. Only Poe and the board—who were periodically apprised of the sheep's condition—seemed to have no recommendations to offer.

Finally, one day Jellybean loped over to the Great Tree where Buddy was asleep, dreaming of his herding days with Farmer Bob.

"Buddy!" Jellybean bleated frantically. "It's Lulu!"

Buddy raised his head groggily.

"I think she's...*dying*!"

The shepherd instantly sprang to his feet.

"The other sheep are out in the pasture working on her," said Jellybean, "but it doesn't look good. She's been having seizures and hallucinating and now she's breathing really strangely. Like a rattle."

Buddy had been out on enough medical emergencies with Farmer Bob over the years to know what that meant. "I was hoping it was just wog," he said. "But I'm afraid there's only one thing that might save her now. She needs a vet."

"A vet?" asked Jellybean. "How can we get a vet out here?"

"I dunno," admitted the shepherd grimly. "But if we don't, Lulu might not be the only one to cark it. They could all go the same way."

"Buddy?" Jellybean said in a stricken whisper. He gulped hard. "I think Flossy's got it, too."

Buddy's ears flattened. He's seen the young buck making sheep eyes at Flossy and knew, along with the rest of the farm, that he was head-over-hooves in love with the comely ewe. "Are you sure?"

"She's been acting moody for a few days. At first, I tried to ignore it, told myself it was just the stress of Lulu being so sick—you know how sensitive she can be—but then she started walking funny. And this morning I caught her out at the fence. Scratching."

"Oh, Jellybean," Buddy said. "I'm so sorry."

They just looked at one another for a moment.

"C'mon," Buddy finally said. "Let's go check on Lulu, and then we'll sort out what to do. We'll think of something, mate."

Long before they got to Lulu, they saw the crowd of animals around her. The sheep were baaing and bleating inconsolably. Gizzabelle, who was standing with Gizmo at a respectful distance behind the sheep, waved them over.

"I think she's gone," she said in a low voice.

Jellybean sat down heavily. Buddy knew he was thinking about Flossy.

"Are the rest of the sheep going to die?" asked Gizmo.

"Gizmo!" snapped Gizzabelle, mortified.

"We're going to do what we can, Gizmo," sighed Buddy. "Maybe if we can get the vet in, he can fix the crook jumbucks. The board's been talking about contacting the humans about the corn. Maybe they're already working on a plan. Let's go talk to Poe. I know we've had our differences lately, but he's always got good ideas. And he is still our CEO."

Gizzabelle nodded. "If anyone can think of something, Poe can," she said, but her voice lacked the confidence of her words.

Gizzabelle and Buddy headed back to the farmhouse. When they got there, Buddy went up to the kitchen stoop and barked loudly. "Poe! Poe!" he woofed. When there was no response, he scratched on the pet door and barked some more.

Finally there was a rustling within and Poe stuck his head out the pet door and hopped onto the porch. "Yes?" he said.

"We're here about the sheep," said Buddy. "They're as crook as Rookwood."

"We've lost Lulu," said Gizzabelle. "And the others are getting worse."

"I was afraid that might be where we were headed," said Poe. "I wish there were something we could do."

"Actually," said Gizzabelle, "we were thinking it might be time to bring in a vet ..."

"Well, now," Poe said, "I don't know if that's smart. We don't know if the vet could even do anything for the sheep. What if we exposed ourselves to the humans and the farm went to Kratchet, and all the sheep died anyway?"

"I hadn't thought of it like that," said Gizzabelle uncertainly. "The vet couldn't save my parents."

"And even if we knew for a fact the vet could save the sheep," continued Poe, "what's the point of saving the sheep now if they just get sold to Kratchet and slaughtered a few months later anyway? Along with all the rest of the animals?"

"But we don't *know* that we'd be discovered," Gizzabelle insisted. "And even if we were, that the farm would go to Kratchet. Maybe we'd get another owner as decent and kind as Farmer Bob. Or maybe the humans would even let us keep running it ourselves. You never know."

"The eternal optimist, eh?" said Poe. "Well, I'll take the matter back to the board and see what they say."

The little hen didn't say anything.

Poe cocked his head at her. "Don't worry, Giz, we'll make the best decision. Trust me. We'll take everyone's interests into consideration."

With that, he hopped back inside the farmhouse, the pet door banging behind him.

Gizzabelle looked at Buddy. "What do you think we should do?" she asked.

"Buggered if I know," said Buddy. "I reckon it's no use arguing the toss."

"Do you think they'll make the right decision?"

The shepherd shrugged. "I dunno. Poe's dinki-di, but that Bandit's as cunning as a dunny rat."

Gizzabelle couldn't come right out and admit it, even to herself, but for the first time an ice-cold ribbon of doubt snaked through her. *Could* they trust Poe to do the right thing by the animals? She'd always been so sure that he was a good bird at heart, that their faith—*her* faith—in him had been well placed, but now she just couldn't be sure. He seemed so different since he'd come under Bandit's sway, more distant and detached with every passing day.

No, she was probably just being overly critical, miffed that Poe seemed to favor Bandit and the crows over her. Besides, she reminded herself, Sausage had seen something worthy in Poe and Sausage was never wrong.

"Poe will do the right thing," said Gizzabelle valiantly. "We've just got to have faith."

CHAPTER 16

It was a beautiful clear day and Gizzabelle was scratching around in the barnyard, trying to enjoy the sunshine and keep her mind off the sheep while Clementine bent her ear about how crotchety and set in his ways Sarge was getting lately and never a kind word or bringing home a worm "just because" anymore when Shylock came streaking across the field, shrieking at the top of his lungs.

"Human! Human!" he screeched. "Human coming!"

Instant pandemonium erupted. Having gotten complacent since they'd locked the gate and put up the "keep out" sign, the animals hadn't been keeping up their drills and now they were rusty.

Gizmo tried to follow the standard drill procedure. "Do not panic. Stop, think, and proceed to your nearest safe spot. Repeat, do not panic. Proceed to your nearest safe spot," he squawked.

Because there had been so many animals in the barnyard enjoying the unusually nice weather, the designated hiding spots soon filled up and the rest of the animals dashed around in circles, lowing and bleating and oinking wildly. Although the chickens didn't need to hide, they were making more fuss than anyone.

Buddy tried to herd the animals who hadn't found a hiding spot, but there was already too much chaos and he couldn't catch anyone's gaze to give them the Eye. His frantic barks disappeared into the din. He looked desperately at Gizzabelle, then back at the road, which was still empty. The human would be there at any moment! He wasn't going to have time!

Suddenly an earsplitting crow shot through the crowd, stopping everyone dead in their tracks.

"COCK A DOODLE DOO!" Gizmo crowed again at full volume. Then, when he was sure everyone was paying attention, "Follow Buddy. He knows where to go!"

Buddy glanced gratefully at the young rooster. "This way!" he barked.

Relieved to have a leader, the animals eagerly fell into line and followed Buddy behind the barn, which was easily large enough to hide them all. Sides heaving, they listened for the sound of a vehicle. Nothing.

Buddy frowned. The car should have been here by now. "Wait here," he said to the others. "I'll have a Captain Cook."

He went back around to the barnyard where the chickens were standing stock still, their eyes trained on the road. Buddy trotted over toward Gizzabelle.

Before he had a chance to speak, Poe landed beside them, the rest of the crows following behind. "Shylock says there's a human coming?"

"Dunno," replied Buddy. "Just had a Bo Peep. No sign of anyone yet."

"Maybe they turned around and left?" Gizzabelle suggested hopefully.

"I'll have a look," Poe said, spreading his wings. Just as he was about to take off, there was a stir among the chickens. They peered at the road. A human on a bicycle had crested the hill and was pedaling their way.

Poe quickly took flight and swooped over the chickens' heads. "Stay calm," he ordered. "Remember, just act normal. You've seen humans before. Just act like you always did."

The chickens dutifully scratched the ground, always keeping one eye on the approaching bicycle.

As it neared, they could make out the bicyclist, a beanpole of a girl in jeans and a T-shirt. She coasted into the barnyard and nimbly dismounted the bike, resting it against a fencepost. Then she took off her helmet, releasing two thick plaits that shone like polished copper.

"*Penny!?!*" shrieked Gizmo, who had catapulted forward, nearly knocking Poe over as he streaked past at full speed and planted himself at the girl's feet.

Penny scanned the barnyard. "Hello?" she called. "Anyone here?"

"Penny, it's me!" Gizmo screeched.

"You know this human?" demanded Poe, keeping his distance.

Gizmo hopped up and down in front of the girl. "Penny, it's me, Gizmo!" he squawked. She smiled down at the hysterical little bird, then sidestepped him to head into the barnyard.

"Gizmo!" Poe said sharply. "How do you know this girl?"

"We're friends," Gizmo said, not even looking Poe's direction. "Facebook friends."

"Facebook friends?" exploded Poe. "Are you saying you've been on the computer with a GIRL? A HUMAN girl?!?"

Gizmo tore his eyes from Penny's back. Poe seemed to have grown to twice his normal size.

"*ANSWER ME!*" the raven croaked.

Gizmo cowered behind his sister. "Yes," he cheeped.

"Do you realize what you've done?" Poe thundered. "You've put the whole farm at risk, you stupid, idiotic chicken!" He looked at Penny, who was wandering over toward the farmhouse.

"No, I didn't," Gizmo insisted. "I was careful."

"You'd better tell us everything," Poe said darkly. "Right now. And I mean everything."

Gizmo took a deep, tremulous breath. "Well, after you showed me the computer for the rally, I started playing around with it at night after everyone was asleep. At first I just looked at the pictures, but as I learned to read, I did more and more stuff online. I got into Farmer Bob's Facebook account and he was friends with Asa, who is Penny's grandfather. And Penny was a vegan and volunteered at an animal shelter, so I figured she must be cool, right? So I made my own profile and IM'd her. We've been friends ever since."

"Whoa," said Buddy. "You lost me. Facebook? Profile? IM'd?"

"Never mind," snapped Poe. "It'll take too long to explain." He turned back to Gizmo. "So what's on your profile? I assume you didn't say you're a chicken? Even you wouldn't be that dumb."

Gizmo scowled. "She thinks I'm one of Farmer Bob's farmhands. A human boy."

"But what do you talk about?" Gizzabelle wanted to know, wondering what a chicken and a human girl could possibly have in common.

"Oh, movies and music and all sorts of stuff," said Gizmo, brightening. "You'd really like her, Giz. She really fights for what she believes in. She's big-time into animal rights. And human rights and worker's rights and women's rights and gay rights and environmental rights. She even founded an eco-group at her school. How awesome is that?"

Suddenly the human in question started walking back toward them. Having found no one in the farmhouse or the garage, she crossed the barnyard and climbed up on the fence to the sheep pasture. Shading her eyes with one hand, she squinted into the pasture.

Gizzabelle held her breath, hoping Penny didn't notice how strange the sheep were acting. The healthy ones were keenly aware of the young human and doing their best to act normal, but the sick sheep, seemingly oblivious to her presence, were scratching and biting themselves and prancing around in that weird high-stepping way of theirs. One was even having a seizure.

Gizmo paced back and forth, grumbling darkly to himself.

"Don't do anything stupid, Gizmo," warned Poe.

Gizmo just huffed.

Sighing, Penny finally jumped off the fence and looked back into the barnyard. Her eyes fell on the barn and began striding purposefully toward it. Seeing where she was headed, Gizzabelle ran ahead to give the animals inside a heads-up while Buddy, Poe and Gizmo stayed with the girl. When Gizzabelle got inside, everyone was safely in their stall and the doors were all shut. Of course, Jock's stall door was shattered beyond repair, but the rest of them looked presentable if you didn't look too closely.

"The human's coming," she said, "but don't worry, everything looks fi—" She stopped. Something in the back of the barn caught her eye. She gasped in horror.

Dashing outside at top speed, she flapped her wings urgently.

"Don't let her in the barn!" she squawked at Buddy and Poe. "The mission statement! We forgot to hide the mission statement!"

Buddy instantly sprang into action. He launched ahead of Penny and planted himself squarely in the middle of the barn doorway. He growled menacingly. Penny pulled up short, then took a tentative step forward. Buddy let loose such a torrent of vicious barks that Gizzabelle couldn't help cringing even though she knew it was all bluster and no bite.

— 234 —

Penny paused uncertainly, but kept looking into the barn. The mission statement was clearly visible on the back wall, proudly displayed where all the animals could see—if not read—it.

"We've got to distract her," Poe cawed urgently. Glancing around, he flew over to a trio of big rusty barrels nearby and landed behind them.

"Penny!" he cried in humanspeak from behind the barrels.

Gizzabelle couldn't believe Poe had revealed himself. She glanced at Buddy, who looked just as surprised as she was.

Penny pivoted toward the barrels. "Who's there?" she called. "Gizmo, is that you?"

"Uh-huh," Poe replied. "It's me. Gizmo."

"*WHAT?*" Gizmo screeched in outrage. He raced around behind the barrels, squawking Poe out at the top of his lungs.

Penny grinned. "It's about time! I was beginning to think you weren't here. I was visiting my Grandpop and wanted to surprise you. What are you doing back there? C'mon out so I can see you."

"I can't," said Poe.

"Darn right, you can't," cried Gizmo. "You can't pretend to be me!"

"Why not?" Penny asked.

"I'm afraid," Poe humanspoke. Drawing his wing across his throat, he shot Gizmo a silencing glare.

"Afraid?" Penny scoffed. "What, that I won't like what you look like or something? Geez. Do you really think I'm that superficial? You should know me better than that."

"Yeah, Penny is *totally* against beauty ideals," said Gizmo knowingly. "It's a media-driven wommmph—" Poe had clamped Gizmo's beak shut with his foot.

"It's not that," he said to Penny, while Gizmo thrashed back and forth trying to free himself from the raven's grip. "You see, I'm not *exactly* who I said I was online..."

Penny's eyes flashed. "You *lied*? About what?" she demanded.

"Well, I don't know exactly how to explain this, but I'm actually not a boy..."

"A *perv*!" Penny cried, jumping back like she'd been burned. "I should have known, with a name like *Gizmo*," she muttered as

— 235 —

she frantically dug into her pocket. "Don't move!" she yelled. "I've got mace...and a cell phone!" She struggled to open her cell phone while also fumbling with the tiny canister of pepper spray attached to her key ring. "I'll tell the cops I've got an Internet predator here and they'll be out here faster than you can say spit."

"No, no, it's nothing like that!" cried Poe. "Hold on, Penny! Don't call the cops! You don't have to be afraid of me. I'm not a... predator, I'm a *bird*!"

Penny stopped mid-dial. "A...bird?"

"Yeah," Poe said, flying up to perch on top of one of the barrels. "See? I'm just a bird."

Penny stared at him suspiciously. "Is this some kind of joke?" she asked, looking around. "Am I being punk'd? Are there cameras somewhere around here?"

"No, Penny. It's nothing like that. I'm telling you the truth."

"There's no one else back there?" she asked. Keeping her eyes glued on the raven and her phone out, Penny made a wide circle around the barrels until she could see behind them. Gizmo hopped out from behind them to stand at her feet again.

"See, it's just me," said Poe.

Penny lowered the phone. "So you're saying *you're* Gizmo?"

"That's right."

Penny arched a skeptical eyebrow.

"Liar!" screeched Gizmo. "He's lying, Penny! *I'm* Gizmo!"

"How can I prove it to you?" asked Poe, studiously ignoring Gizmo's increasingly hysterical squawks.

Penny thought for a minute. "Okay, what's your favorite movie?"

Gizmo cackled, looking at Poe expectantly.

Poe frowned. He hadn't spent much time with the animals watching TV. He knew Gizmo's favorite expression was "Cowabunga, dude!" which he used ad nauseam with the cows, but Poe didn't know what it was from or if that was even his favorite movie. Gizmo also liked to go around practicing his "crane kick," a move he'd picked up from a movie Poe *had* seen.

"Um, *Karate Kid*?" Poe said.

Penny's eyebrows shot up in surprise. "Huh," she snorted. "Could be..."

Gizmo screeched in outrage.

Penny eyed Poe speculatively. "Okay, one more," she finally said. "What's *my* favorite movie?"

"Oh, oh! Look down here!" Gizmo cried, spreading his wings and holding them high behind him, chest out and eyes closed, a dreamy expression on his face. He hummed a few bars of the soaring theme song.

"Easy," Poe said. At the insistence of the hens, the whole farm had had to endure that one, despite it being a raging chick flick. "*Titanic*," he said confidently.

Penny looked like she'd just bitten into a maggoty apple.

"Psych!" Gizmo whooped gleefully. "Penny hates that movie! Her favorite's *To Kill a Mockingbird* with Gregory Peck. You're busted, sucka!" He pumped his wing.

Poe grimaced at the girl's violent tastes; no wonder she and Gizmo got along.

"Just kidding, Penny," he said quickly. "*To Kill a Mockingbird*, of course."

"Argh!" spat Gizmo, smacking his forehead.

A grin slowly spread across Penny's face. "It really is you. That's wild! I can't believe I've been chatting with a raven this whole time. I never would have....*OUCH!*" She jerked backwards. "What the heck! That dumb chicken just pecked me!"

"*Dumb chicken?*" Gizmo cried, his feathers bristling. "Who're you calling dumb? You're the one getting hoodwinked! How could you not realize that Poe is not me? Does he talk *anything* like me? Open your eyes, Penny!" He stopped for a breath, then looked straight at her, willing her to recognize him. "Can't you see it's me?" he said softly. "*I'm* Gizmo."

Penny stared at him and neither spoke for a moment. Then she grinned at Poe. "Boy! The little chicken sure has a lot to say, doesn't he?"

"Argh!" Gizmo screeched. "And here I thought you were *smart*. Boy was I wrong!" With that, he stalked off.

"Hang on a tick," Buddy barked at the retreating cockerel. "Don't choof off. Give her a fair go."

Penny eyed shepherd warily. "He's awfully aggressive," she said

— 237 —

to Poe. "Does he bite?"

Buddy winced. He wasn't used to being considered unfriendly and even though he knew he'd given her good reason to think he was dangerous, it still hurt. He sat down and wagged his tail furiously.

"Oh, you don't need to worry about him," said Poe. "He just gets a little overprotective sometimes."

"Yeah, he looks friendly enough now," Penny said, visibly relaxing. "It's generally not the dog's fault anyway, you know. Usually it's abuse or bad training. He's probably just doing what he's been taught. At the shelter we have a saying: there are no bad dogs, just bad owners."

Buddy's ears drooped, doubly upset that his actions had reflected badly upon his beloved master. "Farmer Bob was *not* a bad owner," he said emphatically, expecting Poe to correct Penny's mistake.

But instead the raven just looked at Penny thoughtfully. "You're right," he said. "I hate to say anything against him, but Farmer Bob's not exactly what you'd call the best owner."

Buddy was instantly on his feet, snarling in outrage. "Shut your gob," he growled.

"It's okay," Gizzabelle rushed to placate him. "I'm sure he doesn't really mean it. I think he's got a plan."

Buddy stopped growling, but he stayed tense.

"What do you mean?" Penny asked Poe. "It's okay. You can tell me. Is he...abusive?"

The raven shrugged sadly.

"I can't believe it!" said Penny. "He and my granddad used to be best friends for years and years before they had their falling out. I met him lots of times when I was visiting Grandpop. He seemed nice. A little gruff, but in a cute, teddy-bear kind of way. I remember when I was little he always used to pull quarters out of my ear and give them to me for candy." She shook her head. "I just can't imagine him being an animal abuser..."

"Well," said Poe quickly, "he doesn't *mean* to be. He's really a good person most of the time. It's just..."

"Just what?" Penny prodded.

Poe sighed deeply. "It's the drinking," he said. "It turns him into a whole different person."

Buddy curled his lip in disgust. "What's he aiming at? Farmer Bob was no boozer."

"It's been getting worse ever since his wife died," Poe confided to Penny. "He's closed off from everyone. He stopped selling eggs and milk, and you saw that "keep out" sign he put out front. And he was drunk when he had that fight with your grandfather."

Gizzabelle listened in awe, amazed by how smooth Poe's story was and how convincing his telling.

"But he's probably glad to have Asa out of his life anyway," Poe continued. "He's finding it harder and harder to hide the drinking these days. I'm sure you noticed how run down the farm is, with all the broken fences and busted doors. He won't let anyone near the place. He won't even call a vet for the sheep, not even after one died—"

"What?" Penny demanded. "A sheep *died*? And he still didn't call the vet?"

Poe shook his head.

"That's awful. That's animal cruelty! We've got to do something…"

"But what can we possibly do?"

"Well, we could try talking to him, tell him he has to call the vet."

"No!" Poe squawked. "You can't do that!"

She paused. "Why not?"

"He'll be furious," said Poe.

Penny frowned at him. "You know, over the computer, you seemed so…different. Ready to take on the world, fight The Man, stand up for the underdog. I didn't think you cared what anyone thought."

Poe's feathers puffed out. "What are you trying to say?" he snapped. "I'm no pansy! I'm not *afraid* of Farmer Bob. I'm not afraid of anybody! It's just that talking to him won't work. He can't stand to be told what to do. It'll just make him mad and make him dig in his heels even more. I guarantee it wouldn't work."

"Oh," said Penny. She chewed the end of a braid, deep in thought.

"But maybe there is another way…" said Poe.

"What?" Penny said eagerly.

"You could call the vet yourself."

Gizzabelle and Buddy exchanged a glance. So *this* is what Poe had in mind!

"You want me to call the vet?" asked Penny.

"Yeah, I think that could work," said Poe slowly, his voice rising with excitement as he spoke. "You just call and say you're Farmer Bob's farmhand and when the vet comes, you take him out to see the sheep. We don't have to worry about Farmer Bob showing up 'cause he's out on a bender and he's never home 'til after midnight when he's drinking."

"But he's sure to find out later, when he gets the bill," said Penny.

"Not necessarily," said Poe. "He might just assume he had another blackout. He wouldn't dare ask the vet because he'd be too afraid it might expose his drinking. And besides, even if he did somehow find out that you aren't a farmhand, he wouldn't know who you are. No one knows you're here, right?" Poe gave Penny a sly smile. "I really think we could pull it off. You up for it?"

Penny grinned. "You betcha!"

Buddy and Gizzabelle marveled at Poe's ingenuity. Not only had he managed to avert disaster but he'd turned the entire situation to their advantage!

Poe quickly filled Penny in on the sheeps' symptoms and she called the vet and relayed all the information that Poe had given her. The animals waited expectantly while she listened to the person on the other end, occasionally answering questions they couldn't hear. "Uh-huh." "Yeah." "No, they're not quarantined." "Uh-huh," she finally said. "I'll be here." She snapped the phone shut.

"He wants to see them immediately," she told Poe. "He's on his way over right now."

Gizzabelle tried not to think about what the vet's urgency might mean.

"Well, I guess we should go unlock the gate," said Poe to Penny.

While the raven and girl set off to get ready for the vet, Buddy and Gizzabelle went around the farm to inform the other animals what was going on. Everyone was nervous about another human coming to the farm, but they were glad the sheep might get the help they needed.

It wasn't long before they heard the unmistakable sound of the warning alarm coming down the lookout chain. A white van drove down the drive and pulled over near the sheep's pasture, where Penny was standing by the gate. Poe was perched on the fencepost, and the crows, who apparently had been roused from the farmhouse, flew overhead.

The vet—a ruddy, disheveled man with a thick black moustache—cut the engine and got out. "So you've got some sort of sheep problem," he said to Penny. He looked up at the circling crows. "You say you lost one already?"

"Yeah," Penny said uncomfortably. "We should have called earlier. We didn't realize it was that serious."

"Well, let's take a look and see what we've got," said the vet.

Buddy and Gizzabelle followed them to the pasture, but the vet closed the gate in Buddy's face.

Gizzabelle looked at Buddy questioningly. Should they follow? They could easily duck under the fence, but they didn't want to draw attention to themselves.

Buddy shrugged. "Let's wait here. Poe can keep an eye on things from the air."

They watched as the vet went around to all the sheep, observing their behavior and occasionally stooping down to take what appeared to be some sort of sample. He sprayed the sheep displaying symptoms with a large red mark. Although there were few surprises, Buddy and Gizzabelle exchanged pained glances whenever a sheep they didn't know was sick received a mark.

After the vet had looked at all the sheep, he went over to Lulu's body. He handed Penny his bag and began dragging the carcass toward the gate and then to his van. Trying to be as inconspicuous as possible, Buddy and Gizzabelle nonchalantly wandered around the van as the vet hefted Lulu's body into the back and slammed the door shut.

"Like I said, we won't know for sure until we get the results of the necropsy," he told Penny as he got into his van. "But in the meantime, you need to quarantine the ones that are infected. I'll give you a call when we've got the results."

As the vet drove away, Poe landed at Penny's feet.

"Maybe he's wrong," she said glumly.

"Yeah," said Poe, equally glum. "You never know."

"Well, I'd better be getting back," Penny finally said. "Grandpop thinks I'm just out on a bike ride. He'll start to worry if I don't get home soon."

"Sure," said Poe. "Thanks for staying this long. You did everything you could."

"No problem. And you'll make sure the sheep are quarantined?"

"Of course."

"Okay, just let me know if there's anything else I can do to help," Penny said as she began walking back toward the barn to get her bike. "I'm just a phone call away."

"Thanks. But the most important thing you can do for us now is nothing. Don't tell anyone about Farmer Bob...or me. The consequences could be really bad."

"I won't tell a soul. My lips are sealed," Penny assured him.

Suddenly Poe, who was flying just ahead of her, gave a strangled screech.

There, in the middle of the barnyard, the message "PENNY, I'M GIZMO!" was scratched out in enormous letters with lots of big arrows pointing to the young cockerel, who was reclining in the dirt with a huge, self-satisfied grin plastered across his face.

"Get rid of it!" Poe cawed frantically. "Get rid of it!"

Gizzabelle and Buddy started over, but before they got near, seven black forms flew over them and dove toward Gizmo.

"What's the matter?" asked Penny, who, even though she hadn't been able to understand Poe's words, had heard the panic in his voice. She'd been so fixated on him, she hadn't noticed Gizmo's elaborate creation.

"It's, um, I thought I saw something on the farmhouse porch," Poe improvised. "I thought it was Farmer Bob!"

Penny's gaze immediately flew to the farmhouse, right past the crows who were busily sweeping away all remnants of Gizmo's message, despite his furious protests.

"I don't see anything," said Penny, squinting hard at the porch in the distance. "Are you sure?"

"It must have been just a shadow," said Poe, satisfied that the

— 242 —

crows had thoroughly obscured Gizmo's communiqué.

"Whew! You nearly gave me a heart attack!"

She set off again toward the farmhouse, scattering the crows and walking right past a crestfallen Gizmo and his obliterated message. He followed behind her unnoticed.

When they got to her bike, Poe landed on the fencepost it was leaning against.

"Thanks again, Penny," he said. "It was really great getting to meet you in person."

"You, too, Gizmo," she said. Suddenly her eyes lit up. "Hey, I've got an idea!" she exclaimed. "Maybe we can have an intervention with Mr. McMann, just like they do on TV. I'm sure Grandpop would be glad to help and then—"

"Um, yeah," Poe said, cutting her off. "That's an idea." He looked up at the sky. "Didn't you say you had to get home soon? It's getting late."

"Oh. Right," she said, noticing the sinking sun. She climbed onto her bike. "Well, I guess I'd better get going. I hope I can get my bike back over the fence; it nearly got stuck when I was trying to get it over coming in!" She pushed off. "Well, see you later, Gizmo!"

"Bye, Penny," Poe called as she pedaled away.

Gizmo watched her recede into the distance. Gizzabelle and Buddy came to stand beside him as she disappeared over the hill.

"Whew, that sure was close," said Gizzabelle.

She turned to find Poe glaring at Gizmo. "There will be serious consequences for you, young cockerel," he said severely.

"It's not my fault," the young chicken said. "I was careful. How was I supposed to know she'd come visit? She doesn't even live nearby."

"Do you have any other contact with humans?"

Gizmo looked down at the ground.

Poe narrowed his eyes. "Gizmo...?"

"Well, I tweet a little..." the cockerel mumbled, his gaze still fixed on his feet.

"Tweet?" asked Buddy.

"Hashtag GizmoRants," Gizmo elaborated, although this illuminated the shepherd not at all.

"What's 'a little?'" demanded Poe.

Gizmo shrugged. "I've got a couple of thousand followers."

"*What?!?*" Poe squawked.

"Will someone please explain what's going on?" Gizzabelle pleaded.

"Gizmo here has apparently been chatting online with *thousands* of humans!" Poe snapped.

"What?" asked Gizzabelle. "What on earth about?"

"Stuff," Gizmo said resentfully. Then, seeing the glowering look on Poe's face, he cleared his throat nervously. "Uh, just stuff I'm interested in. You know, computer games, kung fu movies, hip hop, animal rights..."

"This is completely unacceptable!" cawed Poe angrily. "You shouldn't have been on the computer in the first place!"

"Why not?" snapped Gizmo, back in full-bore adolescent sulk mode. "You don't own it! Why should *you* get to be on it and not the rest of us?"

Gizzabelle cocked her head to one side. Now that he'd put it that way, Gizmo was right. The board *didn't* own the computer, or the farmhouse for that matter. It just seemed like it since they'd moved in and locked everyone else out. But putting locks on something didn't make it yours.

Poe ignored the question, pressing forward with his own. "You knew you were doing something wrong, or you wouldn't have been hiding it, would you? How did you get inside without us knowing?"

"At first, I went in through the pet door at night when everyone was asleep," Gizmo said huffily, still mad but also somewhat proud to reveal his exploits.

"I thought you were visiting Sunny!" Gizzabelle said.

Gizmo screwed up his face. "Sunny? Why would I be visiting her?"

"And after we locked the pet door, how'd you get in then?" Poe wanted to know.

"I started flying in through the window when you're in your morning board meetings."

"You *fly?*" asked Gizzabelle in disbelief. "All the way up to the window?"

"Sure. Why not?"

"Well," Poe said abruptly, "it ends now. From this point forward, you're to have no contact whatsoever with humans."

"What? What do you mean?" Gizmo squalled.

"No contact," declared Poe. "No email, no Facebook, no Twitter, no contact *whatsoever*. Nevermore."

"No! I won't do it! You can't make me!" Gizmo looked pleadingly at Gizzabelle.

"I'm sorry, Gizmo. I have to agree with Poe. It's just too dangerous."

"I know you're getting the rough end of the pineapple," said Buddy, who understood just how powerful the animal-human connection could be. "But you have to think of the farm, mate."

"I don't even get to say goodbye to Penny?" Gizmo said, his lower beak quivering threateningly. "She won't understand."

Poe paused and considered. "You're right," he admitted. "There's no telling what she'd do if you just disappear without any explanation. I guess that leaves us with no choice."

Gizmo perked up. "You mean I can...?"

"I'll just have to keep pretending to be you," Poe said curtly. With that, he took off for the farmhouse.

CHAPTER 17

Over the next few days, the mood on the farm sank to even greater depths. The sheep with the ominous scarlet markings were in a paroxysm of terror and huddled together away from the others in self-imposed quarantine. Except for Jellybean, who wouldn't leave Flossy's side, the rest of the herd shunned the infected sheep, adding an additional layer of guilt to the fear and sorrow they already felt.

Even Gizmo—the one animal who could usually be counted on to raise everyone's spirits—was practically despondent. He wouldn't talk to anyone, not even Gizzabelle. Poe had taken him off lookout duty as punishment, and the animals could see him pacing back and forth on the outskirts of the farm at all hours, ranting and raving to himself.

Finally, after what seemed like forever but was actually only days, Poe called an All-Animal Meeting. He'd heard from the vet.

Everyone gathered in the barn, nervously awaiting the news. Everyone, that is, except the sick sheep who stayed behind in the pasture.

Poe hurriedly called the meeting to order. "As you know, the vet called," he said, skipping any preamble. "I'm sorry to have to tell you, but the test results aren't good. The sheep have a transmissible spongiform encephalopathology."

"A spongy encephalawhatie?" asked Gizmo.

"It's also called scrapie. The humans don't know exactly where it comes from, but it is very dangerous and you can catch it if you get close to someone who has it."

A shockwave of fear ripped through the crowd.

"Can the humans fix it?" asked Jellybean.

"I don't know," said Poe, "but I'm afraid they're the best—the only—shot the sheep have. I've already called and they'll pick up the sheep later today."

"Pick up?" bleated the sheep. "They're taking them away?"

"Why can't they fix them here?" demanded Gizmo, the sheep murmuring mutinously in agreement.

"Sounds like a trick to me," cried Henrietta. "You can't trust vets. Animal hospitals are death factories! You never come back."

"Bull dust," said Buddy. "I had to go to the animal hospital once when I had heartworm. I was sick as a dog and never would have made it through without the vet's help. He worked his magic and I came back right as rain!"

The animals were somewhat mollified.

"And don't forget, scrapie's transmissible," Poe reminded them. "If they stay here, it could spread to the rest of the flock."

That cinched it for the sheep. "They should go to the hospital," they said. "Definitely. Go get fixed up. We only want what's best for them, of course."

Jellybean was quiet. "I'll tell them," he finally said, heading for the barn door.

When he reached the sheep pasture, some of the sheep seemed confused and unable to focus, but the healthier ones stared at him apprehensively.

"Poe heard from the vet," Jellybean said. "You've got a condition called scrapie. It's serious, but don't worry, we're going to do absolutely everything we can for you."

"Can you make it go away?" asked one ewe with large bare patches on her backside. "The itching is so dreadful. I feel like my skin is alive!" She started rubbing compulsively against the fence.

"It's unbearable!" moaned another before she went back to biting at her legs.

"We've called in the humans," said Jellybean, "They're coming soon to take you to the animal hospital."

"They're going to take us away?" the more lucid sheep murmured fearfully.

"Buddy's been there and he says it wasn't bad at all. They just gave him some medicine and brought him right back to the farm. Isn't that right, Buddy?"

"King oath," said Buddy. "Just a couple of shots and Bob's your uncle! It was rough taking a sickie, but it wasn't long before I was bonzer again."

This seemed to satisfy the sheep. At this point, they were willing to do anything that offered an end to their suffering, and the idea of an enforced vacation didn't sound half bad. They went back to biting themselves and scratching against anything that would stand still.

"Jellybean, will my wool grow back?" asked Flossy anxiously. Try as she might, she'd been unable to resist rubbing a few bare spots in her coat, which distressed her to no end.

"Absolutely," he assured her. "It'll grow back even thicker and more beautiful than before."

"Okay," she said looking at him with utter trust.

"Jellybean," Buddy said gently, "you know you can't stay here."

The ram frowned at him. "Why not?"

"It's contagious. You might catch it."

Jellybean glanced at Flossy. "That's okay," he said.

"I can't let you do it."

"It's my decision," said the ram, more firmly than Buddy had ever heard him speak. "It's a risk I'm willing to take."

Buddy contemplated Jellybean for a long moment, then sighed deeply. "If you insist. But at least promise you won't share food or drink from the same bucket. And absolutely no nuzzling!"

Jellybean nodded.

Flossy flounced over. "I wanna play," she demanded petulantly. "Now!"

Jellybean gave Buddy a rueful smile, then dutifully followed Flossy into the middle of the pasture. Buddy watched them gamboling together in the grass for a few minutes. Eventually he turned and ducked under the fence. He went directly to the Great Tree where, after circling twice, he lay down and closed his eyes. A weariness like he'd never felt before swept over him. He fell asleep almost immediately.

The next thing he knew, he was awakened by strident squawking. The chickens on the lookout chain were sounding the alarm. "Human! Human!" they crowed.

Instantly on his feet, Buddy took off for the sheep pasture. When the vet arrived, having someone there to tell them what to do would go a long way toward keeping the sheep calm.

Back in the barnyard, Gizzabelle was headed toward the road to see who was coming. She had gone only a few steps, though, when she was nearly knocked over by a feathered comet streaking past her at full speed.

"Out of my way!" Gizmo screeched as he raced by. "Penny's back!"

Gizzabelle squinted into the distance. Sure enough, the young human was cycling down the hill.

As the little hen started after her brother a shadow passed over her and Gizzabelle looked up to see Poe flying overhead. He easily overtook the sprinting cockerel.

"Penny!" Poe called from the air. "Thanks for coming."

"Hey, Gizmo!" she said, dismounting to talk and walk at the same time. "Glad I can help out. They're not here already, are they? I got held up a little. Had to muck out some stalls for Grandpop."

They had almost reached Gizmo, who had stopped by the side of the road and was struggling to catch his breath.

"Penny!" he croaked between gasps.

You could have knocked Gizzabelle over with a feather. Her little brother...making *humanspeech*! Apparently no one had told Gizmo that chickens weren't capable of it.

Penny stopped.

Gizmo took a deep breath and just as he opened his beak to speak again, he was suddenly clobbered by a blur of gray. He went flying into the gully beside the road and vanished from sight.

"Bandit!" Gizzabelle shrieked. She hadn't even seen the raccoon approach and was stunned at how fast he could move. She'd gotten so used to his usual indolent languor that she'd almost forgotten there was a deadly predator lurking underneath.

"Did you hear that?" Penny asked Poe as Gizzabelle raced over to where Gizmo had disappeared. "I thought I heard my name."

"Sorry," said Poe. "Didn't hear anything."

Gizzabelle reached the edge of the gully and looked down to find Bandit sitting on her brother, his fingers wrapped around the chicken's beak. Gizmo squirmed and bucked, but the raccoon's grip only tightened.

As soon as Penny passed, Bandit put Gizmo in a chokehold and started dragging him off toward the farmhouse.

"Let him go!" Gizzabelle squawked. "Where are you taking him?" But Bandit didn't spare her a glance. She would have attacked the raccoon herself except that the way he was holding Gizmo, she knew he could snap his neck like a twig. She couldn't afford to give him any provocation.

Gizzabelle frantically looked around for help. There were hens milling around in the barnyard, but they were probably too far away to have seen what happened. Besides, what could they do even if they had?

Who she really needed was Buddy. But she knew that by the time she was able to get the shepherd, Bandit would have had more than long enough to do whatever he wanted with Gizmo.

Gizzabelle didn't want to let Gizmo, who was kicking and clawing like a wild animal, out of her sight. Surely Bandit wouldn't harm him in front of a witness, she told herself.

He might not leave a witness.

Gizzabelle shuddered. As much as she disliked Bandit, was he really capable of *that?*

She had to admit she didn't know what the raccoon was capable of. Oh well. At the very least, if worse came to worst, it would be more difficult for him to explain away *two* disappeared chickens, she thought. She took off after Bandit and Gizmo.

Back in the barnyard, Penny had barely parked her bike when an enormous truck came rumbling down the road to the farm. It came to a halt in the middle of the barnyard and, the engine still running, a man hopped down from the passenger side.

"You got some sheep for us?" he asked Penny.

"That's right," she said. "They're in that pasture there. The ones with the red marks."

"Right then. We'll round 'em up," he said, walking back to the gigantic rig and motioning the driver to back it up to the pasture gate. When the truck was finally in position, he opened the gate and the driver backed in and shut off the engine.

The driver got out and both men went around to the back of the truck and lowered a loading ramp to the ground. The driver, the taller of the two men, walked up the ramp and swung open the two gates within, each one flanking the ramp on one side so that they formed a chute.

He strode down the ramp and they set out into the pasture. They wandered among the sheep, carefully checking both sides of each one before moving on to the next.

"Hey, Joe, you found any marked sheep?" the tall man finally called. "I haven't found a single one yet."

"Will ya lookit that," said the short, stocky one, nodding to the group of sheep huddled near the back fence. "The sheep we're lookin' for are all over there together. All in a group!"

They started over to the sheep.

"Okay," Buddy barked, keeping his tone brisk and matter-of-fact. "Here they come. Time to get going. Move along. This way. To the ramp. That's right. Good job. Keep moving."

The men watched in astonishment as the sheep obediently trotted across the pasture toward the ramp. Some had the distinctive high-stepping gait, others the funny jackrabbit hop. A few of the sheep were obviously dazed and disoriented, but they were swept along by the others.

"I've never seen anything like it!" the tall man exclaimed.

Suddenly there was a disturbance in the crowd. Flossy had stopped dead in her tracks and was struggling to break away.

"No," she moaned. "I won't go! Help! Someone help me!"

Out of the corner of his eye, Buddy saw Jellybean race over and charge into the back of the herd, fighting his way toward Flossy.

"It's okay, Flossy," he bleated. "I'm coming!"

"Grab that one!" yelled the tall man, pointing at the ram. "He's not marked."

His partner swooped in and seized Jellybean by the scruff of his neck. "Whoa, there, fella," he said, dragging him over to the side and holding him still while the rest of the sheep passed. "Trust me, buddy, you don't want to go where these guys are going."

Jellybean went berserk. His eyes flashed white, and he began bucking and kicking frantically. But all his struggles were to no avail. The man's grip was like a vise.

"Jellybean?" Flossy shrieked. "Oh, Jellybean! Help me!"

The tall man had grabbed Flossy and was pulling her forward. "This one's a fighter!" he chuckled as he dragged her toward the ramp.

When the last of the sheep had passed them, the stocky man released Jellybean and shoved him back into the pasture. They could still hear Flossy's muffled cries. Jellybean lowered his head, ready to charge.

Buddy ran up beside him. "It's no use, Jellybean. They won't let you go. You're not sick."

At first, Jellybean didn't move. Then, slowly, he raised his head. He watched the mass of sheep disappear into the truck. As the last of the sheep boarded the ramp, he looked at Buddy with a resigned smile and turned to walk away.

Suddenly his hind legs seemed to buckle and then spring up. He caught himself then took another strange bouncing leap forward.

"Jellybean, don't!" Buddy cried, realizing what the ram was up to, but Jellybean continued his awkward rabbit-like hopping, even turning sideways to give the men a better view.

Buddy spun around and raced over to the stocky man, growling and barking and nipping at his legs.

"Easy, there!" the man said, his eyes riveted to the crazed shepherd. "What's gotten into you all of a sudden?"

Jellybean began bleating loudly, but Buddy's furious barking easily drowned him out.

The tall man climbed the ramp after the sheep and closed the gates. "Gimme a hand with this, will ya?"

"Sure," his partner replied, turning away from Buddy to help raise the ramp. Jellybean ran up behind them.

"That's the weirdest job I've ever had," the short man said, as he secured his side.

"I wish they were all that easy," the tall man replied, sliding the latch in place and making sure it was firmly fastened. "They practically loaded themselves. Maybe we need to get ourselves a sheep dog!"

Neither man noticed the ram right behind them convulsing and falling to the ground.

The tall man got in the truck and drove it out of the pasture, while his partner followed on foot and shut the gate behind them.

As the truck pulled into the barnyard, Jellybean slowly stood up. Buddy hurried over.

"What were you trying to do?" he asked. "I know it was hard to let her go, but what could you do? You couldn't save her."

"She was scared," Jellybean said quietly. "I couldn't have saved her, but I could have been with her."

Buddy didn't know how to respond. "Don't worry," he finally said. "They're in good hands. They'll get the best care possible."

Jellybean contemplated him. "I'm not so sure."

"What do you mean?"

"It's just something that man said. I don't know, but I don't think they're going to the animal hospital at all."

"What?" Buddy barked sharply. "What makes you say that?"

Jellybean shook his head. "Nothing definite. Just a feeling."

"You thought that and you *still* wanted to go with her?"

Jellybean wouldn't meet his eyes.

"Oh, mate," sighed Buddy, shaking his head sadly.

"I know everyone thought she was just a silly, spoiled princess," Jellybean said, "but I didn't see her that way." A wistful smile played across his lips. "She wasn't just a crush or a lay in the hay for me. It was the real thing. She had something special, a...spark." He sighed. "I don't know, I can't explain it. Something about her just lit me up."

"I reckon no one can explain love, mate," said Buddy, glancing over to the Great Tree. "It's something you just feel."

Gizzabelle hadn't taken her eyes off Bandit and Bandit hadn't taken his paws off Gizmo's neck for what seemed like an eternity to the little hen.

"Just wait until Poe gets here," Gizzabelle said to fill the growing silence. "He won't tolerate this kind of behavior."

"Oh, won't he?" The raccoon's eyes glittered jubilantly. He was clearly enjoying himself.

"Of course not," she said more confidently than she felt. "It's reprehensible."

"Oh, I haven't done anything reprehensible ...yet." He leaned in to Gizmo and inhaled deeply, closing his eyes in rapture as if the aroma was the indescribably delicious.

"Get your paws off me, you nasty, stinkin' 'coon!" cried Gizmo, shooting the raccoon a lethal glare. He squirmed but Bandit only tightened his grip.

Gizzabelle thought the raccoon was only toying with them, but she couldn't be completely sure. She wasn't about to let Gizmo out of her sight, just in case.

Suddenly they heard a noise from the kitchen. "Hellooo?"

"Buddy!" Gizzabelle squawked with relief. "Come quick—we're in here."

The shepherd appeared in the doorway. "Tell Bandit to let Gizmo go right now!" the little hen demanded.

"Back off, Bandit," Buddy snarled.

Bandit took a step back, but he dragged Gizmo along with him.

"I said, let the chook go."

"I don't think so," said Bandit. From behind a chair, the raccoon pulled out Buddy's nemesis: the vacuum cleaner!

Buddy's ears dropped and he began to tremble, but he didn't back down.

"Your presence is not required here," said Bandit. "Why don't you just turn around and leave the way you came?" His paw hovered threateningly over the "on" button.

"I'm not leaving without Gizmo," said Buddy.

Bandit shrugged and hit the switch.

The vacuum roared to life, sending Buddy bolting across the room. He stood rigid, hackles up, staring at the thundering machine. Still holding Gizmo in one hand, with the other Bandit awkwardly pushed the vacuum in Buddy's direction, driving the shepherd toward the kitchen door. Buddy barked furiously, surging forward briefly before Bandit's next lunge forced him back again.

Suddenly the vacuum went silent.

"WHAT THE CLUCK'S GOING ON HERE?"

Everyone turned to Poe, who was standing beside the electrical outlet, holding the disconnected plug in his claws. In all the commotion, no one had noticed him fly in through the window.

"Bandit kidnapped Gizmo!" chirped Gizzabelle. "He's been

holding him here against his will!"

"I said to bring him here," Poe admonished the raccoon, "not drag him by force."

"*You* told him to take Gizmo?" Gizzabelle repeated in disbelief. "But why?" Bandit smirked at her dismay.

"Gizmo defied a direct order," said Poe, flying over to the desk. "There have to be consequences."

"What kind of consequences?"

"I think he needs to spend some time alone, thinking over what he did."

"What?" screeched Gizmo. "You want to send me to the clink? No way! I'm not going to the hole!"

Poe rolled his eyes. "Don't be so dramatic. You've watched too much TV. Nobody's going to *prison*. You're just grounded."

"Grounded?!?" Gizmo gasped, falling to his knees. "Noooooo! You're tearing me apart!"

Gizzabelle shook her head at her little brother's theatrics. He really *had* been watching too much TV.

Gizmo rolled around on the floor. "You can't! It's not fair! Nooooooo!"

"You know," Gizzabelle said after a full minute of watching Gizmo wailing and writhing in anguish. "He's actually right. You can't ground him."

Gizmo instantly sat straight up.

"I mean," Gizzabelle continued, "I don't think you have the authority. That's for parents, not CEOs."

"Yeah, that's right!" chirped Gizmo triumphantly. "You don't have the authority!"

Poe sighed heavily. "Well, if you want to go strictly by the books, you're probably right. The most we could do is write him up, which is the first step to getting demoted...or fired." He let that sink in. "I thought a little 'time-out' would be a better alternative."

Fired? Gizmo looked truly chastened.

"How about I talk to Clementine and she can decide on an appropriate punishment?" suggested Gizzabelle. "*She* can still ground him."

"Nuh-uh!" protested Gizmo. "I'm practically a rooster!"

Gizzabelle shot her brother a warning look and he wisely shut his beak.

"Well, that sounds acceptable to me," agreed Poe. Bandit's face fell. "As long as she recognizes the gravity of the situation. Gizmo's recklessness put the whole farm at risk."

"I'll make sure he gets some fitting consequences," Gizzabelle promised.

"Alrighty, then," said Poe, smiling broadly. "I'm glad we got that taken care of!"

Gizmo and Gizzabelle were turning to leave when Buddy stopped them. "Before you go, there's something else I need to say..."

"Of course, Buddy, what is it?" asked Poe.

"It's about the crook jumbucks," he continued. "Jellybean reckons they aren't coming back from the vet and I told him I'd fetch him some answers."

"Not coming back?" echoed Gizzabelle, more confused than alarmed. "What do you mean?"

Poe frowned and tapped a claw. "I'm afraid Jellybean's right," he finally said. "There was nothing the vet could do for them. There is no treatment for scrapie. It's terminal in all cases."

"What?" cried Gizmo. "They're all gonna die?"

"Crikey!" gasped Buddy.

"You *lied* to us?" croaked Gizzabelle.

Bandit settled back on his haunches, ready to enjoy the fireworks.

"Look," Poe said, "I know it's a shock. We didn't want to frighten the sheep any more than they already were, and we couldn't tell the other animals for fear they'd let on."

"But if they're not getting treatment, what's happening to them?" asked Gizzabelle.

Poe looked down at his feet uncomfortably. "They're being put down. It was the most humane course of action."

"Humane?" asked Gizzabelle, shooting Bandit an accusing glance, sure he was somehow at the root of this outrage. "Why couldn't they live out their last days peacefully in their own home surrounded by family and friends?"

"That's exactly what they *couldn't* do," said Poe. "Scrapie's communicable. If they had stayed, they could have infected the rest of the flock. We could have lost them all. Is that what you wanted?"

Gizzabelle bit her beak. "Well...I guess not," she finally admitted.

"It was for their own good," concluded Poe, his tone indicating the subject was now closed.

Gizzabelle nodded. With a heavy heart, she started off toward the kitchen, Gizmo and Buddy following behind. As they made their way toward the pet door, suddenly the little hen's eyes fell on something she had missed on the way in, so focused was she on Gizmo and Bandit. Frowning, she hopped closer and her eyes widened in horror.

Gizzabelle dashed back into the main room. "Have you been eating *eggs*?" she demanded, her eyes aflame.

Poe gulped. "Not me," he said quickly, shooting a glance toward the raccoon. "But the others..."

Gizmo gagged loudly. "Gross!"

"You sure pulled a swiftie moving them to the root cellar, ya bloody bushranger," Buddy growled to the raccoon.

"Now, don't get upset," Poe implored. "I know it's unsavory to think about, but the eggs were unfertilized so they never would have become chickens anyway. It's no different than what you do, Buddy. You eat mice, right?"

"Are you *kidding*?" Gizzabelle squawked, her disgust turned to fury. "You can't see the difference?"

"I don't eat any of the farm animals," Buddy cut in. "You don't eat your mates—not ever!"

"Come on guys, you've got to be pragmatic. Don't you think it's better to do something *productive* with them? Wouldn't it be worse to let them go to waste?"

"Stop!" Gizzabelle screeched. "Just stop! I don't want to be *pragmatic* or *reasonable* or *logical* or *realistic*. There are some things that are more important than your confounded productivity. Do you even realize that?"

Poe stared at her dumbly.

"Layoffs, forced retirements, now eating eggs!" she continued. "Where does it end? Is nothing sacred to you?"

"You tell him, Giz! Take that, you clucking scavie!" crowed Gizmo.

"I don't even know who you are anymore," said Gizzabelle. "You're certainly not the bird I thought you were. I would never have nominated you for CEO if I'd known you'd become...*this*."

Poe drew back as if she'd struck him. Gizzabelle's heart clenched, but she didn't back down. She was just sorry Bandit was there to witness it. She hated giving him the satisfaction.

"Gizzabelle..." Poe pleaded, an undercurrent of panic in his voice.

The little hen's eyes bored into his. They just stared at one another, the air between them electric.

Gizzabelle finally spoke. "All this time I thought you were too good for me," she said. "But the truth is, you're not good enough. Not nearly good enough."

With that, she turned on her heel and stormed out.

Gizzabelle couldn't stop replaying the incident with Poe over and over in her head. It had kept her up half the night, given her nightmares the other half, and kept after her even in the light of day. The questions and doubts just wouldn't leave her alone. Had she been too hard on him? Should she have tried to be more understanding? After all, he hadn't had the advantage of growing up in a loving family. How was he supposed to learn if they didn't teach him?

In truth, much of her anger was directed not at Poe, but at herself. Wasn't she supposed to have been his friend? Who else should have taught him right from wrong? Indeed, hadn't Sausage charged her specifically with the task of looking out for Poe?

Had she been so worried about running after him and looking like a besotted fool with a hopeless crush, that she hadn't been involved enough to be the friend he needed? Could she have done more to counter Bandit's influence? Had she failed in her duty to Poe and to the farm?

Then again, maybe her feelings for Poe had made her too accepting of his faults for too long. Maybe she had let her infatuation blind her and trusted him too much, always making excuses for his behavior. Maybe he was just a scavenger after all.

The poor little hen didn't know if she'd been too loyal or not loyal enough. She felt guilty for letting her feelings for Poe possibly endanger the farm and equally guilty for betraying Poe with her doubt and suspicions.

Still—and she always kept coming back to it—Sausage *had* told her to watch over Poe.

Suddenly she stopped cold.

What had Sausage's exact words been?

Watch out for Poe.

A horrifying notion suddenly struck her like a thunderbolt.

Perhaps she had misinterpreted Sausage's instruction this whole time. What if it wasn't a prompting to protect Poe at all, but a warning against him?

Gizzabelle shook herself from head to claw, trying to rid herself of the terrible thought. Surely it couldn't be.

But the idea wouldn't go away.

Watch out for Poe.

Could Sausage have been trying to get her to see past her raging hormones and ridiculous romantic illusions and perceive the reality of Poe's heart of darkness? Was the clever raven capable of some great treachery that Sausage divined in his inscrutable way? Perhaps Poe was not an ally at risk of going astray, but himself a danger to watch out for?

It was past noon when Poe flew back to the farm. He'd spent the whole night out flying over the forest, trying to get Gizzabelle's words out of his mind.

I don't even know who you are anymore.

You're not the bird I thought you were.

You're not good enough. Not nearly good enough.

Did she even realize what a terrible burden it was to feel responsible for the fate of the farm? How hard it was to balance all the competing interests, trying to foresee and avert all possible dangers while always pushing to make the farm as profitable as possible? He was only doing what he had to, what was necessary. And instead of thanking him for all his work and sacrifices, all he got was criticism! He couldn't believe Gizzabelle questioned not only his decisions but even his intentions.

Maybe Bandit was right. The other animals just couldn't understand the demands of management, the tough calls that had to be made. *They have no idea*, he thought as he alighted on the farmhouse window.

"Well, well, look who's back," said Bandit. The raccoon was squatting on the floor surrounded by his usual collection of old padlocks from the garage and a bunch of papers Poe had never seen before. Then he noticed that Farmer Bob's safe was open.

Poe's beak fell open. "You figured out the combination?"

"It was just a matter of time," the raccoon simpered. "It had to reveal its mysteries to me eventually. I am a master burglar, after all."

"What did you find?" Poe asked eagerly, flying down to look inside.

"Nothing!" Bandit snapped, whipping from self-congratulatory to irate in the blink of an eye. "Except for these worthless papers, it was completely empty!"

Poe glanced at the papers strewn on the floor. He picked one up and examined it. "Last Will and Testament of Robert C. McMann," he read. "What's that?"

Bandit brushed off the news with an irritated wave of his hand. "Nothing that matters," he muttered darkly. "What matters is that there was no money, no gold, no stock certificates, *nothing* of any value! So we're in exactly the same situation we were in before you took off on your little joy flight."

"I was only gone overnight..." the raven said, offended by the raccoon's accusatory tone.

"Wouldn't it be nice if we could all just up and take a holiday whenever we felt like it? As it happens, you missed a very important call this morning."

"What do you mean?" Poe asked. "Who called?"

"The vet," Bandit said. "He wanted to know what to do with the sheep."

Poe frowned in confusion. "I don't understand. I thought the sheep were, you know..."

"The bodies," Bandit said, rolling his eyes in exasperation. "What to do with the *bodies*."

"Oh. Uh, bury them, I guess?"

— 260 —

"I suppose we *could* do that..." said the raccoon slowly, "but it wouldn't gain us anything."

"Gain us anything? What on earth could it gain us?"

"Well, they could be...recycled, you might say."

Poe jerked back in horror. "You can't be suggesting what I think you are."

"It's common practice," said Bandit. "It's called rendering. All the farmers do it."

"Feed animals to other animals? That's despicable!"

"Now, *Poe*," the raccoon said. "I know it's unsavory to think about, but you've got to be pragmatic. Don't you think it's better for something *productive* to come out of their loss?"

Poe was repulsed hearing his own words thrown back at him.

Bandit smirked. "Wouldn't it be worse to let them go to waste?"

They locked eyes.

"Absolutely not," Poe said emphatically.

Bandit raised his eyebrows in surprise.

"I told the animals when we started this that no one eats anyone else in a corporation," Poe continued, "and I'm sticking to it."

The raccoon's expression hardened. "We've been over this before, Poe. If you make a decision that isn't in the best interests of the company's bottom line, you can be removed from office."

Poe didn't retreat. "Removing me as CEO wouldn't be in the company's best interests either," he said. "How would you possibly make it without someone who can humanspeak?"

"Since you asked, it just so happens that Shylock has been experimenting with humanspeech lately. He's not nearly as proficient as you, but he isn't half bad."

Poe stumbled backwards as if he'd been kicked in the chest. "Shylock—?"

"Now, now," Bandit tutted. "Of course, we'd like you to stay on as CEO. You're making a mountain of a molehill with this rendering business, don't you agree? After all, in the end, it's just meat."

CHAPTER 18

The next day the animals organized a memorial service for the sheep who had gone on to The Meadow Without End. They gathered in the sheep pasture where they constructed seventeen small stone cairns to remember their fallen friends. Many sheep began bleating inconsolably.

Without Sausage, there was no one to lead the service and give them the spiritual solace he always provided, but a number of the animals took it upon themselves to speak. Jellybean and Ewina shared memories of Flossy, and Gizzabelle noted how the two earnest sheep comforted one another in their common sorrow. She wondered if their friendship might someday blossom into more—she hoped so. Someone should find some happiness.

Poe didn't attend the memorial. Gizzabelle hadn't seen him since their row and she wondered if he was avoiding her. Then again, none of the other board members had come either. Since no one had invited them, it was possible they didn't even know it was being held.

Gizzabelle wasn't sorry Poe hadn't been around. She hoped it meant he was taking what she said to heart. But mostly she was relieved because it gave her time to sort out her own feelings, which were in a hopeless muddle. She still didn't know if she should rekindle their friendship and keep trying to steer him in the right direction or give him up as a lost cause.

When Nimbus announced the next day that the board had ordered nutritional supplements for the animals to be delivered later that week, Gizzabelle wondered if this might be an olive branch. Had her words actually made an impact and prompted Poe to take more of an interest in the animals' wellbeing? Were the supplements his way of trying to put things right?

When the pallet of large, plastic canisters was dropped off in the middle of the barnyard a few days later, the animals hurried in from all corners of the farm and eagerly watched as the cows used their horns as giant can openers to pop open the containers and turn them over on their sides. The animals rushed forward and enthusiastically tucked into the chunky, grayish foodstuff that spilled out onto the ground. The new cuisine wasn't like anything they were used to, but it had at least one thing going for it: it wasn't corn.

For the first time in weeks, the animals looked forward to the prospect of full bellies.

Gizzabelle stood off at a distance, watching the other animals shove one another out of the way to devour as much of the gray pottage as they could shovel into their mouths. Even though she was decidedly peckish, Gizzabelle was still terribly conscious of her weight and felt uncomfortable having anyone watch her eat. Rather than fight the crowd, she decided she'd come back later and eat whatever was left—if anything.

She wandered into the barn where she would be safely out of the sightline to the debauchery outside, and there, to her surprise, she saw Buddy crouched in front of a hole in the wall. He appeared to be hunting.

"Hey, Buddy," she said. "The 'dry-rendered tankage' is here. Don't you want some? Get a break from mice?"

The shepherd straightened up. "I'll eat after everyone else is chockers," he said.

"There may not be much left if you wait," warned the hen.

Buddy shrugged. "I reckon I don't need it as much as some of the others. Besides, that's what it means to be a leader. A leader always goes last."

Gizzabelle shook her head ruefully. "You don't even realize how special you are, do you? If only every leader thought the way y—"

Suddenly Xena galloped through the barn door and skidded to a halt in front of them. Her sides heaving and her breath creating puffs of steam, the cow glared at Buddy and Gizzabelle. Before they could say anything, she dropped a small object at Buddy's feet.

"What do you know about *this*?"

"I dunno what you mean," Buddy said. "What *should* I know about it?"

Xena glowered at the shepherd. "It was in the food—the

'nutritional supplements.'"

"Blimey!" yelped Buddy.

Gizzabelle felt as if she'd been sliced open and gutted like a Cornish game hen. "No," she breathed. "It can't be!"

"You recognize it, don't you?" Xena insisted. "The Clover of Excellence? *Flossy's* Clover of Excellence?"

The horrific implications were almost too much for Gizzabelle to bear.

"I think I might chunder," Buddy said weakly.

"You *swear* you didn't know?" Xena demanded.

"On Farmer Bob's grave," said Buddy.

The cow looked somewhat mollified.

"This has Bandit's pawprints all over it," said Gizzabelle.

Xena looked back and forth between the shepherd and the hen. "Well...?" she pressed. "What are we going to do about it?"

Buddy and Gizzabelle looked at one another.

"Does anyone else know about this?" asked Gizzabelle.

"Not *yet*," Xena said suspiciously. "Why?"

"We need to think before we rush into anything," said the hen.

"What's there to think about?" Xena retorted hotly. "We should run them off the farm! Making us *eat* each other, just like them, those disgusting scavengers! Banishment's too good for them—they should be run *through*!" She lowered her head and stabbed the air with her horns.

"Easy, there, mate," said Buddy.

"Easy? *Easy?*" she bellowed as if he'd waved a red cape in front of her. "It's a travesty! An atrocity! A *monstrosity*!"

"You're right," Gizzabelle said quickly. "It's *completely* wrong. But we have to be smart. We can't go off half-cocked."

"What are you so afraid of? I could crush those puny little creatures with a single hoof! I'm stronger than the lot of them!"

"Now, Xena, violence isn't the answer," chided Gizzabelle. "And we've got to be careful with Bandit. You never know what kind of tricks he's got in store."

"He's a bloody ratbag," seconded Buddy, "and he's like as not to pull a swiftie if we're not careful."

"We should throw that dirty varmint out on his stubby stump of a tail!" bellowed Xena.

"I hear you, Xena, really I do, but can you just hold off until we come up with a plan?" asked Gizzabelle. "This may be our one and only chance and we don't want to blow it."

Xena snorted. Patience was not her forte.

"Just one night," Gizzabelle assured her.

Xena stared at her for a long moment, then nodded reluctantly. "One night. That's it."

"Thank you, Xena. We'll figure it out. I promise."

The fiery young cow turned to go. "I don't know how I'll hide it from the others," she said. Playacting wasn't her forte either; she wore her heart on her hide. "It makes me sick to my stomachs. They're sure to notice something's wrong."

"Don't talk to anyone. Just go to straight to your plot," Buddy advised. "It'll turn out tickety-boo."

"Alright," Xena said. "I'll give it a 'burl.'"

They exchanged wan smiles.

As soon as Xena left, Buddy got straight to the point. "What do you reckon we ought to do?"

Gizzabelle was silent. "I think Xena's right," she finally said. "They've got to go."

"Stone the crows!" exclaimed the shepherd. "You really want to give them the flick?"

"I don't see any other way. Not after what they've done."

"Things are crook in Tallarook," agreed Buddy. "Have been for yonks. But givin' em the heave ho? How do you reckon we do that?"

Gizzabelle tapped a claw thoughtfully. "We've got to get everyone on board or it might not work—or even if it does, it could split the farm and that could be a disaster. The problem is the animals are so petrified that they can't survive without the CEO and the board, I'm afraid Bandit will be able to play to their fears and convince them that there's no other way than to go along with him. I think our best bet is to tell some of the animals ahead of time and make sure they are on our side, then tell the others right beforehand and hope their outrage and disgust is enough to help them push past their fear."

"Right-o," said Buddy. "We've got to have a strong coalition going in; animals who can't be sucked in by Bandit's furphies. Who can we count on?"

It was only when they began trying to identify potential supporters that Gizzabelle and Buddy appreciated the full impact of the loss of their banished co-workers for the first time. Mordecai, ever the outspoken critic, would have laid bare the reasons for revolt while Newton's clear-eyed logic could have plotted them a roadmap to revolution. Peanut's passion could have rallied the animals to the cause and Sausage's support would have imbued it with legitimacy. They had been stripped of four of their strongest allies before they had even begun.

Running through everyone who was left, they were surprised by how few animals they could reliably depend upon to join them. Most of the farm animals, it had to be admitted, were fully and thoroughly domesticated and liked nothing so much as predictability, habits and routines. Rebels and revolutionaries they were not. Throwing out Bandit and his *crow*-nies would definitely be going against their grain and they'd need a lot of help to get them over the hump.

In the end, they decided to pick one member of each species to inform ahead of time, win over to their side, and arm with talking points to withstand any of Bandit's arguments. They selected Millie, Jellybean, Clementine, Hamish, and Jock as the most level-headed and well-respected of all the animals. Unfortunately, they were among the most humble and self-effacing as well and none had the charisma or oratory flair to really rally a crowd.

"That's where I'm hoping Xena and Gizmo come in, and even Henriette if we're lucky," said Gizzabelle. "It's hard to know which way she'll break. She's no fan of Bandit's but she's absolutely terrified of Kratchet. She could go either way."

"Speaking of unknowns…" broached Buddy carefully, "what about Poe? Can we count on him to stand with us? You know him better than anyone."

"I don't know if I do know him anymore," replied Gizzabelle sadly. "If I ever did."

"He still is our best reader and the only one with humanspeech," said Buddy. "If he is with us, that'll go a long way in assuring the other animals. If he's not, it could be the deciding factor. Do you reckon we should approach him before we confront the others?"

Gizzabelle considered the question, which cut right to the heart of the dilemma she'd been struggling with for days.

Finally, she shook her head. "It's possible he would be on our side, but I don't think we can count on him. We don't know where his allegiances lie. We don't even know if he knew about what happened with the sheep."

Seeing Buddy's crestfallen expression, Gizzabelle felt a stab of guilt.

"You don't really think he might've known, do you?" asked Buddy. "He's always been a good mate."

Gizzabelle hated that she was even considering it, but she had to face reality. "It's possible," she said. "It's even possible he ordered it. How else could they even have gotten it done without his humanspeech?"

"I hadn't thought of that," said Buddy glumly.

"And if we tell him about our plan and he *isn't* on board, he might tip off Bandit beforehand. We can't risk squandering the element of surprise."

Buddy nodded in agreement and as the two concentrated on mapping out their game plan for the next day, neither noticed when the dark figure that had been watching them from the barn window spread its wings and flew away.

Gizzabelle was alone in the cornfield. The corn was so tall and thick that she could barely see two inches in front of her beak. She slogged forward, struggling valiantly to bushwhack the dense stalks with her wings, which were woefully ill-suited to the task.

In the distance, she thought she could hear Buddy's urgent barking but she couldn't make out what he was saying. The sounds of other animals in panic began to nip at the edges of her consciousness, an indistinct hum that quickly swelled into a thunderous roar of bleating, bellowing, squealing, and clucking.

A stampede!

Before she could even wonder what kind of a stampede included *chickens*, the ground beneath her began to tremble and a spooked cow bolted past, nearly trampling her in its rush to escape. Gizzabelle dove out of the way and straight into the path of a wild-eyed sheep, who only managed to avoid a collision by vaulting over the terrified chicken. It galloped away at full speed without even a backwards glance.

Desperate to see what was pursuing them, Gizzabelle flapped her wings and was able to get just enough height that she could peek over the tops of the cornstalks. In the brief moment she was aloft, she caught a glimpse of the corn picker zig-zagging crazily through the field, a deranged-looking Bandit at the helm. Animals ran this way and that, trying to get out of the way of the rampaging machine spewing ears of corn in every direction. Just as Gizzabelle started to lose altitude, Bandit suddenly turned her way and looked straight at her, a wicked smile curling his lips.

Landing on the ground with a thump, the little hen popped up and began to run as fast as she could. She could hear the metallic grind of the corn picker behind her. She chanced a look over her shoulder only to see the enormous machine bearing down on her, slashing the corn stalks and sucking them into its depths. Its roar was deafening and she could feel its pulsations vibrating throughout her body.

Just as she was about to be overrun by the giant beast, a voice from above cawed to her.

"Gizzabelle, this way!"

Without thinking, she leapt sideways and covered her head with her wings. The corn picker whizzed past. In its wake, a huge ear of corn rolled toward her. When it came to rest at her feet, the green husk rolled down of its own accord. Where there should have been corn, though, there was a head.

It was Sausage's.

The great hog opened his eyes but he seemed to stare unseeingly into space.

"The way is in the heart," he intoned. "Let your heart lead you."

Suddenly Gizzabelle felt something inexorably pulling her away and Sausage's words echoed softly, as if from a great distance. "Let your heart lead you."

Gizzabelle twitched and her eyelids fluttered open. She was

burrowed in her nest, safe amid the whistling snores of the other chickens. Her pulse was still racing, but she felt lighter and more buoyant than she had in weeks. After weeks of struggle, Gizzabelle finally knew beyond a shadow of a doubt what her heart was saying.

She trusted Poe!

Confident that the dream was an unambiguous message from her Higher Chicken, Gizzabelle determined to put her fears and suspicions to bed once and for all. Certainly Poe had made mistakes, but his intentions had always been pure. All they had to do was make him see where the best interests of the farm lay and he would join with them. She was sure of it.

She hopped out of her nest, eager to go tell Buddy her newfound conviction. They would present their case Poe, win him over to their side, then confront Bandit and the crows together.

As she stepped out of the henhouse and into the sunlight, her fears of the night before seemed like mere phantoms with no more substance than fog. What could Bandit really do to them? He had no actual power other than what they had given him.

She stiffened her spine and puffed out her chest boldly. It was time for them to take that power back!

Striding ahead full of purpose and determination, Gizzabelle had just rounded the corner of the henhouse when she heard a loud crack and then everything went black.

Gizzabelle slowly came to, the throbbing pain in her head gradually receding as she became aware of voices speaking nearby.

"You're crazy if you think *I'm* going to carry them around for you," croaked one.

"Oh, please, Jax," cooed a higher-pitched voice. "I just *can't* leave my jewels behind…"

Gizzabelle opened her eyes and tried to orient herself. With equal parts panic and disbelief, she realized she was in the farmhouse living room, her wings and feet tied together! The bright sunlight streaming through the window told her she had been unconscious for at least several hours.

"You can afford to buy new ones with your share of the proceeds," continued Jax, who was standing nearby with Fae, their backs to Gizzabelle.

Trying to be as discreet as possible, the little hen furtively tested her bonds, hoping they were loosely tied and she might be able to wriggle free and slip away. Unfortunately, the bindings were tight— undoubtedly Bandit's handiwork, she thought. The nimble-fingered burglar was the only one capable of tying such accomplished knots.

"Well, now, look who's awake!" boomed the raccoon, who had appeared out of nowhere as if she'd summoned him into existence simply by thinking of him. The crows cast an indifferent glance in her direction before flying upstairs to continue their conversation in private.

"Glad to see you are back in the land of the living," sneered the raccoon, standing over her and staring down on her prone form triumphantly.

"What do you think you're doing?" demanded Gizzabelle with more confidence than she felt. "You have no right to hold me here. Let me go immediately!"

"Tsk-tsk," chided Bandit. "Enough with the feigned outrage. You're a dangerous agitator and you know it."

"W-what do you mean?"

"Don't play innocent with me. I know all about your hostile takeover attempt."

Gizzabelle's eyes widened and Bandit took obvious delight in her shocked expression. "That's right. A little birdie told me everything."

A little birdie? Had Poe overheard them talking last night? Gizzabelle's heart sank as she rewound the conversation in her mind. If he had, he would have heard her telling Buddy she didn't trust him...could that been enough for him to rat them out to Bandit? Could her betrayal have sabotaged their whole plan?

The raccoon smirked as if he could read her thoughts.

Suddenly Gizzabelle saw something that made her blood run cold. The pads of Bandit's hands were stained crimson and his fur was speckled with dried flecks of red.

Blood red.

A horrible notion took possession of the young hen.

"Where's Poe?" she squawked, her voice shrill in panic.

Bandit narrowed his eyes and observed her carefully before

replying. "He's left the farm. Permanently."

"You're lying! He wouldn't leave us in the lurch!"

"That's not what you said last night," the raccoon said, gloating as Gizzabelle crumpled under the blow.

"What have you done to him?" she squeaked.

Bandit bared his teeth in a carnivorous grin. "Nothing. I assure you he left quite voluntarily." Then, unable to resist twisting the knife, he added, "Can you really blame him after what you said?"

A tear formed at the edge of Gizzabelle's eye. She would have loved to believe Poe had simply left the farm—even if it was her fault—if it meant he was alive and well. But she just didn't think it was true. The evidence pointed to something far more sinister.

"Are you going to kill me?" she asked dully.

"What good would that do? Except to make you a martyr to the cause," the raccoon said lightly, apparently not at all offended by the question. "No, it's better if you're alive—although not essential."

Gizzabelle bucked up a little at Bandit's flippancy. "The other animals won't stand for it! As soon as Buddy finds out, he'll come and rescue me."

Bandit arched an eyebrow. "And who, praytell, will rescue Buddy?" He grinned. "I believe our faithful shepherd is... *tied up* for the time being." It was only then that Gizzabelle registered the faint barking coming from the direction of the Great Tree.

She cast about for another way out. "Xena!" she squawked. "Xena knows about what you did to the sheep! She's already ready to break you in half!"

Bandit nodded, looking decidedly unworried. "As I said, you're more useful to us alive. A little *leverage*, if you will. Xena and the others won't do anything to jeopardize your safety."

"But that'll never work," insisted Gizzabelle. "You can't keep me here indefinitely!"

"You're absolutely right. But we don't need to keep you indefinitely, just until the farm sells."

"*WHAT???*"

"That's right. We're selling the farm."

Gizzabelle felt as if the floor had disappeared from beneath her. *Everything* they had done was to save the farm from being sold.

Now all their efforts would be for nothing.

"B-b-but *why?*" she stammered. "You don't need money. You don't buy food. You don't even seem to like bling. So what do you need money for?"

"Gizzabelle, dear, I'm not a petty thief," he chided her. "Only small timers actually care about the loot." He straightened up proudly. "I'm a *master* burglar."

"I don't understand," she croaked.

"It's not about what the money can *buy*," he explained patiently, as if instructing a none-too-bright hatchling. "Money's just a way of keeping score."

Gizzabelle gave a strangled cheep. "Score? This is just a *game* to you?"

"Of course!" the raccoon exclaimed. "It's the most wonderful game of all! There's nothing like the thrill of pulling off the perfect heist and getting away with it. Proving you're smarter than everyone else, a champion, a *winner.*"

Gizzabelle recoiled. "You're sick!"

He shook his head reproachfully, condescension oozing from every pore. "Of course, *you* wouldn't have any experience with it, but I assure you, once you've felt that rush, you'll chase it the rest of your life. Nothing else comes close—not food, not bling, not rutting, *nothing.* Winning's the ultimate high. And you can never have enough."

Gizzabelle sat back, utterly deflated. There was not a shred of conscience or decency she could appeal to, not an ounce of animal compassion. Bandit was a predator through and through, and she could think of nothing whatsoever that she could offer him that would count for anything in his screwed-up scale of values. Still, she had to try something.

"But, really, haven't you've *already* won?" she said. "You've beaten the humans at their own game. Run the farm right under their pathetic, deficient noses without them even knowing! Made fools of them all. Why not just leave now? Get out while the getting's good?"

"You make a good point," said Bandit, nodding thoughtfully. Then he was in her face, his nose just millimeters from her beak, his eyes glittering dangerously. "But it wasn't the *humans* plotting to throw me out on my 'stubby stump of a tail,' was it?"

Gizzabelle gulped hard.

"No," he continued, "I believe that was *someone else* who wanted to organize the animals to oust me and take over the farm."

"Take over the farm?"

Both Gizzabelle and Bandit looked up in surprise.

"Poe!" squawked Gizzabelle to the raven on the windowsill. "You're alive!"

Poe didn't look at her; he kept his eyes on Bandit, who was staring back at him with equal intensity. Poe flew down and landed next to them.

"What are you doing here?" asked Bandit, his tone carefully neutral. "Considering how you left, I didn't think you'd be back."

Poe shrugged. "Yeah, I was a little...hot when I left. But after I had some time to think about it, you're right. What have the other animals done to deserve my loyalty? Like this one,"—he jutted his beak in Gizzabelle's direction—"having the *nerve* to ball me out after all I did for her. Ungrateful banty."

Gizzabelle shrank back at the venom in his voice. Was he truly angry or just putting on a show for Bandit? If so, he was certainly convincing.

"I figured I might as well come back and help you out with that rendering thing after all. I mean, like you said, why not? They're already dead."

Bandit narrowed his eyes skeptically. "Well, that's quite a reversal," he finally said. "We appreciate the offer, of course, but we already took care of it. Shylock's humanspeech is coming along quite nicely. Nothing extemporaneous yet, but he can follow a script."

Poe nodded nonchalantly. "So what's with the chickabiddy? Why's she trussed up like a Thanksgiving turkey?"

"Shylock overheard her plotting a hostile takeover," said Bandit. "With Buddy and that bull dyke."

Poe gawped. "Really? What are we going to do?"

Gizzabelle thought she saw Bandit relax slightly. Poe's easy, reflexive use of "we" seemed to have eased his suspicions.

"What's the advice I gave you the first time we met?"

Poe frowned. "You mean back at Granny Ann's? Um, I don't know...always have an exit strategy?"

"Exactly! Knowing how—and *when*—to get out is the part everyone misses."

"No kidding. We learned that with the stock market, didn't we?"

Bandit scowled. "No one could have seen that coming," he grumbled.

Poe quickly changed the subject. "So what exactly do you mean, *get out?*"

"We're selling the farm," announced Bandit.

Poe took the news without even blinking an eye. Gizzabelle's heart plummeted; surely no one's acting skills were *that* good.

"We stand to make a pretty penny," continued the raccoon. "Especially with the asset stripping beforehand."

"Asset stripping?"

"We'll sell off the livestock herds separately," explained Bandit. "You get more money that way."

"You won't even keep the animals on the farm?" squawked Gizzabelle furiously. "You rotten, no-good weasely—"

Suddenly there was a commotion from out in the barnyard. It was the chicken alert system sounding the alarm: "*HUMAN! HUMAN COMING!*"

Poe appeared genuinely surprised and Bandit's ears flattened against his head, his fur on end. Jax and Fae came darting down the staircase, pulling up short when they saw Poe.

"What's going on?" cawed Jax.

"We don't know. I'll go check it out," said Poe, spreading his wings and turning toward the open window.

"No," commanded Bandit sharply. He eyeballed Poe, his suspicions reignited. "You stay. Jax will go."

Chastened, Poe sat back on his heels and watched the other bird fly off.

"Where are the rest of the crows?" Bandit asked Fae.

"How should I know?" she asked somewhat petulantly.

"Go find them," he ordered. "We need everyone here."

Fae looked as if she might object, but thought the better of it and took off behind Jax.

An uncomfortable silence descended among the three remaining animals. Gizzabelle noticed that Bandit positioned himself between her and Poe.

After a couple of interminable minutes, Bandit impatiently hauled Gizzabelle up by the trusses and began pulling her toward the low windows that looked onto the front porch. Her ankles bound together, she had to hop to keep up with him.

Keeping one elbow hooked around Gizzabelle's neck, Bandit drew back the curtain and peered out the window. The little hen glanced back at Poe, who took advantage of Bandit's momentary distraction to give her a wink.

Gizzabelle's heart soared! Relief and joy exploded inside her, along with a jumble of questions. Did Poe have a plan? Was the alarm part of it? Was a human really coming or was it just a ploy? Was it Penny who was coming?

When Bandit pulled away from the window with an annoyed, "Can't see anything," Gizzabelle had to quickly rearrange her face and wipe the goofy grin from her beak.

A few seconds later, Jax flew into the room. "It's a man in a red truck," he reported. "Should be here any minute."

"Okay," said Bandit. "Go help Fae round up the others. That dodo couldn't find her way out of a paper bag if you left her a breadcrumb trail."

With a quick nod, Jax headed back outside.

Gizzabelle held her breath as they heard the truck pull up beside the house and its door slam shut. Soon heavy footfalls strode up the stairs to the porch and a loud knock came at the door.

"Bob, you there? It's me, Jim Kratchet."

Gizzabelle and Poe involuntarily exchanged a horrified look. Gizzabelle realized instantly that Kratchet was definitely *not* part of Poe's plan.

"I saw your sign," Kratchet continued. "Want to make you an offer."

Bandit pulled back the curtain again and peeked out, still holding Gizzabelle by the throat. She was able to make out the man's legs and the wooden "FARM FOR SALE" sign he held at his side. The crudely-formed letters were written in bright red paint.

Gizzabelle thought of Bandit's hands. *Not blood—paint!*

"I see you in there, watching me," Kratchet said.

Bandit quickly stepped back from the window and let the curtain fall into place. "Answer him," he instructed Poe in a loud whisper.

The raven hesitated, his glance flickering to Gizzabelle.

Fury ignited in Bandit's eyes. "I *knew* you were faking!" he hissed.

Bandit turned back to Poe and tightened his grip on Gizzabelle's throat.

"Answer him and make a deal or she's done for!"

"No, don't—!" Gizzabelle managed before Bandit cut off her airflow. Locking her eyes with Poe's, she frantically shook her head, wordlessly begging him not to give in to Bandit's threat.

For a moment Poe appeared paralyzed. Then Bandit squeezed so hard Gizzabelle's eyes began to bulge.

"Stop!" croaked Poe. "I'll do it—just *stop*!" Bandit relaxed his grip but didn't remove his hands. "I'm sorry," Poe murmured to Gizzabelle. "I couldn't..."

A tear trickled out of the corner of her eye. Everything they had fought for was lost.

Poe hopped toward the door. "Yeah, Kratchet, I'm here," he said in Farmer Bob's voice.

"Open up and let's talk about this face to face." Kratchet reached for the doorknob.

Poe shot Bandit a *what now?* look and in reply the raccoon tightened his paws around Gizzabelle's throat.

The door opened an inch.

"No!" Poe yelled. "I'm, uh, sick. Yeah, that's it...I'm contagious." He gave a short burst of coughs. "But I can hear you just fine from here. What've you got to say?"

"Well, I know we've had our differences in the past, Bob," Kratchet said in his most ingratiating tone, "but I want to help you out. I can see that the place has really gotten away from you lately. When was the last time you cut the grass, Bob? And your pasture fence is wrecked—it's a wonder the cows don't just walk right out! This farm's clearly too much for you to handle anymore. But I'm

willing to give you a good price despite its condition. You'll entertain an offer?"

Bandit stared at Poe pointedly.

"I believe that's what 'for sale' ordinarily means," said the raven,
unable to keep the churlishness out of his voice.

"Excellent, excellent," Kratchet chortled. "Glad to hear you're
willing to be reasonable. No sense letting personal opinions get in
the way of doing business, eh, Bob?"

Suddenly there was a *rip* and yell. "WHAT THE—?!?"

Poe and Bandit both rushed to the window, Bandit dragging
Gizzabelle with him.

Kratchet was standing with his back to them, a few dangling
threads hanging where his back pocket should have been.

"You've ruined my pants, you bloody bugger!" Kratchet yelled
at the goat contentedly munching on his back pocket. Gizzabelle
gasped. *Mordecai!*

"What's that old crank doing here?" muttered Bandit under his
breath.

When Kratchet stooped to pick up his wallet, which had fallen to
the floor, Mordecai promptly butted him smack-dab in the keister
and sent him sprawling across the porch.

Out of nowhere Buddy bounded up the stairs and grabbed the
wallet in his mouth. He waited until Kratchet scrambled to his feet,
then took off down the porch stairs, still clutching the wallet in his
teeth. Turning to make sure Kratchet was following him, he sprang
away as soon as the man got close.

This scene repeated over and over, Kratchet coming within feet
of the shepherd, only to have Buddy leap away again, mischievously
dangling the coveted wallet from the side of his mouth. Kratchet
trailed after him, filling the air with a stream of increasingly colorful
invective. Soon Buddy had led him to the side of the house and the
two disappeared around the corner.

Poe flew over to the side window to keep the dog and man in
his sights. Bandit dragged Gizzabelle over to it as well, but unlike
the ones overlooking the porch, this window was far higher off the
floor. He could climb on the overstuffed floral armchair and see out
but he wouldn't be able to take Gizzabelle with him. The raccoon

glanced at the hen undecidedly, then up at Poe, perched on the back of the chair and peering raptly out the window.

His curiosity getting the best of him, Bandit released Gizzabelle, crawled up on the arm of the chair, and pressed his nose to the glass.

Her trusses still as tight as ever, Gizzabelle could do nothing but sit there wondering what they were seeing out in the barnyard, what Buddy and Mordecai were up to, and how Mordecai had even gotten there in the first place. Then, out of the corner of her eye, she saw a flash of pink and Peanut materialized at her side.

"Shhhh…" whispered the diminutive pig, ducking his tiny head to the string binding her. He wrapped it around one of his needle-sharp incisors and snapped it in two, then repeated the maneuver twice more. The bonds slipped off and slid to the floor.

Peanut jutted his chin in the direction of the kitchen. Nodding her understanding, Gizzabelle set off toward the pet door, careful not to let her claws clack on the floor.

"Hey, you there! *Stop!*"

Bandit and Poe whipped around to see Shylock, who had just flown in the back window with the other crows in tow, then followed his gaze to Gizzabelle, who had frozen in the middle of the room.

With an enraged growl, Bandit leaped onto the floor, oblivious to Peanut still under the chair, and took off after the little chicken. Gizzabelle bolted for the kitchen. Poe swooped after the raccoon, but found himself surrounded by the crows.

"Not so fast, Mr. Big Shot," said Shylock.

"Always acting like your guano doesn't stink," chimed in Jax.

Poe looked around the circle for allies, but even Fae, Nessa, and Rune seemed set on keeping him corralled. He watched helplessly from above as Bandit closed in on the fleeing hen.

With a prey's sixth sense, Gizzabelle could feel Bandit right on her tail—and gaining. Knowing she'd never be able to outrun the raccoon on a straightaway, she realized her only hope was to dodge and weave like a hunted rabbit. Just as she reached the doorway to the kitchen, she slammed on the brakes and veered back into the living room.

Bandit overshot his target and in his haste to change course,

tripped over his own feet, somersaulted across the kitchen's lino-
leum floor, and hit the cabinets on the other side. Back in the living
room, Gizzabelle scampered behind the couch, and allowed herself
a moment to catch her breath. Her lungs felt like they were about to
explode and her legs were beginning to shake like jelly.

"Gizzabelle, run! He's coming!" squawked Poe.

The little hen shot out from behind the couch and sprinted to the
other side of the living room, Bandit hot on her heels. She darted
between Poe's birdcage and the chair next to it, a space too narrow
for the raccoon. He plowed through anyway, sideswiping the cage's
base and knocking it to the floor with an enormous crash.

Out in the open once again, Gizzabelle was in full-blown survival
mode. Running solely on instinct and adrenaline, her entire being
was focused on escaping Bandit. She raced across the thin rug faster
than she would have believed possible, but it was still not enough.
His four legs to her two allowed Bandit to easily close the distance
between them.

With his bird's eye view of the action, Poe could see from Bandit's
expression that his kill instinct had been triggered and there would
be no stopping him until it had been satiated. There was no doubt
about it, Gizzabelle was running for her life.

"Here it comes!" crowed Fae in a mix of horror and delight as
Bandit narrowed the gap. She squeezed her eyes shut against the
coming carnage.

Poe took advantage of the crow's momentary inattention to
barrel past her and make a break for Bandit. He dove like a missile
and was able to get in two good pecks on the head—allowing
Gizzabelle to squeak out of Bandit's grasp—before Shylock tackled
him midair and the two birds spun out and crashed to the floor.

Gizzabelle kept running. Her energy was flagging and she willed
her legs to keep pumping. Almost immediately, she could feel Bandit
brushing her tail feathers again. There was nowhere to run, nowhere
to hide.

This is it, she thought. *It's over.*

Suddenly there was an awful screeching, hissing yowl behind
her, joined by an outraged snarl and the sounds of a ferocious fra-
cas. Without stopping, Gizzabelle looked over her shoulder just in

time to see Bandit fling Coco against the wall, her body sliding limp and lifeless to the floor.

Barely missing a beat, the raccoon zeroed in on her once again and picked up the chase as if the cat had been nothing more than an irksome mosquito. Gizzabelle turned back ahead and redoubled her efforts, only to realize she was fast running out of room and she'd soon run right into the wall.

Poe, who was in the air again, saw her predicament. "Under the couch!" he cawed. "Run under the couch!"

Gizzabelle took a hard right and darted under the couch. Popping out the other side, she started running in the opposite direction toward Poe, who was hovering in the middle of the room above the overturned cage. She could sense Bandit behind her, but she kept her eyes trained on Poe, whose gaze seemed like a lifeline pulling her forward.

As she ran toward him, she could see by Poe's anguished expression that Bandit was nearly upon her. She had hoped he would give her some direction—right or left?—but the raven, seemingly out of options and paralyzed by fear, was silent.

Then an unmistakable baritone rang out clear and calm.

"Fly, my child, spread your wings and *fly*."

Gizzabelle did as she was told. She extended her wings as far as they would stretch and gave a powerful flap. She was running so fast that she got excellent lift and soared over the cage. Bandit, immediately behind her, ran right into the cage's open door and hit the bars behind at full speed, knocking himself out.

Poe's beak hung open in astonishment. Shaking himself from his stupefaction, the raven slammed the cage door shut and slid the latch into place.

"Jesum crow!" squawked Jax.

Quickly assessing the situation and Bandit's changed circumstances, the crows promptly flew the coop.

However, Poe realized they couldn't count Bandit out yet. Even if the crows hadn't recognized it, he knew that the simple latch would be no deterrent to the masked escape artist once he awoke.

"Gizzabelle, you've got to get out *now*. This won't keep him long," he said to the hen, who had landed safely—if not terribly gracefully—on the other side of the cage. "Maybe you can get Buddy here before he wakes up. Even if he comes to, I might be able to hold him off for a bit longer if I peck at his hands…"

"No!" snapped Gizzabelle. "It's too dangerous. If he wakes up, just let him out."

Bandit groaned and rolled onto one side.

"Gizzabelle, go," said Poe urgently.

"Promise me," she insisted.

The two were locked in a silent standoff when Peanut trotted up, a padlock—one of Bandit's padlocks—in his mouth.

"Peanut, you're a genius!" shrieked Gizzabelle.

Peaunt carried the lock to the cage and working together, the three animals maneuvered it around the bars. But when it came to snapping it shut, they simply didn't have the muscle power.

Peanut pressed his snout against the bottom of the lock while Gizzabelle and Poe pushed on the shackle. It didn't budge.

Bandit shifted and his eyelids fluttered.

"Hurry!" Gizzabelle whispered. "He's waking up!"

Peanut turned and threw his tiny shoulder against the lock.

"On the count of three, give it everything you've got," Poe instructed them. "One, two, *three!*"

They pushed with all their might and the lock snapped shut with a satisfying click. Bandit jolted upright at the sound, still clearly disoriented and struggling to focus.

Gizzabelle sat down with a hard thump, relief washing over her.

"That was amazing!" cawed Poe. "I didn't know you could fly like that!"

"Me neither," Gizzabelle admitted. "I completely forgot that when I molted, my flight feathers grew back. What a birdbrain I am." She shook her head ruefully. "Fences of the mind…"

"Now, Gizzabelle, you are anything but a—"

Suddenly there was an outraged yell from the barnyard followed by an unrepeatable anti-chicken slur, abruptly reminding them that there was another enemy—far bigger and even more deadly—just outside the door.

CHAPTER 19

I'll wipe that shit-eating grin right off his g-damn face.

It was bad enough how he'd been humiliated on the porch, rear-ended by that nasty, numpty goat and sent sprawling onto the ground in such a ridiculous manner. Wouldn't the insolent patsies back in the office have a field day with that? Kratchet down on his hands and knees and taking it in the arse! Oh, how they'd snicker.

There was nothing Kratchet hated more than being made a fool of. He was a man of importance, a man of influence. A captain of industry, you might say. His net worth would make Midas sick with envy. He deserved—was *owed*—admiration and respect. By God, he wasn't some poor schmuck to be trifled with or made into an effing laughing stock.

But now, now he was being toyed with by a dog. A damned *dog*!

Every time he approached the mangy mutt only to have him prance away at the last possible second, always staying *just* out of reach, Kratchet felt his blood pressure hike up another notch. He'd like to have kicked the leg-humping mongrel smack into next Tuesday. Or better yet, gotten out his trusty Winchester and popped the sorry son of a bitch right in the face. See how he liked *that*.

But, no, he cautioned himself, he couldn't be sure he was out of McMann's sight and until the deal was sealed, he had to play nice. People were such sentimental saps, getting their panties all in a knot when you didn't treat their precious pets like they pissed rainbows and shit gold. Kratchet knew better. Animals were animals. A half step up from turnips.

"Here, doggy, doggy," he gritted out through clenched teeth. "Nice doggy." He made another lunge for his wallet and again the canine easily sprang away with his treasure. Scowling, Kratchet glanced back at the window, wondering if McMann was watching. He thought he could see movement behind the curtain. *No doubt getting his jollies at my expense, the prat.*

Well, he'd have the last laugh. The stupid old fool was probably so far in debt that he'd take any amount Kratchet offered and be happy to get it. He had no head for business, never had. Bob McMann was a relic, the last of a dying breed who had stubbornly clung to the old ways and refused to change with the times. He'd run the farm into the ground and now Kratchet stood to snatch it up at a firesale price.

I'll give him five grand less for every time that friggin' mutt yanks my chain, Kratchet promised himself, feeling marginally cheered by the prospect.

"That friggin' mutt" danced back and forth in a semi-circle around him. Then he laid the wallet down and stood over it, his tail wagging vigorously.

Taking a new tack, Kratchet pretended indifference, whistling and oh-so-innocently cloud gazing while inching closer and closer. But when he made his grab, the dog swiped the wallet right out from under him and Kratchet crashed face first to the ground, eating dirt and ripping a hole in his pants at the knee.

Picking himself up while spewing a stream of vitriol, Kratchet suddenly had the eerie sensation that he was being watched. He could've sworn that all the chickens in the barnyard were not only staring at him, but looking down their nasty beaks at him like they were somehow *better* than him. Of course, that was sheer nonsense, but still...

Suddenly a bunch of crows flew over his shoulder and across the barnyard toward the fields. The chickens seemed extremely interested in the crows' exodus, clucking and cheeping excitedly. The dog, too, stared after the birds, the wallet hanging precariously out of one side of his mouth.

"If you don't drop that *right now*," the man growled under his breath, "I'm gonna come here at night and poison your damn Alpo, see if I don't. Then you'll—OUUCH! Why you chickenshit little peckerhead!" Kratchet glowered at the black-and-white chicken who had just given his ankle a vigorous peck. The impudent cockerel stared back at him brazenly.

In fact, *all* of the chickens seemed to be glaring at him with their beady eyes. If he believed in animal sentience—which, of course, he didn't—he would have said that their attitude had somehow shifted from mocking to downright aggressive.

"Stare all you like," he muttered angrily. "The first thing I'll do when I buy this place is send the lot of you straight to the slaughterhouse."

One of the hens started squawking hysterically before falling over onto the ground while the rest of the chickens clucked in indignation and shot him the fisheye, almost as if they'd understood what he'd said.

Realizing the absurdity of attributing thoughts to *chickens*—beasts as dumb as rocks—Kratchet shook his head at his own folly. *Watch it, Jimmy boy. You're going soft in the head. Next thing you know, you'll think the damn birds are* talking *to you.*

Kratchet wasn't feeling so hot; his heart was racing and he felt light-headed. Admittedly he'd gained a few pounds since his collegiate football days, but chasing the infernal hound around the yard shouldn't have him gasping like he'd scaled Everest for Christ's sake. Maybe Marjorie was right; he should lay off the double cheeseburgers for lunch.

He sat down hard on a plastic drum. *I'll just take the weight off for a minute*, he told himself. *No reason not to. Besides, the blasted bonehead probably thinks it's a damn game. If I don't play along, soon enough he'll get bored and drop it.*

But as Kratchet waited for his ragged breathing to steady, the shepherd showed no indication of tiring, bounding back and forth with unflagging enthusiasm. *Bloody hell! At this rate, I'll be here 'til the frigging cows come home...* He was ready to wrap up this shit circus and have a stiff drink. He deserved it.

Suddenly there was a loud cawing from the direction of the house. A hush fell over the chickens. Even the dog froze, his ears perked up attentively. No one moved the entire time the cawing continued.

When the nonstop stream finally ended, the dog abruptly dropped the wallet on the ground and trotted away without a backwards glance.

What the—?

Shaking his head in disbelief, Kratchet heaved himself off the drum and scooped up his wallet. He strode over to the porch and knocked loudly on the door.

"McMann? Bob? I'm back. Just having a little, uh, *fun* with your dog. Quite the prankster, that one." He chuckled over-heartily. "We can get back to business now. So, where were we?"

"Seems to me that where we were was me telling you where you can shove your offer."

Kratchet's mouth worked like a fish out of water. "W-what do you mean? We were just about to make a deal! Why the hell did you change your mind?"

"Don't you recognize sarcasm when you hear it, *Jim*? You know I've stood up to you in city council, written editorials against your despicable business practices, told you to your face what I think of you and your ilk more times than I can count, so why on earth would you think I'd ever sell my farm to you? I'd sooner give it to the animals than let you have it!"

"Now, Bob—"

"Don't you *Bob* me!" bellowed the voice from behind the door. "We're not friends! Never have been and never will be. In fact, I want you off my porch and off my property—pronto! You'd better get moving before my attack cows run you through."

Kratchet snorted uncertainly. Attack cows? Surely the old geezer was jacking with him. He *had* to be joking…didn't he?

Then he heard the hoofbeats.

He turned to see cows flooding the driveway and stampeding toward the barnyard as if Pamplona's Running of the Bulls was right there in the U. S. of friggin' A.

Kratchet clutched his heart and a strangled—if unmanly—shriek escaped his lips.

His truck! His brand-new, fully-loaded Ford F-150 Raptor with a supercharged 5.2-liter V8 engine—they were headed right for it!

With a speed that belied his now-portly form, Kratchet shot off the porch and toward his beloved fully-loaded Ford F-150 Raptor just in time to see the first cow reach it.

"Get away from that!" Kratchet bellowed. "Shoo, shoo, you stupid cow!"

The slighted bovine glared at him, then very slowly—almost deliberately—scraped her horn from the tailgate all the way up the truck's side, never taking her eyes off him.

Kratchet groaned.

By then, the truck was surrounded by cattle. One kicked in a tail light; another smashed a side mirror. When a brown cow gouged the passenger side door, Kratchet doubled over as if he himself had been gored. But when he rose, his expression had changed from pain to fury.

"You mother effer!" he shouted at the offending heifer. "I'll kill you! I'll kill you all!"

The cows—each and every one of them—stopped dead and stared at him, completely uncowed. The one who had first scratched the truck—the ringleader, to Kratchet's mind—lowered her head and pawed the ground as if he'd waved a red cape in front of her.

Ice-cold fear bathed Kratchet's innards and his sphincter control suddenly became questionable. He took a step back.

"Now, see here..." he said in his best attempt at a placating tone.

The cow charged.

Kratchet turned and ran. All around the farmhouse he ran, the cow hot on his heels. Up and over the woodpile and back into the farmyard he ran. The former footballer weaved and veered through the rest of the cattle, who politely moved aside to let him pass un-molested, and raced toward the fence to the sheep pasture, hoping his exhausted legs wouldn't fail him before he could scale it and finally get out of reach of the deranged cow chasing him.

Just as he was about to reach the fence, his Brunello Cucinelli loafer squished into a huge, fresh pile of manure and slipped for-ward, sending him flat on his back in the self-same cowplop.

The cow behind him pulled up short and stood over him, wheez-ing and snorting, but no longer threatening in any way.

Sheep gathered on the other side of the fence. "Baa-ah-ah-ah," they bleated.

Curious cows and cackling chickens surrounded him, including the insolent little black-and-white cockerel who'd pecked him ear-lier. The dog and goat, joined by a braying mule, came over and peered down at him. As outrageous as it sounded, Kratchet knew with absolute certainty what they were doing, all of the infernal, godforsaken beasts.

They were *laughing*.

Kratchet sat up, feeling the warm ooze sticking his shirt—his favorite Brooks Brothers!—to his back. He furiously hoisted himself up and, cutting a path through the smirking animals, stormed back to the farmhouse. Stomping up the stairs, he pounded on the door.

"McMann! McMann, open up! You're gonna to pay for all the damage your psychotic nutjob animals have done to my truck. I'm gonna sue your miserable ass for more money than you've ever seen at one time. You won't have a pot to piss in by the time I'm done with you! *And* I'll have your freaking cows put down for being a menace to society!"

"Try it and I'll post the video of you all over the Internet," the voice from behind the door said calmly.

Kratchet drew back. "W-what video?"

"Those security cameras I've got all over the farm have *finally* justified themselves after all these years. I'll have you from every angle, running like a scared little girl. And that ending—classic! It's sure to go viral. Whadaya think, maybe a couple million hits? Could make me rich…maybe I'll post it after all."

"Wait!" Kratched bellowed. "Don't do that. I, uh, I'll take care of the truck myself. We don't need to get anyone else involved. We're neighbors and I can afford to be generous."

"My, my. You're so *generous*. How about this? You never show your face here again, never contact me in any way or do anything to remind me that you're alive, and that video never sees the light of day?"

"Uh, yeah. That sounds fine."

"I catch a whiff of you and it hits YouTube before you can say Jack Robinson."

"I *said* we had a deal!" gritted out Kratchet, unable to keep the anger out of his voice.

"Then why are you still here, darkening my door and stinking up my porch?"

Kratchet stood there for a moment, clenching and unclenching his jaw. Then, finally, he turned and stalked back into the barnyard. He marched through the cows who were still milling about and got into the truck without even noticing the large bird cage in the bed of the pickup that held one spitting-mad raccoon.

As he peeled out and they careened down the driveway in a cloud of dust, the filthy, stinking, muck-smeared captain of industry cursed cows and cow shit and impudent chickens and know-nothing farmers and security cameras and YouTube and stupid, peeping little nobodies who had nothing better to do with their time but try to pull their betters down to their pathetic level, all the while completely unaware that he was hurtling toward what would go down in history as perhaps the fiercest man vs. raccoon war ever waged, an epic battle of wills and wits that would test the very limits of their cunning, treachery, and pathological need to win—and, ultimately, bring ruin and misery down upon both their heads.

If he had looked in his rear-view mirror, he might have seen the animals in the barnyard—who were no less ignorant of what fate had in store for the feared human and hated Procyon, but would have heartily approved had they known—cheering and waving a triumphant goodbye. But he did not, instead continuing to rant and rave as the improbably well-matched future adversaries unwittingly sped off together in the fully-loaded Ford F-150 Raptor with a supercharged 5.2-liter V8 engine to their mutually-assured destruction.

Watching the truck disappearing down the road from the window, Gizzabelle sat back in disbelief. Could it be true? Were Bandit and Kratchet really gone—gone forever?

"Wow," breathed Gizzabelle. "You did it. You really did it!"

"*We* did it," Poe corrected. "All of us, together." Gizzabelle glanced back at Peanut, who was over by Coco. The cat—though sore and down one more of her allotted nine lives—was otherwise unharmed.

"We couldn't have done it without you," the chicken persisted. "If you hadn't come back, we would've been done for. But even after all those terrible things I said to you, you came back. I'm so sorry for everything I said. I had no right."

"No, you were *exactly* right. You made me realize how far off course I had strayed. I don't know what came over me. It was like I was bewitched. I got so caught up with making money, I lost sight of everything else. I can't explain it."

"To understand things, we must have once been in them, and to have come out of them," said Peanut, coming up behind them. "The one who is still under the spell, and the one who has never felt the spell, are equally incompetent."

Gizzabelle wondered fleetingly if that was a Sausagism or an original saying—a Peanutism. But then she wondered, what difference did it make? Wasn't *all* real wisdom timeless and universal, endlessly recycled generation after generation?

Suddenly the front door flew open.

Gizmo strutted inside. "That was *legendary*!" he crowed. "Did you see the expression on that stinkin' scavie's smug-ugly mug? He was madder than a wet hen! And Kratchet! Man, he about crapped his pants. It was awesome!"

"Gizmo!" Gizzabelle chided, but it was more of a knee-jerk reaction than an expression of any real outrage. Truth be told, she was just as thrilled as her brother. Regardless, as usual, the reprimand was like water off a duck's back.

"What're you doing hanging around in here?" demanded Gizmo. "C'mon—everyone is outside waiting for you."

Poe, Gizzabelle, and Peanut dutifully followed him onto the porch and into the barnyard, where all the rest of the animals were milling around, marveling amongst themselves and recounting— sometimes with comical embellishment—what they had seen and done. No one had all the pieces of the story and they were each trying to fill in the blanks.

When they saw Gizmo and the others emerge, they immediately barraged them with questions.

"Are you okay? What did that beast do to you?" squawked Clementine, rushing over to Gizzabelle's side.

"What are you doing here?" oinked Hamish to Peanut. "How did you get back?"

"Where've you been, mate? Where'd you find them?" Buddy asked Poe, jutting his snout toward Newton and Mordecai.

"What happened in there?" everyone wanted to know.

"Whoa, whoa! Easy! I don't know where to begin..." replied Poe. He thought for a moment.

"Well, I guess it all started when Bandit wanted me to do some things that, uh, weren't in the animals' best interests."

"What things?" squawked Henrietta apprehensively.

Poe's gaze flickered to Xena. What purpose would it serve to inform the other animals of the depth of Bandit's perfidy, the gross depravity in which they'd been unknowingly involved?

Xena gave a barely perceptible nod of agreement.

"That's not important right now," Poe told the panic-prone hen. "What matters is that even though I'd gone along with him in the past, this time I told him no." He stared meaningfully at Gizzabelle and the little hen looked at her claws, too bashful to meet his eye. "But he said if I wouldn't help him, he'd just get Shylock to since he was starting to humanspeak. I realized if I tried to stop him, he'd just replace me as CEO and then I wouldn't have any influence at all. I felt helpless to do anything.

"But then I thought, there was one thing I *could* do. Something to rectify another mistake I made by going along with Bandit. I could find Peanut and Newton and the others, and bring them back. So that's what I set out to do. I didn't tell anyone because I wasn't sure I'd find them, and I didn't want you to be disappointed," he said, again looking right at Gizzabelle.

"Luckily," he continued, "it wasn't as hard to locate them as I thought. I asked all the birds I flew across if they'd seen them. Mules, goats and pigs aren't too common in the forest—particularly when they're traveling together! It wasn't long before I got a bead on where they were living and I found them and told them to come home. They never should have left to begin with." He looked over at Newton and Mordecai. "I'm sorry for my part in it. I never should have gone along with it."

"You've got to stop apologizing," said Newton. "You were just doing what you thought was best at the time."

Buddy jumped in to give Poe—who appeared verklempt—a chance to collect himself. "We didn't know that Poe had gone or where," said Buddy, "and we knew that Bandit was out of control and we needed to do something. Gizzabelle and I had a chinwag about how we could take the farm back from Bandit."

"But Shylock overheard us and told Bandit," said Gizzabelle, surprising the shepherd with that bit of news. "He realized the gig was up so he decided to sell the farm before we had a chance to oust him. That night Bandit chained Buddy to the tree while he was sleeping and the next morning he hit me over the head and took me to the farmhouse, planning to hold me hostage in case any of the rest of the animals tried anything."

"The dirty varlet!" snorted Xena. "Is there no limit to how far he would sink?"

"None at all," grunted Mordecai. "He's as coldblooded a mammal as you'll ever have the displeasure to meet."

The other animals murmured angrily in agreement.

"We saw the 'For Sale' sign on the gate when we arrived," said Poe, picking up the tale again. "And when we got to the barnyard, Gizmo told us that he thought he'd seen Bandit drag Gizzabelle into the farmhouse. We could hear Buddy barking from the Great Tree. We didn't know if Gizzabelle was in danger or how much time we had, so we decided to split up."

"I unclipped Buddy's leash," interjected Gizmo eagerly. "Newton showed me how, but I did it!"

"I understand the mechanism," conceded Newton, "but my hooves are no use. I couldn't have done it without Gizmo." The little cockerel puffed out his chest proudly.

"Meanwhile," said Poe, "Peanut and I went to help Gizzabelle. Newton and Mordecai are too big to get through the pet door, but Peanut could slip right in. We didn't really have a plan, but at the very least, we hoped we could stall Bandit until Buddy could get there. But then, Kratchet showed up.

"That took us by surprise. I don't know what we would have done if it hadn't been for Buddy and Mordecai's crackerjack distraction."

"It was Newton's idea," elaborated Mordecai for the animals who hadn't seen. "I got ahold of the lowlife's precious wallet, and Buddy played keep away with it."

"You should've seen it!" said Gizmo. "Buddy had him running around all over the barnyard! It was killa!"

"Once Kratchet was out of the picture," continued Poe, "we were able to get Gizzabelle away from Bandit and, thanks to Peanut, lock him in the bird cage with one of his own locks," he said, skipping over the feather-raising details for Clementine's—and especially Henrietta's—sake. "When the crows saw that we'd trapped Bandit, they took off."

"I guess they were more attuned to which way the winds were blowing than I ever gave them credit for," said Gizzabelle dryly.

Poe guffawed, then, clearing his throat, he continued on. "That's when Gizzabelle had the brainstorm to get Xerxes to carry the cage to Kratchet's truck. So I cawed for the cows to come and to get Kratchet out of sight of the porch long enough for Xerxes to get in and out unseen."

"Chasing him around the house was perfect, Xena," said Gizzabelle.

"He was shittin' bricks!" Gizmo cackled. "What a frigging scaredy-cat."

"Gizmo," said Gizzabelle severely, "don't ever say that again. Cats aren't cowards any more than chickens are. Coco attacked Bandit when he was after me. She risked her life to save mine." Gizzabelle shot the ebony feline, who had since sauntered off the porch and was sunning herself in a patch of grass, a grateful look. "If it wasn't for Coco, I wouldn't be here. Her and Sausage."

Poe's head whipped around. "Sausage?" he croaked.

"Yeah, where *is* Sausage?" she said, scanning the crowd for the great hog. "I haven't had a chance to thank him yet."

Poe gave her an odd look. "He's, uh, not here."

"What do you mean? Where is he?"

Poe looked helplessly to Peanut, Newton, and Mordecai for aid. The mule and goat exchanged a glance, while Peanut appeared to be lost in thought.

"We don't know," Newton finally said.

A distressed rumble arose from the crowd.

"Why don't you tell them the whole story from when you left the farm," prompted Poe, "like you did me?"

"Alright, I'll try," Newton said, clearing his throat. "After we left the farm, we headed for the forest. We didn't have water or shelter, and the food from the backpacks ran out quick. We had no clue where we were going or how we were going to make it through the winter.

"I don't mind saying, I was scared out of my wits—we all were. Or at least the three of us. Sausage, now, he was calm as a millpond. He just said Nature would provide. But even though he wasn't as preoccupied with foraging for food as the rest of us were, whenever things were at their most desperate, ten times out of nine it would be Sausage who'd be the one that would find a little spring or a patch of mushrooms or whatever it was we needed to tide us over."

"It was the damnedest thing," confirmed Mordecai, with a decidedly out-of-character respect—even an awe—in his voice. "It was more than luck or whiz-bang olfactory. It was like he had a sixth sense."

"Yeah, well, whatever it was," said Newton, still clearly grappling with what he had witnessed, "he saved our hides more than once. But then there came a point when it seemed not even Sausage could scrounge up any food. The ground was frozen solid and everything was picked over. There was not even a single acorn to be found anywhere. I thought we were going to starve for sure.

"As the days passed with no food, we were getting weaker and weaker, but strangely enough, Sausage seemed to be getting stronger. Eventually he was out in front, keeping up a steady pace and leading like he knew just where he was going. It was all I could do to put one hoof in front of the other, but I thought if Sausage could do it, so could I. And then, as if things weren't bad enough, it started to sleet!"

"When it rains, it hails," observed Mordecai in what might have been his life motto.

"Technically, hail's a warm-weather phenomena," corrected Newton. "Hail forms when thunderstorm updrafts—"

"Newton!" barked Buddy. "Don't lose the plot, mate." The rest of the animals glared at the mule impatiently.

"Oh, um, sorry," he said. "I got off track. Where was I? Oh, yeah, we were desperate to find shelter from the storm. Then, just before it got too dark to keep going, Sausage led us through a thicket and down an embankment to a little rock cave big enough for us all to fit in. The sleet hitting the rocks made a real racket, but I was so exhausted, I fell right to sleep.

"In the morning, I woke up early, when the sun was just coming up. Peanut and Mordecai were sleeping beside me, but Sausage was gone. I went outside and couldn't believe my eyes. The cave was on the bank of a little stream, surrounded by a virtual orchard of untouched trees! There were fruits and nuts everywhere. It was like Shangri-La."

"A bleating improvement on *corn*," snorted Mordecai. "Corn, corn, and more corn—*bletch*. Variety's the spice of life."

"*Anyway*," said Newton pointedly, " I went and got Mordecai and Peanut, and we started feasting on apples and pecans. Sausage was still nowhere to be found, but there was no sign of a struggle or anything untoward, so we figured it wouldn't be long until he came back."

He stopped and a shadow crossed his face.

"But he never did," he finished sadly.

"We didn't find so much as a single hoofprint," said Mordecai. "It was as if he simply vanished. We never saw him again."

"No!" squawked Gizzabelle. "That can't be. Sausage was *here*! He was in the farmhouse. He spoke to me—I heard him!"

"When?" asked Poe. "I didn't hear anything."

"When I was headed for the bird cage with Bandit right on my tail. Sausage told me to fly. It was clear as if he was right beside me."

"But it couldn't have been him," said Poe. "How could he have fit through the pet door?"

Gizzabelle pulled up short. She hadn't considered that. "I don't know, but it was," she insisted. "I'm telling you, it was *him*."

"Gone, yet not gone," mused Peanut. "Nowhere, yet everywhere."

Shaking his head, Newton sidled over to Gizzabelle. "He's been like that ever since Sausage disappeared," he said, lowering his voice to a confidential whisper and nodding his chin toward Peanut. "At first, he just about went crazy looking for Sausage but then he went basically catatonic. Wouldn't talk, wouldn't eat, wouldn't sleep... we were really worried. Eventually he came out of it, but he was, um, well, *different*. He was so calm and collected, and half the time he sounds just like..."

"...Sausage," Gizzabelle supplied. "He sounds just like Sausage."

"Only listen," Peanut continued. "He is in the wind, the rain, the rushing stream." Gizzbelle and Newton shared a knowing look.

"Ah," said Buddy, his ears perking up with sudden understanding. "I reckon Sausage is with Farmer Bob now."

"What, you're saying he's *dead*?" squawked Gizmo.

"Nooo!" Henrietta shrieked. "It can't be! He can't be. I'd feel it in my bones!"

"Death is not an ending," said Peanut gently, "only a doorway."

The histrionic hen rocked back and forth as if she hadn't heard. "Doomed," she moaned, curling into the fetal position. "We're all doomed!"

"No, we're not!" Gizzabelle said more forcefully than she intended. "Didn't you hear what Peanut said? Sausage isn't gone. And I *know* it's true because I heard him."

"So what?" bleated a sheep. "Even if he isn't gone, how is that going to save us? So the cows chased Kratchet off for the time being. What's to keep him from coming back for revenge? And bringing the rest of the humans with him? They'll slaughter us one and all!"

"No they won't," said Gizzabelle excitedly. "We didn't tell you the best part yet! Poe told Kratchet that he took a video of him chasing Buddy and Xena chasing him and him slipping in the poop, and that he'd show it to all the other humans if Kratchet ever bothered us again! He wouldn't dare risk it."

"I know his breed. That sort would rather be stung to death by fire ants than be laughed at," agreed Mordecai. "Good thinking, Poe."

"*Oui,*" agreed Coco. "*Quelle bonne idée.*"

"We're just lucky he didn't realize the cameras are fakes," deflected the raven.

"Well, it did the trick," said Gizzabelle. "You saved us...again."

"Sometimes I'm afraid I've done more harm than good," said the raven ruefully. "But maybe that makes up for some of it. And here's something else, something that could save us *permanently.*"

"What?" lowed Buttercup eagerly. "What is it?"

"Before I left to find Sausage and the others, Bandit opened Farmer Bob's safe and inside was a will. That's a paper that tells what a human wants done with his possessions after he dies. In his will, it says that Farmer Bob left the farm to his friend Asa."

"Penny's granddad?" asked Gizmo.

"That's right," said Poe. "His farm is just a few miles away. I flew over it when I was looking for the others. I talked to his animals and they seemed, well...*happy*. Asa, he's like Farmer Bob. He's a good human. And best of all, he raises cows for milk, sheep for wool, and chickens for eggs—no meat!"

"What about pigs?" oinked Hamish anxiously.

"Apparently, he used to raise pigs, too, but he's just gone no-kill so now he he'll only be breeding them for show. Seems he finally gave in to his favorite granddaughter, the outspoken animal rights activist, who plans to take over his farm someday." He winked at Gizmo. "No doubt she's been even *more* outspoken lately after becoming friends with a certain bird..."

"Clutch!" Gizmo cackled. "Penny's the bomb! She'll make sure we're treated right."

"If we let Asa inherit the farm, we wouldn't have to worry anymore about making money or the humans coming and discovering us," said Poe. "We'd be safe."

The crowd rumbled enthusiastically.

"So what would we need to do?" asked Gizzabelle. "How do we let the humans know that Farmer Bob's gone?"

"Well, I don't think we'd want them digging up the grave," said Poe, casting an apologetic glance toward Buddy, who was visibly mortified by the very suggestion. "That would only raise all kinds of questions. But we could make it look as if he'd done himself in. With his supposed reclusive behavior lately, the fight with Asa, the allegations of alcoholism to Penny, and his money problems, I think the humans would buy it. I could even write out some kind of suicide note..."

"What do you think, Buddy?" asked Gizzabelle. "Would you be okay with that? I know it would tarnish Farmer Bob's memory, but for a good cause."

Buddy paused for only a heartbeat. "If it helps others, Farmer Bob would be all for it. That's the kind of bloke he was."

"Alright then," Poe exclaimed. "Looks like that's settled."

Suddenly a quiet voice spoke up from the back of the crowd.

"Excuse me, but I've got something to say."

Everyone turned in surprise.

"Of course, Millie," said Poe. "What is it?"

"The highest manifestation of life is that a being governs its own actions," said the mild-mannered cow. "Isn't that what Sausage told us?"

A ripple of surprise spread through the crowd.

Another voice rang out. "We are not creatures of circumstance," said Jock, "we are creators of circumstance."

"Do not be led by others," declared Jellybean. "Decide for yourself your own path," finished Ewina.

Gizzabelle shot Buddy an astonished glance. They'd underestimated the animals.

Poe scanned the crowd. "What are you saying? You want to keep on running the farm ourselves?"

"Why not?" said Mordecai. "Sure, we hit a few bumps in the road, but we were making it. No reason to go scurrying back to the confounded humans just yet."

"Better even to die free than live slaves," pronounced Peanut. At the word "die" Henrietta began to hyperventilate.

"We're stronger than we think," said Buddy.

"And smarter," brayed Newton.

"And braver," said Sarge, shooting the still-swooning Henrietta a stern look. She gulped and snapped her beak shut.

"Let's do this like Brutus," crowed Gizmo. "Penny's woke and all, but animals *rule*!"

Everyone was nodding and murmuring in approval.

"Well..." said Poe thoughtfully. "Fae and the others did leave their diamonds and other bling behind. We could use that to pay off at least most of our debts. But the way I see it, even without Bandit and the crows, I'm afraid if we keep going as we were, we'll end up no better than before. There's something about the corporation itself...it's like it casts a spell over you or something..."

"We need a different system," said Gizzabelle, "one that doesn't just *say* it puts animal health and happiness first, but really *does*."

"I'm not sure there is one," the raven said bleakly. "If there is, I don't know it."

Gizzabelle's spirits sank like a stone. Poe always had all the answers. If he didn't know, what hope did they have? If he didn't think they could succeed, they might as well not even try.

Don't act so small.

Gizzabelle gasped. She looked around for the speaker, knowing she wouldn't find him. None of the other animals seemed to have heard a thing.

You have wings. Now fly.

The little hen frowned. Fly? What did that mean? Where was there even to fly to?

Then—slowly—a smile spread across her face. She hopped up onto a nearby pile of rocks and faced the crowd.

"We don't need a new system," she declared with sudden confidence. "We know what to do. We always have."

The animals exchanged looks of complete bewilderment. How could she say they knew what to do? If they knew anything at all, it was that they didn't know anything at all.

"The way is in our hearts," Gizzabelle continued, undeterred. "We just have to listen."

"All know the way," pronounced Peanut, nodding earnestly, "but few actually walk it."

"That's right," the little hen said, "we've known all along what we should do, we just didn't do it. C'mon, did anyone *really* think it was right to give some animals more corn than they could possibly ever eat while others got nothing? Or to kick animals off the farm because they weren't 'productive' anymore?"

"It's monstrous! An atrocity!" screeched Henrietta, well aware she was no spring chicken herself.

The other animals rumbled loudly in agreement.

Gizzabelle didn't stop there, though. "And do you really think it's right not do your fair share of work and force others to work harder to make up for it?"

Even though she didn't look at anyone in particular, several of the sheep and chickens suddenly wouldn't meet her eyes.

"Or to lord your bling over others?" she continued. "Or grab the best plot of pasture for yourself?"

There was more head hanging and tail drooping.

"Or spend more time watching your shows than with your babies? Or put the interests of your own species above everyone else's, like they're not as important as you?"

By now, everyone was staring at the ground.

"The hard part isn't knowing what to do," Gizzabelle said. "The hard part is actually *doing* it."

There wasn't a peep from the crowd.

"You're right, as always," Poe finally said. "We knew—*I* knew all along what was right. I just told myself I didn't." He sighed. "Maybe it's not the system. Maybe it's us."

"Well, it *is* us, but I wouldn't let the system off the hook either," said Gizzabelle. "You couldn't follow its rules and your conscience at the same time. They're incompatible."

"No one can serve two masters," said Peanut.

"So how would it work without a system?" the ever-practical Newton asked skeptically. "We'd have to make everything up as we go?"

Poe looked at Gizzabelle tentatively. She gave an encouraging nod. "Well, the way I see it," said the raven slowly, "we wouldn't have to do everything differently. It's more a matter of resetting our priorities. We'd make every decision with the long-term welfare of all the animals in mind."

"If that's our North Star, we can't go wrong," said Gizzabelle.

"Now, it won't be easy," warned Poe. "It's not just picking a new system or a new leader, and sitting back and expecting that to fix everything. It will mean each and every one of us pledging to do our part and become the animals we were meant to be. All of us, every single day. Are you willing to make that commitment?"

He surveyed the crowd. They were not the same animals they had been just a year ago. They no longer had the blind faith and naïve optimism that had fueled their first venture. They had known great hope and crushing heartbreak. They had stumbled and fallen and gotten back up. They had lost much...but they had learned more.

"I reckon we give it a burl," said Buddy finally.

"*Qui n'avance pas, recule*—who does not advance, recedes—*n'est-ce pas?*" purred Coco.

"Of the animals, by the animals, for the animals—for real!"

chirped Gizmo.

"Of the animals, by the animals, for the animals," repeated Mordecai.

"Are we all in agreement?" asked Poe.

Everyone nodded in unison. Not a single animal abstained.

"It's official then," cawed Poe. "Animals, Inc. is hereby dissolved. Now we're starting, uh, well..." He stopped uncertainly.

"...*something else*," finished Gizzabelle. Their eyes met and an electrical charge flashed between them, stronger than ever before.

"That's right," said Poe, shooting her a crooked grin. "Something else."

The little hen's heart soared.

From the crowd, there was no chanting or clucking or braying or bleating. There was no stomping of hooves or flapping of wings. Instead of a frenzy of frothy excitement, there was a blossoming resolve, powerful and firm. They didn't know where the journey would take them, but they would choose the path themselves. No longer were they creatures of circumstance. They were masters of their own fate, stepping out to meet their destiny.

THE END

and the beginning

APPENDIX

The discerning reader will no doubt recognize among the Sausagisms found herein the words of a great many prophets, poets, philosophers, and sages of human extraction. This raises the titillating prospect that there exists a Universal Mind or collective transspecies trough of wisdom which Sausage was able to access though his many years of deep meditation, or alternatively that he had existed in a prior lifetime as a human mystic before reincarnating into his higher porcine form. After digesting the following passages, the gentle reader may pass on their insights to others, thereby securing his own reputation for enlightenment, or he may achieve essentially the same effect by following the sound advice of Sir William Ousler: *"Look wise, say nothing, and grunt."*

"We are not creatures of circumstance;
we are creators of circumstance."
—BENJAMIN DISRAELI

"The way is not in the sky. The way is in the heart."
—SIDDHARTHA GUATAMA BUDDHA

"The wise talk because they have something to say;
fools, because they have to say something."
—PLATO

"The opposite of a correct statement is a false statement.
But the opposite of a profound truth may well be
another profound truth."
—NIELS BOHR

"A foolish consistency is the hobgoblin of little minds."
—RALPH WALDO EMERSON

"There is no such thing as chance;
  what seems to us as merest accident
  springs from the deepest source of destiny."
  —JOHANN FRIEDRICH VON SCHILLER

"The tongue is like a sharp knife;
  it kills without drawing blood."
  —SIDDHARTHA GUATAMA BUDDHA

"Death is not an ending."
  —WALT WHITMAN

"Nature wants things to be round.
  The bodies of human beings and animals have no corners.
  The universe itself is circular, and made up of earth,
  which is round, of the sun, which is round, of the stars,
  which are round. The moon, the horizon, the rainbow—
  circles within circles, with no beginning and no end."
  —LAME DEER

"For life and death are one,
  even as the river and sea are one."
  —KAHLIL GIBRAN

"There is no death.
  Only a change of worlds."
  —CHIEF SEATTLE

"One must be a god to be able to divine success
  from failure without error."
  —ANTON PAVLOVICH CHEKHOV

"The only real failure in life
  is not to be true to the best one knows."
  —SIDDHARTHA GUATAMA BUDDHA

"The deeper the sorrow the less tongue it has."
—THE TALMUD

*"The embodied soul is eternal in existence,
indestructible, and infinite, only the material body
is perishable."*
—BHAGAVAD GITA

*"A wise man sees as much as he ought,
not as much as he can."*
—MICHEL EYQUEM DE MONTAIGNE

*"There is no greater love
than to lay down one's life for another."*
—JESUS OF NAZARETH

*"Be wary of freeing a camel from the burden of his hump,
you may be freeing him from being a camel."*
—G.K. CHESTERTON

*"It is not its length that gives life meaning,
but its depth."*
—RALPH WALDO EMERSON

*"The highest manifestation of life consists in this:
that a being governs its own actions."*
—SAINT THOMAS AQUINAS

"Satisfy your need, not your greed."
—MAHATMA GANDHI

*"I discovered the secret of the sea
in meditation upon the dewdrop."*
—KAHLIL GIBRAN

"Nature never hurries,
 yet all is accomplished."
  —LAO TSE TUNG

"Nature is harmony."
  —EMILY DICKINSON

"Never does Nature say one thing and Wisdom another."
  —DECIMUS JUNIUS JUVENALIS

"A domesticated lion is an unnatural lion,
 and whatever is unnatural is untrustworthy."
  —AFRICAN PROVERB

"The goal of life is to make your heartbeat
 match the beat of the Universe,
 to match your nature with Nature."
  —JOSEPH CAMPBELL

"Life must be lived forward,
 but can only be understood backwards."
  —SOREN KIRKEGAARD

"Your task is not to seek for love,
 but merely to seek and find
 all the barriers you have built against it."
  —JALĀL AD-DĪN MUHAMMAD RŪMĪ

"You were not meant for crawling, so don't.
 You have wings. Learn to use them and fly."
  —JALĀL AD-DĪN MUHAMMAD RŪMĪ

"Corn cannot expect justice
 from a court composed of chickens."
  —AFRICAN PROVERB

"Only from the heart can you touch the sky."
—Jalāl ad-Dīn Muhammad Rūmī

"What is in the end to be shrunk must first be stretched.
Whatever is to be weakened must first be made strong.
What is to be overthrown must begin by being set up."
—Lao Tzu

"Laws are like cobwebs, which may catch small flies,
but let wasps and hornets break through."
—Jonathan Swift

"Money is like manure,
of very little use unless spread around."
—Francis Bacon

"It was the incarnation of blind insensate Greed.
It was a monster devouring with a thousand mouths,
trampling with a thousand hoofs;
it was the Great Butcher—
it was the spirit of Capitalism made flesh."
—Upton Sinclair

"As I would not be slave, so I would not be master."
—Abraham Lincoln

"The attempt to combine wisdom and power
has only rarely been successful, and then only briefly."
—Albert Einstein

"By three methods we may learn wisdom:
first, by reflection, which is noblest;
second, by imitation, which is easiest;
and third, by experience, which is the most bitter."
—Confucius

"For what shall it profit a man,
if he gains the whole world,
but loses his own soul?"
　—JESUS OF NAZARETH

"We do not receive wisdom; we must discover it ourselves
after a journey no one can take for us or spare us."
　—MARCEL PROUST

"The greatest danger—the loss of one's self—
may pass off as quietly as if it were nothing;
but every other loss, that of a leg, five dollars,
a wife, etc., is sure to be noticed."
　—SOREN KIERKEGAARD

"To whom much is given, much is required."
　—JESUS OF NAZARETH

"Who looks outside dreams.
Who looks within awakens."
　—CARL JUNG

"Be kind, for everyone you meet is fighting a hard battle."
　—PLATO

"The greatest wisdom of all is kindness."
　—HEBREW PROVERB

"You, yourself, as much as anyone in the entire universe,
are deserving of your love and compassion."
　—SIDDHARTHA GUATAMA BUDDHA

"The faults of the burglar
are the qualities of the financier."
　—GEORGE BERNARD SHAW

"Men have become the tools of their tools."
—HENRY DAVID THOREAU

"There is more to life than increasing its speed."
—MAHATMA GANDHI

"The greatest wealth is a poverty of desires."
—LUCIUS ANNAEUS SENECA

"What is essential is invisible to the eye."
—ANTOINE DE SAINT-EXUPERY

"Returning violence for violence multiplies violence,
adding deeper darkness to a night already devoid of stars.
Darkness cannot drive out darkness; only light can do that.
Hate cannot drive out hate; only love can do that."
—MARTIN LUTHER KING, JR.

"Goodbyes are only for those who love with their eyes.
Because for those who love with the heart and soul
there is no such thing as separation."
—RAINER MARIA RILKE

"Your heart and my heart are very old friends."
—JALĀL AD-DĪN MUHAMMAD RŪMĪ

"I am not born for a corner.
The whole world is my native land."
—LUCIUS ANNAEUS SENECA

"Peace I leave with you;
my peace I give to you....
Let not your hearts be troubled,
neither let them be afraid."
—JESUS OF NAZARETH

"Better even to die free than live slaves."
—FREDERICK DOUGLASS

"Do not be led by others,
awaken your own mind,
amass your own experience,
and decide for yourself
your own path."
—THE VEDAS

"There is a voice that doesn't use words.
Listen."
—JALĀL AD-DĪN MUHAMMAD RŪMĪ

"To understand things,
we must have once been in them,
and to have come out of them.
The one who is still under the spell,
and the person who has never felt the spell,
are equally incompetent."
—HENRI FREDERIC AMIEL

"All know the way, but few actually walk it."
—BODHIDHARMA

"No one can serve two masters."
—JESUS OF NAZARETH

ANIMALS, INC. STUDY GUIDE

Prompts for
Further Reflection

A Suggestion for Discussion Groups: Do not attempt to tackle all or even most of the questions in a single session. Digging deeply into a select few questions is more worthwhile than a cursory, superficial exploration of many. Pick just a few discussion prompts or consider having each participant present the one that they found most provocative.

1. What most struck you about the book? What was the most personally relevant? Have you had any experiences in the workplace/corporate environment that relate?

2. What character would have made the best leader— Poe, Buddy, Sausage, or someone else? Why? Would the outcome been different with a different leader?

3. What would a society (economy, government, religion, etc.) based on maximizing wellbeing/happiness instead of productivity/prosperity look like? How would it differ from our own?

4. Does overwork decrease your ability to just "be"? Do you have trouble doing nothing without feeling bored or anxious?

5. Poe encourages the animals to follow clock time rather than the rhythms of nature. How might your life be different if you got rid of your clock and relied upon your natural rhythms? Is that even possible in modern life?

6. Sausage says money is the root of poverty. What do you think this means? How might it relate to anthropologist Marshall Sahlins' statement, "The world's most primitive people have few possessions, but they are not poor....Poverty is a social status. As such, it is the invention of civilization"?

7. Do you think the book is anti-capitalist or critical of a particular style of capitalism? Do you believe an ethical or people-focused capitalism achievable or a logical impossibility?

8. Margaret Thatcher famously used the slogan "TINA" (There is no alternative) to describe modern capitalism. Do you believe this is true? What are the effects of such a belief?

9. The book suggests spirituality is not just outside of, but opposed to the economic system (the "monster" of Capitalism/ greed). Do you believe a spiritual outlook is compatible with our economic system and the driving force behind it? Why or why not?

10. What does it imply that Sausage quotes from all the main world religions? Do you believe all major faith traditions share a common foundation? If so, can you articulate what it is they all share?

11. What is your favorite Sausagism? Why is it meaningful to you?

12. Gandhi said: "The greatness of a nation and its moral progress can be judged by the way its animals are treated." What do the conditions on Kratchet's factory farm say? How does how we treat animals relate to how we treat other humans?

13. Is the book a call to vegetarianism/veganism? Why or why not? What do you think morality demands in regard to eating meat and/or animal products? What are your personal practices?

14. When you are born into a system, it often seems natural, inevitable, and inalterable because it is all you know. Seeing the animals create their social structure choice by choice, did it enable you to realize that certain aspects of your society that you had thought were natural are, in fact, constructed and therefore, subject to change?

15. There are genuine difference between species. Does that make the "species-ism" more acceptable? What do you think this says about racism or nationalism within our species? Do you think it is acceptable for our species to decimate— and even eliminate—other species? Why or why not?

16. How might an ethos of "enough" rather than "more" changed the outcome?

17. What does Bandit represent? What motivates him? Do you know people like him? What drives people who earn more than they can ever spend to keep seeking more?

18. Bandit claims all property is theft. Is he wrong? What is "ownership" of nature/land based on? How could society function if this fundamental premise was questioned?

19. The animals have to devise an "income" distribution system. Ideally, should everyone be equal or should there be differences? If so, what should differences in income be based on? What are they based upon now?

20. The book satirizes Western culture. Do other cultures around the world organize their life/work balance differently. What are your thoughts on different approaches to the way we live?

21. Is it fair to consider playing the stock market gambling? Why? Is gambling wrong? Why or why not?

22. Are alcohol, TV, bling and accoutrements necessary to our economic system or merely incidental?

23. What is the book's perspective on science and technology? What does the cornpicker-caused unemployment represent? What does the fact that the cornpicker runs out of gas symbolize? What does it mean that Newton, as an "unnatural" cross between a donkey and horse, is sterile?

24. Mordecai is critical of the human practice of monoculture. Is Big Agriculture exploitive of the soil in ways that are similar to how factory farms treat animals? What issues are you aware of related to current industrial farming practices?

25. Do you think the decision to render the sheep is wrong or just being productive/practical? Is efficiency the ultimate value? If there is any higher value, what is it?

26. Do you believe most people are interested in self-governance or do they prefer being controlled by strong leaders and familiar systems? How would society be different if self-determination was, in fact, something everyone insisted upon?

27. What assumptions and purposes are served by saying that it isn't "realistic" to believe people could be motivated by something other than money and self-interest? Are you personally motivated solely by self-interest?

28. In the original ending, Poe never renounces his allegiance to the corporation. Do you think this is more or less likely? Why?

29. Was the ending realistic? Do you think the animals would have revolted against the corporation or stuck with it? Why? If you were one of the animals, would you have been on the side of revolution or status quo?

30. What do you imagine would happen after the novel ends? How could the animals structure the farm to best fulfill their original mission to provide all the animals with a good life? Do you think they would be successful? Why or why not?

Suggested Resources

Selected Books:

Alperovitz, Gar. *What Then Must We Do? Straight Talk About the Next American Revolution.*
Analyzes the deep systemic problems with our current economic model and possible alternatives for democratizing wealth and power.

Bakan, Joel. *The Corporation: The Pathological Pursuit of Profit and Power.*
A potent indictment of the world's dominant economic institution and how it has metastasized into a dangerous and possibly terminal cancer.

Berry, Wendell. *The Unsettling of America: Culture and Agriculture.*
A timeless 1977 text eloquently linking our estrangement from the land with the cultural and spiritual impoverishment of post-industrial American society.

Eisenstein, Charles. *The Ascent of Humanity: Civilization and the Human Sense of Self.*
A provocative and far-reaching polemic arguing that the converging crises facing humanity are an inevitable result of mankind's attempt to separate from and control nature.

Korten, David. *When Corporations Rule the World.*
The ground-breaking classic exposing the global impact of multinational corporations, their role in the economic colonization of developing countries, and the existential threat they pose to democracy and life.

Jackall, Robert. *Moral Mazes: The World of Corporate Managers.*
A penetrating investigation of how corporations and the pursuit of short-term profit shape and deform the moral consciousness of those within them.

Reich, Robert. *Saving Capitalism: For the Many, Not the Few.*
Examines the clandestine alliance between Washington and
Wall Street that keeps powerful interests entrenched and
offers an array of possible correctives for a system that works
for everyone.

Roberts, Paul. *The Impulse Society: America in an Age of
Instant Gratification.*
Explores how the self-centered consumerist ethos of the
marketplace has infiltrated every aspect of our society
including our very character structure.

Films:

FOOD, INC.
A disturbing exposé of the horrors of factory farms and
the food production industry.

INEQUALITY FOR ALL.
This documentary featuring Robert Reich is a quick primer
on the current economic forces at work in our society that
are creating massive inequalities in wealth and political clout.

THE CORPORATION.
Based on the eponymous book (listed above), this award-
winning film makes the compelling case that we accept and
applaud actions from corporations that are considered
psychopathic in individuals.

WE ARE ONE.
A thought-provoking reflection on the links between our
attitudes toward and exploitation of animals, the environment,
other humans, and ourselves.

Periodicals:

YES! Magazine
A hopeful, life-affirming monthly publication offering real-
world solutions that are not just theoretical but actually
being implemented now to create a more just, sustainable,
and compassionate world.

Acknowledgements

No book is born in a vacuum and a book of ideas has an especially rich heritage at its back. My first nod of acknowledgement must, of course, go to George Orwell, whose *Animal Farm* was its inspiration. Knowing Orwell to be an outspoken promoter of democratic socialism, I believe that if he were alive today, it would be the excesses and brutalities of predatory capitalism that he would rail against as the greatest threat of the age. One lazy summer day, I whiled away the time by imagined Orwell retooling his immortal classic and recasting the greedy, cruelly exploitive swine at the end as capitalist pigs, an impromptu thought experiment that eventually culminated in what you have before you. *Animals, Inc.* is the book I fancy Orwell might have written—or at the very least, I hope, would have been honored to have sparked.

I am also heavily indebted to the countless thinkers and writers—several of whom are listed on the resources page—who have shaped my understanding of corporations, capitalism, consumerism, and the impact of our current economic system on not just our livelihoods and social arrangements, but our values and character. My intention is that *Animals, Inc.* will give form and life and even wider exposure to their ideas.

A special thanks goes to Sara, the novel's midwife, first champion and most stalwart cheerleader; the many early readers—including Lucy, Julie, the "other" Julie, Christine, Ally, and Christina—who gave their time and invaluable feedback to make the story better; and Jessica and Kathy, the outstanding publishing team who helped launch the book into the world.

Finally, I am most profoundly grateful to my family, for giving me roots, and my husband, Chris, for helping me find my wings.

About the Author

Upon graduating from The College of William and Mary with a highly-practical degree in English literature, Catherine Arne's first job in the "real" world was with a startup management consulting firm in New York City, whose primary aim was to find ways to downsize the workforce of its client companies. There she helped create a computer program in which workers would rate each other daily on their performance using an ever-increasing standard of expectations that was unattainable by design. After learning the company's founder had been convicted of leading an abusive, brain-washing cult in the 70s, she realized he was intent of bringing many of the same nefarious techniques to the business world (including his own company) and promptly quit.

Following a short stint at *Ladies' Home Journal*, she went on to work at two established, mission-driven companies—a prominent inspirational magazine and a church-funded family counseling program—where the culture shifted beneath her feet as profit edged out their original *raison d'être* in the span of only a few years. Deeply discouraged, Catherine decided to take some time off from gainful employment to pursue a M.A. in creative writing at Wilkes University, where she wrote the first draft of *Animals, Inc.* as her master's thesis.

After graduation, Catherine set a course for assured downward mobility as a self-employed ghostwriter, screenwriter, and escape room designer and owner. When her husband's lucrative but soul-sucking career in upper management grew increasingly intolerable, they resolved to make their break from The Man complete. After following the tenets of the FIRE movement for several years, in 2018, they quit their jobs, sold their home, loaded their two cats and two dogs into an RV, and hit the open road. They have been happily nomadic ever since.

CPSIA information can be obtained
at www.ICGtesting.com
Printed in the USA
LVHW020813271021
701667LV00003BA/393